Seesaw

The Only Way to Go is Up

LISA PORTOLAN

Barringer Publishing, Naples, Florida
www.barringerpublishing.com
Cover, graphics, layout design by Lisa Camp

ISBN: 978-0-9961973-5-9

Library of Congress Cataloging-in-Publication Data
Seesaw / Lisa Portolan

Printed in U.S.A.

Dedication

For my Gigi Bee

1. Valentine's Day
14th February

That's right, it's that fucking internationally commercialized day of the year where women everywhere are supposed to be all loved-up and romantic, sipping Veuve Clicquot from champagne glasses, eating dinner at some Michelin Star restaurant in Sydney or the Northern Beaches, wearing elegant but slightly skanky black dresses, staring longingly, albeit slightly intoxicatedly, into the eyes of their beloved men who—please take note—have planned the whole thing, probably to get inside those skanky dresses, but also for something more—because there is more … Right before dessert is served (some decadent delight, of course), the beloved lovers of these fucking adored women are suddenly leaping from their seated positions—gallantly, but nervously at the same time—a look of perfect desperation and longing in their *eyes—and the women, well, they're continuing to look sexy but coy; watching, waiting, with the utmost level of surprise—as they whip open little black boxes—yes, the ones that hold those things that us women call rings, and not just any ring, but a fucking enormous engagement ring which, may I just add, had previously been concealed inside the pockets of their Armani jackets, and the men start spouting those magical words. Those magical words that every lady has been waiting for in every relationship, those four little words that every woman has dreamed of hearing since she was just a girl. Just four words! Nothing too extravagant, but nonetheless timely; "Will you marry me?" Yes, that's right, fucking Valentine's Day. That's what's happening to all of those women, all at the same fucking time, and, well, it should be happening right here, right now, for me!*

Shit. Abominable start to the evening! I actually swear loads, don't I? Not only does my mouth swear, but my inner monologue does, too … So fuck it, shit again, who cares anyway? I'm past caring full stop. I'm sitting here in my sweats, downing vino after vino like there's no tomorrow, watching episode after episode of *Keeping Up with the Kardashians* on Pay TV in my rented apartment in Potts Point (Yep, Potts Point—by no means is it Kings Cross) on Valentine's Day evening … completely and utterly alone!

That's right. No elegant but skanky dress, no reservations at some Michelin Star restaurant, no charming *love of my life* wearing Armani at the opposite end of the table, no flashy wedding proposal. Nothing. Zip. Nada. Nil.

Not even some Australiano, sweet but folksy, boyfriend to spend the evening in with, eating some order-in on our laps, whilst watching some sci-fi mini-series or football game. None of that even!

Just me. Just ye old *Cecilia*, home alone, watching the Kardashian clan living their lives. So yes, it is just *moi*, staring aghast at the screen as more Kardashian booties are paraded about—large, high, prominent. Like built-in seats really …

But that's what the men want these days, isn't it? Built-in seats. Big booties. Pert ones that smile at the sun! *Hello, sunshine.* Did you know that there are ladies out there that are actually getting bum implants, right this second probably! Can you believe it? Bum implants to make the old buttocks that little bit more pert. Silicone, or something. That's what they use.

Must get up! I am very much rising to my feet now, swaying slightly, the potential effect of a bottle and a half of Shiraz *perhaps*; goblet still in hand, ready to inspect my own derrière. Twisting my spine at an obscene angle, trying to catch a glimpse of my bottom. It's difficult. I guess I should have been paying more attention in those yoga classes. Or that one class I took … What did the instructor say again? "Rotate, twist from your coccyx." I think that was it, and so I shall twist, twist … Twist, god damn you!

Finally, I can see it, but only after potentially causing severe damage to my spinal cord which, may I add, I will not know until the morning once the Shiraz has worn off. I am managing the smallest of looks, a glance really, and to be quite honest, this is enough. *Sigh.* Flat as a fucking pancake! Certainly nothing of the Kardashian variety, not really in the same ballpark! Butt enhancement, hmm? NO!

Sigh. Now that I'm up, I may as well fix myself a drink. Why not? After all, it is a special occasion. Well, at least it is for all those proposed-to women. And my glass here is almost empty. I shall drain the rest of the content whilst heading to my kitchenette. I'm so trying to maintain stability and hand-eye coordination with objects. A little trick I've learnt over the years, it's called the "not fall flat on your flat ass when tipsy" technique.

Kitchenette, such an outdated word. I think my real estate agent referred to it as a "galley kitchen." Makes me think of boats and sailors—but there are certainly no sailors here! Feeling triumphant at having made that semi gag! Worth a titter methinks. My humour standard has dropped somewhat over the past several hours though, and it's likely to be a direct correlation to the amount of alcohol I've consumed.

I'm considering the bottle of red staring back at me, perhaps a quarter of its contents remaining. If I consume two bottles of red on a weeknight (notably a sorrowful day which occurs every year—Valentine's Day if one needs to be reminded), then that would quite possibly make me an alcoholic.

What to do at this point? To drink or not to drink? That sounds so Shakespearean, doesn't it? I'm totally cultured … *To drink or not to drink? That is the question!*

Seconds have passed, maybe moments. Impasse reached.

Wait, light bulb moment! Epiphany! I shall fix myself a cocktail instead. So much more awesome and fanciful than draining the bottle of red like some lonely wino. No way, not tonight. Tonight it's cocktails and sophistication for *moi!*

Pantry door open, and a series of measly shelves scattered with random products revealed: an exorbitant amount of instant noodles; health bars (never consumed, most likely out of date); half a packet of Shredded Wheaties; flour (again, never opened, nor consumed—perhaps purchased at a stage when baking seemed like a distinct possibility; I mean you just don't bake for yourself do you?); a tiny shred of chocolate, proudly left in an 800 gram packet (still holding onto the notion that I've not consumed the entire lot in one sitting, because as long as something remains, there is hope. Not a chocoholic, and similar to wine *bottle theory*, I am not an alcoholic either—not even close); lots of condiments: ranch dressing, olive oil, lemon juice, tomato sauce, mint sauce, HP sauce, mustard. Dear lord, why so many condiments? And finally ... Tabasco sauce.

I'm reaching for it like it's my saving grace. Oh, it feels good in my hand, a nice temperature, and I can grip the whole way around the bottle. No decent Bloody Mary can be made without a big splash of Tabasco. I know that much at least.

I am scanning the contents of my pantry now in more detail, and even through my drunken haze, it is clear that there's not much to scan; three shelves hardly does a pantry make. I should inform my real estate agent that this place was falsely advertised. I seem to recall a specific reference to *a pantry, a large open-planned living area, balcony and potential sunroom.*

Well, for $700 per week in Potts Point (that's right Potts Point, not ever going to be Kings Cross), that's what one would expect. But in fact, *non, c'est ne pas* what one would expect. Far from it actually! My one bedroom in Potts Point features a delightful two-by-two metre living area (combining dining and living—perfect for entertaining, might I add, with a wistful, ironic semi-smirk, on an occasion like Valentine's Day); a cat's bedroom (by cat's bedroom, I mean that only a cat could possibly deem it an appropriate size for its living quarters, yet ironically enough, one could not swing a cat in the space); a balcony, which faces out onto another seedy terrace; and that sunroom, the one the real estate agent sold the flat to me on … Well, let's just say the sunroom is merely an expansive window which lets in some light in an otherwise dim locale. Of course, there is my pantry—not a walk-in food cupboard, by any stretch of the imagination, but a bi-fold door that conceals three shelves.

As much as I like the thought of having one, I don't need a pantry. After all, there's only one person living here, just one. That's me. A well-stocked shelf would serve me just fine. Look, don't feel sorry for me! It's not exactly just me, myself, and I; it's me, myself and my moody Cavoodle, Fred—named after an ex-boyfriend who bought him for me after yet another breakup. Yes, one buys puppies now in recompense for breakups, and then the said broken-up with lady names the said puppy after the man who broke her heart, or at the very least shattered her ego … Why? Not quite sure. Was it a memento of the relationship?

Je ne sais pas!

And where is *said* dog at this *said* moment when one needs him? Just like his father, or *giver*—whatever you'd call it—hiding out somewhere, afraid of Mummy's erratic drunken behaviour, potentially with some statuesque blonde!

More like hiding out behind the couch at this point.

Where's the Worcestershire sauce? Good, got it … Need you mister pepper pot, some sugar, and tomato juice—not chilled—but at the very least available in my pantry. Must have considered making Bloody Maries at some point in the not so distant past, given the currency of ingredients native to the Bloody Mary in my possession. *Convenient.*

Moving on from my pantry with a nice firm clap of the bi-fold, clutching my ingredients like a drowning man with a flotation device, I find myself here, in my galley kitchen, *kitchenette*, whatever you call it these days. Ingredients now ready and waiting on the counter, it's time I inspect the freezer for the vodka, non? Let's say, the most salient ingredient—Oh, and ice cubes to compensate for the tepid tomato juice. I love it when a plan comes together.

These cupboards are a mess, and whilst I am still clattering and searching for a pitcher, it has just dawned on me that I have no pitcher. That's right, no pitcher for my sophisticated cocktail, and come to think of it, there are not any other worthy containers to stir this up in. Unless —a punch bowl *could* work, couldn't it? But it serves twelve, which rather seems too much.

There's the vase option. I'll go for that instead. Said vase—likelihood of use for flowers, purchased for *moi* by some handsome man—or *any* man—highly unlikely … But temporary stirring place for alcoholic beverage—much more likely.

This sort of throwing ingredients together doesn't require measuring, but exceedingly inappropriate quantities, of course, not skimping on the Vodka by any measure. Focusing on the stirring allows the thought that my elegant mid-week cocktail has been degenerated into some sort of garden-quality drink brewed in a vase. Just keep stirring. Just keep stirring.

My phone ringing? No, I must be hearing things. On the evening that is Valentine's? Surely not! But it is!

"Fuck." I just dropped the f-bomb for the fourth time this evening. Erm, it may have been more than that, if you count my inner monologue, but who's counting? It's not the only thing dropping … Uh-oh, slow motion; I want to save it, I really do—not happening. Half of the contents of the vase has tipped over the counter and a fair splash is on my

Ugg boots. It's not a pretty sight—but still worth a smile because there is enough to make a girl happy still sloshing around in the vase.

Where's the cordless? And who is so persistently calling at this hour? It must be gone eleven! I've been watching Jenner and Kardashian drama in an inebriated state since I got home from work. Could be four to six hours worth? Have reached brain-dead reality television quantity.

Staggering, still with the vase clasped in my arms like it is a child needing protection, I pick up the phone.

"Hello!" Green button pressed and I'm trying really hard to contain my semi-slurred voice, as this could potentially be work (some sort of inordinate advertising emergency on Valentine's Day perhaps?), or some sort of relation or friend who will take badly to my alcoholic state—more possible!

"Cecilia speaking." I always do this, a grimly pronounced greeting with a slightly jaunty note and unlikely-British accent, given I haven't been to the UK for more than two days at any one time during my lifetime.

"Oh hello, *Cecilia speaking*, it's your mother speaking." She's attempting to mimic my tone, but is not quite as convincing.

Oh fuck. Why did she have to call at a moment like this? Fuckity-fuck, fuck, fuck, fuck. A little worried that one of my expletives may slip out, I try to compose myself further, setting my vase baby down on the counter slowly, just in case she senses that I am holding it, nursing it, stirring a beverage with high alcohol quantity in a container intended for flowers.

I wouldn't be surprised; the woman has telepathic qualities, I'd put money on it!

"Oh hello, Mother." I'm still putting on a slightly affected, stuck up tone of voice. Not my usual voice at all, rather my, *I've been caught out drunk, planning on getting more drunk, stirring up Bloody Maries alone on Valentine's Day* voice.

"Are you okay, Cecilia? You sound ... you sound a little bit strange." She's prying as though she's trying to spy out exactly what's going on.

"I'm fine, Mother," I say, faking a reassuring titter of a laugh, but it has come out as a half snort. "Just at home, looking over some work for tomorrow."

"Really?"

I can tell she's not buying it. I know her, and I know that she knows me too well. I can picture her now, standing by the phone, peroxide-blonde hair poofed up in some sort of suburbs, *du jour* do, wearing clothes one size too small, and giving Brad, her soon-to-be husband, a look equipped with an all-knowing raised eyebrow. And I wouldn't doubt that it is that very eyebrow that makes her telepathic. Brad is likely to be propping himself up by the fridge, after having grabbed his VB from inside: a drink he describes as a *"brewski"*—And he's probably sipping away at his brewski, wondering why the hell his wife-to-be is looking at him like this, with the eyebrow, and he probably doesn't give a fuck what in god's name she's trying to convey through said expression.

"Yes." Power-on now, Cee. Bamboozle her with all sorts of nonsense, just for the hell of it. "Yes, we have a new creative director, and his work is so far off the mark I have to keep looking over it thoroughly before I provide it to the client."

There! I deserve to high-five myself, no make it a high-ten—both hands to thin air, but only symbolically, or I'd drop the phone. A lie; always better when stitched with the truth, right? Makes it more realistic.

And we do have a relatively new creative director, and he is a cretin, and he has been causing me grief. Well, he had been, anyway, so truth'ish.

"Is he a man?" She's snapping, and quickly, on the scent of new blood: a potential eligible bachelor for her unmarried daughter.

"Yes, he's a man." *Sigh*. "Why is that of interest to you?" Like I don't know!

"Well, I'm just keeping my eyes open for you, darling, because I love you and I'm your mother. You're thirty-two now, not a spring chicken anymore. You really need to get in there fast if you want to secure a good one soon," says the woman onto her fourth marriage. "And really, darling," oh there's more, "spending Valentine's Day alone … " I imagine she is shaking her head at this point. "Always alone," I'm not sure she needed to add that, "it's just not right."

Oh, she has stopped again. My turn to speak, I gather, my part of this dialogue that is so very riveting and so unpredictable. *I am fucking busy drinking, goodbye.* That's what I want to say. Instead, I'm just going to reassure her as per usual.

"I'm fine, Mother." I think I've said this fifty times this week. "Completely fine. I'm having a fabulous time." Okay, I'm lying, and this one has no weave, no embellishment and no stitch of truth. I am *not* fine. Completely not having a fabulous time, and I can now see that my cocktail is drying out to a sticky stain on my new Uggs. Not fine at all!

"It doesn't sound like you're having a fabulous time. Working on Valentine's Day? You're young," she's contradicting the *spring chicken* comment, you see I do listen to her, I just don't like what she says, "You should be out having a good time, not working on a weeknight. Not working on Valentine's Day!"

In reality, I'm doing neither, but nonetheless I shall defend.

"I'm fine!" My modus operandi of defense, only this time I have injected some more energy into my tone. "It's just another day in the year, Mother, and unfortunately I just have to get this work done."

"What about the creative guy?" She is a persistent one.

"Oh, Mother, he's a douche. Another creative one, too many tattoos, one too many ideas. Not my type really," I say honestly, envisaging him in my mind to give more credibility to my words.

"Don't be too picky. No one's perfect, you know? Hanging out for *Mister Perfect* is not going to get you anywhere." I can hear a strange crunching noise in the background above her high-pitched, Australian accent, and I'm suspecting it might be Brad shoveling in some chips, perhaps semi-interested in the conversation, providing subtle prompts in relation to my sketchy romantic life.

"Yes, Mother, we've had this conversation before, but I'm not going to surrender and decide some tattooed Yank twat is up to standard."

"He's from the States?" Selective hearing. "I love an American accent. Very Ridge Forrester on *Bold.*"

I am totally holding my tongue and not going to tell her this guy is no Ridge from *Bold*. "Mother, if you love American accents so much, you can approach him after everything falls on its head with Bradster. I hear fourth time is the charm." The comment's rude, disrespectful even, but the filter's gone post a bottle and three quarters (let's be realistic, not a half, plus that swig of neat vodka that I have omitted to mention or acknowledge to myself until now), and I really want her to get off the phone before she realises I'm plastered, and only narrowly holding it together.

"That's very unkind, Cecilia," she's telling me. "Not any way to treat your mother." Here comes the sob story. Violins at the ready to play a sympathetic symphony. "I was really just checking in on you to make sure my only child is okay on Valentine's Day, given she's had a very recent breakup, and she's working hard, and she's alone … Always so *alone!*"

The sob story—It's not so much the words as it is the tone, and I know what face she is pulling, too. And in true form, she still has to add that dagger into the back. Alone!

"Again, I'm fine, Mother. Not about to top myself at any point. Don't worry, I haven't been Googling how to make a noose on the Internet." I know I sound insensitive.

"Really, darling, I don't know why you have to be so crude. This is why you don't meet any eligible bachelors—because you make such awful comments! Not everyone prescribes to your sadistic humour." She is sounding hurt now. Probably fake though.

"I'd hardly call it sadistic," I say, holding the vase in one hand. Yes it's back, it's my child, and I'm nearly ready to down the entire thing in one swig.

"Well, whatever … I'll stop bothering you then." She is still speaking with the same pitiful tone, but I'm over it. "Just remember, you're due at my place on Saturday morning to help make the wedding invites."

Oh shit. Double shit. Not *wedding-invite Saturday* with Mother, potentially Bradster, and Char (that is short for Charmayne you know?) —Mother's strange little best friend.

"About that …" I say, trying to wheedle my way out. My befuddled alcohol brain is struggling with an excuse. My energy is done on this. Fuck it, I'll have to go, and this is where her *my only child* comments count, because I'm going through guilt and obligation, a sense of duty to her. I guess that makes me a pretty good daughter right now.

"No!" Oh, she's quick, sharp, speaking now in that schoolteacher tone of hers. "No excuses darling, you'll be here, bright and early and bushytailed on Saturday. No excuses."

"But I have to drive all the way to Wahroonga," I'm pleading in my most childish tone, now falling into our mother-child or teacher-student dynamic. But who am I kidding, huh? I am already there.

"Yes, you will. Not my fault you decided to live in Kings Cross after having spent your entire life on the Northern Beaches."

"I live in Potts Point, Mother—not Kings Cross. And it really isn't Kings Cross."

"Same difference, darling! You live in Kings Cross. I blame that friend of yours for this."

"Do you mean Chris? You should know his name by now, we've been friends for ten years." *Sigh*. Not quite sure why this Chris-Mother dichotomy continues after all this time.

"Yes Chris. He's a terrible influence. You can't be a gay man. You're a woman, for god's sake," she's telling me authoritatively—expert advice of course—like I have been trying to be a *gay man*.

"He's not trying to make me into a gay man, Mother. After all, I do have a vagina." I've a small smile on my face, knowing that she's probably grimacing at the very word. And it's a nice one, too—Yes, I have a nice vagina, but I'm not going to say that. It's a little too crude even for me.

"Why would you say that?" she's whispering, like we've been caught out smoking by the headmistress behind the toilets, and she's not the teacher anymore, but my naughty friend assisting me in discarding the evidence. She is so shocked by the word *vagina*. VAGINA! I've heard her say way worse than VA-GI-NA before—way worse! I know she's just trying to play the innocent card this evening. The woman usually swears more than I do. Well, possibly not more than my mind, but more than I verbalise.

"What?" I ask, pretending to be bemused. "Do you mean, vagina?" I'm saying it louder now and with higher intonation than a usual question, as though I am actually squeezing my vaginal muscles as I speak.

"Stop it now!"

I am picturing the look of panic on her face, like I've literally placed an unknown vagina right in front of her. Imagine that! A random floating vagina is taunting her right now! The Bradster would choke on his brewski for sure.

"Mother really," I say with an exaggeratedly bored tone from *moi*. "You have one. I have one. Chris wishes he had one. It's not like I used the word pussy or cu-"

"Don't you dare say that vulgar word." She's giving me her warning and a slightly alarmed tone.

"What word, Mum? Do you mean C-" Oh how rude, she's hung up, and before I've finished speaking, "-UNT." There, just a word! Mwah. Yes, I have just kissed the phone—A little V-Day love, you know, because mission accomplished. End of the most boring, annoying call since her last one! Who would have known that the humble vagina was the key all along?

I can now return to my Bloody Mary ingestion, and to Caitlyn Jenner and those juicy junk-in-da-trunk Kardashians. Yes, returning to such musings does make my world a happy place.

SEESAW

2. Still Valentine's Day

Potentially 2:00 a.m. (Not sure if it's Valentine's Day anymore, is it? It's actually post-Valentine's Day. I'm waking up, yes at 2:00 a.m. Slightly dazed, location unknown, Fred the dog sleeping almost on my head, celery stick pasted to my face, phone ringing … Again! Really?)

Cannot possibly begin the day after Valentine's Day with swearing. Cee, do not say *shit*, or *fuck*, for the entire day. It's hard enough stumbling to my feet without having to deal with indignant groans from Fred the dog, who may I add shall from now on just be known simply as *Fred* … Because there is no *Fred the boyfriend* anymore, is there? So one does not need to state if the said Fred is the canine form or the human variety, hence wiping Fred the ex from mind completely. The day is looking good already.

Oh, what's that? Hand to face, in bid to accomplish new morning duty

—the un-sticking of celery stick from right cheek. Think this may have been the Bloody Mary stirrer. It smells like Bloody Mary. Must have been.

Emergency? Oh no! Why else would someone call, and so persistently, in the middle of the night? I left the phone on the kitchen bench after that call with Mother featuring the errant reference to vagina. Too much? Enough to give her heart palpitations or potential stroke? Oh no, I've killed her with the word *vagina*.

Affected superior tone, with slight British accent switching on! It's so ingrained now.

"Hello, Cecilia speaking."

"Oh hello, my lovely English vixen. It's Chris speaking." Similar curt, affected tone, and some smothered laughter. Love him.

"Yes, *Chris speaking*," I'm hissing. "It's 2:00 in the morning, why are you calling?"

"It's 3:04 in the morning to be precise, and doll, it's Valentine's Day. Not technically anymore I know, but I'm still up, so I wanted to check in on you."

"No, I haven't topped myself," I'm confirming grimly. How long is this conversation going to go on for? How long will I need to endure? Everyone seems to have this thing about checking in on me, like I'm the top of some *top one's self* list.

"Good news! Just making sure you weren't hanging from the banisters somewhere random."

So it would be okay if I were hanging from the banisters of somewhere *not* random then?

"There are no banisters at my house."

21

"Metaphorically speaking, babe."

"Whatever. I wouldn't have answered the phone if I was dead, non?" I'm smart, even at this hour.

"I know, doll. I tried your mobile like ten times—the landline was my final desperate call before the police."

"My mobile is on *silent* to stop crazies calling me in the middle of the night." I'm acting like I don't care that he cares, but indeed I do. Totally care for him, too. Just pissed off he's called so late!

"Are you inferring that I'm a crazy?"

"Infer what you will." *Sigh*. Yes, go on. Infer. Who else calls in the wee hours of the morning on a weeknight? Repeatedly, and using all available contact devices? A crazy person, that's who!

"Okay," he's responding with his *I know it all manner*. "I'm hearing *tired—I had too many beverages this evening—and grumpy … I'm also hearing middle-aged hag.*"

I'm hearing *fuck off prima donna,* but it's best I brush that comment aside. This is how he communicates. Jibes. If he weren't being sarcastic, ironic or rude, I'd know I didn't have a connection with him. But I do, and life would most likely be easier if he were straight. But Mum is right about one thing: I'm not a gay man.

"All of the above is very true. And no, I did not cry my eyes out into a pillow while doing some ritual voodoo spell over that asshole's photo or his left-over possessions." *Asshole*, of course, referring to the *said* not-be-named—Not to be confused with the one that purchased my flat-mate … But my newest and most recent ex, who broke up with me approximately twenty-nine days prior to Valentine's Day in no uncertain terms. Something along the lines of, "Babe, you're just not the right person for me. And to be frank, I want to meet other chicks." That's actually what he said …

And he didn't even have the decency to buy me a dog.

"I don't know about sobbing into the pillow, but some voodoo? I am hoping you did some of that this evening." He positively has a slight perversion in his tone.

I'm giggling softly down the phone. *That Chris*, such a lovable interrupter of sleep. Love him.

"So close—I'm fine, or at the very least, I'm as well as one can be after having consumed one and three quarters bottles of wine and an unmarked amount of disgusting Bloody Mary ingredients, which actually didn't really taste anything like Bloody Mary. Oh, and that wheel of Camembert; I ate that, too."

"Good. Sounds like your evening went swimmingly," he's saying resoundingly, as though there's no concern to be had in my words or the possibility of his friend potentially becoming a binge drinker or eater. Just another midweek late night for Chris. "Now do you have time to talk?" he asks, his tone becoming earnest.

Oh, right. Not at all a check-in call for *moi* then, more like a debriefing about something relating to his personal life, thinly-veiled in concerns over my well-being. Sounds just like Chris. Typi-*bloody*-cal.

I don't even get a word in before he launches straight into it.

"So I was down at Canary Yellow with Greg the new BF. So we'd just had dinner, right?" I have ensured I squeeze in a "hmm" so he knows he has my full attention, and then there's more. "We were super relaxed and happy. You know that sort of night—wine and food coma had set in, and I was like thinking *OMG, I just adore this person, like properly think he's lush.* Just awesome, right! Then I'm like *why didn't I meet him sooner?* And I'm thinking we'll just have a few more drinks and then I'll head off with him to have a wild night of sex!"

He has paused, probably for air. Oh, he must be waiting for a response. A response to that string of utterances! Do I recognise this state of mind? Vaguely. Not quite sure though. My last pseudo-relationship was with a born-again Christian (financier nonetheless), who was abstaining from sex, but broke up with me to meet other chicks. Not entirely sure I am the most qualified, and not really even sure what he is asking!

"Cee?" Chris is now petulantly interrupting my thought pattern, and possibly because I have remained silent for too long—not allowed on phone calls apparently. "Are you still there? Or are you slumped over the counter in your drunken state?"

"I'm not drunk." I'm sounding perhaps a little indignant and potentially rich. "I was drunk, but am drunk no longer. And I was considering your question so I could give you an appropriate response. What was the question?"

"Forget it. Your response time was way too long, so I'm just going to finish …"

"I'm really tired," I'm whining.

"Yah, I get it. Camembert, vino, Bloody Mary, *sad life* coma—I get it," he's responding snappily, "but this will only take a minute."

"Fine." I'm tired, and I know his minutes, so there's good reason for me to be scooting over to a stool to take a seat. Should I finish that one-quarter bottle of vino left while listening to Chris? Does that make me a real wino? Like potential alcoholic, AA meetings, the whole thing? Does it? If I'm slugging it down straight from the bottle, maybe it does, but surely if it is executed with an ever-so elegant sipping from a nice wine glass it would be fine? And surely I would be excused, given the magnitude and expected length of this conversation.

"So I'm in this mellow state of mind, and I'm all like, 'Oh, I love you,' and then on our third gin and tonic he says to me … Are you reaching for more wine?"

"Why did he say that?" A bit confused as to where his story is heading.

"No, I'm talking to you! Are you reaching for another glass of wine?"

Damn! How did he intercept that? How does this man know me so well? What do I say?

"No," I say, hand still touching the bottle.

"You're holding the bottle right now," he's saying so smugly.

"Bullshit!" I'm nothing but a caught-out drunk.

"I knew it. I can hear you bloody clunking around. I don't care—who am I to judge? I'm not your regular Pollyanna. In fact, I can pop around and we can finish that bottle together if you like. Remember, I'm just down the road—whenever you need me!"

How can I forget?

"No really, the phone conversation is enough. I really need to get to bed. I've got an early meeting tomorrow." Whoops, lying again. All these fibs and swear words … Wow, the things I've been pushed to during the last twenty-four hours. Although maybe I do have a meeting … Fuck, can't remember!

"Bullshit!"

How does he do it? He's better than any medium I've visited, between him and my mother they could rule the world.

"But fine, if you don't want to see me. I'll tell you the story again face to face over lunch tomorrow … But just before I go, let me get it out now before I forget the fresh details. You know how they leak out of your brain if you sleep on it?"

Vaguely. Yes, maybe that one's true. Time to pour the red. The colour of love! Very apt!

"So back to my story—Where were we?"

We were nowhere. You, however, were about to have wild sex with your new BF.

He starts continuing without any prompt from me, "We've had a few drinks at Canary Yellow, and then he starts talking to me about this other guy."

Oh shit. Here comes some threesome story. I'm not sure I can deal with ball-brushing, ass-slapping chat. Maybe this is how Mother had felt when I had raised the vagina conversation. Nothing a large swig won't fix. Alcohol consumption warranted, given the potentially disturbing details about to be unleashed. *Gulp*.

3. 9:20 a.m. 15th February

*R*unning disturbingly late for meeting after recalling that said meeting was not actually a ruse to dispose of Chris quickly on the phone last night, but an actual reality. I had felt it vaguely in my mind, but wine had taken over. I'm not looking forward to this bus ride to work—vomit-worthy. Feeling bloated and middle-aged—even though not middle-aged, despite Chris's jibes. Standing on bus now at 9:27 a.m., clinging to the rail, swinging at whim because no male has seen it necessary to provide me with his seat. Age of gallantry is gone. Only one thing to do really … must keep eyeing off each of the able-bodied men with my death stares. They're all averting their eyes quickly, looking back down to Smartphone or newspaper or anything, even down at their scrunched up crotches in clear desperate attempt to avoid drawing death stare from crazy-eyed woman. Swinging motion and sudden jerking stops of the bus doing nothing for dirty hangover condition. Vomit probability

increasing by the second. Feel the urge to barf. Love the word barf. So
American! Very Homer Simpson—certainly apt for situation—BARF!

More swinging, and all the way round onto Miller Street in Pyrmont.
Going to the doors now, got to get off first. I'm in desperate need of fresh
air—this is my focus. Fresh air. Shove *you* out the way, and you, another
passenger move on for *moi*. Possibly acting in an unladylike manner, but
must get to work before 9:30 a.m., or 9:30 a.m. on the dot, or at the very
least a reasonably late time after 9:30 a.m., like for example any time
between 9:30 a.m. and 9:40 a.m ... or even 9:45 a.m. Any time after that
is completely unacceptable. Unless it is just by one minute after maybe!

Weekly WIP with directors, other account directors, and creatives
working on specific projects is always on at 9:30 a.m. They all must be
used to the fact that I've been consistently late to these meetings. Getting
to work on time, or anywhere on time, has never really been my strength.
It's not even a sleeping-in issue. It's more of a random, hanging about flat
for no reason, time running away from me issue. Today is more of a
sleeping in due to grotesque hangover, due to a post-Valentine's Day vino,
cocktail, or the semblance of a bucket of Bloody Mary issue.

Whoopee, I'm at the front, ready for this bus to lurch to a stop a few
blocks away from my office. The doors mechanically spring to life like
geriatric robots. *Phew*, fresh air. Now my focus is 9:30 a.m., hence the
hurling of myself in the general direction of the street, flinging my bag
onto my shoulder as I go, go, go ...

Running now, in some sort of demented high-heeled, short-skirted
sprint. A maniacal expression on my face—I can feel it, I am forcing it
even. Luckily, there's hardly anyone on the street, so less like an obstacle
course. But of course, there are less people on the street because said

people who would usually be blocking my trajectory are currently, most likely, comfortably seated in their office chair, swigging a soy latte and noshing on a *skinny* muffin, catching up on their emails or watching some cat video on Facebook.

Rounding the corner now, not dissimilar to Carl Lewis on his final turn, I'm metres away from my work place. It's in my sights, I see it, and I can also see a few stragglers outside the front of the building, Styrofoam cups in hands, placid smiles on faces. They're wearing mustard hipster pants—rolled up to reveal bare, sockless ankles; floral, nonchalant dresses with jean jackets, like an updated Courtney Love from the days when Hole was *du jour* (yes, I remember Courtney Love, Hole, and that goddamn wonderful song "Malibu"—a sign of my advancing years); and fagging away like nothing could kill them because they're hipsters and, well *cool*, or something.

Their presence is making me conscious of my walk, so pulling up abruptly, trying desperately to slow to a casual saunter as I'm approaching them, pushing the hair out of my face, trying to affect a look of calmness and zen. Hair not moving, persistently sticking to sweaty face! Oh shit, my short skirt is shorter than I remember it being before I alighted the bus. More than slightly flippy, definitely flippy! *Sigh*. Think I may have just flashed my underwear to those cool hipsters. Well, I have been running, a morning exercise of sorts, even if it has been in a potentially inappropriate manner.

There's that bloody creative. The American. Hmm? Trawling brain. Mental dictionary of names … *What is he called?* It's something hip, which matches his hipster attire and general nonchalant behaviour. He's like some sort of man-child. Behind his mustard pants and sailor shoes, tats, and current haircut, I can spy his advanced age ... potentially as advanced as my own. Yep, definitely early to mid-thirties.

And in this industry, that's advanced. Anything over twenty-nine is over the fucking hill.

He's looking at me with a sly little smile on his face, like he knows ... well, like he knows *everything*: the fact that I have been running like a lunatic because I'm late for a 9:30 a.m. meeting, the fact that I'm desperate and dateless and have spent Valentine's Day alone wallowing in my sorrows over Kardashian re-runs and consuming copious amounts of alcohol, and perhaps he even knows my advanced age as well.

I can't help but look his way right now, and he's just given me this random head nod. Some sort of primitive, yet cool, salutation. I'm trying to return the nod, but my neck isn't allowing it, as if I am hardwired for non-coolness.

"Hi," I say, opting for a greeting paired with my slightly snooty tone instead, the one that says *my shit don't stink, but I bet yours does,* and *I fart rainbows and butterflies—but you don't.* Yes, very mature indeed—helps to keep my advanced age down.

Great, he is following me into the building. This monolithic, judgmental, creative, American being behind me. Perfect time to swish my hips a little then, just enough for the skirt to flip again ...

Surely he's not heading to the lift as well. *So* hoping he'll turn off in another direction. Pressing the *up* button and turning, with an expression of aloofness on my still clammy face, ever so slightly to check if he's still present.

He still is. He's right here. Hands in mustard jean pockets, flexing his meaty tattooed biceps. Are they biceps? Not sure, wasn't paying sufficient attention during physical education. Can't recall if biceps are on top of arm or beneath. You know, the flabby tuck-shop arm area? They are on top actually. I recall a chat with Chris about biceps and bisexuals now. Can't remember the exact content of the conversation, but distinctively remember biceps are the bulgy bits.

"Lift's here." He's already in the lift, holding the door open.

I am looking up at him, for longer than a glance, away from my muddle of former thought pattern. "Right." That was supposed to sound calm, although it's come out as a semi-sob.

"Level two?" he's asking me with his sweet American twang, eyebrow raised like he thinks I don't know whether I'm *Arthur or Martha* and don't know what floor I'm going to.

"Yes." I am purposely being prim. In fact, I do know it's two. *It's my bloody floor, you wanker!* Exclamation mark, exclamation mark! It *is* your floor, too, you tosser! Exclamation mark.

Best to stay silent and just keep looking towards the doors as they are closing again.

He's not speaking now either. Obviously having concurred that I'm a lost cause. He's leaning an arm against the side of the lift in his *too cool for school* manner.

One, two … *Ping* … *Phew*, the doors are slowly swinging open.

Instead of looking to check if he's walking out—because these days, as ascertained on the bus, the age of gallantry is over, and he could very well be advancing past me already—I'm just going to walk … stalk, in fact, through the doors slightly aggressively.

I am inhaling air, as if preparing myself for the day, and more importantly, this meeting. Smoothing my blonde hair down now, in what

I hope is a Cameron Diaz-esque glory of a bob, whilst still stalking somewhat, heading in the direction of said meeting room. Focus, Cee. Forget that American meat cake in lift, forget diabolical journey to work, and ignore that you are very much still secreting alcohol through the pores in your skin. Impress. You're a smart, capable woman. Perhaps not top of your year at school, but very close, fourth to be exact! Perhaps not graduating with first class honours, but honours nonetheless. Go get them, tiger!

Walking, less stalking, holding head high—Own this, Cee. Own this.

Meeting room twelve is the designated area for weekly WIP, and turning the corner, there are ten heads swinging in my direction, all seated, perfectly poised, and wearing equally irritated expressions on their faces. That must be my doing then.

And so here it comes, that influx of negativity. I can recover myself though, I know I can, with a flash of a jaunty smile. Easy … Oh, how *odd!* It's not working. The irritated expressions have remained.

Locating a free chair. Heading there now, but a difficult task, ascertaining which seat is free, isn't it? Same as in a waiting room, or even at a theatre when you have an allocated seat. Just a little awkward cocking your head to locate that spot that makes you feel less of a spectacle. Spectacles. Ha, well done, Cee. I'm not wearing glasses, because too vain, and as a result, I can't see a fucking thing until I am within two metres proximity to said free seat. A stumble is fine, nobody has seen—I'm sure of it. Grabbing of the chair has saved me, but shit, that's more than slightly unfortunate, as it seems that *Americano* has been behind me the whole way and now is taking the only other free chair next to me.

It's best that I don't look at him. Instead, I'm focusing on recovering myself. I am still smiling sweetly, and this time in the direct direction of the Director. That sounds funny. He must think I'm cute; after all, I'm cute right? Yes you are, Cee! Even though slightly aged (but not archaic); surely he is being taken in by my inherent charm?

"You're late!" His voice is stern.

Not quite then. The smile has failed me it seems. He's a portly man, age unknown. I suspect between fifty and sixty. Could potentially be younger with a whole lot of hard living behind him. He's an obtuse individual: British, loud, boisterous, has some sort of strange flaky skin condition, and is on the brink of being obese (portly is my kinder descriptive option, but he's pissed me off now, so today it's *obese)*, his shirt straining at its very seams on most days. Usually, I have him on my side. We're two flamingos amongst a group of sparrows, pigeons and other semi-colourful birds. He likes me, and I like him—sort of. In that strange, I sort of understand where you're coming from way, even though you're rude and need to buy larger shirts to avoid buttons bursting on a daily basis.

But not this morning, I can tell. He hates tardiness. Abhors it. Especially when it's on his time, which is more than a couple of grand an hour.

My smile is still fixed, hoping it's going to bide me time so I can scan my mind for potential alibis other than *I got really drunk last night and then woke up with a terrible hangover, late of course* … and then the public transport in this goddamn country was terrible and slow … or something to that effect! Still scanning—scan, scan, scan. But nothing is jumping to mind.

Really, Cee? After all these years of hard drinking, breakups, binge eating, jobs unfinished, work hours limited, and you still have nothing?

I'm aghast.

I'm suspecting there's a look of utter panic on my face right this second. Yep, sure of it. I have been feeling the creep of it for a few moments, almost as if I've slowly been peeling away a latex mask.

"We went to get a coffee … but the queue out there is ridiculous. Longer than anything in the States." Americano has jumped in, his voice solid, calm, and regular … breezy really. The rest of the group is tittering, ha-ha funny, anything that comes out of his mouth is so fucking funny because he's American and so wonderful, of course.

Looking at him with a quiet smile on my face, eyebrow skeptically raised. *I'm onto you.* You are not funny, Mister Americano. That wasn't even a clever quip, and … and … anyway, you're a liar!

Note to self: Beefy over here is a liar. Will say anything to keep himself out of trouble: making an excuse for fagging away outside instead of being here on time, making himself late to an important meeting with directors and the like.

"I can't imagine anything being longer than queues in the States," Ian is chiming in, a benevolent smile playing across his chubby cheeks.

Aww … I see, *all is forgiven.* One crack from this guy next to me, and it's fine, is it? Really!

"You've gotta be joking," *Beefy* is continuing with a ready grin and casual tone. "You guys are the worst for queues … and coffees!"

And now they're all laughing. Rip-roaringly. What is he saying? I can hear their thoughts: *We make the most amazing coffees! How could this American say anything but? Him and his plunger coffee! So funny!*

Or something of the sort … but the fact is, they're laughing. And I'm finding myself laughing along with them, too, even though I want to stick something sharp in my eye and in his. This is the game, Cee—can't you see it? Play along! Be liked. And if you're not liked, side with the person who is liked.

That's life though, isn't it? Schoolyard tactics.

"You're a funny guy, Jai," Ian is scoffing, belly shaking in between guffaws. A life of its own, that midsection of his.

Damn, *Jai*, that's it. Jai, aka *Beefy*. Sounds like some prefix of a French phrase more than a proper name. I may well stick to *Beefy*, or *Americano* or *Twat*.

Happy citizens and workers all round so it seems, and I'm still laughing, even though my internal grimace is growing, but externally I'm playing the game too—a portrait of grace and zen am I.

Zen beginning to crumble slightly. Shit, did I just not dress properly this morning? I must have cursed myself for thinking about Ian's popping buttons! How can I do my shirt button back up without anyone noticing? How to re-button and maintain grace and zen? Help!

"So let's get started." Ian is clapping his hands together like his voice isn't booming enough and an extra sound is required. "Let's talk about our top jobs this week."

Distraction. Top button done up, that was some kind of ninja move from me; nobody has noticed my arresting of the potential bra flash. At least I remembered a bra today, which would have been pretty embarrassing if I was sans brassiere.

Why am I glancing towards Americano again? I think I can sense his testosterone because he is sitting so close. He is the *real* distraction, and he's clearly not interested, staring straight ahead towards Ian. In fact, they are all showing Ian their undivided attention.

Let's start with the men, shall we? Mustard pant Account Director—

no, not worried about my near wardrobe malfunction either—staring at Ian. Other mustard pant Account Director—no—staring at Ian. Burgundy pant Account Director (a bit of a change, but still of the hipster ilk)—and no—staring at Ian.

The ladies. Account Director, floral dress, cardigan—NO—still staring at Ian. Floral dress jean jacket creative examining notes—no! Other garment lady … No, no, NO … Ahh, Elsie, she's meeting my eye with a smirk on her face.

Yes, fucking Elsie. I have to smile back, and it's my most demure smile. She has her hands wrapped around her mug and is bringing it to her lips for a sip. It almost looks seductive. No doubt it is hot water with a sliver of lemon, because that's what Elsie has in the morning. Cleanses the system apparently—that and a few rocket leaves and potentially some almonds. It's likely she doesn't even know what a Bloody Mary is.

She's still looking at me. We're competitors. Both Account Directors, both of a certain age, both looking to move onto Director-ville …

Gawd! Feeling like could vomit in my mouth, that's how perfect this woman is, and also because I am still hung over. She's wearing the right clothes, has the right shade of tan, and her hair parts in just the right way, falling down her shoulders in a magical combination—Sofia Vergara cross Jennifer Aniston—Starlet meets girl next door.

And her skin's all dewy and fabulous. And she looks like she's some sort of natural beauty, no makeup or effort of any description.

Farrrrk! How am I supposed to compete with that?

The outfit I've chosen today is worth a consideration, non? I'm trying really hard for no one else to recognise that I'm glancing down towards my attire: black, flippy skirt bought who knows when and who knows where, certainly not a label, or not at the very least a high-end one; random black shirt, no sleeves, with buttons—that often pop, previously popped moments ago to be precise, revealing an inappropriately coloured bra. Potentially peach? Who knows what I threw on this morning. It was 8:30 a.m. when I woke up. No time for the usual wardrobe plan. But I did manage to throw on something that was clean and available. That's initiative.

Overall, I have the definitive look of a woman, potentially Account Director from the early nineties or maybe later if I'm lucky—certainly not hipster charm.

"Cecilia!" *Snap.* I can hear my name being called loudly. Ian! Staring at me sharply, as though he may have said my name a few times prior to this.

That sweet smile is back and I'm recovering myself.

"Ce-cil-ia," he is enunciating again in that highbred British accent that comes out all arrogance and aging Prince Harry.

"Yes?" Oh god, he really did just ask me something while I was staring off into the distance wondering if my outfit was hipster enough for this office and planning revenge against that goddamn perfect Elsie.

"Cecilia, I know you must have had a big night last night, given it was Valentine's Day and all." A few titters rising from the group, because of course they're all convinced I was off shagging some so-and-so given that I'm single, in my thirties, and in that *free love* category. "But we really need you to come back to earth. You're off with the bloody pixies this morning."

They are all giggling now, slightly furtively, some with evident pleasure. Not like their chortle with Jai. This is different laughter, and Elsie, well, she is covering her mouth politely as though she's too demure to laugh out loud, but her eyes are grinning with pure mirth. *Beefy* is laughing solidly at my side. Big American raucous laughter, and I am not laughing at all.

"Yes, I'm listening. What was the question?" I say, trying to keep the crossness out of my voice and instead injecting it with some Marilyn Monroe breathlessness.

"How is that new yoga account you're working on going?"

Shifting in my seat, I'm trying to recollect where it's up to. A yoga franchise, some Swami or other, who wears orange robes and has massive following here and in the States. Now looking to us to increase his following even further, make him a household name in every reasonable hipster house in Bondi that there is.

Flash! I'm waiting on the creative. The sun shines once more. A glorious light beaming into my consciousness! It's not me holding up the progression of this, it's *Beefy* sitting beside me. Brilliant.

"I'm waiting on the first draft from the creative." *Ha!* There Elsie, you perfect little hipster-come-Account-Director, I am on top of things despite the roaring headache.

"Jayyyyy, how's that going?" Ian has made Jai's name sound like a cleaning product.

"Oh, yeah. Done. It's on Cee's desk. Finished it up this morning."

Smug little shit. I'm not going to look at him again, blinking my eyes a few times trying to think of a way of confirming or denying. Nothing has sprung, or is springing to mind.

Besides, how dare he use my nickname? I don't call him *Beefy* to his face! But he thinks he can throw *Cee* around like we're casual friends, slurping lattes down at the café together. Not on my watch, buddy. Not today, Beefy. Not ever!

"Right," Ian is snapping again. "Cecilia, get it together and send it across to the Swami before we lose his yogic business."

"Sure thing." Think unfrazzled, Cee. Refined, on top of things. Focus.

Luckily he is moving on to his next victim. He's like a shark circling his prey, darting at any sign of inefficiency like he's smelt blood. He's taking a few punters down right now with a prod—a pounce—and a pound.

Mustard pants to my left is virtually quaking in his seat under Ian's direct line of questioning. It's amusing to watch now that it's not me under the depths of his wrath. Breezy creative with peroxide blonde hair and pink tips looks as though she might cry. *Boohoo.*

Who's next? Oh, the perfect Elsie. The look on her face is everything I would have wanted on mine a moment ago, completely zen and at peace with the work. How does she stay so composed? She should be taking the yoga account, not neurotic drunk over here—That's me, unfortunately.

Oh, it seems she perfectly knows where everything is perfectly up to. Perfectly concentrated to utter per*fuck*ion.

Sigh. Relief. Glad that the weekly grilling is done. Ian is busying himself getting to his feet. Large gut bulging over the table, a button unfastened, revealing the straining semi-pregnant growth itself, along with a few tufts of aging body hair. It's not just me attempting to, but failing to, avert my eyes. It's like some grotesque train wreck. Sometimes you just can't look away. So wrong, yet so enticing!

"Okay, little people." So PC and everything, isn't he? "Time is money, and in fact, my money, so get moving. Don't just sit there gaping."

He clearly has no idea about the shirt, but the thing is, even if he knew about the shirt, he wouldn't care. Money beats anything else in the *rock-paper-scissors* game of life, including obesity and grotesqueries. Dr. Frankenstein's creation would have been a hit if he had a few million to burn, a home in Rose Bay, holiday house in Ibiza, and was a Managing Director of an advertising agency. But poor Franky had none of that.

We are all scrambling to our feet because his words are like a command to move, tripping over ourselves to see who can get up faster, grabbing iPads, bags and lattes in some manic dance to prove our worth and initiative.

Here we go again, it's like the bloody bus, I'm totally getting squeezed out of the doorway by a couple of ever-keen hipsters, and I am falling behind big time ...

"Big night then, Cee?" Who's that? It's an American someone, who's standing behind me. I'm looking up to see the gloating little smile on his face. People are still pushing past me like the last life raft from the sinking Titanic is on the other side of the door. *My heart will go on and on* ...

"Yeah, something like that. By the way, it's Cecilia." I have to throw that in for good measure, in an aloof tone of course.

"My apologies, Cecilia." He's pushing in front of me and now letting me through in a gentlemanly fashion, a sly grin on his face. Sly like a fox ... Like an American fox. Does America have foxes?

I am doing that stalking again, right past him, but he's sharp on my heels.

I'm turning in at my office, all six square metres of it. There you go, bag. I'll dump you down in your rightful place—my desk, next to his bloody designs; those designs that are all ready, and waiting, sitting flatly on my keyboard. Prick; was he looking to make a fool out of me at this morning's meeting?

Really. *Oh, go away.* He's dangling at the door. *Act unaffected, Cee; just continue booting up your computer.* I can't completely ignore him. I can sense he knows that I know he's here, so raising a quizzical eyebrow and looking at him, I am just going to wait until he speaks.

"Did the boyfriend take you to dinner?"

Is this man, all American charm and swagger, looking to expose me with such a question? Need to gather what's left of my wit and sagacity in this post-alcohol binge haze. "Yes, in fact he did. We went to Fratelli Paradiso in Elizabeth Bay."

Credible, *non*?

What the fuck is Elsie doing standing at my door now too? Both of them looking at me with that bronzed combination stare and their matching zen smiles and knowing eyes. Like I need this now.

"Oh, that's right." She is speaking all cheerleader-like and adorable, mug still in hand, flicking that mane of hers. "That would be close to your house in Kings Cross?"

"Potts Point." These two small words have left my mouth through clenched teeth.

"Right. Like I said, Kings Cross. New BF then, Cee?" She's asking me this like we're *besties*. More like beasties. Clinging onto the table now, my knuckles have started turning white. "I thought you just broke up with that other guy, the finance guy?"

Sigh. Yes, the finance guy. Does this woman eavesdrop on my conversations? Apparently, she does just that.

"Yeah, new guy," I'm confirming, nodding my head. Taking that almost maniacal nodding to my screen, not wanting to respond to her other than perhaps jumping up out of seat, flinging my body forward over my desk in some Lucy Liu move, skirt flipping above my ass, buttons popping and revealing (possibly) peach bra, arms forward, hands in grip position ready to throttle her tiny little bird neck, or just mess up that perfect fucking hair. I'm guessing that's all rather inappropriate. "Lots of work this morning." I'm hoping this mantra-like delivery will give *Beefy* and *Cheerleader* the hint to take a hike.

"Oh, sure," she's saying so breezily. "You're a fast mover." She's turning on her heels, obviously always wanting the last word. "Hope this one's a keeper."

Ah! There it is. Knife wedged into back. In between shoulders. I might reach an arm around to see if there is an actual real dagger there instead of a metaphorical one. Oh no, arm not quite there. Had I taken a few more yoga classes with the Swami, perhaps I would be able to reach it instead of looking like some primate swinging my arms behind my body.

Damn! Beefy's still here—just watching silently!

Americans need more of a nudge, don't they? "See you, then." I'm not even going to say his cursed name.

"See you, Cee." He clearly has to say mine. "By the way …" He is purposely pausing, clearly for dramatic effect, and I'm looking up wondering exactly what this will entail.

"Nice knickers," he says grinning. "Candy pink?"

Random twitching happening on my face. Involuntary. As though I might have a stroke. Feeling blood rushing to my head simultaneously.

He's spluttering with laughter and he is leaving. *Fuck off, prick!*

Good. He's out of my sight, and I'm glancing around now making sure there's no hangers-on. Time to check under my skirt, slowly peeling it up just enough to see that … Damn! Candy pink indeed. Must have flashed him and that couple of other colleagues when running down the street post-bus journey.

The horror. The horror. The horror.

There are probably memos circulating about my candy pink knickers at this very moment. Ping from the computer. Instant message. The pinging is starting to play everywhere. Yes, memo shared!

And I have become the work laughing stock it would seem.

Is it wrong to drink at 10:15 a.m.? Is it wrong to keep a bottle of Bombay Sapphire stowed away quietly in my bottom drawer, waiting for eventualities such as these? Well, is it?

4. 11:30a.m.

id not consume Bombay Sapphire as had initially intended. Decided that slide into alcoholism has become too pronounced, and have two meetings this afternoon—one with the Swami and another with ex-football-player-come-restaurateur. Eligible bachelor of the year, of the decade, potentially of the century. Marriage number two now concluded, embarking on some rash franchise of single restaurant, looking for advertising skills to assist—and think, arguably, new wife. Must be on form for this meeting, that is, no slurring, flashing, or floating off into another dimension with thought pattern. Bombay Sapphire would not assist in this enterprise.

Furiously typing an email reply to Chris. Not exactly work, but it's this or the gin …

"Yep, I'll meet you for lunch. No drinky-poos though, love. Meeting marriage material after lunch, and if you want to ensure your place on my post-marital yacht, you won't encourage me. Greg's a complete tosser if he wants anything but your ass.

Speaking of ass … May have flashed colleagues …"

Unfinished. Interruption. Knocking at door. Glancing up, I'm annoyed. I'm sick of interruptions today. No glasses on—so frowning like crazy person to make out the figure standing in the doorframe. It's a young thing. Brunette, hair perfectly coiffed, figure outstanding, short skirt, large belt, flat ballet slippers, eyebrows thick and styled, can't make out the rest of her facial features from this far away. Very *du jour* and young! Vomit in mouth, must be an intern.

"Hi, Cecilia?" She's bold with her question, and broadly smiling. The fact is she should be saying it apprehensively, with fear in her voice, given she's talking to someone firstly, so advanced in years, and secondly, advanced in career (sort of). Well, it should appear that way to someone of her age. How old could she be? Nineteen? Twenty?

Eyeing her warily. Delaying my response, just because I am a little delayed in all actions, verbal or otherwise today.

"Yes." I'm waiting now for her to elaborate.

"I'm your new intern!" *Of course you are.* Intern! I knew it, but my intern? What the? I don't take interns—ever! When the intern lottery happens I keep my hand down. Very down. Down so low nobody could ever possibly see it. I don't *like* interns. I don't do interns. I'm not interested in interns. All that youthful enthusiasm reminds me of failed dreams.

"No," I say, remaining resolute. "There's been a mistake. I don't have an intern assigned to me." Best to return to my keyboard, hoping she'll just go away. Email to Chris sent. Good.

Eyes flitting up … not good. Geez! Really? She is still very much here, in my office, with her whole internship-ness contaminating my personal space.

"I'm definitely assigned to you. I just went through the whole induction process, and I have your name written here, right on this slip of paper. Cecilia Binner?" She is holding the paper out to me, taking steps forward ...

Not apprehensive steps, not timid steps. Big steps. Confident steps. Towards my desk. Handing me the paper with a smile, but I'm not smiling. I'm squinting at the printed emails. Eyesight is failing me.

There it is, *my name*, against the word "supervisor."

No, this can't be right.

"Again," I repeat. "There must be some sort of mistake. I'll sort this."

I wave her towards the minuscule table and chair in the corner of my office. I'm calling Ian directly. No need for middle management, he'll sort it.

I can feel the sickly sweet smile fixed on my face and she is smiling, seemingly sincerely, back to me, clearly unbeknownst to the fact that I'm trying to desperately discharge her, or better still, confirm this is some sort of bizarre accident. *Christ!* After all, haven't I made it clear enough I won't be responsible for interns? It's my mantra ... Well, one of them.

"Binner?" Ian has answered. I was semi-expecting his EA, and now this has thrown me off instantly. She's probably off buying a coffee, or diet pills, or having injectables deployed into her face. It's good it's him, though. He knows me; he'll sort this bullshit.

"Well hello, Ian." I pause for a moment, still trying to regain my thought pattern. What was I going to say in the first place?

"Yes, Binner? What do you have to say for yourself? After all, you called *me."* Tone of British disdain, followed by off-putting chewing sound. What is he eating at this time of the morning? Brunch? Eggs and tomatoes; some sort of crispy bread with tapenade? Oh, I'm bloody hungry!

"Why yes, I did, sir," I say coyly. Flattery always works.

"Don't flatter me." He's talking in between gulps of air and chewing of some sort of ingestible.

"Well, Ian, I have an intern here." I am purposely sounding flat—It's all in the tone, you know.

"Right. And?" *Chomp, chomp, chomp.* There must be some sort of crispy bread involved. I'm actually salivating at Ian's crunching sounds, tummy rumbling now, crying for solid food.

"I didn't apply for an intern. I didn't request one," I say, hoping to keep the plaintive tone out of my voice. No luck, it's definitely there.

"I understand." He's paused, and there's a pause in eating also. "But we felt you needed one."

"I don't need one." I may sound snappy and hasty, but this is ludicrous, and I'm somehow still managing this sweet smile at the intern. She still clearly has no idea what's going on; her smile says so.

"Well, we thought you did."

Who is this royal "we" he's referring to? I have no idea—him and the other execs, or just him? I'll refrain from asking.

"That's very kind of you, but I don't have time to train an intern. Not at all. I'm very busy. As you know with the yoga account, and that restaurateur, not to mention … "

"Yes, I know perfectly well what you have going on." He's just cut me off. "That's why we felt an intern would be of use."

"But you know how it is, Ian," I'm desperately appealing. "You spend half the time training the intern rather than the intern being of assistance to you." I don't care that she is present in the room. She doesn't seem to notice anyway.

"Cristina's very clever. Top of her class at school and university. I'm sure she'll catch on quickly."

"I don't think that's the case." I'm choking here, totally feeling the intern noose settling around my neck. "They're all the same. Complete rookies."

"Binner." He always interrupts, and with such authority in his tone. "You will deal with that. No further questions asked."

Stuttering inelegantly and watching Cristina shifting in her seat—I think she is more aware of the nature of this conversation now.

More stuttering, unable to put together a rational sentence. No words are coming out, just random, almost rodent-like sounds.

"This is your weakness, Binner—people management. You need to find your style, whether it's kind and motherly, best friend or complete tyrant. You don't have one now because you refuse to manage people." Here we go, pause, adding of that predictable dramatic effect. "This is your chance! Don't mess it up."

"I ... I ... I don't want a chance!" I can feel the impending doom coming on. This battle has been lost, hasn't it? Once Ian gets something in his head, there's no changing his mind. The only changing of his mind happens when he gets another thought in his head.

"Yes, you do!" he is roaring down the phone at me, and there we have it. He's hung up.

Sitting here thinking. Hunger passed. I'm still clinging to the phone, eyes wide, trying to digest the conversation. Time to return to the room and to Cristina, who is watching me with an *I told you so* expression, arms crossed and legs crossed, foot tapping knowingly against the ground.

Tap. Tap. Tap.

My smile is hopefully more dignified in manner than it has been since she entered this room—*my* office.

"Well, apparently you're my intern," I say, placing the phone back on the deck.

"That's what the paperwork says." She's so cool with her response, flicking her immaculately coiffed brown hair, which flows like a pure chocolate sheath: lustrous, brown, thick and straight.

I'm getting one of those interrupting, sudden visions, one that shows me what I must appear to her to be like: My "Blondie-esque" hair awry, no time to give it a straighten this morning (not that it would have made a difference to my wiry, untamable locks, which have the appearance of one who has stuck their fork in the toaster), face tired, potentially puffy as a result of alcohol, outfit outdated, personality bizarre and non-descript, trying to get myself out of motherly intern duties.

Now I'm wishing that I'd ingested that Bombay Sapphire as initially intended.

"So," her voice is so crisp, "where should I begin? Should I set up in here?'

Glancing around in a panicked state at my tiny office, barely enough room to house one being, let alone two.

"Aren't there some desks out on the floor?" I'm waving her in the direction of the floor, the egalitarian area where most people sit, separated only by partitions. A place I had so desperately tried to leave, and successfully have, only to have this jumped-up little girl infringe on my space.

What is she shaking her head at?

"No, I checked." Oh, did you indeed?

Sigh. "Fine, set up there."

I wish she'd wipe what appears to be a genuine smile off her face. Youth of today, so quick to forget any past scorns.

"Great!" She's talking again and starting to unpack what she has with her. A skinny laptop, a notebook, some pens. "Can I bring some more things?" Somehow she's been lured into a false sense of safety and security in my presence.

"Like what?"

"Oh, you know, just a few odd bits to make it more homely in here. Maybe a plant?" She's glancing up at me, face filled with promise.

A plant, for Christ's sake!

"No." A neat flat response should shut her up.

"Oh, okay …" She's conceded, and is continuing to unpack, hopefully without another word.

It's 12:20 p.m. I'm saved. Hunger returning. Lunch. Starving actually.

Stumbling to my feet and grabbing my bag, I need to get out of here. "Lunch. Starved. Must go." I have to be careful to keep my thoughts locked away from articulation now that I have her lurking around here.

Door in hand, I hear her voice. "Wait!" It feels like some sort of command.

Turning slowly, feeling perturbed, I can't quite be sure what's waiting expectantly behind me.

"What am I going to do in the meantime?" she's asking, looking desperate, her enthusiastic little face crumpling.

"Go to lunch." For fark's sake, self-explanatory, non? Who is this person?

"It's just ... "

Her sentence is trailing off, and I'm running late. Spit it out! She's probably deterred by the look on my face, which must be somewhere between food deprivation and homicidal.

"Well, go on!" Impatient prompts often required with moaning interns.

"It's just ... they only keep one of us," she says, shoulders slumping.

What the hell is she talking about? I'm just looking at her waiting for some more dialogue to babble forth from that pretty little mouth of hers.

"At the end of the internship, they only keep one of us—and ... and I want to stay, so I need to start learning as quickly as possible."

Sigh. The burden of the *driven* and *conscious!* If only I could shoulder some of it for them. Come on, Cee, soften up. She thinks her whole career is hanging on this internship, on this very day. *Sigh.*

"We'll start working—after lunch!" My hungover mind is rattling through the things I had been planning on doing after lunch: online shopping, stalking ex-boyfriends and friends on Facebook, perusing the adult learning section on university websites, whimsically thinking that one day I'll take up an art course or language class—All of these beautiful possibilities have now been thwarted with the advent of this little person.

But she looks like she is brightening slightly, presumably at the thought of starting proper work this afternoon.

"Go make friends." Good advice, methinks. "That can be your first assignment. Remember, it's not what you know, but who you know." Spouting all this wisdom is giving me more of an appetite. Not sure where it just came from, and don't care, because food deprivation is really setting in.

She's sitting up straight, with that enthused expression on her face, and I can tell what she's thinking: *I thought this mentor was bust, but she's shrewder than I expected.*

Or here's to hoping.

Turning again for the door, intending to actually leave this time, but oh no, because Cristina is making another sound, and it's, "Oh!"

I'm turning around again, ever so slowly …

"By the way, I just thought I'd let you know," getting to her feet quickly, coming up to me, standing ever so closely and now whispering desperately, "that there's a rumour going around about you this morning that you're wearing pink underwear."

She is looking at me pleadingly. She's trying to get in my good books, isn't she? As an act of solidarity—it's painfully obvious. Clearly, she's thinking, *tell your gruesome mentor the truth, so she can at least be aware why people are snickering at her when they walk past her in the office. It's only right that she should know, and perhaps it will endear me to her.*

"Really should have had that Bombay Sapphire earlier."

"What?"

Oh, I said that out loud.

"Well, Cristina," I say using my best Marilyn tone, "I do have pink underwear on, and it's lacy, too!"

With these words, I am very much sliding away from her with my best Marilyn forward slash Marie Antoinette walk (or at least how I think such vixens would have walked). Oh, the devil is speaking to me, that little vixen on my shoulder. It's making me do inappropriate things like raising my skirt enough for those very much talked about candy knickers to peek out and say *hello Cristina,* pink and lacy indeed. I really want to turn around to see her face, so I can show her my mischievous smile. Chris will be proud.

If they want to talk about my panties, let them talk about my fucking panties!

5. 1:00p.m.

owning a gin and tonic with Chris, waiting for lunch. I know I said I wasn't going to drink, but the intern thing has tipped me over the edge. Lamenting sorrows. Sitting at Poncey, hipster locale in Newtown. Thinking I shouldn't be drinking at this point, but Chris's dialogue and my revelations that I've flashed underwear to colleagues, have sent me spiraling towards an unrelenting path of alcoholism. It's like a juggernaut, really. Even though I purposely showed my intern, she is not technically a colleague. More of a growth, a parasite perhaps.

"So what do you think?" Chris is asking again, expectantly, sipping on his cocktail. He's wearing a tight, checkered shirt, rolled up to his biceps, showing off his tanned and muscular arms. The shirt is tucked firmly into a pair of those signature mustard pants. Why is every hipster man alive wearing them? Mustard! It is the colour of newborn baby shite. And now they've even crossed tracks from the hipsters to the homosexuals. When will the mustard pant plague end? When! WHEN?

He just crossed his legs, a pair of Hugo Boss shoes peaking out from beneath the table. No socks of course. His face is perfectly bronzed, his eyebrows perfectly shaped, too perfect! His green eyes warm, if not slightly tired, an evident sign of his shenanigans at the Canary Yellow last night.

He's a handsome man, no denying it, and masculine, too. The *gaydar* would really have to be switched on to the max. But to the gay-connoisseur, like talented *moi*, having lived the majority of my adult years in Potts Point (yes discretely close to Kings Cross), it's evident.

The truth is that *everything* is just too tight. The clothes are one size too tight, the biceps are too exposed, the shoes are too shiny, the eyebrows are too perfect, the hair is too coiffed … It's just too *everything*. It's a sure sign of being in gay territory.

Perhaps I could impart this knowledge to my intern? It's valuable stuff. After all, it could save her a lot of time while browsing in this town! Non? But I hardly think a type like hers would appreciate such insight into Sydney's gay world.

"So, should I have the threesome or not?" Chris is blurting out loudly at the same point that our sliders are being placed in front of us. The waitress is beaming down at us with a judgmental expression—all *holier than thou* is she, whoopee fucking do.

"Who's having the pork and mustard?" she is asking so prim.

"That's mine," Chris is replying, but not even looking up, obviously unaware of any social *faux pas* which may have occurred.

I'll follow his lead, methinks, and switch on my Monroe aspirated tone.

"Mine are the *meaty* balls sliders."

"Meatball sliders," she is correcting my smuttiness, oh so righteously as she pops my very meaty balls onto the table.

Oh, thank god for greasy food. Thank god for sliders. Thank god for the person who decided to transform greasy, unhealthy burgers into something slightly petite and fulsome and *du jour*.

"Stop looking at your food and salivating, and answer my question." Hearing him talking, but food is taking priority. "One day you're going to get a booty!" Ha! Here's hoping it'll be a nice, juicy Kardashian one.

I can focus on conversation and food at the same time. I'm biting into one of these things, and no one, not even a friend in need can stop me.

"People are getting ass implants these days," I tell him pointedly, with a mouthful of meatballs.

"What does that have to do with my threesome dalliance?"

"You said I was going to get a booty, and I was pointing out that these days, it's all the rage. People are even getting ass implants."

"Only ghetto girls."

"Kim Kardashian probably has ass implants and she's on the cover of Vogue," I say, sneaking in another bite of a slider. Previous one did not touch sides.

Food, glorious food! Yum, yum, yum, yum!

"You're not married to Kanye."

"No, I'm not Chris, but perhaps I could be … *if* I had ass implants."

He is staring at me, maybe assessing my comment. He's relinquishing, presumably knowing that he'll get no sense out of me if he doesn't accept the direction the conversation has taken.

"Fine, booties are *du jour,*" he has decided to say.

"I concur." I'm going with smugness, starting to hoe into my lunch now in a big way.

"So?"

"So!" So what?

"So, what do you think about the threesome? Sheesh! You really do have the memory of a goldfish."

Sigh. I usually find that the *memory of a goldfish* technique serves well, especially when you're trying to avoid difficult and persistent questions delivered by Chris. I hate being involved in questions that relate to his relationships. Somehow I always end up being the bad guy.

If I say *go with the threesome,* when it all falls over (and it inevitably will), he'll tell me it was bad advice in the first place, he should have never listened to me, given that I have a bad track record, and *then* he'll not talk to me for a fortnight. He'll finally withdraw from his cave with a peevish expression on his face and a warning that my actions have been noted and forgiven, but not forgotten.

On the other hand, if I say *don't go with the threesome,* he'll tell the new boyfriend that this was my advice, resulting in a hex on me from said new boyfriend and strained contact between the three of us for the next few months or so until the relationship hurtles again to its inevitable conclusion. The end. Goodbye. Finito.

Oh, and after the inevitable, I'll be the one that has to spend weekends with Chris, holding his head over toilet bowls as he cries and vomits himself into oblivion and discretely trying to flush pain relief medication down the toilet intermittently so that he doesn't take them all in one hit.

Lose-lose situation. Conclusion drawn: Chris should refrain from any sort of relationship and potentially take on life of abstinence in Buddhist monk fashion. Full stop. Period. Endnote.

"And?" he's asking me again.

"Well, what do *you* think?" Thrusting it into his direction, and thrusting more meatballs in my mouth, hoping he'll talk himself into his own conclusion.

"On the one hand, I'm not adverse to a threesome, as you know …"

Yes, too well. Too many details recounted. Too many times!

"… But," he's continuing, "the threesome is usually reserved to drunken dalliances, when you don't know either of the parties that well and won't ever have to see them again, or you know, for further down the track in a relationship, when things have become stale and you need to liven up the boudoir. I've never encountered the threesome so early on in a relationship, and frankly I think it doesn't bode well. Is he that bored of me now already, or is he a serial threesome haver?" He has concluded, and is pushing his food around the plate.

What is he *doing* with his food? Opening one of the sliders! Oh, he's spearing a gherkin out with his fork. "I adore gherkins, non?" he says holding it up in front of his face, and now he's chewing on it.

I am really trying hard right now not to draw any hasty sexual parallels linking gherkins to cocks, but it's a natural comparison … not the colour necessarily, but definitely the shape, even the bumps and veins; too phallic not for it to enter my mind, and it's there in that direction, and it's difficult to recover from.

"Maybe he just wants to get all the sexual craziness out of the way now and then move onto a serious relationship?" Now we all know this isn't true, but when a friend is in need, one feels a desperate desire to prop them up with idle fantasies.

"I doubt that's the case." He's not having any of my idle fantasies today.

"Where did you meet this guy anyway?" Perhaps some circumstantial evidence and context will help in the threesome decision-making.

"On Grindr."

Hmmm ... This doesn't bode well either. Not well at all!

"What was his profile name?"

"I see where this is going ..." He's letting out a big sigh, like I've asked what cock size his new BF is, which actually he'd probably be more happy to answer. "You're trying to paint a picture of him as some sort of sexual deviant. Yes, I met him on Grindr ... So what!"

Someone is looming over me. I can feel it. An awareness has come over me that I'm being watched while I shovel my food in and wash it down with gin. It's that bloody waitress, I bet. She's going to get one pissed off expressions. Here goes ...

Oh, not said waitress it seems. Instead Jai is staring down at us with an entertained expression. Even with my furious kicking towards Chris's leg under the table, he is continuing on with his trail of smut, regardless.

"But no, his profile name was not *lots-of-cock-for-you*, if that's what you're thinking. Arguably, the word 'cock' *is* in his personality description, but I hardly think that's a hanging offence. After all, it is Grindr, a hookup website for gay men, doll, so one needs to put their best foot forward, or in this case their best cock forward ..."

I'm screwing my face up, and at last he's paused his cock narrative. I think he has become aware of Jai's presence, too, as he is very much looking up at him now, and it seems he's not at all embarrassed.

"Oh, hello," he's saying airily.

"Hi there," Jai has responded, all swagger and American accent.

"Do you know this lovely gentleman?" Chris is asking me with a flirtatious tone in his voice. Oh, Christ, could this get any worse? I feel like crawling under the table.

"I do," I say in a prim manner. "We work together. Chris, *Bee … I mean*, Jai. Jai, Chris." I can't believe I just nearly called him *Beefy*, unsure if they have noticed. They are kind of nodding in a cool acknowledgement to each other. Men. Gay or straight. Hard fucking work.

"What a treat!" Chris is declaring with as much enthusiasm as if he were enacting a scene out of a Broadway musical.

"Yes, indeed," I say, but I'm scowling with my words and not smiling at this point.

"We were just having lunch over there." Jai is gesticulating to a table near the window. Thankfully out of earshot of any smutty discussions. Who are *we?* I'm struggling to see the other figure moving towards us. Focus eyes. Shit! I think I'll wear glasses tomorrow. Maybe not, actually so vain, would prefer to just squint beguilingly at people and be completely unaware of anything that's happening outside of my peripheral vision.

Shit! It's Elsie! So it turns out that things do get worse then.

"Oh hello, darling," she is cooing, looking from Chris to me quickly, evidently assessing the nature of our relationship. "This isn't the gentleman you went to dinner with last night, is it?"

Another swift kick to Chris's leg under the table, just in case he goes into some sort of verbal diarrhea about me not having a date at all. I am completely ignoring his expression and opting for talking breezily over the top of that slight wincing sound he is making. I have perhaps bruised his shins, methinks. Whoops.

"No, no," tittering, with that fixed grin again. "This is my good friend Chris."

"Oh, lovely," she is saying, very prim, but I see her smugness.

"Best friend, confidante, neighbour, soul mate … It's a bit like Catherine and Heathcliff," Chris is piping up all good-naturedly, but with some random bullshit.

And I'm just staring at him. Yes, *just like Catherine and Heathcliff*, without that crucial sex part!

Jai is grinning away, having a grand old time with all of this, I imagine. *Yank prick.*

"Oh wow, you got the sliders!" Elsie has remarked, a tone of disapproval in her voice masked by fun and mirth.

Yes, we got the sliders—now fuck away with you both. Oh, how I would love to tell them to do exactly that.

"They're absolutely wonderful here," Chris is enthusing. "We always have them. The perfect hangover remedy." And he has finished off with a flourish, crossing and uncrossing his legs. "What did you have?"

"The quinoa and rocket salad—Actually, we both did."

Of course you both did. I literally am staring a hole into Jai's stupid face; my eyebrow is well and truly raised. Quinoa and rocket salad. Emasculating much? He doesn't seem pleased by this revelation.

"Elsie's a clean eater," I'm telling Chris, like she can't speak for herself. "You know, vegetarian, vegan, no carbs, no sugar, no caffeine …"

"Soon they'll be telling us not to eat at all!" Chris is quipping, and he's making me laugh. Jai is smothering his laughter, too, while Elsie is looking perfectly perturbed, like she's just swallowed a piece of meat and doesn't like the taste or consistency of it. *Oh, no meat, it's a dead animal, it's been cooked in it's own body fat, little remnants of blood still oozing out in the juice.*

"You have to look after your body; it's the only one you've got!" She is trying to invoke her usual singsong quality, but there's a tone of alarm in there, too.

"Yes, I couldn't agree more," Chris is managing to say whilst winking at Jai. Oh dear god, no Chris, the reference to body does not instantly mean sex. Although I know it does for him. It's like my gherkin-cock association, it just happens.

"So," Elsie has clipped quickly, obviously looking to change the topic, "I hear you have an intern."

"I do, indeed." And indeed, I do, wishing indeed that I don't. "News about anything and everything seems to travel quickly in the office. It's like a sieve," I say, pointedly looking at Jai, wondering if he is the originator of the *pink panties* rumour. Not that it's actually a rumour really, but you know what I mean, the person who tattled.

He is raising an eyebrow, evidently amused.

"You have an intern?" Chris is crying out loud. "Good luck." He's spearing another green cock, I mean gherkin.

"I have one, too," Elsie has already injected, clearly not happy that her role in the discussion has diminished. "I think it's going to be awesome. A little mini-me! I'm sure she's going to be the one that stays."

"And then you can be her mentor forever and ever after. Sounds a bit like a modern day fairytale." Chris's laughing, and I can see Jai's lips turning up at the ends.

Evidently he's on *team Elsie,* otherwise why would he be having lunch with that clean-eating, shiny-haired, eastern suburbian twat? It's an affront for him to be laughing at my jokes!

"I know you like to joke, Cee, but really it's so important for their growth, you know, to have a good role model. It will give them a head start, and their first experience in an office environment should be a positive one."

Oh, please. Shouldn't this be accompanied by some sort of liturgical dance? And why the hell is she calling me *Cee*? I don't call her *El*!

"Oh, you're probably right, El. I should get rid of that bottle of Bombay Sapphire under my desk and stop having cocktail hour every afternoon at three. Might set a poor example."

Chris is in hysterics, Jai has turned away from us, I'm suspecting he needs to hide his laughter (stop laughing at my jokes, goddamn you!), and Elsie is glowering.

"Yes, very funny. Alcoholism is such a joke," she is saying crossly. "Probably time for us to head back to the office, Jai, so much work to do, and I want to focus on my intern." She is annunciating the words carefully to clearly show ownership. I feel sorry for her poor intern! "After all, I want to make sure she's the one that stays." She just has to have the last word. She then proceeds to turn on her heels, and without as much as a *ta-ta* of any sort, saunters off. She's not the type to stalk, at best she'll saunter. Not like *moi*, I definitely stalk.

"See you later." Jai is turning to follow her. Whatever.

"Ciao!" Chris has cooed

"Was she setting down a gauntlet?" I've waited until they are out of earshot before I say this.

"What do you mean?" Chris has asked, still watching Jai in the distance.

"Well, only one intern gets to stay. Did she mean her intern against mine? Her intern stays and mine gets thrust out into bigger Sydney to find a job?"

"I think you're reading into it too much," he is saying absently.

"No, I'm totally not. She said it, you heard her—twice! She said it victoriously, didn't she? As though it's evident. Her intern gets to stay!"

"I think you're going all crazy bitch now," he's saying, chewing meaningfully on his cheese.

"I am not." I'm defensive, and rightly so. "That little green eater …"

"I think it's *clean eater.*" Same thing, methinks.

"Whatever! She's a vindictive little so and so. She's pushing my poor defenseless intern out!" I find myself snapping, potentially now sounding a little crazed.

"Hmm, if only I cared, sweetie. Meanwhile on *Planet Me,* that Jai is a nice piece of ass, non?"

I'm actually a bit alarmed at how quickly he's changed topics from my vengeance and interns to Jai being *a nice piece of ass.*

"I think *non.*" Cold response from moi.

"Are you just saying that because he was at lunch with your little nemesis Elsie? Or is it El?" he's asking provocatively.

"No, those two deserve each other. He's started some rumour this morning about me wearing pink underwear, I told you in the email, and now the whole office is a buzz with it. My intern told me, like she was doing me a favour, like she wanted me to be aware that everyone was talking about me, so I could do something to ameliorate the situation, or at the very least hang my head in shame." Slightly out of breath after ranting, must start doing more cardio.

"Hang on, what's this? He started a rumour about your panties! I think if he's talking about your panties, that's a good sign," he's saying, eyebrow raised, in a resolute tone as if he's resting his case.

"No, it's not like that. Besides, it's not actually a rumour. This morning I was running to work …"

"From home?"

"No, from the bus stop …"

"I thought so, running to work does not sound like you."

"Indeed," I say, acknowledging his interruption, otherwise there's no way to go forward, "and there were a few of my colleagues outside the building. Anyway, whilst running, my skirt must have flipped up, revealing the pink underpants I'm wearing … And he remarks on it at our morning WIP meeting!"

"In front of everyone?"

"No, later, as an aside."

"I was going to say. Fit ass, but asshole."

"Next thing I know, everyone's talking about it!" I say, finishing with a flourish.

"Well, you don't actually know if everyone's talking about it," he has concluded. But I do know, don't I?

"My intern knows about it. Potentially the least connected person in the office!"

"That's true. Maybe everyone does know about it. Are they at least nice underpants?"

"Yes, really nice, but that's not the point …"

"Darling, better to be caught wearing nice underpants than none at all, or, dare I say it, *dirty ones.*"

"I just said that's not the point, and it isn't … The point is that he spread this rumour." He's so frustrating. Sometimes it's like talking to someone who's having a completely different conversation.

"It's not really a rumour, though, is it? After all, it did happen …"

Sigh. "Yes, I said that, and yes it did happen, but he didn't need to tell everyone," I'm hissing now, blood pressure rising. Where's my gin? Shit, glass is empty.

"It could have been someone else. There were other people who saw the incident."

"I just know it was him. I know it. He's looking to discredit me!"

"You're acting a little *cray-cray* today, my dear … Look, at worst he told people that you flashed some pretty pink underwear. You have a nice pair of legs despite all those vinos and sliders, so what do you have to lose? You might turn into the office *vixen.*"

"I don't want to be the office vixen."

"Oh, darling, don't lie to me. Everyone wants to be the office vixen." He's using his omnipotent, all-knowing voice.

If I close my eyes, he may disappear. Closed. Peeling open again. No, he's still here, but this discussion is going nowhere fast.

"Anywho," he's starting breezily again, "about the threesome then …"

6. 2:30p.m.

n ow lying to self, it's more like 2:45 p.m. ... Or a few minutes past that and I'm flying back into the office after long lunch. Extremely prostrated lunch, which, to my dismay, continued with much threesome discussion. Still managed to remain non-committal with responses to pointed questions. Feeling satisfied with outcome, however know that it will likely come back and bite me on the bottom because it involves Chris and a relationship. Now running, jogging, skipping along towards office, may be flashing more takers my underwear, but no longer care. I actually like the breeze on my butt cheeks. Afternoon meetings are upon me—no time for trivial flasher thoughts. Will take up my role as office vixen with panache and ingenuity. Long live the office vixen! Here—Here! That could be the gin and tonics talking, yes I ordered more.

Turning into my office slightly breathless, and here's Cristina. Sitting at the tiny table, straight backed, laptop ready, pens and paper expectant, eager expression on face.

"You're back!" Her tone is so excited.

"Yes, very observant. I am back." It's out of my mouth before I can stop it. Last thoughts in taxi, heading back to work, were that I would be kind to the intern, pseudo-loving, somewhat motherly in approach. I will teach her everything that I know in some vague attempt to ensure she is the intern to stay on, instead of Elsie's intern. I've not met Elsie's intern, but I dislike her by default and her associations with *Missus Perfect*.

So I must oust Elsie's intern at any cost. Even if it means developing relationship with own intern.

Have failed initial attempt.

Running around to desk and quickly bringing computer to life. Tapping in password. Right, check meetings.

"Both of your meetings are rescheduled for tomorrow," she's saying crisply.

"What?" I ask inelegantly.

"Both your meetings this afternoon are rescheduled. The first one with Swami Krishnananda is now on at two o'clock tomorrow, and the meeting with Chad Thompson, the restaurateur, is also rescheduled. Now on at four-thirty tomorrow instead." She has just listed it off all astutely, in true intern fashion.

"Oh no," I'm muttering, "I was hoping to do a studio cycle class tomorrow at 6:00 p.m."

"Oh, I'm sorry," she's tittering nervously. "Where's your gym? You might still be able to get there on time."

The two little words indicating where my gym is form in my mouth, but I just can't manage to spit them out. Kings Cross. Not that I live there, but it's the closest gym to my home in Potts Point.

"That's fine ... I'll just go to the class at six in the morning."

That's a lie, it's not fine. The last time I went to a morning gym class was in 1998, when my mother dragged me there in one of her classic desperate attempts to lose a couple of pounds. But no matter! My aim is to sound energised and fit, with a life functioning to a perfect schedule. Here's to hoping she's suitably impressed.

"Meanwhile ... How did you know all of that?" I'm glancing suspiciously at my computer. Surely she couldn't have accessed my emails? I can see in front of me at least fifty unopened messages, a number of which are from Ian and are likely to be *urgent*.

"They called through, and I answered your phone. I hope you don't mind." Her desperation to please me is not at all unsettling. In fact, perhaps interns are more useful than initially anticipated. I go out for an extended *slider and gin* lunch with gay friend discussing threesome dichotomy, and she stays here answering my calls. Not bad, not bad at all!

"Not at all—In fact, feel free to answer my calls if I'm not about."

Looking down at the red button bleeping on my phone, I obviously have a number of recorded messages. Maybe I could get her to clear those, too!

"Oh great!" She's clapping her hands together—apparently the notion of being a glorified receptionist or lackey resonates well with her.

"Did either of them say why they needed to reschedule?" I'm slightly peeved that the meeting with restaurateur is now tomorrow. He's slowly slipping out of my grasp. That said, at the very least, I get an opportunity to put together a slightly more stylish outfit and tame the frizz that is my hair.

"Yes, Krishnananda …"

And I've almost said flippantly, *Who cares about Krishnananda?* But I'm managing to keep that indiscretion to myself.

" … had a clash, a Kirtan seminar that he had forgotten he was holding."

"Had a what?"

"Kirtan. It's a type of yogic chanting. Very popular at the moment—Kirtan studios popping up everywhere … And now that Russell Brand is doing it too, it's definitely becoming super popular."

Note to self: completely out of touch with popular culture.

"And the restaurateur?" I ask, prompting more information.

"Oh, right. Sorry. Some sort of abrupt court settlement meeting with the ex-wife. Sounded very apologetic on the phone."

Looking promising …

"Great … Right!" I say, getting to my feet and trying to inject some enthusiasm into my otherwise lethargic self. Potential need for a coffee coming on.

"You can come to the meeting with Krishnananda tomorrow." She looks ecstatic at the thought of this and begins clapping her hands together in that infantile gesture again. "But not the restaurateur meeting."

Hardly think it would be appropriate for her to be meeting with Chad Thompson. After all, she's young and impressionable and may throw herself at him. In reality, having her in the room might allow for the mutton and fresh lamb comparison. Without her, there will be no basis for comparison.

She doesn't seem to notice the slight. Good. I'm warming to her.

"Thank you so much for the opportunity! It will be so awesome working on Krishnananda's account. He is so huge at the moment! Do you practise?" she's saying excitedly as I take a seat near her little table.

Practise? What exactly? What is she referring to?

"Practise?" I'm unable to get myself out of this one.

"Yeah, yoga."

"On the odd occasion." The last odd occasion was probably six months ago … and it was the first and last occasion, but that's a fair description, non? The one odd occasion!

"Me, too! What type?" Evidently she thinks she's stumbled upon common ground. My head is reeling now. There are types of yoga? *Really?* Wracking the brain, trying to think of any signs I may have seen out the front of the yoga studio in Surry Hills I frequented on that "odd occasion," but nothing is presenting itself.

"Oh, you know … the normal type." I say straight faced with a flicking of my electrified hair, as though I know exactly what I'm talking about. *Is there a normal type?*

She seems unfazed.

"Like Hatha, right?"

I'm nodding. Yes, like Hatha. Who knows what Hatha really is, and let's hope she hasn't thrown in some furphy name to expose me as the yoga-naïve that I really am.

"Yeah, I like Hatha. But I'm totally into all other sorts of yoga really. I like Yin but love Bikram and Power yoga. You know the heated types? They're so awesome! Have you ever done hot yoga?"

What the farrk is hot yoga? Obviously it's some sort of craze that I should know about that has blitzed western civilization. Surely in all those episodes of the Kardashians I've watched it would have been mentioned on some occasion, non?

The Kardashians don't strike me as the yoga types. The exercise types. The outdoor types. Actually, I retract; Kendall and Kylie could potentially be outdoorsy. Oh wait, she's looking at me expectantly, waiting for a response.

"No, I haven't."

"You so should!" She has placed major emphasis on the word so. I get the feeling she's trying to transform me into her *bestie*. "It is so *awesome* ..."

There's that word again. Apparently everything is awesome in her world. If only everything was awesome in mine. Wouldn't that be something?

"So it's done in like forty degree heat and seventy percent humidity, and then you go through a series of yoga poses. It's really quite grueling, but it's so soothing at the same time, and when you finish, you feel ah-mazing. Ah-mazing, like a million dollars."

Her eyes are widening with each word. She wants me to understand doesn't she? Really wants me to understand—but that doesn't sound like a soothing experience at all. In fact, at this moment I'm frightened of the notion, and frightened for her, too. She might just drop dead while she's practicing.

"Yes, sounds great!" I lie.

"Oh, we should totally practise together then!" she's telling me ... And here's the bonding moment. I'm sure in her mind, or in some management book, she's been told she needs to bond with the mentor. Find a common interest, and then bond over it, out of work preferably. There's no way in hell I'm going to be fronting up to one of those classes, but that's fine. Whatever makes her comfortable! If the thought that I'll be attending a Bikran, Bikram, Bik-whatever-it's-called-sesh with her, makes her feel like she's ticked something off on that internal intern list, then I'm happy to entertain the illusion.

"Sure, why don't we?" I say so breezily, and laidback in response.

"Fab! My local studio is in Bondi, but I heard around the traps that you live in Kings Cross, so we could totally go to the one in Surry Hills."

So many things in this statement concern me. Number one on the agenda: *Kings Cross*. Number two: the traps. How is this girl so well connected? Already! Number three: Bondi. Of course she lives in Bondi? Where else would a stylish girl of her age live?

"I don't live in Kings Cross," I hear myself saying for about the fifty-first time this week (let it be known that it's usually this many times every week.) "I live in Potts Point. And yes the Surry Hills studio will probably work better for me."

"Noted!" she says, nodding her youthful head. "I'll tee something up!"

"Great—So, back to business." Anything to get myself out of this dialogue!

"Great! I love the business!" Seriously? And again, more nodding. I feel a moment of reflection coming on; perhaps I have provided her with too much confidence. Have I created a monster in doing so? Already!

"I'm going to lay it out for you, Caroline …"

"Cristina," she corrects me.

"Cristina," I correct myself. Shit! Really one too many gin and tonics at lunch.

"You're going to be the last one standing at the end of this internship."

Here comes the *ra-ra*. I can do the *ra-ra*. If I had to rally troops before going over the trenches I'd be all over it. Like a rash. The *ra-ra* is my strength. We are going to take down that Elsie and her intern, and any conversations about my panties if it's the last thing I do at this agency!

"We are going to take you from intern to agency superstar. You are going to outperform each and every one of those interns. They'll be so far behind you that they'll be eating your dust. I don't have any time for that Namaste bullshit Buddhist stuff in this office. In this office we are ..."

I'm borrowing from her lingo in this moment of genius ...

" ... awesome!"

Let's follow that with a confident nod of my head, *thank you*—and she is nodding hers too, eyes focusing on mine like a disciple. I can tell she's drinking all this down, and so it's time to give her some more, because she seems ready for it—right here, right now. "There is no way you're leaving this internship without a job," I say, pausing. "No way." Ending!

I think it is a sensible decision of mine to keep out any dialogue about Elsie and her intern. Perhaps mention of them would not be prudent and make me seem psychopathic ... not that I am—because I certainly am not.

I'm feeling another pause would be apt ... for more dramatic effect.

"Yes, great!" Euphoria is spreading across her face as she is speaking. "We are so totally on the same page. Completely!"

"Good to hear it." How I'm going to pull this off is completely beyond me, but it's great to have the enthusiasm, non?

"I'm so glad you said that," she's continuing. "I was so worried before because I'd heard all these rumours that you're like so not the intern type, and totally wrong for this, what with the late lunches, and late starts, and early leaving …"

Oh no, no, no, Cristina. Time to cut you off with a gesture. A big one: hands up in the air, eyes closed, pairing it with a look of *stop right there, little lady.*

What the fuck? So who has been saying all that about me, huh? I have clearly been under the deluded impression that everyone in the office had the utmost respect for me! For farrk's sake, I've been around this industry for over a decade—smothered it with my knowledge and my eager Marilyn breath, and that's commitment. That's like a lifetime in this business! It must be that fucking Elsie. Surely it's that little clean eating bitch spreading this stuff about me. Oh—who am I kidding? Could have been anyone, even Ian himself.

It should be basic industry knowledge that moments of brilliance need to be accompanied by a late lunch and a beverage or two (or more) if it helps the cause. Creative thinking is not about hours spent behind the desk, no way. It never has been, never will be, not on my fucking watch. Some of us either have it or we don't!

She's looking at me expectantly … What does she fucking want now? I best give her something …

"No matter." I'm being theatrical now. "We are going to win. Win. Win." Because my *petite fleur,* I am a winner.

"I love winning!" she's crying out, and there's a semi fist pump, too. Really? She's a fist pumper?

Sigh.

"Okay, so let's get started."

She is grabbing at her pens already, expectant to learn. And I ... well, I am worrying as to what the fuck I'm going to say! What am I going to impart to this person? What do I even know?

"So today," I begin slightly shakily (Think Cee—THINK!), "is just about really getting to know each other." A moment of brilliance, I have so many of them, and she is buying it. "It's about finding out your strengths and weaknesses. So ... so tell me a bit about yourself."

Good start, Cee. It looks like that's exactly what she has been expecting.

"Sure. So, I have a Bachelor of Communications majoring in advertising and a Bachelor of law from UTS ..."

What the? Bachelor of law? Oh—My—God ... Total overachiever. I can sniff it out from a mile away! Why couldn't I have been saddled with the single degree type? Made it through by the skin of their teeth, but made it through nonetheless. You know, the battler? The slight underdog even, anything but this.

"I have wanted to work in advertising my entire life. Particularly television, but now with everything moving to social media I'm totally across all of the viral campaign strategies ..."

Good that you are, because I'm very much not. And what is she talking about *her entire life?* She's barely a woman. I'm one of those dinosaurs, one that has been working in television for years—an advertising velociraptor. And let's face it, everyone keeps saying that *television is dead* and it's all about *social media.* My limited understanding of social media is Facebook, so she might come in handy after all. *Whoops.* Oh Dear, how long have I been zoned out? What have I missed? Something about her thesis! Good, she's moving on to the personal details.

"I live in Bondi. My boyfriend and I just bought a place there with ocean views …"

With ocean views! *Bought it*, with what exactly? Why do you have that kind of money, eh? Oh no, bile is brewing and rising from my stomach. How could this girl have bought a place with her boyfriend in Bondi? She must be all of twenty-two! Is that possible, or even *legal?* How do two only *just* adult humans buy what no doubt is a million dollar property? A million. While I can barely pay rent on a monthly basis!

Maybe he's a sugar daddy? Non? Could be possible—after all, she is very attractive. Or super, as she would say, and energetic, totally befit for Viagra these days.

"My boyfriend and I went to school together and we've been together ever since …"

Well there goes that theory. Unless he was the head-teacher!

"We were both class captains."

Nope. So he wasn't her teacher. Not a sugar daddy. Oh boy, that bile is churning up. Vomiting is still very much a possibility, but I know this is when any normal person would interject a cutesy comment. Luckily I'm prepared.

Almost tasting the bile, as I'm cooing, "So cute."

"I know, right?" Lots of nodding. "So he's proposed, but we haven't bought the ring yet. It's so hard, so many cuts and colours. I totally want to buy a pink diamond, but his mother, and she's so on-trend, thinks it will date. But you would know all about that right?"

She has just glanced down at my hand. Where there's no band and no diamond. And now I'm even becoming self-conscious about my nails, which need a manicure and shellac. They're peeling over here and no doubt preppy princess over there would have noticed the state of disrepair. No doubt she's thinking *that's how they fly in Kings Cross.*

"Of course!" I *would* know.

"So, yeahhhhh," she's finishing off with a prolonged *yeah.* "So, so, so excited about this internship, and working with you. I can just tell you're totally amaze right from the onset. Super excited!"

Was there a little squeal in there, too? I think I heard a squeal. Yes she squealed.

I'm nodding. Trying to conjure up some words. The fact is, I fucking hate this girl from the get go. With her perfectly groomed eyebrows and hair, gorgeous outfit, house in Bondi, boyfriend, wedding ring—what can I say that won't sound psychotic and aggressive?

Luckily, another office intruder is saving me. Ah, not so lucky, it's *Beefy.* Here you are again, standing at my door. Blocking my chi. My day has been blessed with so many of your intrusions, all American and beefy, all clean eating and snarky by association with that bitch, Elsie.

"Yes?" I say, looking up at him like he's some sort of pest. Which he is!

"Hey," he's nodding to both of us.

"Hey," responding, as is Cristina … That's her name! Points to me for remembering!

So no one is going to speak then. A moment or so has passed already, and this is boring. I'm arching my eyebrows up at him.

"Were you going to introduce us?" he asks, gesticulating towards Cristina. Of course he wants to know who the young, beautiful thing is. She has a fucking boyfriend, ocean view apartment, and soon a rock on her finger, so no I'm not going to fucking introduce you!

Sigh. I best not say that stuff. Here go the pleasantries. "This is my intern Cristina. Cristina, this is Jai." Yes! Got both of their names right.

They are nodding their heads towards each other, sweetly smiling. Oh, fuck! Double vomit. The beautiful people are talking in sign language now, leaving out the pink panty flashing velociraptor over here—it's only *my* fucking office.

"And?" I'm asking Jai rudely.

"Oh …" He's clearly remembering himself. "I was coming to see if you'd had a chance to look at the Swami creative?"

I'm shaking my head. Disinterest full stop. "No, it's been a busy day!"

"I bet." And there's his slightly derisive tone.

"I'll get back to you tomorrow," I say simpering.

Bloody creatives, think the world revolves around them. Well, here's a news flash for you … It doesn't!

"Sure, looking forward to your opinion. Not sure if they're quite right …"

Whatever! Please leave. Not the slightest bit interested in what *Beefy* has to say—not now, not ever.

"So I'll see you two tomorrow." Good, he's getting my *fuck off out of my office* message, but still has that cute smile on his face.

"Yep—Ciao." I'm looking back towards Cristina because she is annoying me again too, with her being here … She is wearing some blissed-out expression on her face. *Really?* Wasn't she just talking about the boyfriend? So now she has a hankering for *Beefy*, does she? How very interesting!

He is out of vision for us both now, around the corner, and it seems that she has finally remembered that I'm here, too. I'm waiting for eye contact, come on Cristina, my eyebrow rising at the ready for her to notice.

"What?" She's all sheepish. "Even though I'm taken doesn't mean I can't look, right? Besides, he's so cute," she has added with an adoring smile.

Not this again. First Chris, now Cris-*fucking*-tina. Sluts.

"Looking leads to touching." I'm purposely delivering this pointedly, like a school matron. "Here, start writing this down. I'm going to impart some of my wisdom …"

Getting to my feet, I stand over her looking down, creating presence, and all for dramatic effect. Pacing would work too, non? Starting to pace, it feels good—powerful, I like it! And it's working. She is scrambling for those pens again and some paper like I'm going to say something important. Which, of course, I am. Just haven't quite decided exactly what yet.

"Never date the creatives," I'm telling her.

Good, she's scribbling this down.

"Why?" she's asking, all gorgeous arched eyebrows.

"Because they're usually losers living in Redfern with ex-wives and children that they don't mention. Means a lot of maintenance." Rubbing my thumb and forefinger together to indicate money. "And they're usually spliffed-out. All about the art, doll. Trust me, it's a nightmare."

Does that sound like personal experience?

"Spliffed?" she's asked.

Oh really, what are the young people saying these days? Think, Cee.

"Spliffed—You know, ganja, Maryjane, the pot, and the like?"

Why is she still looking so blank? Thought she had a degree in law.

"Marijuana?" I've decided to supply.

"Oh, right!" She's finally looking at me with understanding on her face.

"Oh yeah, right," I'm nodding. "Now," I declare, "first project!"

She's shuffling her body taller in her seat.
"How do you feel about reviewing creative?"
"Oh, yes! Please!" And lots of clapping!

7. 6:30p.m.

us trip home. Exhausted. Effect of G&Ts, sliders, afternoon sun, and emotional distress due to underwear issue, Chris, run-in with Elsie and Jai over lunch, and intern all starting to set in. But no matter, have renewed sense of gusto for turning life around in positive direction. Potential consequence of spending parts of the day with Cristina. Suddenly spurred into action after discovering child—well fresh out of uni, is a child in my book—is more successful than I am. Highlights my washed-up has-been status. Trawling through bag, looking for mobile.

Wallet. Scarf. A dozen crumpled receipts. Gum stuck to the back of some random ticket stub. More gum. More receipts. Pad. Tampons. And off one flies. That's right! Loose tampon very much journeying out of my bag and almost falling onto the person sitting next to me. They are shifting uncomfortably, and I'm keeping this smile demurely fixed on my face. Ah, mobile!

Small victory. Have found mobile. *Note to self:* should probably clean out handbag later on this evening. All part of project *organise Cee's life* and *empower Cee's life.* Project commencement time: 6:00 p.m., 15th February.

I have to phone Jess—my other pseudo best friend, alongside Chris of course. First met at the production company I worked at after university. We were both fresh starters with similar mindsets, a penchant for boozy lunches, and lax working hours. As you can imagine, we hit it off almost instantly. Chris maintains a wary friendship with Jess, holding firm that he's the original *bestie* (given I met him a few years earlier at uni), and Jess is just a very poor imitation of himself.

"What up, buttercup?" she answers ironically. This is how she always speaks, slightly detached, ironic, like there's nothing in the world that you could possibly say which would surprise or entertain her, like she's on some funny, hip, American comedy set in New York. Ever since her split with Pete (now ex-long term partner), her dry tone has gone into overdrive. Like Sahara desert overdrive.

"Hey, sweetheart," beginning, I can hear a rustling on the phone and subsequent chewing, "where are you at the moment?"

"At home, why do you ask?"

"I can just hear rustling, that's all."

"Oh, yeah. That's the Doritos packet. I wish they had spreadable cheese in a container like in the States that I could use as dip. Instead I have to microwave shredded cheese until it turns into a puddle—but then it coagulates quickly into a solid, so my efforts are wasted. *Anyway …* "

Hmm—sounds like my Valentine's evening last night. I am picturing her sitting on the couch, messy hair, shoes kicked off, plunging into that

Doritos packet like it's her last day on earth. I can almost hear her thought pattern as well: *who cares anyway if I put on another ten kilos? I'm already in the large category, what does it matter if I become an extra large?* And yes, she is in that large category. Not quite as large as Ian, but still!

"I know I shouldn't be eating this. But I honestly cannot be fucked. Those diet protein bars we bought the other week taste like cardboard, and I need to have five of them in one sitting to actually feel full-ish, which, I think, might negate the purpose of them anyway."

"Tough day?" I'm reading between the lines.

She just let out a big sigh, and probably some Doritos crumbs, if they dare to escape, that is. "I don't know. Just another day, I guess. Got some goddamn awful email from Pete about wanting to collect some of his stuff from the house this weekend, and if I'll be around so he can come over. So I had to lie and say no, because of course I can't let him see me in this advanced disheveled and obscenely fat position. Told him we're heading off to a winery in Pokolbin with some lads …"

"Pokolbin?"

"Yeah, it's in the Hunter Valley."

"Did that lie just spring to mind spontaneously?" Impressive if it did!

"No, and this is how sad it is, I spent nearly an hour Googling plausible lies that might make me look fab and on-trend."

"Who are the lads?"

"I didn't elaborate, just thought that I would try to knife him at the same time. So I alluded to other company, of the male variety of course. Not that he'll even care or notice—he's so *moved on* now, you know dating and all? I see his Facebook page all the time, new girls commenting and the like—and the other day he updated his status to *in a relationship.* Not enough pizza and ice cream in the world is going to fix that," she's finishing off smoothly.

"Hmm! You need to stop looking at his Facebook page." I am counseling her because she needs it, knowing at the same time how difficult that can be. I probably devote the first half hour of my day going through exes' Facebook pages, hoping they've gotten fat and ugly, or some misfortune has occurred—Usually, I just find the smiley faces of new partners and updates about beer, enough to send me spiraling into self-loathing.

Note to self: must not look at exes' Facebook pages. In fact, should de-friend all exes this evening as part of broader strategy and *Cee-Project.*

"I know! God—it takes up so much energy. I spend more time on his Facebook page than on mine." More crunching and swallowing.

"So listen," I'm trying to shift the subject from self-hate to strategy forward slash Cee-Project exclamation mark. "Tomorrow morning, I thought we could do a spin class together," I say, throwing it out there with a happy, sing-song voice to go along with it.

"Haven't been to the gym in about two months. I might have a heart attack under the stress of vigorous exercise."

"I have my first aid certificate so I'm sure I can be of assistance—and most gyms have defibrillators anyway. I think it's part of their policies." Trilling. Who knows if it's part of their policy? I'm the last person to know, but need to sound confident and convincing to lure Jess into a sense of assuredness about the gym.

"You're probably right …"

"And it's studio cycle, not RPM. You know, the dumbed-down version for gym naives like us. All you'll need to do is push those pedals around, and then you'll be able to enjoy those Doritos and melted cheese snacks guilt free tomorrow." Wow, this is good stuff. You can tell I'm in advertising, can't you? Just beautiful, and I think it may well be working.

"Hmm, I won't want Doritos tomorrow. I'm already salivating at the thought of Tex Mex. Why are there so many Mexican restaurants and take-out places in this goddamn city? Makes it so much easier to ingest food."

"So what do you think?" I say, trying to keep her on track.

She has fallen silent, not a bad sign, as not an outright *no*. I'm waiting …

"What time?"

Oh, and here's the hard part, the part I know she'll rail against. "6:00 a.m." Delivered confidently, of course, as though it's not at all a ridiculous time to do anything at.

"Six in the morning!" she is screeching down the phone at me, like I've just discussed some murder strategy with her.

The person next to me can hear it, they must be able to. He is shifting uncomfortably in his seat, as though sitting next to me has become such a chore he would prefer to stand up for the rest of his sweaty way home. Go on then … stand away!

"Yes, 6:00 a.m.," I repeat, maintaining cool and calm persona.

"What's gotten into you?" she's demanding suspiciously. "Who have you turned into? One of those *fitinspo* bunnies?"

"Not quite!"

"Who else would suggest something like that?"

Clearly *only a crazy person* are the implications of those words. Says the lady who is eating melted cheese, distressed it will solidify before she can dip yet another Dorito into it.

"Listen, I have two late afternoon meetings tomorrow, one with the Swami and one with the restaurateur, and I want to squeeze in some exercise at some point to ensure I don't go into cardiac arrest at the tender age of thirty-two."

"That sounds all very organised, Cee, and somewhat militant. Exercise, meetings—Should I be concerned?"

God forbid that I be organised in my approach to life.

"I am trying," stressing the words, "to turn over a new leaf here, Jess. *Project organise Cee's life* is what I've decided to call it—*Cee-Project* for short."

"And what brought this on? Usually you only go into meltdown around the holidays! You know, Christmas, New Year's, and then of course your birthday—significant dates with exes, times when exes announce new relationships on Facebook …"

She is still going on, and I've got to block out the noise. This shit! Okay, so I go into meltdown on a semi-regular basis. Is that so terrible? Doesn't that make me more human?

"Look, I'm not in meltdown," I'm hissing at her now, attempting to break up her continued litany on other previous meltdown scenarios. "Hang on a sec—here's my stop, hold on."

Buses are crap at stopping, and I'm crap at standing to my feet without swaying—I'm clutching my phone to ear, and handbag close to my body. But I'm still swaying precariously, trying desperately and graciously to get past the middle-aged man sitting next to me. Oh shit, was that his foot? Swift and ladylike moves, Cee. Lurching forward with the momentum of the bus, almost ass planting into his lap. Lucky fellow! Another outing for the pink panties. Great! You can recover from this,

Cee! Composure. Elegance.

"So sorry," I'm hearing myself murmuring, scuttling past. And even with the potential knicker flash, he is glaring at me with a look of complete hatred. Whatever, mate, like that wasn't the only action you're going to get for the next year or more—potentially lifetime. And I know for a fact that you'll be thinking of me later in some sordid affair with your own mind, and maybe your hand.

"Excuse me. Excuse me." I have to keep pushing past these people or I'll never get off this thing … Man with headphones, *move*. Old lady, *move*. People staring at phones with dull expressions, *move, move, move!* Freaky, they are somehow beginning to shift like zombies, clearing a path for me. I can see the door—it's open within my sights, but the step … not so much in my sights. I drop unceremoniously out onto the pavement, and manage to style out my stumbling with a little leg kick. Nice, Cee. Very nice. Points towards your *project*.

Wow, it's hot, stifling even on the Kings Cross street. So much noise and clamminess. My hair is starting to slowly part in various directions reacting to the humidity. I can feel it. Attractive, I think not.

Home. Walking towards it and looking forward to … Shit, Jess is still on the phone.

"You still there?"

A prolonged grunting sound ensues and she's still chewing. "I'm onto Smith's salt and vinegar now."

Where were we? Trying to recover the point where we had left off in the conversation, but it evades me. "Today," announcing instead, "I was assigned an intern."

"Oh, poor you. They're always such nobs."

"Exactly! Thank you! Not sure what this girl is. Overly enthusiastic, yes. But anyway—when she was telling me about herself, she announces that she's had a boyfriend since school, they're getting engaged, they've just bought a place in Bondi, and then she's talking to me about types of diamonds! And I'm just thinking *I have no idea what you're talking about because I've never been close enough to that part of the relationship where said mate proposes!* Not like all those women last night. Of course, I didn't reveal this to her. Oh, and ..."

"Wait, who proposed last night?" Jess is interrupting.

"Everyone ... no one ... forget it. Anyway, she's also a yogi!"

"So you're wound up over the intern?" Jess has deduced correctly.

"No! Well, maybe. Yes ... I don't know!" Shit, it's so frustrating. Turning down my street, at last my day is nearly done. "All I know is this girl is half my age, well not quite, but she's a kid, and she has everything, and her life is in order. Meanwhile, I'm thirty-two, renting a place in Potts Point, been through a series of broken relationships, no potential relationships in sight, not happy at work, and not even doing a good job. Today I flashed my colleagues my pink underwear for Christ's sake! Could it be any messier or free form?" There, a triumphant finish, moi thinks. And home at last, but I'm not moving. This is a moment for a stop, a hand on the hip, and a demanding look at the pavement outside of my apartment.

Jess is tittering. "Who *hasn't* flashed their undergarments to colleagues? At least your flashing was discrete I bet, and not some crazy standing on a table pulling shirt over head at their Christmas party after one too many vodka martinis."

"Ahh, the great drunken Christmas party of 2006." She has me laughing.

"That's right. And at the very least, I had a nice bra on—and breasts underneath, which weren't saggy, and a relatively flat stomach. I look back at that day and think—I wish I hadn't been fired over it, but nonetheless, seize the *fucking day!*"

I'm not sure where this is going now, and I'm thinking that Jess might be in some carbohydrate haze and not able to follow logical patterns of thought.

"Where is this going?" I have to interject. My feet are starting to hurt from heels, need to get inside and remove shoes. Need to park ass on sofa.

"The point is you're in no way, shape, or form some washed up has-been. You have a good job. You never, ever, were a good example in the workplace, nor did you aspire to be one—and yes, you're thirty-two, but you still look good. You're still thin, and blonde. You even remember to get your re-growth done on the occasion. For Christ's sake, your clothes still fit despite the alcohol binges and penchant for greasy food!"

That's true. This lady knows me too well. I am still pretty hot.

"I, on the other hand …" Oh shit, here comes the slide into self-pity. "I've completely let myself go. My size fourteen clothes don't fit anymore. Like *literally*. I busted a pair of pants this morning. There was this death defying tearing noise and then half my ass was hanging out. Has that ever happened to you?"

"No, but I have torn an old pair of pajamas."

"*Humph*—probably because they were threadbare and would have yielded at the slightest of touches! This was not the case, Cee. These were sturdy pants. Made of sturdy material. My ass literally, quite literally, tore

90

the fabric—completely. Anyway, you say you have no potential relationship in sight but what about the restaurateur?"

"Oh, please," I say, scoffing. "I mean realistic ones, not fantasy ones that occur in my mind."

I'm leaning on my metaphoric fence now … and on the real one because my feet are screaming! May take shoes off here and now. Is that disgusting? If feet make contact with street in Potts Point will possible hepatitis ensue? It is kind of close to Kings Cross. But my feet are made of tougher stuff than that, a lifetime of wearing heels and showering in public places (gyms, pools, etc.) without thongs probably means feet have built up enough calluses and immunity to withstand the barrage of germs from street situated in Potts Point—*not* Kings Cross. I'll be quick, but not so discrete removing these shoes from my crying feet. Now off, shoes in hand, phone call can commence.

Ahh! Liberation! Feet can finally breath again. Thank fuck for feet.

"Did you hear that?" Jess is quite frantically calling down the phone. Evidently she is waiting on some response, and as she's not received one, she is clearly realising I have succumbed to internal dialogue with *moi*, myself and I.

"No. Sorry, babe, was taking shoes off."

"I said," she starts to repeat (Oh shit, really? This is going to take forever), "maybe you can't get the restaurateur, but I'm sure there are other pretty ships on your horizon."

Pretty ships! What sort of metaphor is that? Carbohydrate haze is now definitely setting in. She may well lapse into a coma soon if she carries on with the chips.

"But what about me—I spent near on ten years with a bastard I met at university! Always thinking he was going to marry me! On and on he went about not believing in the institution of marriage—because he was such a rule breaker, such an anti-conformist, such a Chardonnay socialist … such a wanker!"

Oh, for fuck's sake … Not this again! And lord, I understand, I really do, that she's been hard done by, but it's been six months, and I've heard this over a million times. I've been there through the tears, tantrums, endless binges—I've even woken up more times than I can mention at her place and had to wipe excess pizza off her face while pulling her into a dignified sitting position.

"… *Oh no, we can't get married,* that's what he told me, *but I'm completely committed to this relationship. So committed, in fact, that we should move in together. We should start trying to have a baby*—a baby! And then, of course, because I'm in my mid-to-late thirties and my ovaries have already packed it in, dried up, wasted away …"

Oh the visual! The horror of it. Please no more. I beg of you, no more!

"You're thirty-four," I quickly correct her. *Never let a lie get in the way of a good story,* Jess would say. But this, I'm very sorry (for myself) to say, is far from a good, or new story … Frankly, it's fucking boring! Heard it all before, thank you very much!

"No matter," she's brushing it aside. "The gyno told me that my ovaries are in decline after twenty-seven. After twenty-seven, for Christ's sake! I wish they would have told me that while I was beavering away trying to finish my degrees!" She is screeching again.

"Because you were always the studious type." I can't help saying this ironically.

"Don't be cute, Cee. *Anywho,* you know the rest." Yes, I do know the fucking rest … Now give it a rest, will you! But she's still continuing …

" … He supports me in getting IVF, I get fat, emotional, and broke as a result of the process—and then he leaves me—leaves me, just like that. *I can't deal with this anymore Jess,* he tells me. *None of it's fun anymore.* Of course it's not fun, you MOTHER FUCKER!" she is yelling, and now I'm certain that it's blown my right eardrum—Semi-deafness has kicked in. Maybe if I hold the phone away from me about half a metre … Nope, I can still hear her.

" … Of course it's not fun! You're not the one who's getting a million and one injections and swelling up like a whale, having uncontrollable mood and binge swings just to carry your *mother fucking* baby!"

Oh, I think it's safe to return phone to ear. She's stopped. Silence. Waiting a few more seconds in case there's more. I'm being cautious, my ears are delicate. *Phew,* the storm seems to have subsided.

"I know, right? It was all a terrible affair, non? He was a real mo-fo, eh?—Now … " I'm good at this shuffling of conversations back to the original intention: my focus, my life, not hers! This is the reason for the phone call after all. " … What about tomorrow morning? Will you do the six o-clock class?"

"Fine." I like what I'm hearing, and her resigned tone is giving me a feeling of power, of persuasion—all good points towards my *Cee-Project.* "I'll do the 6:00 a.m. class, even though it might kill me, because you're my best friend and you listen to my rants endlessly."

Ahh—a bit of self-realisation it seems. Nice, Jess. But for the record, I don't always strictly listen, but *anywho.*

"Fab—See you there at six. Don't go to Tex Mex tonight, otherwise you might vom in the middle of class." It's good advice I'm giving her.

"Oh, the humanity!"

"Ciao," I say, pressing the red button before she has a chance to say another word, just in case she rethinks her response or goes into another paroxysm about Pete and their finished relationship.

I feel a sense of relief right now, progression; gym tomorrow, and my brain is calming after that chaotic chat. Welcome pause. Well needed stretch of my neck. I don't often take a moment to look at the teeny view of water and quay from this location. It's no bigger than a square, but it's there nonetheless. Oh, that breeze is picking up somewhat. I like how it is ruffling my feathered hair and cooling the sweat on my neck, almost like it's caressing me. Don't mind if I do *breeze*.

Great, a nice swift end to my moment of reverie—here's one of my neighbours: a middle-aged man inaptly named *Phoenix*. So wrong, right? right? It's as if he has just magically appeared at the gate—wonder where he's going? He's looking down at my bare feet; he's bringing his gaze up … No, his eyes are flitting right back down to my bare feet. And his gaze is raising again … Will he stop here? No, not a word—no acknowledgement! He is going. It's a walk, but it's quick paced.

"Oh hello, Phoenix." Why do I do this? I just can't help calling after him. "Beautiful evening, isn't it?"

No response.

8. 5:45a.m.

*B*arely made it to gym on time. Sailing through doors like crazed person. Hair askew, clothes askew, mind, as per usual, askew. Hand girl at desk (perfectly coiffed young thing with pert breasts) gym pass, have already dumped contents of bag out, again, rifling through receipts, gum, used gum, pads, tampons, wallet, and there it is—gym pass. Girl is looking mildly alarmed, although not put out, must get this sort of behaviour often at this time of morning. Realising I should have emptied out bag last night instead of eating microwave popcorn on lounge, drinking Sav Blanc, and online clothes shopping (not purchasing anything, just browsing and then being crushed by indecision given too many options and indecision over what my new look should actually be: aging hipster, sophisticated sheike business woman, slutty business woman, edgy creative woman—It's a difficult decision, non?).

Nonetheless, have at very least managed to pack bag with work clothes for today, plus makeup. Reasonably suitable outfit, methinks, for meeting with Swami and restaurateur. That is, an *ensemble* mixed between conservative for the former, and sexy for the latter. Or is it the other way around? *Anywho*—Not all, as they say, is lost.

So now I've stowed my bag in the change rooms and am now headed to cycle room, which is surprisingly full at this time of the morning. I'm very much wondering where I'm going to park my bottom because this room, in fact, is full to the brim. So full that there are no spaces at the back of the room, or in the middle of the room, just right at the front— directly opposite the teacher: a beautiful brunette wearing colour coordinated fashionable gym gear, hair pulled into jaunty ponytail, flicking through phone, idly pedaling, waiting for stragglers to arrive. Waiting for me. Waiting for Jess! Where is she?

I've no choice, have I, other than to colonise one of those bikes right in front of her. Towel on ground, water bottle in water holder, slowly pulling myself into seated position on bike. Slightly inelegant, but here nonetheless.

Why is she looking at me? It's only briefly, with a lack of animation on her poised face. She can't, even if she thinks she does. Never been to her class before. Good, she evidently doesn't.

Feet in pedals, trying to pedal idly. Cooley actually. Just waiting for the class to start. Not at all checking out the other women in the class or their outfits. My three-quarter length tights are not the thing to wear it so seems, everyone else appears to be wearing short shorts: tight, brightly coloured and patterned, exhibiting perfectly muscled and spray-tanned legs.

Note to self: need spray tan. Starting to look pasty. Actually, always look pasty.

"Cee!" Someone is hissing my name, startling me from my clothes and spray tan reverie.

It's Jess. And about time, too! She is standing really near me, clutching her towel and looking slightly desperate and crazed. Her dark hair is pulled into a messy ponytail, her round face quivering like I'm leading her out to battle with the potential of being hung, drawn and quartered.

"Hey, babe! Trilling, as though we're regular gym buffs and this is our usual meeting spot.

"Why are you so close to the front?" she is still hissing at me. Great, now the instructor is looking in our direction seeing as how Jess has inadvertently drawn her attention.

"There were no other seats, babe." I'm remaining placid, smile playing on my face, avoiding words like *down the back* or *where we can hide*. Acutely aware that the teacher is watching, and potentially some of the other students, too.

"I don't want to sit here!" Jess is hissing again, now petulantly, look of desperation on her face. "We're too close to the front—and to the teacher!" She is gesticulating towards the woman like she's not even there, and I can tell she is listening.

"Oh, you'll be fine!" I say, eyes wide, trying to tell her through osmosis that she's drawing attention towards us. Clearly the message is not getting through all of that cheese trying to seep out through her pores.

"I won't be fine. I haven't been to the gym in a century and ..." she is leaning in even closer, I guess this comment is for my ears only, "I had the Tex Mex last night. On top of the chips, on top of the cheese ... and the ice cream! This could be brutal."

"Ladies," the instructor is referring to us cheerfully, "it's time to get started. What's your name there with the green track pants?" She's smiling. And staring.

Oh shit, she's referring to Jess. I'm just watching as Jess quivers and clutches at her towel even tighter now like it's her security blanket. All eyes are on her. Feel like terrible friend, possibly worst friend in the world. Have just brought potentially clinically depressed friend with eating and weight issues to 6:00 a.m. spin class and sat her down the front. Quite literally thrown her under the bus, to the vultures, to a twenty-something-year-old teacher who doesn't know what it's like to be rejected by Pete the pseudo-socialist after a ten year relationship. Plus those hormones—Jess has had enough of them to make any other woman spontaneously burst forth in the immaculate conception—not to mention the Tex Mex—the one I warned her against!

"Jess," she is saying quietly, like the fat kid in school about to get picked on by a cool kid. She might need to go back to a counselor after this session. Shit!

"Right Jess, you'll be fine. Just hop on your bike next to your friend there." *Phew*, it's lucky for me that she hasn't asked for my name. Yes! Still flying slightly under the radar. "I'm going to keep my eye on you during this class."

Oh, double shit. The thing is she's trying to be all attentive and sweet, but really it's the worse thing she could be doing. Calling attention to Jess's ample derriere as she is clumsily climbing onto this bike.

"We are going to get through this together, and you're going to feel fab after this class!" She is still talking at Jess, and pedaling.

Oh no, the *ra-ra!* Jess hates the ra-ra. I hate it unless I'm giving it. Jess doesn't respond well to it, and now she's just staring forward towards the teacher with an almost maniacal expression on face. It's Stockholm syndrome, I can tell already. She's bound by her kidnapper, unable to look away or stop following orders.

"Okay, here's the music ladies." And on it goes, thumping through the sound system, and there it is—the sudden whirl of feet on pedals, almost as loud as the music. "Welcome to Thursday RPM!" Lots of enthusiasm—Who are these women? And why are they so enthusiastic? And did she just say RP-*fucking*-M?

"RPM?" It's spilling out of my mouth before I can stop it. Fucking verbal diarrhea! It gets worse in situations of abject panic. "I thought it was studio cycle?"

She is looking straight at me, and her smile is continuing to spread, although her forehead is slightly creased, like this is an untoward change in her usual routine, a rogue question.

"Nope, RPM," she's just boomed. "It changed about a month ago. We really need to update the website!"

Oh, fuck. I have to glance at Jess, and while I'm whirling my feet around as quickly as I can. I knew it, silent treatment—she's saying nothing, just staring ahead. Stockholm has set in now. Panic is fast setting in for me. RPM! I can barely do studio cycle on a good day.

"Okay, ladies, pump it up, resistance on, we are going to burn some calories this morning. Are you ready? Come up. If your resistance isn't on, it's like you're wasting time—no point being here, right? You should have just stayed in bed!"

Out of the corner of my eye, I can see Jess mechanically leaning down and turning her resistance up. She is already panting and perspiring, her legs working overtime.

"You down the front. *Blondie*, next to Jess." Oh no, please no. If I just glance up slowly at her she may move on to somebody else.

Her eyes just met mine, and she isn't moving them away. This is worse than knowing my name. She has a nickname for me now.

"Turn your resistance up, Blondie! I can see your legs just whirling around—I can tell if your resistance isn't up."

How can she talk so much and pump so hard? She is still staring at me, in a meaningful way, like she's the Santa Claus for RPM and knows if I'm being naughty or nice, or in this case, lazy or hard working. Why can't I be lazy? I wish I could ask her out loud, to that *I've hardly broken out in a sweat* face of hers. I'm paying for this for Christ's sake! If I want to be lazy, well I should be allowed, non? It's not like I'm going to get a bloody gift after this session!

I better look like I'm *turning up my resistance,* leaning down and turning the knob up by one—I'm figuring that is plenty.

"More, Blondie! More!" she's yelling. Why does everyone yell? And enough already with the nickname! I'm a bit alarmed. She's glaring at me with the same maniacal expression that Jess has obviously acquired.

Fine, I can turn this knob a few more notches, stupid name calling instructor, bossy bitch.

"Good. Feel the burn! Feel the burn!"

Yes, I can feel the fucking burn. I wish I couldn't, but I can feel the fucking burn. Oh, that's fire. That's internal combustion; that's a burn on a burn.

6:00 a.m. RPM. What was I thinking? It's all that intern's fault!

9. 7:10 a.m.

C hange room. Post-class. Sitting on bench. Jess next to me. Both staring ahead. Women around us, a whir of activity, bustling about, blow drying hair, showering, applying makeup. Talking, laughing. "Great class!" and the like. Big grins. Don't think I can move. At all. Not any muscle. Including eye muscles. Mouth muscles. Hand muscles to wipe sweat. Need to wipe sweat. Leave sweat dripping. Just staring silently ahead.

It has been a fair few moments, but I think I may be able to move again, something, even the smallest body part, in the tiniest of ways. Come on. Move, Cee!

"When I'm able to move again," Jess has begun, "I'm going to kill you."

"I give you my full permission," I'm spluttering out. How can it be that my face hurts? Oh yes, the instructor did say not to tense the face, no frowning; *your frown can't help you now.*

"So you admit this was the worst fucking idea you've ever had in the history of your fucking ideas, including that time you talked me into a longboard lesson in Hawaii?"

I don't know how she even has the energy to string those words together.

"Yes—worse than longboarding. Way worse than longboarding. At least the instructor was a hot piece of ass for the longboarding."

"Agreed. And despite coming off the board and cutting my head on a low lying rock, this still remains a fucking worse experience."

"Well, at least you spent the next hour with the said *hottie* pressing an ice pack to your forehead," I'm responding, though face and every other part of me still hurts.

"Indeed. But do you think Tania would press any ice packs to me now? No, I think not."

"Who is Tania?" I ask, glancing at her. Her face is beetroot red, as though it might explode at any point, or at the very least she may have a stroke. Not nice. Hair is pasted down in a myriad of directions by sweat on her very red face.

I know my face is just as bulbous and red right now. That mother fucking resistance.

Jess is looking at me perplexed. "The instructor."

"Did she tell us that?" Who knows, it was a whirlwind of things and comments and yelling and barking—Who knows what she was saying half the time!

"Yes, she told us that." Jess always hisses, it's so annoying. "She said it at the start of the class. Were you even listening?"

I can only manage a faint smile, but its sensation is big inside. Wish I had the energy to laugh loud in my best friend's beetroot face. "You love her," is all I can muster.

"Fuck off. Say that again and I'll hit you. I'm just offering her the respect she deserves as a qualified trainer. You lady, have no respect."

"You love her!" I manage to jump to my feet quickly because I know she's going to swing at me. It is true what *they* say: that you can do anything for survival.

The pair of us dissolve into laughter. The ladies around us are beginning to stare, all stopping in half motion, drying hair, putting on underpants, mascara, toweling down. Like they are frozen in the moment. A tableau.

Oh, the laughing hurts. Hysterical now. Both of us.

10. 8:50a.m.

*S*itting at desk. Have not been at work this early since, since—not sure, potentially ever. Feel, like, awesome (decided to acquire Cristina's word) businesswoman: on time, on schedule, sipping latte at desk before 9:00 a.m.—despite having forgotten knickers at home (were not packed in otherwise studiously packed gym bag). No matter, have longish, past knees pencil skirt on, and nobody will be able to tell the difference. No chance of flashing in conservative black pencil skirt and blouse. Hair swept up into elegant chignon (care of Jess, who ditched homicidal tendencies forty-five minutes after class and decided to assist in beautifying project given meeting with restaurateur forward slash ex-football player, and potential fantasy relationship). Makeup also perfectly applied, although shade of foundation could not possibly cover red post-class glow, which has not since subsided. Look slightly pink, like I have been perhaps sitting in sun for too long, or just had *unlimited early morning shagging session and am glowing as a result. My imagination will certainly opt for the latter, and all in all a wonderful start to my day.*

Facebook status updated with cool little quip: *RPM session with Jess this morning. Tough, but amazing!* Held back from including little smiley face with halo around head indicating "feeling blessed." Might be a little too trite given advanced age.

"Hey, Cee." Startled from happy reverie by Jai. Oh, my inner voice seems to have re-categorised his name as his actual name. Interesting, maybe a glitch, only time shall tell. He's leaning on door coolly in his faded jeans and tee, tattoos and muscles exposed. *Seriously*, does the man even own any long-sleeved shirts?

"Jai," responding calmly, latte in hand.

"You're early. Actually, I'm not sure I've ever seen you in the office this early."

My smile is fighting the clenched teeth. "In fact, I'm here at this time often." I'm lying. "Maybe you're just in here later."

Smiling, too, and revealing his perfectly white, straight teeth, there's no denying he does have a cute little grin. The brain is a strange thing because I'm finding it difficult not to think how perfectly constructed his grin is—a little boyish, and also a little cool. The smile sometimes speaks without speaking, and it's speaking now: *Hey, I think you're funny, but just a bit funny.* Maybe he practises it in the mirror in the morning.

"I'm sure that's not the case." *So you don't practise?* Oh, what is he referring to? Mind has been wandering. Doing so well earlier, Cee, back on track please.

Best to not respond in such situations. Just smile back charmingly and take another suppressed sip from my latte, rather than glugging it down like water as per usual.

"So, did you get a chance to look at the designs?"

Oh, the fucking designs again; this guy never lets up about his creative. Creatives are always like this. Think the world spins on its axis because of their design work.

"No, but Cristina took a look last night. I, myself, have otherwise been engaged."

"The intern's reviewing my designs?"

"Is that too lowly for you, Jai?" I ask him rudely. "Is she not up to looking at your designs? The girl has two degrees, for goodness sake. Is that not enough for you?"

"Of course it is!" His voice is brusque, as though he couldn't possibly be thinking that. "I just thought it was an important account and you would look at them first."

"Hmm …" I murmur, getting to my feet—I do it slowly, calculatedly, whilst smoothing my skirt down. Yes, finally, in a position of power with Jai, and not looking completely incompetent or ridiculous or remotely slutty or late—I'm on top of my game, early, RPMed, and I feel like now is the perfect time to pick up my glasses, holding them loosely in hand, hoping to exude intellect and sophistication with chignon and pencil skirt combo working with me. I shall ignore the little internal memo that spells out in big red letters *remember commando nature of underwear*. Luckily my blush is likely to be disguised beneath the well-applied makeup and the crimson exercise glow.

It does, however, feel a little breezy in here now, particularly down there, and so I think I'll return to a seated position. Still with a touch of authority about me, and with more calculated movement. Very businesswoman-like. Good preparation for meetings.

"It's a good developmental opportunity for her," I'm telling him. "She'll give me her feedback and we'll go over it together. Then I'll speak to you before my meeting with the Swami this afternoon."

Can't believe it. Did that just come out of my mouth? Developmental opportunity? Did I just sound as competent as I feel? Do I have a strategy and plan in place for the creative and subsequent meetings? Practically squealing with delight inside, but holding back external rejoicing. So proud. Crossing right leg cautiously over left knee. No, not going to work. Resuming safe closed leg position.

"Okay, that sounds fine," he's saying to me, hands in pockets, looking down, like he's taken aback, too, or … Wait, has he been put back into his box? Methinks it's a distinct possibility. In you go, *Beefy*. Oh, and there's the *also-known-as name*, stay in there for a bit. Oh, and maybe pop the lid down while you're at it. Now, there's a good creative.

Time to return to my keyboard tapping, basically dismissing him. Starting to email Chris, like busy, important person with lots of things to do.

"What-up A-hole?"

Yes, very mature. I'm allowed—it's Chris.

Why is Jai loitering still, huh?

"You know you look different today?" he's just piped up suddenly.

"Oh?" Re-picking up glasses in classy, elegant manner. Is he about to say that I'm charmingly dressed, perfectly coiffed, empowered, darling of the workplace, perhaps all of the above!

"Like a little flushed …"

Oh, fuck off.

"Have you been out for a run or something?"

I'm afraid to speak because I know I will swear. Composure! "No," responding flatly instead. Not filling in the gaps regarding early morning RPM gym training. Let him think that I've been up all night having wild sex with some beautifully handsome man, or whatever fucking conclusion he wants to draw.

So he is frowning at me now, okay, like he's trying to figure something out.

Oh, and saved by my mignon. Here comes Cristina, all dark hair, big eyes, glamorous clothes and enthusiasm. The girl does have impeccable timing though. At least I have to like her a little for that.

"Here's Cristina!" Trilling like we're besties, and ready for another exciting day at the office with exciting work.

She is clearly finding it a challenge containing herself, and she's bubbling over like frothy champagne thinking *The boss likes me!* "Hi, Cee!" she's crying. "Oh, I got you a latte just like you like it." She's holding it out to me, pushing past Jai at the door like he's an old shoe. A girl like this understands—suck up to the people that can help you.

"You already have one ... " She's clearly slightly bemused—like she also can't believe I got here at this time, and had a spare moment to purchase coffee. What has this girl been hearing about me?

"Thank you, *Tina*," I say, giving her a nickname. Not sure if she goes by Tina, or if she likes Tina at all, she's certainly never mentioned it to me ... But it seems a nice way to reinforce our close relationship, and my competence, and empathy towards people to said loiterer, Jai, at the door. "I'll have it a bit later on," I assure her, taking it from her delicate hand.

"Oh, great!" She's only just managing not to clap her hands together in mirth, but I can tell it's a real stretch for her and that she has to physically hold them back.

"Jai," I say, getting to my feet again, "Tina and I need to get started. We need to talk creative. I'll see you later." I'm loving acting like I'm too busy for eye contact, not even a glance.

"Sure, see you later," he says, oh, a little crestfallen, and heads off in all his muscly, tattooed, American manner.

11. 11:00a.m.

he thing about Beefy, aka Americano, is that he's an awesome creative. Beyond awesome creative, actually. Potentially fucking awesome creative. And as much as I hate to admit it, even mentally (and never would I say it out loud), I know it. It has been a bit difficult to dismiss. Especially when sitting in front of his three options for Swami Krishnananda's creative and finding it difficult to pick a fault with any of them. No matter how earnestly, desperately I have tried, nothing has sprung to mind. In fact, worse still, it has been difficult to pick between them, to make a choice. Vomit worthy really. Couldn't there have been at the very least something that I could point the finger at? That I could criticise if for?

"They're just all so awesome," Tina is telling me, because now Cristina has died, been buried, and resurrected in my mind as Tina. And it is Tina that I prefer, because I am moulding her, making her a Cee clone.

Note to self: her language is starting to invade my dialogue. Recall using the word "awesome" in thoughts not so long ago. I have embraced it—becoming a desperate thirty-two-year-old pseudo-hipster.

"They're *not* all so awesome," I'm telling her. I have a feeling of obligation to moderate her youthful enthusiasm. Downing my second latte for the morning and feeling the milk curdling inside my stomach as a result of the vitriol.

"But really they are. I know you told me last night to narrow it down to two options, or one at best. But all three of them are so suited to the audience, so targeted and creative at the same time. I can see them all turning into a memorable brand."

Indeed. So can I. No matter how hard I try to squint and see a negative, it's just not happening. Shit!

"Well, take me through the options again. We can't show Krishnananda three options. Like I said, give the client some leeway and they'll take a mile. They all think they're brilliantly creative minds, even if they don't have a creative bone in their bodies. We can't show him three. Only potentially two, and we drive in a particular direction. Got it?"

She is looking at me with slight desperation now, as though there's no way she's going to pass this task.

"The options," I say, snapping my fingers. Wow, where did that come from? Snapping fingers? So not my thing, but apparently my new and improved, gym bunny, organised and sophisticated thing. *A Cee-Project thang.*

"Well, the first is based on the lotus flower and the one thousand petals philosophy. It's the concept of Sahasrara—the top chakra. The chakra that links man, or person, really—like a river to the ocean. The thing that connects us to the ... "

"... *Rest of the universe.*" Yes! I've heard the chakra bullshit once before. Soon I'll be as well-versed as a yogi.

"But the clever thing about this is it becomes the logo, and it uses a palette of psychedelic colours, like fusing an old school Indian painting with new contemporary art. It's dynamic and bright, and the brand extends into a number of colours and forms," she is pausing to salivate, potentially for effect, not sure, "which are still relatable to the original. *Which* suggests longevity for the brand."

It does suggest longevity for the brand. Oh shit, who is this person, and how did she become so well rehearsed in the lingo? Isn't she supposed to be a graduate? She could sell this better to the client than I could. I don't need to let her know that though. No Cee, keep her down, or she'll be grabbing at your job.

"It's a little colourful though, isn't it?" I'm adding—unhelpfully.

She is staring at me again, right in the eyes as though she's not quite sure if I'm a fool or a genius, but she must be thinking it's the latter because she has started to scribble the thought down as though it's something really profound. It does sound like something a client would say. Her mouth is opening. No, it's closed again. Holding the boards of the second creative idea firm, she looks like a woman possessed, hair swirling, face animated. Expressions slightly crazed. My suspicions have been right all along—she's not of this world.

Okay second idea done, waving at her with rapid arm movements onto the third without commentary.

"The third is a stylised image of Swami Krishnananda, executed in black and white. While less visually pleasing than the rest, it certainly has some graphic gravitas. It's memorable, and could extend across a number of mediums including *television* and social media ..."

"There's no television in this campaign." She is looking rather startled at this thought. And what's this perplexed expression she is sharing with me, hmm?

"Yes, but it could still be used across television ..." she has continued nonetheless.

"Yes, but never say that in the room with Krishnananda. The client will always latch onto the thing they want to hear, even if it's out of context. You say television, and he'll be demanding television. He wants television already. He's an egomaniac, he wants to see himself on the big screen, but it's completely wrong for this campaign. He needs to be seen as subtle: a guru, a man of religion, not a used car salesmen flaunting himself on ... televison!" I like these dramatic finishes. Getting to my feet, I begin pacing the length of the room, seemingly deep in thought.

"Do you always put the client in the enemy zone?" Is she asking this with irony? Or is Tina actually waiting for sage advice?

Sage advice, apparently, pen poised on the paper.

"Always. The client is the enemy, Tina. They always want more than their budget can stretch to. They always want to use the mediums they prefer; they always want television—because television is the fix all—and they're terrible with creative."

She's scrawling this all down, semi-frowning in concentration.

"Oh, I'm learning so much." She has admiration in her eyes.

"Great. Now listen, we're going with one and three. That's one, river meets the sea ..."

"The ocean," she has supplied.

Whatever, waving the correction off. "And three, stylised image of the guru."

Job done. I saunter over to my desk with a sense of achievement. Obligatory and somewhat abrupt checking of my emails ... Chris:

"So hungry right now, just had epic fuck match this morning with love of life. Are you ready for lunch yet? I'm quite literally starving. Soon I'll cannibalise and eat one of my minions."

Respond:

"Ready. Where and when, buttercup?"

Ping. Almost instantaneous response—love him—he must have been paused at the keyboard:

"Let's go big, greasy Italian on Norton Street. Pino's?"

Fingers poised to tap out a response:

"Done and done. Big. Greasy. Italian and Pino's. Famished from cardio session at *sparrow's fart*, and subsequent hard work (at work—in case you needed to be reminded)."

Waiting! Evidently long message will be with me in a moment—He's a man who touch-types like a beast.

Ping. At last:

"I believe in the words 'big, greasy, Italian' ... and none of the rest— Cardio at sparrow's fart and hard work at work? Non! *C'est ne pas possibile.* Is this Cee I'm talking to or the intern?"

I respond quickly:

"Cee, and I'm quite literally walking out the door. Don't keep me waiting."

Chris:

"Never. Ciao! For now ..."

Grabbing for my handbag, I notice Tina's large eyes are staring at me … She really is a gawper.

"Yes?" I'm asking.

"Are you going to talk to Jai about this? I mean, you mentioned you'd provide him with feedback."

Oh, god. She's a serial finisher. *Must finish everything.* If it has been mentioned, even in passing commentary, then it must be done. A completer. Leave no sentence, book, movie, love affair, recipe, friendship, and you know the rest—unfinished. I know the type—and I'm not the type.

"No," I tell her … But she needs more, to hear something further. I can tell from the expectant look on her face. "No, the creatives always have inflated egos. Let them sweat a bit. Also, Krishnananda might not like either of them, in which case we'll need to go back to the drawing board, so no point telling Jai we have a winner just yet."

Nice! Another strategy. Even if it's a false one. Feeling super strategic today.

"Very practical," she's telling me, shaking her head as though she herself cannot quite believe the genius she's stumbled upon.

"Today is the day that we sign them up: lock, stock, and barrel. No more vacillation on the strategy. I want their agreement."

"So," I continue, and she has started doing that sitting upright thing, readying herself for instruction, back straight as an arrow, arms poised in elegant gesture.

"Yes?" Expectant tone.

"After lunch, I'll meet you at the boardroom. Krishnananda and his lackey will be brought up to the room from reception."

"He has a lackey?" She seems slightly concerned.

"Yes, they all have lackeys, Tina. People who suck up to them and basically make their days as comfortable as possible. His lackey is a particularly …"

Oh, how to describe Adriana? Dutchy-McDutchy? McDutchy-McBitchy? These are the usual descriptors I use for her behind closed doors and with the likes of friends, Chris and Jess for example. She is also a semi-crazed, direct, militant Dutch yogini with flaming red hair and an expression like a thunderclap. Even the tie-dyed clothes don't soften her otherwise impenetrable exterior.

"Particularly?" Tina is searching. I must have paused for an extensive period.

"Particularly strident in her commentary."

"Bitchy?" Tina offers.

"I like how we're both on the same tangent," I say, nodding my head. I can tell she thinks she has just received a gold star.

"So, I'll talk through the communications strategy. Again. Because they've heard it a few times and keep insisting we include television, even though it's completely the wrong avenue and we won't sign off on it."

"Completely the wrong avenue," she's echoing me.

"And then to throw them off the chase, you'll present the two concepts."

"Me? Present the concepts?" She is looking panicked, like she's a vampire and she's just stepped out in the sun, only she doesn't shimmer like Edward, she's more burning to a crisp Dracula style.

"Yes, you'll present the concepts," I say, repeating myself, thinking time is getting away from me now and Pino's *Gorgonzola gnocchi* are calling, oh so loudly. Come on girl! Agree!

"I'm not ready!" *What!* We are far from agreeing.

"You totally are. You had me sold, and I'm a far worse cynic than Krishnananda and his assistant." Maybe not the assistant, but she doesn't need to know that. "Keep it up, you know the river meets the sea ..."

"The ocean," she has corrected me again.

"Yeah, whatever! That stuff. It works—It'll distract them. And every client likes to see creative. They like to see pretty pictures. It always throws them off the chase."

"Okay," she's saying shakily. *Gnocchi, I'm almost there!*

"You'll be fine. Birth by fire, non? No better way to start, earn your stripes, find your feet." Whatever, because Pinot Grigio is singing now.

"Okay, I'll do it!" She's back to her enthusiasm now.

"Great!" I exclaim, giving her a slight fist pump. Yes, I'm fist pumping, too, along with snapping my fingers. Desperate times call for desperate measures, and *hunger* is a sure desperate measure.

"Oh my gosh! I'm so excited!" She is basically yelling at me. I'm sure half of this floor can hear her!

I'm creating a monster. And I think I quite like it.

"Maybe a little less enthusiasm." Time to creep out, slide away with food and vino as my incentives, and because I've suddenly become a little afraid for my very person. Her expressed fervor is too much for me.

I'm nearly out of the door, and she's nodding, and now writing it all down. Probably something like, "Moderate enthusiasm."

12. 2:00p.m.

*S*ailing into office. Again running late. Fuckety fuck fuck fuck. Was sure had left sufficient time after my tiramisu and limoncello to break into an Olympic sprinter-style run, get into a taxi, who would no doubt drive like one of the characters on Fast and the Furious, another under ten second sprint, and would have been back in the office with five minutes to spare, leaving moi ample time to powder nose and organise notes. Instead, Olympic sprint was more like pedestrian shuffle, and driver was a seventy-year-old man who could barely see over the steering wheel, and the speed of vehicle peaked at around fifty kilometres rather than two-hundred. He also bore no resemblance to Vin Diesel. As a result … I'm late. Or exactly on time, which means late for Dutchy-McDutchy and Swami because their concept of "on time" is early. Note to self: pencil skirt also hampers Olympic sprint-style running.

Sweat is now on neck, hair has swung slightly out of chignon in what I hope is a slightly *Bridgette Bardot* manner rather than *slutty*, late so-and-so manner. Turning the corner leading to the boardroom, and I best slow down to a *normal* pace. Smoothing skirt, patting hair back, affected, placid, in control, smile fixed, and now I'm ready for that meeting … In I go!

Oh, nice, three faces looking up at me: Tina, wide-eyed and still excited, creative boards spread around her, face down, with pink sticky notes demarking certain points she'd evidently like to remember; Swami, wearing his orange robes, hair long and grey, beard long and grey (imagine a tanned Gandalf), some sort of smear at centre of eyes, which are dark, peaceful, centered, and vague, with a smile on his face, looking as though he might spontaneously levitate off ground; and McDutchy, bright, curly red hair a tangle around her, wearing tie-dye, her long horse-like face also wearing a somewhat angry expression, eyes focused, burning a hole into me. Not nice.

She has just sprung to her feet with the agility of a lion and is now extending her hand. Oh, what's this? The expression on her face is still slightly maniacal, but I have come to learn that this is not an expression, as much as it is her actual face, and so I refuse to allow it to be a reflection on anything I've done or haven't done in the last two minutes.

She has a strong handshake, her eyes fixed on mine.

"Cee, lovely to see you again," she's saying to me, her voice a strange tone, as if it were spoken through the teeth, as though she's telling me, "Let's go to the deuce," like in the ye olden days.

"Lovely to see you …" I'm hesitating because I should be saying her name, too, but *McDutchy* almost just flew out of my still open mouth.

Close it. Yes, clenching of my teeth is vital at this potentially awkward moment. Perfect—a show of clenched teeth solidarity, smiling with a closed mouth. Adriana, for god's sake! Her name is Adriana!

"Adriana." Why did I say it? An inappropriate amount of time has lapsed.

"Yes?" She must think I'm asking her something. Shit.

"I just wanted to say you look fabulous."

"Thank you."

Phew. Fucking *phew* for that.

Now it's the Swami's turn, I guess. He is slowly getting to his feet. Frail, old, he really looks like he's about one hundred and fifty years old. I have no idea how old he is, but ancient would be an accurate description. I'm not going to be thrown off by his ancient, calm, happy demeanour. This man is a whip! I've seen him in negotiating action before.

He is super slowly bringing his palms together into a prayer position, and he is now bending from the waist, acknowledging my presence. You took your sweet old time about it! Should I do the same? I normally do when we have these meetings. Here goes … Feeling a little awkward, my yogic acknowledgement comes out like more of a strange Christian Génuflexion. I'm a little stuck here, must remember not to wear said pencil skirt on next Swami meeting … Swiftly moving on then …

"Swami." *Phew.* Have managed to stand back up straight.

"Cee, lovely to see you again." His voice has a beautiful breathy quality that makes it ethereal and melodic at the same time. No doubt affected, but a nice touch.

Turning towards Tina, I am hoping she understands the meaning of my nod, but she's clinging onto the table tightly. Otherwise, she might quite literally take off with excitement, I suspect. I quickly take my seat near her and hope she's had the common sense to introduce herself before my arrival.

"How was your lunch?" McDutchy has asked boldly, no doubt seeking to draw attention to the fact that I'm late. For me, though, that was supremely running *on time*, because I was only one or two minutes over.

"I wasn't at lunch," I'm lying again, and so smoothly.

"Cristina mentioned you were at lunch." Oh, bloody Tina, no idea when it's appropriate to lie or not to lie. The poor girl is shifting in her seat as though she can feel my wrath from a metre away. Good, feel it! I want it to taunt you for a little longer.

"I was at lunch," I say, lie forming in head as I'm speaking, "and then I returned and was called into an urgent meeting with our executive. I've just come from there."

"Oh," is all McDutchy has managed. Swami is continuing with those nods of his Gandalf head and swaying slightly with a placid expression.

"So," I begin (you are organised and on top of things across this project, Cee), "it's lovely to have you back in the office again."

"It is indeed a pleasure to see you again, Cee, and meet your lovely friend Cristina," Swami is whispering, hands in prayer position again. Little bow towards me, little bow towards Cristina.

He is throwing me off. Do I need to bow again, too? Not sure, so I will. He is bowing again. *Fuck*, and what do I do in response, *bow again?* What's the social convention in bowing? I'm stopping because I'm afraid I might fall into some alternate loophole of bowing. A vortex of yogic appreciation; I have no time for such nonsense!

"The education of our children is the most important thing in the world, Cee," he's continuing. Oh shit, what's this about? "Educating them in the right way, ensuring they conduct their work into the future with integrity and spiritual mindfulness."

What? I don't have any children. Purposeful pause. Smiling pretty … hoping he'll continue on and shed some more light on this riddle.

"I'm so glad you have welcomed Cristina into your world." Ahh Cristina is my metaphorical child here apparently—Anyway it's Tina … I like her better! "People think of those like *you and I*, childless in a biological way, as barren. As not contributing to society …"

WTF? Yes, that does stand for *What The Fuck?* So wish I could share these choice non-yogic words with Swami over here, but not in keeping with project. I know this! Still! Why is he bringing my womb and ovaries and eggs and such into it? *Barren!*

"But in reality, we contribute on a daily basis. And we find other children to teach and inspire. This is really the meaning of life, ensuring that our knowledge, our quietness of spirit and mind, is passed on through the generations."

I hope he's finished. I'm staying quiet, just in case he has some more nonsensical babble to impart. He's staring at me now, as though he's waiting for me to acknowledge his sage intellect and words of wisdom.

I almost start with *Heavenly Father* … but have bitten the words back.

"I couldn't agree more, Swami." So professional, aren't I? "Educating our children is, in fact—" Pause, *what is it?* Not sure, say something, anything. They'll seek the profound in even the most ridiculous. "—is, in fact, the root cause of our existence … of *all* existence." Oh, powerful stuff. Had to repeat that last bit with a touch of airy breath, and I think it has worked beautifully.

Yes, it has, his smile says it all. His whole face is now beaming and McDutchy, well, she still is very much emulating a thundercloud.

"I'm so glad we're on the same page, Cee. This is why I always wanted you on this project. I can sense a spiritual side to your nature, which is so very brilliant and unique."

I'm glad someone can.

"Indeed." I'm unable to come up with a more suitable expression at this point.

"What do you have for us today?" Ah, Dutchy McDutchy can always be counted on to make abrupt statements and bring the conversation back to business. Despite her thunderclap countenance and guttural tones, I tend to like the lady.

"We'd like to take you through the strategy one more time, because today is when you'll need to sign off on the approach … "

"What do you mean sign off?" McDutchy is intervening, leaning across the table aggressively. I'm used to her conversational demeanour, and being forced into some kind of homicidal stance.

"Well, it means give the go ahead," I'm responding smoothly and with confidence. Hopefully this is instilling said confidence in them, too.

"Is there any signing? You know, pen to paper?" she's asking me, taking an invisible pen in her hand and scribbling on invisible paper.

No, there's no signing, McDutchy. Don't worry, you won't be signing yourself away in blood. This isn't the portrait of Dorian Grey, and no, you won't be signing away your soul to maintain your youthful appearance, although it would appear Swami did that a few decades ago, given that he could potentially be well over a hundred years old. And McDutchy … Well, you could use some signing away the soul for a bit of youthful collagen around the eyes.

"No—It's a figure of speech. No literal signing on paper. But I guess you could say it's a gentlemen's agreement, that this is our way forward."

I regret these words as soon as they start spilling out of my mouth because McDutchy is looking increasingly alarmed and I am beginning to feel myself being drawn into another dialogue around the term gentlemen's agreement, which, I'm suspecting, will be less forgiving than the former. She is now speaking directly to Swami. Double Dutch, literally, it must be, I can't understand a fucking word. Swami speaks Dutch, too? He is conversing with her in what I believe to be fluent Dutch. I guess when one reaches the advanced age of one hundred and three, which he must be at least, then one has had the time to learn a number of different foreign languages.

So not in on the conversation. I may as well pick at a nail. Oh, it's gone quiet. Time to look up.

"I see," McDutchy is saying. "Good." And now she is waving me forward with a sweep of the arm like she is herding cattle. Ahh, so it appears that the Swami would have a full and accurate understanding of what a gentlemen's agreement is. Good, we can proceed.

"And after that, we'll be presenting the creative concepts for your campaign," I tell them, nodding towards Tina, who is looking slightly more alarmed and less enthusiastic than when the meeting first started.

"Good. Good," McDutchy has declared in her clipped, heavily accented, slightly guttural English. "Proceed."

She is sitting back in her chair ready to be wowed, and Swami continues sitting poised with an expression of calm—happiness playing across his ancient features.

"So, as previously discussed, this campaign is going to be heavily focused on social media," I begin … And here it comes, the usual litany. I've said it to them so many times it feels like a sermon, and they're never happy with it, which makes it feel even more like a sermon.

"The reason we've chosen this medium is because the Swami is a credible, religious practitioner—one you hear about through *word of mouth*. For example, 'Have you heard of that great yoga studio in Bondi? Krishnananda's yoga studio?'" This is a great point to stand on, so I will. It adds dramatic effect. In comes my acting ability, re-enacting the role of some Bondi hipster. "'It's *awesome*. The most *enlightening* experience I've ever had!'"

Is that what the yogis are saying these days? Sounds about right. But how can I really be sure having never had a discussion with one? They must say *awesome*, and *enlightened*, and shit like that. Just keep going, Cee!

"And then they press *share* on their social media accounts. Facebook. Twitter. Instagram. Storify. Youtube. We'll be all over every digital medium you can imagine, posting snippets of the Swami, comments he's made, a look into one of his classes, and it'll spread like wildfire … It'll be in every hipster's and wannabe hipster's account by morning."

I just said *hipster* and *wannabe hipster* aloud, didn't I? They appear to be nodding, one sagely, the other aggressively, but nonetheless nodding. These nods are good for making me feel encouraged to keep going … And besides, am all over the social media stuff now, no television dinosaur here thank you very much. I am a woman of the people, a woman of pop culture … one of trends!

"We'll build him up like a cult."

Lots more nodding.

"And then we'll combine this campaign with some well-placed print adverts and local radio. All underground, of course. No overt advertising. Nowhere will the Swami be coming out and saying, 'Hey! Look at me, I'm Krishnananda!'" I am raising my arms and thinking this has ensured that the full impact of this statement is understood. And I'm sure the more I'm saying, the more they're loving it ...

"No, wait, he'll be the person behind it all, but the people advertising it will be his converts. People like Tina," momentary eye flit to said intern, "and it'll be those whose lives have changed in a spiritual, fulsome, and complete direction as a result of practising the Swami's yoga."

This is going well, and there is still more. I can't stop spewing this shit.

"After all ..." I actually feel buoyed by their captivation. Think I may throw in some social and spiritual commentary. Am virtuoso at this point. " ... that's what they really want, a sense of being *whole*, of being *complete*, of purpose ... Why else do they buy all that stuff? All that materialism and consumerism? It is a cry for help to anyone that can help! Help me!" And ... I'm yelling. "Help me! Make sense of my *hopeless* life."

So dramatic, so powerful, yet soft and breathy at points. So totally virtuoso. Like a conductor at the stalls.

"So right, Cee," Krishnananda is profusely nodding. "I knew you were the right person for this campaign; only a truly enlightened mind would make sense of it all."

And I'm joining in with the nodding now, closed eyed, in unison. But this needs something more. Something which will transform them—not just from the converted, but to the preachers themselves. It may come to me if I sit down. Oh, I have it—it's on the tip of my lips—I can drag this out. I'm feeling pretty satisfied, and know it's showing in my expression.

I'm itching to utter the words, knowing I've sold the campaign now.

"You'll be bigger," I need a pause here, "than Bikram." The words have shattered the silence, and the pair of them are looking alarmed, leaning forward, unbelievably on edge, like I've just asked them to have an orgy in this very room.

"Bigger than Bikram?" the Swami has asked, quivering, evident composure lost.

"Yes," I say, reinforcing it. "Bigger than Bikram."

A day ago I didn't even know who Bikram was, but after being shamed by my enthusiastic intern who revealed my limited knowledge of popular culture, yoga and potentially my client … I did a bit of Googling—Yes, I can search just as much as the next person. You know, here and there, it can be squeezed in between lattes and gin and tonics, and well, I know more about who Bikram is as a result, and I know how to use him to win over a client.

I know Tina is holding her breath behind me, too. I can almost hear her thoughts. Maybe with all this new businesswoman power, I'm tapping into my inherent mind reading ability, like my mother? She's thinking - *Who's bigger than Bikram. No one!*

Yes, this is unchartered territory, my little intern friend. Welcome to the world of advertising. Welcome to the world of *sell, sell, sell.*

"Even without television advertising?" McDutchy has said. I'm frowning at her. Really? Fuckety, fuck. We're back to the television ads, are we?

But today, unlike the other three occasions I've pitched the idea, I'm ready to sell it like never before. They better hold onto their hats … or tie-dye and orange robes in this case!

"Yes, without television. Bikram never had television."

Now I don't know if this is for certain, but I can certainly assume it's the case. And really, I know it's the clincher, so how can I possibly hold back from using it? Besides, I just already did!

"Never had television ads?" McDutchy's words come out almost as a sigh. I know what type of sigh it is, too. One of defeat.

No more nodding from me. I'm shaking my head now with real conviction, and my line of sight right on her third eye … that little space between her actual eyes. I'm focused. I am nailing this!

"Never?" Swami has asked, too. Of course he probably thinks I would be less likely to lie to a Swami, what with him being a religious man and all, but the fact is I would quite happily lie to the pope at this point to get this account done and dusted.

"Never!" I repeat with conviction Confidence. Go, Cee!

Why with the Dutch again? McDutchy clearly can't help herself, and is saying something to Krishnananda. He is responding, but I'm not getting anything from his expression, and certainly not from the Dutch dialogue. Of course I know we're *in*. We must be! Slowly getting to my feet again, with an air of confidence, reaching for one of the raspberry muffins shining up at me invitingly from the centre of the table—They're here for the clients, but I want one, and I'm having one. Plate in hand, this little cake is helping maintain my patience. I have all the time in the world to ever so slowly sit back down and peel away the paper wrapper from this alluring muffin, oh so methodically.

More Dutch. More Dutch. More Dutch.

Chewing thoughtfully.

"Nice muffin, Tina." She's still looking deeply alarmed. "Would you like one?" She shakes her head, eyes fixed on the dynamic duo as they are continuing to Dutch it up.

Silence.

"Cee?" It's the Swami; of course he would be the one to speak to sign the deal, not McDutchy. Not the lackey.

"Hmm?" I'm murmuring absently, mouthful of muffin.

"Where should I figuratively sign?" he asks with a cool and calm demeanour. *And* we're back up and running. I knew it!

"I'll send you the first bill."

I know these Swamis too well, even though I really only know this one, but they all want to be rock stars. Spiritual enlightenment is just a path for them to the limousines, satin suits, fedoras and adoring fans.

"Would you care for a muffin?" I ask them, extending the plate and napkins towards them.

The Swami takes one quickly.

"Bigger than Bikram?" Why is he asking this again?

"That's right," I respond casually.

He's sitting back, more relaxed now, and allowing a breath of pure ecstasy to escape him.

"Are these gluten free?" McDutchy has asked, aggressive stance.

"Yes, only the best for you two."

Who knows if they're gluten free, just fucking take a muffin already! She is clearly hungry; she just snatched one. Vulture.

"Now," I say, clapping my hands together (oh my god, I'm starting to really take on Tina's mannerisms), "on to the creative choices."

13. 4:00p.m.

Back in office after hugely successful meeting with Swami and Dutchy-McDutchy. Tina has gone to buy me a latte, double shot, full cream milk, two sugars. Splurging now, in mood to celebrate. Would have a shot of Bombay Sapphire if didn't have meeting with restaurateur, aka future husband, in the next half hour. One to Cee; Universe, zero. Feeling like buzzing, awesome, sophisticated businesswoman, sealing deals and making the world a better place. Correction, making my world a better place!

Checking Facebook. Might change status to something breathy, excited, and in touch with the universe. Stick *that*, Christian ex-boyfriend nobody. I am liberated, successful woman who went to the gym in the morning and mastered a grueling RPM class, and then … Well, signed a spiritual guru to her advertising agency! And the day isn't even done!

New status: "Feeling awesome." *Note to self:* use of hip and cool word *awesome*, like the young people are doing these days. "Fantastic workout at the gym, followed by fabulous day at work. On top of the world."

Cheers!

I don't fancy answering my ringing phone, wishing I could let it go to voicemail, which is non-existent because I've never bothered to program my message. No, not answering it. Mind you, I can't let it ring out because it might be restaurateur rescheduling. Again! *Sigh*.

"Cee speaking."

Pause.

"Cee?" Oh dear god! Really? Why is she calling me at work? "Cee, you sound awfully serious when you're answering the phone. You really need to work on being more upbeat."

"Hello, Mother." *Sigh*.

"Hello, yourself. Don't sound so vexed. I did, after all, bring you into this world."

"I know, Mother … I'm just at work. Busy. Busy." I can tell, even though there's no mirror in front of me, that there's that maniacal look on my face.

"Busy little bee, I know. But I knew you wouldn't answer your mobile if I called, what with caller ID and all, so I thought I'd give you a burl at work."

"Indeed." Clicking back on Facebook, scanning my page, and waiting for the *likes* to begin. Anything to distract me from this call!

"I did call you the other day, too, while you were at lunch and I left a message with your assistant. Charming girl, really. You should start using a phone manner much more like hers. Did you get the message?"

In fact, Tina had passed it on, but of course one does get busy at work in between Facebook updates and lattes, and somehow it has slipped my mind to return the call.

"No, she didn't," I'm lying instead. "She might have a nice phone manner, but she's a silly little thing," responding as the person in question is turning the corner with serial killer enthusiasm written all over her face and handing me a latte.

"Strange though, she did seem so diligent," Mother is musing.

"Indeed," I say, smiling back at Tina—who has no understanding of what's going on, given the permanent euphoric look on her face.

"So Mother ... " I say, interrupting her. I have to before some other long torrid story ejects from her mouth. " ... what where you calling about? I have to dash to a meeting shortly."

"I was just making sure that you were coming on Saturday to help me and Char make the wedding invitations. You know how very much I'm counting on you and your creative vision."

Oh shit, the wedding invitations. I can't quite see how gluing diamantes with a glue gun to cheap paper is in any way evidence of me being creative, but given I've done it twice before, I am potentially one of the most experienced people in the country for the task. But really, not again? *Sigh*. Do I have to sit through a whole day with Mother laughing, drunk over mimosas, listening to terribly inappropriate sex stories?

Yes, even when I'm there she talks about her sex life, and this is not only highly inappropriate coming from the woman who almost had a seizure when I said the word *vagina* the other night, but mostly because she is a seventy-year-old woman who shouldn't be having more sex than me anyway! I'm feeling a cold shudder run through me, not a nice thought, *her at it*. Oh god!

"Cecilia?"

"Yes, Mother?" I say, recollecting myself.

"There was an awfully long pause there. And if you are hoping to concoct some wildly unbelievable lie to get yourself out of assisting, please remember that one, I'm your mother—and know that's your coping mechanism, and two, I'm your mother—and you owe me, not only because I gave birth to you, but because I raised you, alone, might I add, sans husband, because your bugger of a father had already remarried that Italian woman ..."

Must hold back from saying, *But Mother, you do remember that you left him?* No point, wouldn't have a chance to get the words out. It's like a juggernaut now, a torrent, an unstoppable churn of ridiculous logic, which won't halt until I agree that I am, in fact, going. Oh, she is still talking, surprise.

" ... but also because you're my daughter, and you should love me! And you should want to be a part of all of this. And after all, you are the maid-of-honour!"

Can't she give it a rest? Feeling like I want to scream really loudly! Maid-of-honour, again Mother, really? Like at wedding number two, and three—both failed weddings: one when I was nineteen, and the other when I was twenty-five. Somehow she pulls them in! And somehow she spits them out.

"Yes, Mother, I can confirm I'll be attending."

"How are you going to get to Wahroonga at 10:00 a.m.?"

Oh yes, I vaguely remember this conversation from the other night, and shit, 10:00 a.m.! On a Saturday! Please god no! Can't you be appeased by the fact that my alarm went off at 5:20 this morning?

Couldn't I possibly sleep in on a Saturday? Besides, she thinks this will throw me because there's no way I could get to Wahroonga on time, given the start time is that early, using public transport, without getting up at 5:20 a.m. again, and, of course, I have no car.

I'm doing that thing now where I am really trying to stop myself thinking, but it's there in my mind already. The thought exists; it's going to manifest before I have the chance to block it: I bet Tina drives a car. Probably a Mercedes SLR or Z4 BMW that some parent bought her for her university graduation—definitely a coupe. I can see her luscious hair flying in the wind behind her, and now the thought has description, imagery—shit!

"Cee?"

"Yes?"

"How will you get there on time?"

"Oh, I'm borrowing Jess's car." I'm lying. Although, I'm sure I'll have to. Will need to make a groveling call later on today, perhaps alongside a taco home delivery.

"Oh, *fabulous!* She's such a dear girl!"

"Indeed."

Oh—new *friend request;* clicking on the happy *one* digit above the people icon on Facebook. I'm so social network savvy. Love a good friend request: long lost ex or school friend …

Jai Rodden.

Sigh. Why is he sending me a friend request? He's probably one of those serial frienders who friends everyone so that he can achieve some mythical number of friends, like maybe a thousand. I tried doing that once, but failed at around the seven hundred mark, and it all got a bit depressing because I was friending like I was some kind of friend desperado and that is not cool!

"Did you hear that, Cee?" Mother is asking. Oh shit, we're back to the conversation, and no, I didn't hear it!

"Pardon, Mother, I missed it." Trying to work, remember!

"I said," she is sighing as though she knows she should have taken me to be tested for ADD as a child, "why don't you bring Jess with you? I love that girl, she's just so fabulous!"

"Mother—You're really too old to be using that term."

"What term?"

"Fabulous."

"Like they didn't say fabulous in my day!"

"Not with the same reference."

"Darling, they did—and why can't I be youthful and spritely?"

"Because you're neither. You're in your seventies."

She has paused … No wait, here comes her rather stiffly response. "*Seventy* is the new *forty.*"

"Is that right?"

"Yes, I read it in *Vogue* or something …"

"*I* didn't see it."

"That's because you don't read *Vogue*, darling."

Sigh. Did this woman really give birth to me?

"So?"

"So what?" responding vaguely, and staring at that friend request intently … What should I do now? It would be wrong not to accept, or to ignore it, because then he'll really think I dislike him. Not that I don't. Because I do! But at the end of the day I need to maintain some form of collegiate rapport. If only I had some policy, like don't be friends with colleagues. I don't. I'm Facebook friends with Ian, and that bloodsucker Elsie (just so I can keep my eye on her). But if I accept Jai as a friend, then I'll need to maintain exciting statuses, and photos, too, so that I don't truly seem like some down and out thirty-something-year-old, but rather, an awesome, hipster-like doll.

"Will you invite Jess?" Mother is saying earnestly. I'm glad she has finally learned to pause in between my thought patterns.

"I hardly think Jess will be interested. She's just split up with a long-term partner. I don't think she'd want to be around the wedding thing."

"She would love it. It's just what she needs. She needs a girls weekend …"

"It's not a weekend." She is getting carried away, and may well turn this into some pajama wearing, cocktail drinking event at her place with Char.

"You know what I mean," she's speaking primly. "She needs to be out with the ladies."

I'm considering telling her that she's not of our age group, and this is not some night out on the town picking up lads. Rather some grueling match of stapling, cutting, tying bows and using glue sticks, guns if you're lucky, to create somewhat gruesome wedding invites. Last time we did this, I ended up with two calluses on my fingers.

Noting time, almost 4:30 p.m. and need to apply another layer of lip gloss and some blush at least to help pasty complexion before meeting with restaurateur. Need to close this convo ASAP.

"Sure, Mother." I sound convincing, methinks. "I'll invite her."

"Oh, wonderful. Fab. Too excited!"

"Indeed." Need to get her off the phone. "I'm super excited." There, that should do it!

"Oh, glad to hear it, honey! I knew you'd come around."

"Okay, Mother, must go. I have a meeting to run to."

"Of course, my busy little bee!" Her voice is shrill, and I'm hoping that Tina hasn't heard from her spot at the table where she is still taking notes furiously. On what? Haven't a clue! Most likely still penning stuff from the meeting with Swami and McDutchy.

"See you then!" I'm crying with feigned joy for dramatic effect.

"Ciao."

Got to hang up before she can say anything further. Dear god—The weekend has just been swallowed by this Char, Mother, gluing, and stapling event.

Staring at friend request. A swig of coffee will help. Oh, to hell with it! *Accept.*

Note to self: must from here on out exhibit fabulous life on Facebook, filled with inspirational quotes, selfies (which show my true supermodel status of course, correct angle, flattering lighting), and parties … Lots and lots of parties.

Fictitious life? Muchly. But that's what Facebook is for, non?

In need of lip gloss application. Must prepare, potential husband up ahead!

14. 4:45p.m.

Footballer-come-restaurateur is late. Have been waiting rather impatiently in boardroom for at least fifteen minutes. Crossing and uncrossing legs. More the shins than the legs, due to length and tightness of skirt, and commando state underneath said skirt. Adjusting shirt and skirt. Adjusting hair. Adjusting posture. Adjusting in general. Trying to recall which, if any, of my sides are more complimentary. I seem to have the recollection that I look better from left-hand side. Trying to remember previous photos taken, and if they were disproportionately angled towards one side of body and face from an attractive perspective. Nothing is springing to mind. I'll stick with the left.

A plate of fresh muffins has been brought to the table, chocolate on this occasion, and some strawberry Danishes. As well as the ever present coffee and tea apparatus—cups, saucers and spoons.

I'm famished, despite Gorgonzola gnocchi, multiple lattes, vinos, and several muffins consumed after meeting with Swami and McDutchy. Damn exercise. It might be all the brainpower I've been using today, too! *Note to self:* using brain frequently, alongside regular exercise, could lead to overeating.

Is it wrong for me to consume food intended for the client before the client has arrived? Think it potentially could be. But what harm could it do? There are more than enough muffins and Danishes to go around. It's not like I'm going to alienate his choices, and wouldn't want stomach to make highly unprofessional growling sounds during meeting. That has happened to me before. Very unpleasant. Basically a deal breaker. It was my stomach, but think client may have categorised it as flatulence.

Decision made, and I'm already lunging for the plate of Danishes, swiftly collecting the largest, most buttery, and most decadently smeared with strawberry. Mouth watering, taking a mammoth bite now, and nobody here to witness unladylike behaviour. He might not even turn up, and if he doesn't, then who needs him when I have this lovely pastry?

Nothing goes better with pastry than coffee. Leaning over table to collect plunger and a cup and saucer, a bit of milk, a dash of sugar, and I'm sorted. Afternoon snack in process …

Is that someone clearing his or her throat at the door? Oh yes, it is! Looking up, I'm confronted with our strange receptionist—some forty-year-old former opera diva with some sort of subsequent penchant for drama disorder. Seriously, the woman is up and down like a manic-depressive on speed, and has a more active imagination for plots against her than some Shakespearean character like Hamlet or Othello. She is looking aggrieved at this point, leaning on the door jamb, arms crossed, headset on.

"Your 4:30 p.m. is here," she's telling me, ushering through the man behind her.

My heart is pounding just at the sight of him stepping forward. This is definitely the most handsome man I've ever seen, like ever. Without a shadow of a doubt! He's moving towards me, more like gliding, and "Hungry Eyes" from the soundtrack to *Dirty Dancing* comes to life in my mind. Oh, so not good. The song has taken me to a place of unwelcomed distraction—It was used by a burger commercial. Think of more appropriate song, Cee …" She's Like the Wind."It's playing in my head as, *he's like the wind,* whatever, same difference.

He is leaning over now, as if in slow motion. He must want to shake my hand, very similar to the feeling I get on the tennis court when I suddenly realise the ball is heading in my direction, that it will clear the net and I'll need to take some sort of swing at it …

And just like in the tennis scenario, I'm panicking. Not good timing! Because I do take a swing in tennis, and I do usually hit the ball straight into the net, miss it completely, or watch it sail over the base line and towards the back fence.

"Lovely to meet you, Cecilia," he's saying to me, and I'm quite literally almost peeing my pants. He sounds like Ridge on *Bold and the Beautiful,* sans the American accent (Mother would be proud), or like Tom Hardy in almost everything (except when he was Bane, in which case he was completely incomprehensible), all gruff and masculine, but bittersweet at the same time.

"Lovely to meet you, too …"Nearly said *restaurateur,* but have managed to recover myself. " … Chad."

Extending my hand, we shake. His hand is broad, worn, and steady. I can imagine those hands on me. I am imagining them on me right now, and feeling a little flustered at those thoughts and images. Oh no, another image flashing in my mind. Oh, it's lewd, and I'm aware again of commando status. Shit! Focus, Cee, he's a client.

Suddenly recall psycho Desdemona receptionist is still standing over there, looking aggrieved, like a gargoyle of sorts, fixed expression and stone still.

"Thanks so much." I'm being so sickly sweet, so fake—Now heading her way in an endeavour to close the door because she's a crazy bitch and I'm not quite sure what she might say.

"Those Danishes and muffins," she says, eyeballing me psychotically, "are meant for the client."

"Thanks again," I'm trilling, and ignoring the comment, even though it was loud enough for sex-on-legs behind me to hear. *Sigh*. Door closed in said receptionist's face. Returning my attention to said sexy man.

Adjusting shirt. You, Cee, are a wildly clever, ingenious businesswoman who just closed a deal, and who also did a 6:00 a.m. RPM class, and you have this! It's in the back of the net, or I've touched down … I'll get better at the footy lingo if I need to, just like I did with the yoga!

Turning fully towards him, and my smile, bright but demure at the same time, is climbing all over my face. I'm literally smiling from my eyes, and my body, as well as my lips. "Sorry about that."

"No problem," he says calmly. "She did seem a bit unhinged."

He seems astute, comfortable, already having taken a seat. Must not tell him to stand back up so I can assess his height. I didn't get a good enough look, totally been distracted by his baby blue eyes, full head of dark hair, sharp jaw, and beautiful smile (all toothy and sparkly white).

Note to self: Google height later on. Loving search engines!

"Oh, dear," responding, and taking my seat opposite him; crossing my hands on table in front of me to resist tearing my clothes off and also to indicate left hand and lack of wedding band. Subtle brilliance. "That doesn't sound good."

"Oh, it was fine. There was just a lot of sighing when she got up from the reception desk like she had more important things to do than take me to this room, you know, her actual job."

Speak, bright angel! I can almost hear trumpets going off around him.

"Oh, well, you know Facebook, online shopping, Instagram, stalking friends … I can only imagine."

Oh, good start for moi, he is laughing at my little joke. It wasn't that great either, was it? But he seems to think otherwise.

"So can I try one of these Danishes, or were you planning on finishing the plate?" He's sort of funny, in an interesting way, I guess. I was expecting him to be dumber, so this definitely makes things more noteworthy.

"Well, I was planning on cleaning up those Danishes, so if you wouldn't mind starting on the muffins, that would be great."

He's laughing again.

"A lady with a sense of humour and an appetite, that's uncommon." He's reaching across for a napkin and muffin.

"Really?"

"Mmm …" He's biting into his muffin. I wish he would bite into me instead, right into my shoulder, or a nuzzle on the neck, right here, right now … But I'm keeping control of slutty behaviour given it's not even 5:00 p.m. in the afternoon, and the last vino I had was hours ago, and he's a client that I need to bring in. Focus. But the way he is treating that muffin!

Cee, pull it together. Remember you're at work. Try to ignore ongoing background music, the best hits of *Dirty Dancing* still playing in mind, and focus on the business.

"So, it's our first meeting. Tell me a bit about what you're hoping to achieve here."

He has just nodded, chewing thoroughly, in a slightly undignified manner now, which I shall choose to ignore, and is now wiping his mouth (I bet that's how it's done in the *league*, although I don't know if he was in league or AFL or NRL or rugby or if those codes are one and the same thing—Must Google later).

"Since the end of my football career, I've dabbled in all sorts of things: sports commentary, presenting, different home and garden programs— and you probably know I have a home and garden project in the pipeline for next season. *Living Large?*"

I definitely don't probably know that, I just don't know it—but I best nod my head anyway because he seems to need some positive reinforcement. After all, why are we talking about this and not the restaurant? *Note to self:* he was, and will soon be again, a prominent television celebrity—another bonus. And there it is, the image in my mind of myself at glitzy after show parties on Chad's arm with Burt and Patti Newton. Perhaps not the most exciting of party friends, but nonetheless iconic. Focus, Cee! Focus!

"Great, you've heard of it! Good to hear the word is out there, although you do work in the advertising industry so no doubt offay with all the changes in the industry?"

Nodding again. Hate the word *offay*. Has strange *Bogan*, redneck quality about it. Low quality. Well, one must make compromises even when they do meet their *man-of-dreams*. Overlooking some slight imperfections is not unexpected.

"So for a while now, I've been running a restaurant in Freshwater ..."

Finally, we get to the restaurant.

"Right on the water, beautiful views, regional Venetian dishes. Venice is probably my favourite place in the world, a city on water, amazing don't you think?"

"Couldn't agree more," I'm purring now, but not as a pet, hopefully as a business minded and seductive feline female.

"Have you been?"

Oh shit, why do I always have to open myself up to these questions? I could have chimed in the seduction at some other point, but it was the cat thing, it felt good. Where to go from here? *I do have an Italian stepmother, but oh I've never actually been to Italy*. In fact, on my last European trip, spent with Jess after we finished our communication degrees, we steered clear of Italy. Jess had gone on some rant about it being dirty and full of lotharios and food, and she'd already put on enough weight during this goddamn trip ... pretty much comparable to whale-size status, and she really needed to lose a few kilos before she returned to Australia and to Pete. Pete who, at the time, was no doubt expecting to see her return as some sophisticated European siren. Not an Italian mamma. *Let's go to Romania instead*, she said to me. Off the beaten track; *Vlad's Castle, you love Dracula*, she had supplicated. *And I bet they have shit food there, and even if we do eat something, we'll pick up a stomach bug of extraordinary proportions, which will reduce us to Kate Moss thinness in no time.* Oh shit, he's looking at me expectantly.

"No," responding, "but I hear it is stunning, amazing, breathtaking." Lots of descriptive words, Cee. Pile it on just like Jess's pounds.

"Exactly." He's smiling broadly, shaking his hands towards me like we are totally on the same wavelength. I'm noticing that it doesn't take much to impress this guy. "It is utterly amazing. I went on my honeymoon—It was winter there and completely breathtaking ..."

Is he using my descriptive words? Maybe we are on the same wavelength?

"We saw the opera, we ate squid ink pasta ... Well, I ate squid ink pasta; Grace Rose didn't eat anything at all because she never ate *anything at all*. Of course she hated it, every moment. *Italy's too full of Italians* she told me! What the hell? Of course it is! After all, it is Italy! Could you imagine?" I'm staring at him attentively and he's gliding into a more relaxed position in his chair, shaking his head, evidently vexed. Grace Rose! That's obviously the ex-wife. What a bullshit name; it's worse than *Cristina*, worse than *Elsie*, an unmistakable flake.

"Totally ridiculous," I'm reinforcing. "I could go for a plate of squid ink pasta now, maybe with a marinara sauce," I say, salivating at the thought.

Hat trick. He's laughing for the third time, throwing his head back as though it's the funniest thing he's ever heard. "After your Danish?"

"Listen, I did RPM this morning."

More laughter. Now I'm laughing a little, too.

"Sorry, she just makes me crazy. How can you marry someone and not realise how different you are? Not just different, but polar opposites?" He is leaning forward now, no longer sinking back. I just caught a whiff of his woody cologne; it's almost enough to make me weak at the knees.

This man is so *Prince Charming*.

"Beats me! You know, you should have realised as soon as she told you her name. Grace Rose! Such a bullshit name."

Motor mouth—Did I just say that? Shit! Complete verbal diarrhea! Will no doubt be fired! Have even used *shit* word with client. Oh wait, it seems all is not lost, he's in hysterics now, laughing up a storm, giving me enough time to survey his outfit: neat white shirt tucked into black jeans. I like, I like it a lot—no evidence of hipster, Bondi, organic green juice sippage, Bikram perspiration to be seen. Just a whole lot of sex-on-legs!

"You're right! It's a total bullshit name."

I'm laughing. You may not have had me at *hello*, but I'm yours at *bullshit*.

"So back to business." I'm oozing confidence, sexiness—a total businesswoman who keeps things on track. "Your business is highly profitable and you want to expand across Australia?"

"Australia, and possibly the States. May have an opportunity in L.A. An old friend of mine, we played together, Craig Derning?" He's looking at me expectantly again as though I should know the name, and so I must nod profusely. Nodding.

Not sure who Craig Derning is, but can't admit, as am going along swimmingly at this point. I am woman of great understanding of football, of Europe and of food, and also of garden television programs.

"He's living over in L.A. at the moment. Malibu. Beautiful house right on the water, beautiful wife, beautiful kids ..." He's looking a bit wistful at this point. If I were Tina, I would be writing in my notes—*envious of friend Craig Derning. Wants to settle down and be married with kids.*

"Anyway, willing to invest, potentially wants to open one of my restaurants in Malibu, maybe Santa Monica."

"Awesome." I'm scrawling the locations down in my notebook thinking potential junkets on USA horizon.

"You think?" Even though he's smiling, I'm sensing a level of uncertainty. As though he's not quite sure. As though he's never had anyone fully believe or validate his dream.

But this, my new friend, is the world of advertising; we believe in every dream. And advertising (and potentially some clever product placement) makes dreams a reality. Has Cinderella met her Prince? Or has the Prince met Cinderella?

"It sounds wonderful," I'm gushing, and his face is lighting up. There's the validation he's been wanting all along. Meanwhile, still need to keep hands in safe places to avoid ripping my clothes off … or his. Have noticed rippling biceps, pecks, and quads under thin layer of clothes. Now if only I knew which muscle group was which!

"So I need you guys to work on an advertising campaign while I start expanding these deals and networks."

Did he say *you guys?* Are we in? Am *I* in?

"Do you want television?" You know it—Television is the thorn in my side.

"Of course! Is that a problem?" he says with a confused look.

"For you, I'll do television." I'm smiling … and he's smiling back.

And apparently we have an agreement.

In the office, of course—but if only it would extend to the bedroom, his or mine, either would suffice.

15. 7:00p.m.

In house (or apartment really), dialing Jess on mobile. Have been dialing Jess and Chris repeatedly for the last two (potentially three) hours, not sure, may have left ten to twenty messages on each phone like crazy stalker person. But it's warranted! Have even thought about contacting Mother, or resurrecting another old friend from the depths of ex-friends, just so I can talk to someone! Anyone—Must talk to someone! Absolutely exploding with joy ... or something!

No answer. Damn! I'm hanging up without leaving message because a twenty-first message might be too much, non? Ahh yes, shall pour myself another Chardonnay bought from local liquor store. Splurged and purchased forty dollar bottle given that may potentially soon be dating highflying ex-footballer/restaurateur/Australian personality, and will need to know the difference between wines.

Tastes exactly the same as ten dollar bottles I've been drinking, but nonetheless feel the palette maturing.

Fred is staring up at me mournfully, but sitting patiently. "Are you waiting for more food?" Doggy voice essential! I have already fed him, but he's the skinniest Cavoodle in the world, even though he eats like a Labrador in heat. "Well, buddy, given I have no one else to share this fleeting happiness with, or to dissect the ins and outs with, I'll at least pass on some joy to you."

Refilling his bowl with kibble and he's looking ecstatic, tail wagging, smiley face on, as though he can't believe he's going to be fed a second time around. "There you go, Freddy-weddy." Food in front of him now— And he's shoving his face in as though he fears even a moment of hesitation will make it vanish.

Happiest dog in the world! If only it was so simple for humans? Oh, hang on, it is. Think of Jess drowning sorrows in Doritos and Tex Mex food, and my own Gorgonzola gnocchi—a beacon of light, an indication of what was to come, an epic, awesome, beyond *epic* afternoon!

Losing power with adjectives given number of Chardonnays I've consumed. From here on out, I'm going to either refer to things as awesome or epic. After all, it's how the world should be.

Where are those two best friends of mine when I need to gloat and dish? Are they ignoring my calls, or just busy? Those two are perennially attached to their phones. It seems unlikely that they wouldn't be answering or texting back for two hours? Maybe they've befriended each other and are suddenly in league together and have exposed me! For what? A crazy consumer of cheese and vino?

Paranoia is fast setting in. That's what I need—cheese to assuage alcohol consumption.

Open fridge. Booze. Booze. More booze (Evidently didn't really need astronomically priced bottle of Chardonnay—unless you listen to the refining palette argument). Coke Zero. Orange juice. An exorbitant amount of fluids! Hmm! Pasta salad. Tomato sauce (why in fridge?), mushrooms (looking a little sad and shriveled—probably a result of some purchase I made a fortnight ago when thinking it would be wise to include more vegetables in my diet—and of course, none ingested since), ahh—cheese—halloumi, and some smoked cheese, even if only a quarter of each remains in its pack …

Happily dishing out some cheese and crackers and finally, the ringing I've been waiting for happens. Scooting over as quickly as is humanly possible. Smiling at Jess's name flashing on the screen.

"And where have you been?" I'm allowed to be demanding, it's my right as her best friend.

"Is this how you're answering phones now?"

"It is to friends I have been trying to call for the last two hours or more, who haven't been responding to my calls. What if it was an emergency?"

"Was it?"

"No, but that's beside the point. I could have passed out and Fred might have been trying to eat my face off because he's a relentless, desperate eater." I'm staring down at him, and he's looking up at me with a heartbroken face, like he knows I'm talking *smack* about him.

"Really? Fred?"

"Yes, really. Or … I could have been choking on a … " No choking instruments are coming to mind, struggling … Oh wait, this is a good one. " … on a Brazil nut!"

"A Brazil nut?"

"What, are you parroting back everything I say now?"

"No, I just find you choking on a Brazil nut a bit far-fetched, considering you don't have any health foods in your house. I'm pretty sure all you stock is cheese and vino."

Trying to ignore the mental image that springs up of the contents of my fridge.

"Anyway, where were you?" I shall completely avoid the cheese, vino, Brazil nut discussion.

"If you want to know so desperately, I went to sleep, and my phone was in the other room."

"You went to sleep when you got home?" I say, totally incredulous.

"Yes, that's right. I was tired because I got up at *sparrow's fart* to do some ridiculous RPM class."

"Of which you loved every second!"

" … Of which I thought I would suffer severe cardiac failure at any second, and then spent the rest of the day completely dazed and confused because I'd endured extreme rush of blood to the head at 6:00 a.m. So when I got home, I went to bed because I was tired, and because I wanted to avoid another Doritos-cheese-Tex Mex binge."

"Seems semi-plausible." Sarcastic tone.

"Because it is! Now that we have that over with, what did you so desperately want to talk to me about?" She has an annoyed tone.

"Well, now I hardly feel like telling the story because you're in a shitty mood," I say, feeling dejected.

"I'm not in a shitty mood at you. I just woke up. I'm always in a shitty mood when I wake up."

This is true. She isn't a morning person. Semi remember being on a tour with her around Spain and having to shake her awake regularly in the morning so we could catch the 7:00 a.m. bus with the rest of the tourists. To which she would regularly respond, "Fuck you, bitch," but was, however, desperately apologetic at the 10:00 a.m. mark.

"Fine, I know that much! Well, I was calling because I met the restaurateur today!" Excitement is creeping into my voice with each word.

"Potential husband/ex-footballer?"

"Yes, that's the one!"

"And? Was he potential husband material?"

I can hear a popping sound, followed by a metallic scraping.

"He was indeed!" I almost feel like squealing, but this would be very Tina-like and immature for a woman of my age and business acumen, wouldn't it?

Chewing ensuing. Not mine, hers.

"Oh my god. Tell me everything."

Evidently food helps speed up the waking process.

"What are you eating, Jess?"

"Toast and butter, yum—so good."

"Nothing like toast and butter; I want some now."

"So make some."

"Can't, have nothing but cheese and vino in the house, plus some tomato sauce and a power bar. Not exact content of pantry but close enough."

"So tell me more. What exactly happened?"

"Well, the details escape me now because I've had a few vinos, but he thought I was immensely funny, and that we were on the same tangent.

And you'll never believe what he said to me when he left …"

"What??" Sounds like she's on the edge of her seat.

"He said," pause for dramatic effect, "'You're really something, aren't you?' Can you imagine? Have you ever heard a man say anything like that? It's like something from a Hollywood film!" Gasp.

"I wouldn't know. Pete wasn't really the *sweep you off your feet* type. But it sounds kind of impressive." More chewing.

"What do you think? Do you think he's just a charmer and says that to everyone, or do you think he might, potentially, you know, be interested?" I want an answer, come on Jess … Concentrate on me, not the toast!

"Hmm, not sure! I mean, he's the footballer type, right? Bit of a celebrity! Probably has women fawning over him all the time. Did you fawn?"

"I did not fawn," I say, and I didn't. Surely staring at him adoringly wasn't fawning, and he didn't catch me looking at his groin that one time.

"Are you sure?"

"Yes! Why, do you think I would fawn?" Feeling a bit concerned that a close friend thinks I'm the fawning type.

"No, not at all. But you know in the presence of even a minor celebrity, the average Joe can, at times, crawl, fawn, act desperate. That sort of thing."

"Yes, I agree. It's an interesting phenomenon! It happened to me once when I met that B-grade (or really C-grade) celebrity from *Big Brother* in Byron Bay, you know the one with the rather large breasts. Had terrible attack of being starstruck, even asked for a photo with her." Yes, have certainly been starstruck before. It could happen to anyone of us!

"When was this? You never told me that! What was her name?"

"I didn't tell anyone because I was so embarrassed. I do have the photo somewhere ... I seem to recall she had some sort of stripper name."

"Candy!" Jess has cried out.

"Bingo! That's it."

"Oh yeah, I remember her—Really? How could you?" she says with a tone of disgust.

"Not sure, uber embarrassed. Hanging head in shame now just recalling the incident."

"Okay, well if you've fawned before and recognised it, and think you weren't fawning this time, I think it's a good sign. Maybe there was a little something-something between you two."

Feeling pleased with the verdict; must withhold the desire to fist pump.

"He is so hot, Jess. Like *beyond* hot. Complete and utter sex-on-legs."

"I get that he's hot." She's chewing on something else now. Not going to ask her what it is.

"Like Prince Charming. Bluer than blue eyes, chiselled jaw line, a head full of dark luscious hair, and a body ... ripped, indeed!" Feeling the urge to tear clothes off just describing him.

"I hear you—hot! Don't get too carried away with hot though, because usually they're hot *and* dumb." Her tone is deferent, like she's imparting words of wisdom.

"I don't care. For once, I just want to have hot sex. With a hot man. Haven't I suffered enough with the Christians and the weak hipsters?"

"Well, maybe you have."

"Getting another call, one sec!" I say, looking at the caller ID. Chris. I wonder what his excuse will be. Probably hot sex.

"Chris?"

"Yeah."

"Okay, well I'm off to bed again before I devour the entire kitchen."

"Oh, by the way, babe. Two things. Do you want to come on Saturday to make wedding invitations at Mother's house with her friend Char? Say *yes*. She desperately wants you to go—You know *you're such a lovely girl, blah, blah, blah.*" Talking really fast now because I know I've moved into con man territory, but how else can I convince this woman to come to Mother's house to make wedding invitations? Damn, it's blackmail just like my mother! "Also, we'll need to take your car. If you don't want to come, can I borrow your car?"

Pause. Long silence. No response.

"So?" I'm prompting.

"Are those the two things?"

"Yes, they are. Mother's house. Invitations," which involves sticking diamantes onto hideously cheap paper stock with a glue gun and two geriatrics. Halfway during the day you semi feel like shooting a diamanté through your eye to end it all, but realise the glue gun doesn't have the power to do anything dangerous enough to warrant you leaving. "And borrow car on Saturday … Mum really really wants you to go. Loves you more than she loves me really." It's probably true.

"Will you take me to dinner next week? Meal on you?"

"Sure." Sounds like a small compromise. "Where do you want to go?"

"I don't know, but I have a hankering for Tex Mex."

"Again?" *Sigh*. How many beans and tortillas can one possibly ingest?

"Yes, *again.*"

"Fine."

"When should I pick you up?" Glee in her tone already at the Tex Mex potential; can't imagine it's because of the invitation making.

"Eight."

"In the morning?"

"Yes."

"I'll be testy!" she's warning me, like I don't know she hates mornings.

"Oh well, testy is the only way to be for me too, considering one is making wedding invitations for one's mother's fourth marriage, when one remains marriage-less."

"Very true," she has conquered with a crunch of something edible, *I hope.*

16. 11:00a.m.

Sitting in office tapping on keyboard. Tina, it would appear, is going through her notes. Not feeling as sprightly as yesterday at this time. No morning cycle class today. Instead, slept through alarm, got to work disastrously late, had to fling on clothes in my regular "find anything that's clean" fashion, and then sprinted (again, Olympic podium finisher style) to the bus stop, and later sprinted (again, Olympic podium finisher style) to work. Colleagues were, again, congregated outside of building and witnessed erratic entrance. Including Beefy, tattooed Americano, who threw me what seemed to be a cheeky grin, which I quickly ignored. Luckily wearing jeans today, casual Friday, no potential of flashing the troops!

Feeling resolutely tired and not looking forward to weekend with Mother and Char. Trying to think of possible excuses to extricate Jess and I from invitation making, but to no avail. Aged mind is letting me down. That, and emails bouncing to and from Chris who has agreed to go ahead with proposed threesome this weekend. Am prepared to listen to extended conversation over lunch regarding what one should wear to a threesome, how one should address the third companion (or *interloper*, as Chris has been referring to the poor sod), and, of course, what do I make of threesome etiquette? How does one not get left out in threesome? Mind is spinning with variants.

In the background of all of this, I have managed to continue Googling *Chad Thompson*. Have discovered that he's been married twice (okay, knew that already, but now have names to go along with both ex-wives: Madison and Grace Rose—both bullshit names), no kids (thankfully), grew up in Cronulla (slightly off-putting, Sutherland Shire boy, wonder if he has Southern Cross tattoo anywhere), lives now in Freshwater (wonderful improvement). Has played in several teams (still have no idea what league or code or whatever the fuckety fuck they call it—also too embarrassed to ask Tina). Has appeared in several television programs. Has slightly mortifying news story associated with him where in between marriages he was seeing a model and appeared naked on the balcony of her Bondi apartment (unfortunately penis has been pixilated in all photos so can't make assumption on whether or not he is well hung—sent photo to Jess and Chris anyway to see if they can make anything out. Shortly after receiving, they concurred, *unable to make out penis—shape or size*, but otherwise ripped, and incredibly hot in all other respects). Has a Labrador named Apollo.

Am envisaging dog play dates with Apollo and Fred while we sip lattes in the background and canoodle on the beach. Yes, in my fantasy we're on the beach.

Online stalking has since continued, and is now being interrupted by email from Ian, titled unimaginatively: *Friday afternoon drinks.*

"Team,

To celebrate this wonderful week, new interns, and several new accounts, I'd like to bring everyone together for afternoon drinks.

Usual place, usual time (5:00 p.m., boardroom), will organise the rest.

Don't be late.

Ian"

How pleasant. I particularly like the somewhat veiled (but not *really* veiled) threat of being late. I've heard there's a list Ian's receptionist keeps of people who skip out on afternoon drinks. Ian does not take kindly to his invitations being rejected, ignored, or even overlooked due to prior engagements—of any nature.

"We're going to afternoon drinks today, Tina," I say, not looking up from my screen.

"I know! I just saw the email! How exciting, right? It will be great to meet everyone in Ian's team!" There are littered exclamation marks all through her tone. Ahh … the enthusiasm!

"Yes, won't it?"

Email popping up from Chris:

"Early lunch. Need extra long break to discuss *operation threesome,* rules and regulations, and the like."

Oh, it's a tough one, but which is worse? Staying in the office another moment, or listening to drones of penis talk? Neither is better. Complete flat line. No upper hand.

"I don't think there are any rules and regulations to threesomes," I best type back. "Isn't that the point?"

"Well, there's how I know you've never had a threesome before. There are book loads of rules. Like number one, who goes first?" he responds.

"I have too, been in a threesome!" Oh, I *so* have not. But he doesn't need to know everything about me, especially where I've been and who I've been with … or how many times and with how many people, in this case!

"You're lying!" he responds.

"Am not." Okay, so he just knows anyway!

"Are, too."

"I have. I just never told you."

"With whom, where, when?"

Oh, this is too damn hard. I am not going to make up a threesome story to appease Chris.

"You're right, I lied. I've never been in a threesome before, so will be unable to assist in describing the threesome code."

"Not true. You always have good advice, Cee. I NEED A SOUNDING BOARD."

"Lunch. Where?" This man is relentless, as always.

"Fancy some Friday sushi at Timmy's?"

"Done."

"Tina," I say, startling abruptly to my feet, "I'm heading to lunch."

"No worries, Cee. Should I take your calls?"

"Yes." Of course you can take my calls—That's better than an answering machine! More personal, more professional, all aligned with the *new* Cee. "Please!"

Who would have thought intern thing would be such a treat?

17. 3:00p.m.

Rushing back into the building. Trying to ignore the irony of returning at three after all the threesome conversation. Threesome conversation has made head spin. Could be a result of the number of sakes downed in effort to ignore threesome conversation, or at very least to numb the pain associated with it. Is this what modern relationships in our thirties have turned into? Introductions to threesomes? Dissections of threesome protocols? I shudder to think. Lucky no hangers-on outside the building, hence am able to sweep in without too many people noticing the extent of long lunch.

Making my way towards office … Hang on! Who are those few people milling about over there near my office—Hmm, strange! Has Tina died in there? Haven't seen this many people hanging about my office since that time I found a very cute rat in there nosing around.

Sensing some nosing going on in this case, but what about?

Should've known Elsie would be one of them. Now only a few feet away so can recognise other participants of said nosing. Elsie, her intern, another girl I don't recognise, and another. Well, at the very least I recognise two.

"Ladies, slow day?" I say, nearing my door.

"Not at all." Elsie is always quick to respond.

"Well, why the sudden interest in my office?" I'm turning in. Brushing past, looking down my nose at Tina.

Tina's not dead. *Phew!* Who else would take notes and messages and clap hands enthusiastically at me? She is still sitting at the table, tapping away on her laptop, with a pile of yellow post-its sitting next to her. Messages no doubt.

"Tina." I'm purposely sounding totally businesswoman indeed, striding towards her, ignoring gaggle of annoying girls behind moi.

"Cee!" she says, getting to her feet quickly, super enthusiastically. Well, something is going on. Have I been fired? Not enjoying being stuck in the dark here. Shed some light please, Tina!

I have been fired, haven't I? Oh, that thought certainly has flitted across my mind. But wait, what is that? An epically large vase with around two-dozen red roses on my desk! Oh, well, there you have it. A single person in the office has got flowers, and of course that has probably been the gossip of the place all afternoon.

I can imagine the instant messages pinging about the office right this moment. Twice this week. Instant messaging gossip subject. Once for candy-coloured underwear, and once for flowers. If only the gossip topics had been more interesting, like Elsie had walked in on me having sex with Ian perched on my desk. There's a ghastly visual! But nonetheless gossip worthy. Candy underwear and roses, hardly. Hardly people, hardly!

"Oh, roses!"

I can feel the vultures stepping in closer to the door to hear who they're from.

But who the fuck are they from? Who would send me roses? Crazy Christian, realising what a mistake he's made—wanting to revoke it all, and make me his little wife? Chris? Thanking me for listening to threesome dialogue for the better part of this week?

Sort of plausible, but not really.

Trying to contain myself, wanting to snatch the envelope off the cards and rip it open. Stay cool, like I always get flowers. Have so many admirers. Haven't you noticed?

Opening envelope calmly. Predators leaning in, about to topple over each other in anticipation.

No! Really? I can't believe what I am reading. Having to literally re-read the card over again, finding it hard to contain look of surprise and glee from crossing my face.

"Who are they from? Your date on Valentine's Day?" It's Elsie, badgering in the background. Such a little gossip merchant.

Were it not worth it, I would contain this little secret, but it is, it truly is. It is something they'll gossip about for a lifetime. I am going to turn into an urban myth. Go, girl!

Yes, fuck you Elsie—perfect, preppy, hipster! Read this card and weep.

"*Cee,*

You're a breath of fresh air. I'd love for you to meet me for dinner at my restaurant, Sabbia, in Freshwater. Saturday 7:00 p.m.?

Chad"

"Thompson." I best say it out loud, just in case they haven't picked it up.

Elsie is so obviously shocked she has taken a step back. Quite literally. More of a little stumble. The other girls are looking like they may have peed their pants.

"Chad Thompson," one of the young ones has murmured. "Like the footballer?"

"Yep!" *Like the footballer indeed*, I think, smoothly sitting down at desk like this is not at all an eventful incident—even though it really is! Wow! Logging in to laptop. "Like the footballer ..." Verbal confirmation required, I kind of like how it feels, rubbing that jealous salt into their gaping wounds—ha!

Hello, *man-of-dreams*. Hello, red roses. Hello, dinner at Sabbia. Hello, party with Burt and Pattie Newton, as well as doggie dates on beach. Hello, hot sex! Hello, hello, hello!

That's right, bitches—Step away from the door and get instant messaging.

"Ladies, would love to talk," I'm so aloof, and they're standing there, mouths drooping open, "but Tina and I are super busy this afternoon. So really, no time."

"Super," Tina says, reinforcing me by holding up the post-its.

The two younger ones are stumbling out quickly, but Elsie is just staring at me, and there's a look of anger, real hostility in her eyes. That's right, bitch. Cee, two. Elsie, ZERO. Universe, zero. Walk on out with your floral skirt and denim cardigan and early nineties sheike. Off you toddle.

It's as if she can hear my thoughts, and she's silent, not a word, for a fucking change, just wondering away. Speechless.

"And ... " I'm holding up the card towards Tina, "'that is how it's done."

Am remarkable businesswoman, filled with acumen and sensuality. Just went from Valentine's Day lonely alcoholic binge to date with hot ex-footballer and new tycoon on Saturday night.

Oh, how a girl's luck can change. How it can change indeed!

18. 5:30p.m.

rinks. On top of the world. Am most desired woman in office. Red roses are visual proof. Have date on Saturday night with not just any would be man, or Christian for that matter, but sort of famous, stud of an ex-footballer. Sealed two accounts this week. Well, one and a half really. Just had a gin and tonic, feeling fab, sashaying about and flicking hair like Marilyn Monroe. So confident, unaware that reality of it is probably far more unsavory. Men in office staring at me in predatory fashion—now that I'm a wanted commodity amongst the high end of town. Women in office look jealous and psychotic. Except for Tina, of course, who looks super enthusiastic. After all, she has tied her fortunes to the Cee ship ... the best mothership of all. And let's face it, the Cee ship is very much making up territory this week.

Food also looks unsavory. The usual cheese plate and meat dishes have been setup by psychotic receptionist, standing at side of room, leaning on wall, headset on, arms crossed. Staring obtusely. Shall steer clear from the food, methinks. Instead, I shall collect a glass of champagne to compliment my previous G&T.

"Cheers, Tina." Even though she's clutching a glass of what looks like water, may as well celebrate.

"Cheers," she has responded, big smile.

"Not drinking?"

"Oh no, I don't drink." She's smiling still, and I'm staring at her for a moment. Why? Up to her, I suppose, don't want to ask her. Otherwise, I'm sure she'll launch into an extended discussion about how alcohol is terrible for you, killing one brain cell at a time (no wonder I find it so hard to focus these days), will make you gain weight spectacularly fast (similar to cheese—no surprises there), and probably something about it being non-Buddhist or Hindu.

"Mmm," I murmur, taking a sip of my champagne. "It's been quite a week!"

"Oh my gosh, hasn't it been?" she's gushing back to me. "I have learned so, so much. Like, this has been such an awesome experience so far."

"How long is your internship anyway?"

"Only four weeks! It's short compared to other internships. Really short, some offer three months, six months or even a year. But this agency's policy is you can learn the basics in four weeks, and they can discern their stellar candidate in that period of time."

"So I guess it was a bit of a risk coming here, huh?" Businesswoman deduction on my part, all over it!

"Yeah, it was super competitive, too. We had to go through so much, online applications, produce a video, interview ..."

"Produce a video?" I've just spluttered a bit. Shall ignore. What are they making these kids do these days?

"Yeah, so after you got through the written, they selected an object for each candidate and told you to make a video to show how you would use it with a client to ensure you sealed the deal with them."

"What did you get?" This is in intriguing stuff.

"A shovel." I'm laughing now, almost spitting out champagne in unladylike manner. That's funny!

"So what did you do, dig them a hole so you could shove them in, or lop them over the head with it?"

"Not quite." She's so gracious in her response, looking at me with unease. "I don't think that would have gotten me into the program."

"No, I suppose it wouldn't." I am imagining Ian's horror as he watched the video. Although, I'm sure he had some lackey watching said videos. Lucky in my day, there was no video component, or any other component, just a random resume and in you went.

"So what did you do with it?" I really want more about the shovel.

"Well, actually, I did an interpretive dance integrating the shovel." Must not laugh again. Shit. Too late. Hysterical, in fact. The type of laughing where you have to bend over and clutch your side. An interpretative dance with a shovel? What the fuck? How did that get her into the program? How would that get you in the good books with the client? Clearly we were recruiting incorrectly.

Whoops. Methinks I've offended, she's looking alarmed by my laughter. I really want to shovel more shit on this discussion—See what I did there? Oh, but here comes Elsie, appearing almost from a puff of smoke at my side with her intern—Not quite sure of the name, have heard people saying something like *Alaria*.

Today is no different from every other time Elsie has floated up to me, like she's gliding on water, a bit like Jesus Christ, but actually it's more ominous, like a green fog or something.

Alaria (if that's her name) is standing next to Elsie, legs up to her neck, and a sheath of perfectly straightened blonde hair falling to the small of her back. A playful, well-practised smile on her face.

"So I hear you're going on the date with Chad Thompson this weekend," Elsie says to me smoothly. She's on the water, too, clutching her glass in her hand. Alaria's not even clutching a glass of water. Water probably bloats.

"Well, I don't think you heard that." Is it too much that I'm emphasising the word *heard?* Too late! I'm loving this. "I read the bloody note out to you from the flowers in my office."

"Yes," she's hissing, evidently not liking my tone. "The note was inviting you out on Saturday, but I've since heard you accepted. Texted him or something?"

Did Tina tell her? My intern betraying me? She is the only possible person who would have known that. About half an hour after I'd received the flowers (careful, so didn't look too desperate) I had texted him. I'd gotten to my feet in office and announced, "I'm going to text him and say that I'm going!"

Tina had looked up at me, eyes wide, too excited to conceal it, and then evidently told everyone. *Where had I gotten his number?* From his file of course, guys. Really, that's what they should be teaching the young ones to do. How to find potential husbands' forward slash clients' numbers on files—Don't worry about the shovel.

I'm giving Tina a recriminating glare, and she is looking alarmed as always, like she might start shaking at any moment. Really, she shouldn't worry. It was a well-orchestrated plan. Why else would I have announced it aloud and stood up to emphasise the statement? To ensure the office was buzzing with it by drinks. Advertising genius at work!

"Indeed, I'm going," I say, relishing this totally.

"I thought you were seeing someone?" Elsie's prying away.

Oh, had forgotten tale about Valentine's date. Hypothetically speaking, even if one is seeing someone, if someone of Chad Thompson's caliber sets upon you, you would clear the decks. It is human nature, non?

"Oh, yes. It's nothing serious though." I'm being airy, blowing it off like I'm a girl about town and date men non-seriously all the time, not at all obsessed with nailing down husband, given aging appearance and condition of potentially shriveling ovaries.

Who is this I see? *Beefy!* Jai is loitering behind them, eavesdropping evidently. What a crowd. They live for this sort of thing.

"Besides," I say, feeling super self-assured woman about town, "I don't think Chad's at all interested. He just wants to show me the restaurant."

Was not at all looking up wedding couture this afternoon on Internet, am perfectly poised lady, who never lets imagination get out of hand. But it would be rather awesome, fabulous, epic if I were to be in the not-so-future future floating towards him in some stunning designer gown.

"Oh please, Cee …" She's throwing her head back and laughing at me. I want to tip my glass of booze down her throat … What would she do? Probably run out screaming and feeling impure due to involuntary alcohol consumption. "We both know a man doesn't send two dozen red roses if he wants you to go check out his restaurant for purely business purposes."

I agree, thanks for the reinforcement. He would have just called me on the phone. Jai is edging closer, he's almost touching Elsie now. Soon he'll be standing in the middle of our circled conversation, but think he's pretending he's not part of it. He wants the gossip just as much as they do!

"You can read into it as much as you like!"

Oh, and now there are more, well one, but a large one, namely *Ian*— his monolithic build pushing between Tina and I. Feels quite snug. It also feels like he is somehow metaphorically siding with moi. I'm going to ignore that slightly unbuttoned girth leaning into the circle, and am instead concentrating on the vino in his hand. Good! He's celebrating, too. And he obviously hasn't been holding back from the beverages. Cheers!

"She's not reading into it, Cee," he's booming. Oh Christ, really? Who told him! "You've evidently charmed the man. I'm not surprised, you're a charming lady, but remember he's a client." He's peering down at me like a giant ogre.

He's so loud, too, his voice is booming out like he's corralling the troops.

"Well, there are no rules at this agency about dating clients, Ian. I seem to recall someone telling me that at my induction." I'm speaking primly, and totally aware now that everyone's listening. Jai has even dropped the pretense of being involved in another discussion and is looking straight at us like we're putting on a show.

"I'm glad you held onto something from the induction, and I'm not surprised it's that, rather than the fire drill or the code of conduct."

We have a fire drill policy? He might be acutely rude, ridiculous, and mean at times, but there is something endearingly funny about him, and of course sharp like a whip.

"I wish we had included something about dating clients now, but it did seem outrageously patriarchal at the time." He's swigging down his drink, part of his beverage dribbling down his shirt, leaving an unsightly wet patch. Not sure if he's drunk or being his usual crass, disgusting self.

"Indeed," I say, my go-to word. Always.

"In fact, I don't care what you do with this Chad Thompson. As Rita Ora would say, *Fuck who you want, fuck who you like.*"

Completely inappropriate for the workplace. Tina has literally been caught unaware while drinking her water—She's starting to gag. Even Elsie is sharing a look of alarm. Given I'm used to such niceties from Ian, and have endured threesome conversation over lunch, I'm just looking at him placidly and I've even taken a sip of champagne during what seems to be a prolonged shock of silence from the group. I don't care he's used the word *fuck* twice. All in a day's work. Cheers again.

"You certainly are with the times, Ian." I think his comment is worth acknowledgement.

"Well, I have teenage daughters. And rather disturbingly, they *worship* that Ora. Could think of better role models myself, but you know, I'm not of that generation ... and the point of the Rita Ora comment was ..."

Oh shit, there was a point? Let's hear it then, may as well!

" ... I don't care what you do with Thompson. What I do care about is the account. And the associated money. Relationships, or whatever you want to call this thing, always make business messy—People sleep together, then they're in love, then they can't work together, then they either break up or stay together—but the inevitability is that the client leaves." He's looking at me sternly, and it's a far way to look up for me, because he's such a tall and portly man. I'm inescapably at some wrong angle.

I'm silent, but it seems he has more coming …

"Moral of the story *is* I don't care what happens, just don't lose the account." He's booming down at me like some overbearing father with ridiculous ideals.

"I really think you're going overboard with this Ian." I've just noted a slight intake of breath from those around me, thinking *Career Limiting Move*. But I wouldn't say it if I didn't know Ian, and this is by no means a CLM, rather *out* than *in* with someone like him. Usually appreciates the frankness. They are all just hipster lapdogs, not me! I say it how it is! "The man invited me to dinner, he's hardly down on one knee."

Oh, but that would be brilliant if he just proposed. No, stop it, Cee! *Dirty Dancing* music switching off …

"No, he's not," he says, swigging the rest of the vino down like a sailor would, "but he's certainly made his intention clear. A man doesn't send two-dozen roses with no purpose. Do you know how expensive roses are, Cee? They're *fucking* expensive. And two dozen are very *fucking* expensive."

"Hmm." I can barely articulate with all his fucking this and fucking that, you'd think I'd be fucking used to it.

"Okay." He's just slapped me on the back in a *matey* fashion. Of course his meaty hand has projected me forward, so I'm stumbling about abruptly. Must hold on to dignity and glass of champers. "Glad we have an understanding."

What understanding? What fucking understanding?

"Anyhow, nice work this week, Cee." Another momentous clap on shoulders and I'm lurching forward like a drunk person, barely keeping upright on this occasion. "An account sealed with that crazy Swami character and another VIP one in the pipeline. You should be watching this lady carefully," he's telling the interns. Alaria (or whatever her name is) and Tina are both looking scared out of their wits.

"She knows what she's fucking doing." And he has started to walk away ... "Where's another wine?"

I'm semi-anticipating another momentous beating from him, but he's gone. Straighten shoulders, Cee. Dear god! What a crazed person. *Note to self:* if fling with Chad Thompson works out, must find new job, or at very least become lady of leisure.

Oh, it's happening again. Can't deny this image of myself cooking squid ink pasta in the kitchen overlooking the beach. Oh right, remember, can't cook. Reality.

"Well, there you have it." I'm holding my arms up a little, like it's an announcement, bright and breezy does it. "I think I need another drink."

Right, need to push past this little crowd of people that has formed around me and Tina. They have all evidently been transfixed by the Ian spectacle, but I have more important things to deal with, like heading to the booze table. Decide to make another G&T because the champagne's not going to cut it after that episode. Sloshing in half a glass of Tanqueray here and a splash of tonic there. Looking forward to drinking you down.

"Are you going to have any tonic with your gin?" *What does he want?* Jai is standing right next to me, and rather closely, too. Probably because the room is filled to the brim now, and personal space is rapidly reducing.

"This is how I like my G&Ts." I'm just going to ignore his jibe.

"Strong." His tone is so ironic, and he's reaching for another beer.

Who does he think he is? This is a long pause and a bit awkward—I'm guessing he can't think of anything to say, and I'm obstinately refusing to speak because he's an annoying individual who constantly insinuates I'm an alcoholic. *Prick!*

"You never told me which creative execution the Swami preferred."

Oh right, that's what this is about, is it? The man surely has some ego. Constantly wants to be praised for his work. Always loitering in my office or invading my personal space.

"The one of the stylised version of himself."

"Not surprised." He has let out a sigh.

"You sound despondent."

"They always like the one that represents themselves. Makes me wonder why I even bother with the rest."

Clever. I'm giving him one of my raised eyebrows. Agree.

"So, what are you up to this weekend?" he asks. Surely he just heard what I am up to. He has one hand around his beer, another shoved into his jean pocket. He's wearing faded denim today, with a chain linking the front pocket to the back, t-shirt and black beaten-up vest. It's all very *Sons of Anarchy,* and is he flexing his bicep, I swear he is, but trying to look casual with it. No, he's definitely flexing … Well, it's moving, is that flexing?

"Did you just zone out?" He's leaning in, like I might be having a stroke.

"No." I'll inject a rude tone into my response so he thinks his comment is absurd. "I was just wondering why you were asking me such an arbitrary question. Very un-creative really!" I'm recovering, and we're back to our usual antagonistic banter.

Time to sip my G&T. Fuck, almost knocked my socks off, and not wearing any socks to begin with.

"Just engaging in the usual social pleasantries." His response is so all-American drawl and sarcasm.

Or trying to expose that the only interesting thing I have on this weekend is my date with Chad Thompson. Hate the arbitrary weekend question, always makes me feel like a loser because I never have exciting plans like everyone else, who is usually jet-setting off somewhere, going to the new *it* bar or club, generally leading action-packed lives while I defrost my fridge (because I have a fridge old enough it needs to be defrosted) or give myself an unfortunate pedicure with the pedi spa my mother gifted me for Christmas.

No time to make up some fabulous weekend now, have spent too much time thinking mindless crap!

"I'm going to my mother's Saturday to help her make wedding invitations, and then I'm going to dinner with Chad—You probably know about that one because the whole office does."

He is smiling, all big and cute. Oh fuckety fuck, brain is running off in unwarranted direction. "What about Sunday?"

"Well, on Sunday I'll probably go to brunch with my friend who you met the other day in Kings Cross, because I live in Kings Cross … Well, not in Kings Cross, but very close to it. And he'll probably spend three hours regaling me with the details of the threesome he got up to the night before and asking me advice about his next threesome, which I'm really unequipped to respond to because I've never had a threesome before, and the details of his threesome kind of make me want to vom—

and then I'll probably go home to remove images of three men making fervent animal-like coitus. I'll probably make sangria, which tastes more like Bloody Mary (because wouldn't have ingredients in house for sangria … that would involve fruit), and then watch mindless reality television till I fall asleep on the couch. Hopefully, my Cavoodle won't kill me by falling asleep on my face. So not much."

Hmm. That was all very out loud, wasn't it? Not sure why have regurgitated this information, in this way, at this speed. Possibly because gin has gone straight to head (along with champagne and other gin and tonic), *flexing* thought and *cute smile* thought also have caught me by surprise because have previously only had negative, hateful thoughts towards this man generally, even though it is clear he has always had muscles and is good looking. Shit, I'm doing it again. This has been verbal diarrhea of the uttermost worst variety.

He's laughing, though. Probably because have revealed myself to be incurable lunatic with tragic social life.

"You don't strike me as the type who has never had a threesome," he says, continuing to laugh.

I'm staring at him, a stone stare, this conversation is over! I'm done with it. Sipping gin.

"I'm leaving now, and going to find more interesting people to talk to." I'm trying to push past his bulky being.

"Wait." He's grabbing my arm, why is he touching me? "I'm just joking. I thought you of all people could appreciate a joke."

"Yes, of course," but I actually can't, because I'm sick of always being the brunt of them, "because I'm the *funny* lady."

"What's wrong with that? You're the funny lady. There's worse things you could be."

"Well, evidently, as revealed in this conversation, I'm also a sexual amateur, but nonetheless, here's a tip: most women would prefer to be described as glamorous or gorgeous rather than funny." Trying to eye off my exit route. No way out. Slightly dazed from gin consumption. Slightly smothered by his oozing testosterone and bulging muscles and in need of ESCAPE.

"That's a shame, isn't it …" What's with his long pauses, and that intent staring, like he's trying to communicate some thought to me by osmosis? Not sure what exactly. Hmm. Awkward. "You can't seriously be going on a date with that Chad Thompson."

Really? He thinks he can also weigh into this debate. Enough already. Who is he anyway?

"Why would you say that?"

"The man … " His brow is beginning to furrow and he seems to be looking for the right word. Hmm! Alcohol hampered, or just unable to string a sentence together? "The man's an ex-footballer, he probably has the intellectual equivalent of a pygmy!"

"Well, to start with, I think that's kind of racist, because pygmies could very well be a highly evolved tribe of people …"

"I meant pygmy possum." He's intervened before I can see my argument through.

"They have pygmy possums?" Oh, I didn't know that. *Erm*, where to move on to from here?

"Yeah, right here in your country. In Australia." The sarcasm again! Piss right off! I can't know everything, can I? I'm not a vet, or a zoologist, or a wildlife person.

"Okay, well thanks for the lecture on my country's flora and fauna—

Chad is quite funny," and he is, and he's hot, too, "a quality which I seem to recall you thinking of quite highly." So there!

"I doubt he's funny," he says, rolling his eyes. "You were probably distracted by his guns and thought he was funny."

"He was wearing a long-sleeved shirt, so I couldn't have even seen his guns. Besides the fact, I don't get distracted by 'guns.' In fact, I don't even look at 'guns.'" I'm making little quotation marks with my free hand. And I'm lying. I do very much look at guns, that is, if *guns* are the same thing as biceps, which I think they are.

"Well, I seem to recall you potentially looking at my guns at the start of this conversation. In fact, you seemed to lose your chain of thought."

This guy is completely arrogant. And he's completely … can't think of descriptive words, must really have had too much to drink. Okay, back on it. This guy is completely insufferable!

"Whatever!" That was so not a clever retort, but can't think of anything intelligent to say and need to back away from this conversation quickly. Where's my escape? "I'm leaving now."

"*Whatever.*" Very mature. "Have a good Saturday night," he's telling me sarcastically.

"You know what? I will!" Walking away now, and sticking my middle finger up to him, but only in my imagination. Keep stalking, Cee. Taking another sip of drink.

Insufferable man! Where does he get off telling me who I can, and can't see? Bizarre! And then to point out I was staring at his guns. Maybe I was. It was a blip. Like being transfixed by the sun.

Have had one too many drinks. Need to leave the building quietly before any further damage is done. Escape route located, focus on making exit, Cee.

19. 11:30a.m.

other's house. A pleasant little cottage-like abode in Wahroonga *with timber floors and French provincial styling. Purchased after* *the untimely death of her second husband, Harold. Three mimosas already* *down, on the dregs of the fourth. Have been assigned to remedial duty of* *stabbing a heart-shaped pin through the top of each invite, thereby holding* *together an ugly piece of cardboard, in a hue of maroon, which went out of* *trend about two decades ago, and a piece of frosted, almost translucent paper* *where the wedding invite details have been printed.*

"You have been cordially invited to the wedding of Francis Jane Read (surname of dead second husband. Original husband and father-to-me had the unfortunate surname of *Binner*, and third husband was *Rizo*, although since divorce my mother 'Franny' has reverted back to dead husband's name) and Bradley James Streeton ... "

Pin through the two sheets, sticking the pair together. And repeat.

"How are you doing over there, Cecilia?" Mother is asking me as she's stumbling to her feet, I imagine heading to fix another round of mimosas.

"Mother, really? When am I going to graduate to a more important role? Why does Jess get to put the sequins on and Char the ribbon? I have the worst task." I'm being petulant, retuning to a childlike state, but rightly so. My task is mundane, even when aided with mimosas.

"Because, darling, you have big hands, and you know they're not made for the glue gun or ribbon. Do you remember what happened the last time you were on ribbon duty?" she's saying pointedly, hand on hip, leaning into the fridge in an attempt to wedge another champagne bottle out.

"Those ribbons were perfect, Mother. I don't know what you're complaining about." Ahh, the ribbon saga that ensued from the *Rizo* wedding.

"You know they weren't. They were all misshapen. I had people calling me up and saying, 'Franny ... Lovely invitations, but who tied those ribbons?' It was absolutely humiliating!"

She's telling me this, like I've not heard it before, while pulling the cork off the champagne abruptly. It springs up to the roof like a rocket and leaves a solid little dent. She is staring up at it as though the sheer willpower of her eyes will remove it. I wouldn't put it past my mother ... Moving matter with her eyes—something she does on a regular basis.

"So," she's sashaying over to us in a drunken manner, holding the champagne, "who are you ladies bringing to the wedding?"

Oh fuck! Standard question from Mother when we're making wedding invites. It's like she's looking to further shame us into the understanding that she'll be married for the umpteenth time while the rest of us are perennially single. I don't understand how Char puts up with her. Sometimes I think she's afraid of her—living inside mother's shadow and threatening tone for a lifetime.

"Char, you start," Mother is instructing her. Char is sitting up straighter in her chair, shifting upwards as though she's been prodded by an electrode, looking from face to face with desperation.

Mother is pouring her another glass of champagne, adding a splash of orange juice, and now she is filling the rest of the glasses. She's at my glass now, thank god! Oh, typical, the champagne's almost gone, and Char is still struggling to speak. She's a bug-eyed, skinny thing, with a heap of blonde curls. I think she stays so thin because of anxiety—caused by Mother, of course.

Mother is dribbling the rest of the champagne into my glass. "Sorry, darling," she's mouthing at me in a slightly psychotic, drunk manner. *Sorry!* These drinks are the only tolerable aspect of today, and I get the dregs, the dribbles!

"Mother, really." I have to say something, maybe petulantly again, but sometimes things need to be said. "When are we going to graduate me to the big girl drinks? You know, I could really do with some spirits."

"I'll make cocktails after lunch, you little alcoholic." She's sitting down heavily, but her words come out smoothly.

"Well, who do you think I take after?" I'm waiting for her answer as she raises her glass of champagne (and splash of orange juice) to her lips.

"Your father." Her response is abrupt, eyes glaring, boring a hole into my very being.

"Dad hardly drinks." *It's true,* he doesn't!

Here comes the snorting. "He does now that he's married to that little *I*-talian hussy. Vino *every* night." More snorting. The way she has just emphasised the "I" sound in Italian is blatantly racist. Just ignore her! I'm not going to stand up for Maria (father's Italian hussy) though, given she's nuts, too.

Unfortunately, father drew the short straw on both occasions. *Crazy,* I guess that's how he likes them.

"Back to you, Char." Mother is gleeful again, returning to sticking addresses on sateen envelopes. "Who are you bringing to the wedding? I didn't put that plus one on your invite for nothing."

Char's eyes are batting fiercely, she's thinking, for sure. I reckon the cogs are turning in her mind as she is trying to come up with a response Mother will be happy with. *Good luck to her!*

"I—I— I really don't know," she is stuttering out finally.

"Oh, come on, Char," Mother is yelling at her, swinging a hand about violently. Char has just sat up quickly and even taller. "There are lots of men who are interested in you."

She might be saying this to intimidate Char. Or could she be making fun of her? Surely not even Mother would be up to something like that. Is my mother that cruel?

"Not really, Franny," she's responding, hand fluttering to her neck as though she feels she might be choking, or at the very least protecting it from a stinging blow delivered from Mother's unhappy hand.

"What about that chap at the local RSL?"

"Which one?"

"Oh, don't be stupid. You're so blind, Char! You wouldn't know if a man's interested if he were down on one knee. No wonder you've only been married once."

Keep quiet, Cee. Don't say, *No mother, that's probably your influence. Now that she has one crazed companion*, why would she need another? After all, Char and Mother do everything together. Shop together, go to the movies together, sun at the beach together; they're inseparable. Wherever Franny goes, her slightly decrepit, sorrowful shadow Char follows. Sad really. Char is like her PA, or her intern.

"I still don't know who you're talking about," Char has continued, still staring around the room perplexed, looking desperately for answers in our eyes. What to do? I know! I'm just going to shrug my shoulders at her. Easy. Safe. It says, *Sorry, wish I could help, but you put yourself voluntarily in this situation—I can't get away from her, she's my mother!* Jess has followed suit with a slight shrug of the shoulders.

"You know the one, Char. Vietnam vet. No hair. Always sits near us with a schooner and a schnitzel. He's only got eyes for you. I can tell. Always staring." She's laughing, as though she can't believe Char hasn't noticed.

"I think he has a glass eye."

"Nonsense," Mother is scoffing. "He doesn't have a glass eye. Beautiful blue eyes—but no glass eyes."

"I'm sure he does," Char is speaking back shakily, as though she's doubting her own recollection. "The glass one always stares in our direction, but that's because it's fixed."

"Don't be daft, Char! He doesn't have a glass eye! Honestly, sometimes you make up the strangest stories. Right, well, from here to the wedding we're going to make sure we seal him as your date." She sounds triumphant in her decision.

I'm not sure what Char wants me to do with her frantic and pleading expression in my direction. Are you stupid, Char? She is my mother! I can't do a damn thing for myself, let alone for you, doll! Enough already with the pleading eyes. Right, okay, I'll try …

"Mother, really?" Starting well, methinks. "I think Char is perfectly capable of forming her own relationships. She doesn't need your help. And if she's not interested in a man with a glass eye, she's not interested." There, that was nice, supportive to Char, but still respectful to Mother.

"He doesn't have a glass eye!" Mother is yelling at me. Why does she always yell!

Hmm. What now? I shall return to my shrug of the shoulders, this time it says, *See, I tried to help.* Think she's got the message, she has nodded back to my shrug. She is now grabbing for her drink, a little sip perhaps, no she's has just downed it in a single slurp.

"Isn't this fun, ladies?" Mother is trilling. "We'll all have dates for the wedding. On to you, Jess. Who are you bringing, and don't say my daughter. She's not a fucking lesbian, and she needs to find a husband. She's spent enough time hanging around that gay boy, Chris. Luckily now she has a more suitable prospect …" She is gesticulating towards Jess. "So … Speak up! Who are you bringing?"

Oh god, the gloves are off now. She's swearing like a sailor, and she pretends to be put off by the word *vagina*. Who is this woman kidding? Not me, that's for sure.

Feeling terrible for Jess at this moment, and no amount of Tex Mex is going to make up for it. *But can't you see Jess? This is my life! I had to grow up with this creature.* Like I can say that aloud, never going to happen, not here anyway, not right now.

"Oh, I'm not really up to dating yet." Jess's response was just calm, acceptable I think, as though she's talking to an adult. Because, you see, she has *normal* parents.

"Nonsense!" Mother is yelling at her now. "Everyone is up to dating."

"No, really," Jess has continued, "I really need a bit more time."

Both Char and I are hanging our heads at this response because we know exactly what's to come. We've seen it all before! Here it goes ... The shark, aka Mother of course, has smelt blood, and she's coming in for the kill.

"When exactly did Paul leave you?" Mother's tone is superior.

"It's *Peter,*" Jess has corrected her.

"Peter, Paul, Luke or fucking John," Mother's laughing. "They're all the same. When did he leave you?" Her inquisition is continuing.

"He didn't exactly leave me as such ..." Oh shit! This is terrible. I think Jess is starting to unravel, and she has those big staring eyes on, like with the RPM instructor. Stockholm syndrome is taking hold. With this behaviour, you'd think that it was her who has had the fucked-up childhood. Oh, I know that face, she's scanning the kitchen for food. *The only thing that will help now is food.*

"He left you," Mother is still yelling. "He left you for another woman."

Oh shit! Fuckity, fuck, fuck, fuck. Springing to my feet and heading to the kitchen. Focus, Cee, operation *find food for friend.*

"Well, that wasn't quite the case ..." Jess has responded quicker this time.

"He left you, Jess. Stop trying to pussy foot around it. He dumped your tired ass because he'd had enough of your caboose—a whole ten years of

186

it—and thought he could go back to the buffet and sample himself something fresher, something sweeter."

OH MY GAWWWWD! Grabbing for cheese from the fridge, pasta salad, prosciutto, and salami—anything I can. I'm carrying an *ala Carte* menu here.

"It was just over nine years." Jess is almost crying now.

"Nine years! Nine fucking years and no ring on the finger?" Mother is shrieking now. This is the apotheosis. The moment she becomes the preacher—and believe it or not, converts people. Sound a bit like someone? I'm not proud of it! "Nine fucking years, and he leaves you!"

I've made it back to the table, dumping everything at centre, including a bread stick, but no, have I failed? Yes! It's too fucking late—Jess has *gone*, she's enthralled, she's nodding away like this is Jesus Christ himself speaking the message of our Lord. Earth to Jess! Don't listen to her— Snap out of it!

Somehow through this trance state, she has managed to grab the breadstick. *Carbohydrate reflex* is what I call it. And she's good, fast, and accurate, from peripheral vision, smell sensors alert, arm reach and hand to mouth consumption, all without looking. Amazing!

"You better get yourself out there," Mother's telling her. "You better get yourself out there and start dating ... fast!"

Jess is biting into the breadstick like a woman possessed, severing its head as if it were a serpent, and she was a serpent eater. Chewing, looking thoughtful ...

"Well, I suppose I could get Pete to come."

Oh, shit! She did not just say that. Did she? Mother is going to finish her off like a ... Oh, hang on a second, Mother's into the Camembert now and seems reasonably calm. What just happened?

"Why would you bring *him?*" she's asking in between devouring hunks of cheese. "Isn't he the man who left you?"

"Yes, but he does help out periodically," Jess is continuing, calmer now, too, probably the food kicking in. "Like he fixed my washer a month ago, and helped me take scrap metal to the tip, and …" she is leaning forward conspiratorially now, mouth full of food, "he even did me a few weeks ago."

"What the fuck?" I've kept it in way too long, my inner yell is released … and it's louder and more aggressive than Mother's. What the? What is this information? I didn't know about this. How could I not know? How could Jess not tell me and then suddenly do the big reveal to my mother of all people? How could Jess do this at all? She's been moaning about what a terrible person Pete is for months now, eating for ten large humans, and has practically been on suicide watch for the full extent of time—and suddenly, just like that, she sleeps with him again? *He even did me,* what is that, like his doing her a favour! Mortified. Fucking horrified this second.

But in true form, Mother is looking like the cat that got the cream, or in this case, the woman who managed to extricate the information. She's even managed to lower a hunk of cheese, and now she's smiling ever so smugly at Jess. Puke in mouth moment. The shame!

Jess, on the other hand, has continued munching down on the bread like it's the only thing that's going to save her now. I feel like ripping that baguette out of her hand and bopping her over the head with it to see if there's any sense left in her.

Okay, calm down, Cee. Calm the fuck down. Let's try to get to the bottom of this; maybe you heard incorrectly.

"Jess," trying to whisper, but even I can hear a homicidal tone in my voice that I can't get rid of, "you slept with Pete again?" I'm looking at her hard, jaw is hurting a little from tensing and teeth clenching.

"Yeah, I did." She is so avoiding eye contact with me right now. She's just staring forward, eyes fixated on mother. Honestly, I don't know how this woman does it … How does she convert these people to disciples in such a short period of time? It must be something to do with her hypnotic voice? Maybe it's happening on a subatomic level, like communication between dolphins. Perhaps I'm not picking up on the sonorous waves? Maybe I'm immune after all of these years.

"When did this happen?" Doing well, Cee! So biting back the series of accusatory questions, which are springing to mind like little jumping beans. Why didn't you tell me? After all I am supposed to be your bestfriend! I have been listening to all the other crap for months. *How does one just forget a minor detail like "He even did me."—HOW?* Not *how* did he do her, I don't want to know that!

"Well," she continues, still avoiding eye contact, "I'd just had this terrible day at work, and he called me to see if he could collect a few things, and as per usual I couldn't come up with a good excuse …"

"What about that Hunter Valley excuse you came up with for this weekend?" I'm indignant—like really, *who is she fooling?*

"Oh god, I'd been formulating that one for weeks. Ever since *the incident.*"

"Is that how you're referring to it?" Letting him do her is the incident. "The incident? Sounds like a doctor's appointment, or maybe losing a possession. Fuck Jess, it even sounds like the name of some dodgy crime movie. I actually don't think it's quite right for this scenario, and if it were a book or a flick, I think something like 'the travesty,' or 'the biggest mistake of my life,' would be more fucking apt, don't you?"

She's looking at me now, face all quivery and panicked.

"I'm calling it *an incident,*" she's saying in a calm tone.

I can feel the burning of my mother's stare—Her eyes are going back and forth between me and Jess like she's observing a game of tennis. I get the feeling she's going to spring to her feet any moment and start cheering for her favourite player. I almost forgot Char was sitting over there, looking all pleased now that she's out of the spotlight, but still slightly alarmed, possibly knowing that she's signed herself up to securing a date with one-eyed thingy-ma-Bob for the wedding.

"Okay, so can you tell us a bit more about *the incident?*" A haunty tone leaves my mouth. It's the totally wrong phrase. I'll use it, but she knows it, too, and I bet Char and Mum think the same, like it's the pink elephant in the room now, so need to acknowledge it.

Like there are not bigger or bolder pink elephants in the room. There are! Fat fucking ones. With saggy knees, and long trunks full of crap.

"Well, he dropped around to collect some things, and I don't know, I guess we indulged in some nostalgia, and then it just happened." The baguette's almost gone now, and I can see her eyeing the prosciutto with the precision of a preying beast.

"It just happened?" I hate it when people use that excuse! "How does it *just happen?* How does one just have sex randomly? You both just happened to be naked at the same time, or he tripped and it just slipped in?"

I can tell she's peeved—But she really has no right to be peeved at this point, she's been concealing this mammoth secret for weeks now, and instead of telling me about it, she's been talking non-stop about Doritos, Tex-*fucking*-Mex, and how her body has taken on the consistency and size of a baby whale. Baby whales are big!

"You know we were together for a long time—Some things are just familiar, you know. I wouldn't expect you to understand."

Giving her my death glare. Is she having a go at me because I haven't had a relationship which has lasted more than two minutes, and so I can't possibly understand the intricacies of adult interactions? Methinks so! And wondering why she's shagged cheating Pete, and wondering why she's failed to share this information, but she clearly thinks it's okay to resort to bitchiness. Well, I'm not holding back, if she wants some kind of argument in the middle of Mother's hideous wedding chaos, she's got herself a deal! *No, Cee!* Remember your yoga breath! Remember your roses. Remember *Cee-Project*. Of course, I need to conduct myself demurely, rise above this farce.

"I'm not going to deem that with a response." I've opted for snootiness. It's a response I suspect someone like Elsie would give in a situation like this. Not that she would be in a situation like this because she's been in a perfectly functioning relationship for years I'm sure, but you get the gist. I can't imagine her going all crazy bitch. Instead, I can see her being highly evolved, logical, cold even in situations like these.

Project affect Elsie's behaviour beginning.

"So are you thinking of getting back with him?" That's good, staying calm.

"No, not in the slightest. He's moved on, anyway, and he's seeing someone else. It was just an isolated ... *incident.*" And there's that big pink word again, and she's stuffing a piece of prosciutto in her mouth now.

Oh no, murderous thought alert crossing my mind. Imagining her choking on that prosciutto, like the *Wolf of Wall Street's* friend after their drug binge, only unlike the Wolf, I don't administer the Heimlich Manoeuvre. Instead, in this fleeting thought that is growing into an incident of its own, I am standing back with a sweet little smile on my face while she chokes. Harsh, I know! Turning into psychopath. Maybe partway there, so not much to turn until completely a fully-fledged psycho. Result of several mimosas and no food—That's my excuse, along with infuriating mother and recently learnt about friend betrayal and stupidity.

"I might start making some cocktails," Mother is announcing. "Does anyone feel like a pina colada?" she asks, getting to her feet.

"Yes," Jess is answering in a strangled tone, swallowing the prosciutto like a wild person. I'm relieved she hasn't choked, despite vivid daydream of her doing so.

"No Mother, really?" Does she know nothing of follow-up drink choices? "The cream or milk or whatever pinas are made with will curdle in our stomachs after all that champagne and orange juice. Make something sensible like G&Ts or cosmos."

"Fine, darling. You really do have only child syndrome though, Cecilia. Always want to have your own way. You know, I always wanted another child, but the trouble I went through birthing you—the trauma of it, I never really got over it."

Isn't it too early in the morning for the birth guilt to begin? The dialogue about the twenty-hour labour and then the c-section. I'm over it! *Never really got her figure back again,* she'll say, shaking her head, as though it didn't in anyway have anything to do with her sweet tooth, all her boozing, or complete aversion to exercise. Shit, sometimes I feel crap at my descriptions of her because I see the similarities ... except, of course, that I'm no serial bride, and will probably never be a bride, as she keeps reminding me.

What's the time? It's ticked past twelve—I guess it is late enough for the birthing nightmare discussion to begin. But hang on! She's distracting me from the real task at hand. Clever mother, indeed! Jess and the "incident" is where my attention was, and this is how said incident shall be known from here on after ... Still can't get my head around *penis slipping into a vagina* as an *incident.*

"So, are you trying to tell me that you would actually take this man back after all the heartbreak if he wasn't in a relationship already?"

"No ..." Jess is letting out a sigh, as though she is revising her answer. "No ... I don't know."

Well, that's a formidable response!"

"I don't know what you expect from me, Cee. This is why I didn't tell you in the first place," she is very much hissing at me. "You always want things to be so black and white. And if they're not, then you make judgments."

"Me, judgmental?" Complete shock right now! "I just spent the better part of my week listening to Chris justify his threesome. I hardly think I'm judgmental!"

"She is judgmental," Mother is interjecting from the kitchen where she's pouring ingredients into a blender and stirring them with a wooden spoon. The result is some muddy mess, not sure what she's making, but that's neither a pina colada, nor is it a cosmo … And it most certainly is *not* a G&T.

"All I'm saying," she's beginning with a calm tone, apparently reasonably measured now after having ingested an entire baguette and a whole pack of prosciutto, "is that after you've been with someone for a long time, there's just feelings that you can't really get rid of. There just are."

"So you're going to be sleeping with him intermittently for the rest of your life, even though you both might be in relationships at the time?"

"Don't be absurd. I didn't say that."

"She's always absurd," Mother has supplied, carrying a tray of some muddled drink, although it's in cosmo glasses, so one can only assume she has made cosmos. Char is following closely behind her with another tray. Mother is handing Jess a drink, her eyes warm and motherly, as though to say, *Drink up. I know you have a terrible friend, but imagine having to endure her as your only child?*

She is now handing me one, shaking her head at me like she just can't believe my behaviour.

"I'm just saying things are complex," Jess has supplied, and is now taking a slug of her cosmo-esque drink.

"Okay, well I can deal with that. But I don't have to listen to the constant dialogue about Pete then. The hating on Pete, the demanding to know why he left you, the demanding to understand *why, why, why.*" Dramatic maybe, but it's fitting, methinks, so I'll go with it. "The depressing rants about how you're going to slit your wrists because nobody in their right mind would ever again consider you relationship material, and you're going to end up an old maid. Ovaries all dried up, etc., etc., etc.—I'll just refuse to listen to any of that," I conclude, taking a sip of the muck Mother has just served me. All I'm getting is a mouthful of tequila. Wow, it is strong.

"Mother, one doesn't make cosmos with tequila. And why are they brown? There's no cranberry juice in this, is there?"

Mother is just ignoring me, drinking away, and supervising the continued progress of the wedding invite assembly, which has come to a standstill except for Char, who has kept beavering away at tying those damn bows, probably afraid to draw attention to herself.

"Well, if that's the case, maybe I'll stop listening to your diatribes about work, the intern, that poor girl Elsie you've taken a vendetta out against, Chris, and how he's so self-centered and has spent the entire week pontificating over a threesome, and, oh yes, how wonderful Chad is, and how he's your future groom even though you even haven't been on a date with him yet."

Oh shit! Oh shit! Oh shit! She's inadvertently dropped the C-bomb. Chad. The one thing I was hoping to keep away from Mother's prying mind for at least a few dates, or if first date was complete disaster, could have potentially never mentioned him, and by so doing, not had to listen to her bang on about her daughter being a relationship pariah, and not even being able to hold onto someone as good as Chad Thompson for more than one date.

Maybe she hasn't noticed. Hopeful. Desperate. Maybe, she's so hyped up on champagne and tequila that she hasn't heard.

"Chad? Who's Chad?" she's asking suspiciously.

Oh! Who am I kidding? This is my mother, a woman who has been snooping around me since I was twelve years old in order to find evidence of me dating, all for the sole purpose of marriage, so she can finally have a married daughter she can talk to Char and her husband of the day about.

"No one, Mother." Just going to refocus on pinning the sheets of paper together, almost spearing my index finger with one of the pins. *Note to self:* not a task you want to be doing semi-drunk.

"He sounds like *someone,*" she's continuing on nonetheless, glaring at me, as if by hook or by crook she's going to extricate this information.

"I don't know what Jess is talking about," I mumble, successfully avoiding eye contact with everyone.

"Jess," Mother is saying, directing her questions Spanish inquisition-style towards her because she knows she'll buckle … She's sending her sonorous waves right at this moment, instructing her to speak again. "Jess, darling, who is this Chad?"

Jess is staring at me desperately, because despite the biff, I know she knows she's gone a step too far.

My look is one of submission. "There's no point resisting," I say quietly, a nice whisper to best friend, attempting to avoid Mother hearing. We are two minds under siege communicating. "She's onto it now." Too late, and I know this is not going to end until Mother gets what she wants—the information!

"I'm so sorry," Jess is mouthing to me now. Yes, indeed.

"Chad Thompson." Ahh—She's going to sing like a canary now. "You know, the ex-footballer, a bit of a television personality. He has a popular restaurant in Freshwater. He sent Cee two-dozen red roses. Apparently he's a bit taken by her. They're going to dinner tonight."

And there it all is … Just like that, poured out onto a platter, ready for

Mother's dissection.

"Chad Thompson!" Char is stirring to life.

Wow, she has spoken. We are all staring at her. I'm surprised that she's actually part of this conversation, thought she might have fallen into a coma of sorts. "Well, he's a bit of a catch, isn't he? Nice looking man. I love him on that house and garden program!" she's saying excitedly, and clearly she recalls where she is, looking at Mother, who is watching her with a displeased eye, as though this sudden demonstration of personality is totally uncalled for ... And just like that, she has looked down again, back at the bows, so obviously pretending to busy herself with the task.

"I've never heard of him. Mother's sniffing as though she can't believe that she doesn't know who this person possibly is, but somehow socially inept and repressed Char does.

"He's really not that popular, Mother, just an ex-footballer with a restaurant," I say, in an attempt to water down the situation.

"No, really," Jess is interjecting, like she really needs to spill more to Mother, methinks not! "He's pretty big, been on loads of television programs. You would recognise him if you saw him."

"So sorry," Jess is mouthing again. Yeah, I get it, you got carried away. No change there then. What's wrong with shutting the fuck up, can't you get carried away shutting up?

"And you say you're going on a date with him tonight?" Mother's looking at me intrigued, and disbelieving, as though we might be having a go at her at this very moment, so implausible is the situation.

"Yes, Mother, we're having dinner tonight."

"Well, how did you meet this *celebrity?*" She's still in a state of what looks like shock and disbelief. "After all, you don't exactly move in the celebrity circle."

"How would you know what circles I move in?" Pissed off!

"Oh darling, please, you're certainly not having brunch with the Packers," she's scoffing.

"Oh, and you are?"

"Well, let's just say I have more chance of rubbing shoulders with celebrities here than you do in Kings Cross."

So used to the Kings Cross jibe, just going to ignore. Ignore! Anyway, how exactly has she developed this elevated sense of self, and how in god's name does she maintain it?

"Yes, of course, because you have such an active social life, what with the RSL and all. Definitely the type of place that Burt and Pattie Newton would be frequenting." Giving her the sarcasm now ... Well, she deserves it.

Why are Burt and Pattie Newton always my go-to celebrities? Very strange!

"Funny, dear, but could you just tell me where you met him?" Mother's giving me the daggers.

Sigh. "We met at work. He's a new client, wants to expand his restaurant business. We had a laugh, and he sent me flowers and invited me to dinner. That's the long and the short of it." Done, said, nothing more to share!

"Interesting," she's watching me carefully, "and you didn't think about telling your mother this—that you're now dating a celebrity?"

"Mother, I'm not dating him. We haven't even been on one date yet— and I didn't want to get your hopes up." *Like I knew you would.*

I bet she is already thinking about shopping, because she'll need a new wardrobe now that she's going to be rubbing shoulders with celebrities. And she'll need handbags, of course—to match the new shoes that she'll have to buy to match the new clothes for the wardrobe.

"Well, don't be so defeatist, darling, come on! That's why things always end badly for you, because you go in there thinking they will. You need to be thinking this man is a marriage prospect from the get-go ... "

Like I need her assistance with that one! Oh, there's more ...

" ... And then you need to start formulating a plan as to how you're going to *ensnare* him," she's saying, finishing off her cocktail.

Oh no, sensing another sermon coming from her end. They usually coincide with the finishing of a drink, but unfortunately for mother, they don't work on me. Have somehow become immune, having endured potentially millions of such sermons during childhood.

"Mother, he's not a rabbit. I'm not going to try to ensnare him."

"Suit yourself, Cecilia, but that's exactly what you're doing wrong. All the clever girls who were married ten years ago to eligible bachelors and now live in expensive houses in Mosman with a soccer team of children had a *plan*. Trust me. Men and diamond rings just don't drop into one's lap. One needs a plan. Look at Jess, darling." She's gesticulating towards the poor creature, and I'm feeling like she's very much gearing up for some terrible insult ... "Nine years with the man! Wasted the best part of her twenties, her looks and her figure, on him. Now what's she going to do? She's not twenty-two anymore. Her hair doesn't part in just that right way, cascading down her shoulders in come hither waves, and well, let's be frank, she doesn't have a come hither figure anymore, either."

I'm horrified. Jess is looking seriously horrified, too, but less at Mother and more at the situation. Mother has this way of revealing some goddamn awful truth about you, and then making the bad part out to be the goddamn awful truth rather than the person who has uttered the words. It's a real skill.

"And you know why that happened, Cecilia?" Mother is asking, and I can tell the other two ladies are waiting for a response with baited breath. They're dying to know what Mother—*the relationship extraordinaire* — has diagnosed.

"… It's because she *didn't* have a plan!" And there you have it!

"I didn't have a plan," Jess is echoing. "She's right. I didn't have a plan!"

"She didn't have a plan," Mother is saying again, like it's some sort of mantra, gesticulating towards Jess with the unspoken message, "I told you so."

Sigh. As much as the other ladies think they've just heard some golden relationship advice, I'm still unconvinced, and I'm sure that going into a first date with the expressed desire to snare some man with a master plan is likely to be perceived as a little crazy. A little cuckoo. Wouldn't you say?

I can't be bothered to say anything. Just staring at her with a raised eyebrow. She knows the preaching hasn't worked. I can tell, and good!

"Fine—You don't want to go into this with a plan that ends with a diamond ring on your finger, don't then. It's a mistake though … Tell me at least when this date is, so that I can project some positive vibes in your direction."

"Please don't." She already knows that it is tonight! Maybe she wants the exact time! "I hardly need you here doing some little incense ritual in a desperate attempt to ensure I capture a man."

"You need all the help you can get, and Jess, and our meditation instruction." Char clearly knows that "our" means her, too, and she has looked up again, her expression slightly aggrieved." ... A little positive energy goes a long way! When's the date?"

When she's on to something, there's no point trying to circumvent. The only way is through the issue. Don't I just know it!

"'I said *tonight* earlier, Mother."

"Tonight!" she's gasping, covering her mouth in alarm like it's the first time I've said it. Maybe she just didn't hear due to her drunken state and extreme advanced age.

"What's so wrong with that?" *Why always so dramatic?* "Too soon for you to enact some sort of voodoo spell with Jess?"

She's clearly ignored the jibe. "Tonight?" she's repeating again, incredulously.

"Yes, Mother." Surely she heard me the first and second time! "Did you suddenly have a stroke or something?

"And you're going like that?" she's asking, horrified tone still evident. She is waving a hand towards me and clasping the other over her mouth.

"Well, no," I'm looking down at the jeans and tee I have chosen to wear for this gluing extravaganza, "I'll change outfits and do my makeup of course." Not really thought this far ahead!

"Darling, that's not enough. Sometimes I wonder if you hit your little head as a child or something," she says, giving me her exasperated tone. Is she trying to tell me that she dropped me on my head? Wouldn't be the slightest bit surprised, probably struggling holding baby daughter at the same time as stirring up a cocktail.

"What do you mean that's not enough? What else would I be doing? Buying a ball gown? Taking elocution lessons? What?"

"Don't be absurd. See Jess, she's always absurd." She's looking to Jess for support, who's now fist deep in some mozzarella picante, and is just managing a string of "hmms."

"Darling, you're living under a rock. These days, girls get fake tans, fake eyelashes, their hair done, and their makeup done. The whole kit and caboodle for a first date."

She's gone totally mad. Definitely this time!

"He's seen me before, Mother. Don't forget he was 'taken with me' after seeing me at work in my dowdy work gear," I say, starting to feel slightly paranoid. I was wearing that tight black pencil skirt—hmm? What am I going to wear?

"The girl's lost her mind!" She's slapping her knee enthusiastically, as though she can't believe what I'm saying. "Darling, this man's a celebrity, he's going to be expecting fake tan, tits to match, acrylic nails, sumptuous hair … "

"Sumptuous hair! What does that even involve?" Confused *dot com*.

"It means big hair, darling. *Big, big* hair. Like those Kardashians. Men love hair. Do you know why? Because they don't have any, and men always want what they can't have. She is looking around as she speaks, clearly searching for affirmation from the group. Char is nodding slightly, looking scared, and Jess is nodding even more vehemently in her cheese-induced haze.

"Well, Mother, I can't get any of those things done by 7:00 p.m. tonight. Certainly not the tan and acrylics—and most definitely not the tits. I hear there's a few weeks recovery time after they pop those babies under your skin." I'm grabbing my boobs as I speak.

"Jess," Mother is beginning … Oh no, she's going to drag her into this for support, isn't she? Jess has already looked up, a little entranced, with cheese smeared on her chin. "This man's a celebrity, and you know he'll be expecting everything or nothing."

Jess is clearly thinking about this, frown on face, giving it some real conscious thought. "Yes—Sorry, Cee, but the women he usually dates probably do wear a lot of fake tan, and probably do have fake tits. Not to mention veneers. All those girls dating the celebrities have fantastic teeth."

"Show me your teeth," Mother is demanding, lurching forward and trying to grab my chin. I move back abruptly, brandishing a pin at her. Get away, crazy woman!

"Move any closer and I'll stick you." *I actually will.* "I'm not bloody showing you my teeth … Besides …" *Phew.* She's returned to a comfortable position in her chair, away from me. "… I'm your daughter, you know what my teeth look like."

"Just smile for a second," she has asked anyway.

I can't muster a smile. She can have a grimace instead. So forced. Teeth showing.

"Well, they're nothing to write home about." She lets out a huge sigh. "You're so unprepared, girl. Just promise me one thing—you won't take your clothes off in front of him until you get a fake tan done. Jess, make her promise." She's waving a hand in front of Jess.

"I'll promise no such thing." Why should I? Not that I have been planning to strip down on our first date or anything (but stranger things have happened).

"Really, Cecilia, look, I didn't want it to come to this … but you're a bit lacking in the breast department. What are you a B cup, if that? I mean, men like Chad think that double D's are the norm. At least get a fake tan done before he sees you naked!" She's shaking her head.

I'm lost for words, and that doesn't happen often, right? Okay, so I'm lacking in the *breast department,* as mother would call it. Did I need that to be pointed out to me hours before a crucial first date? No, I did not!

"I have nice legs," I tell her,. And I do! I'm sharp with my responses to her now, *nice legs*—that's something at least.

"And you do, Cecilia," Mum has concurred. Wow! Did she just compliment me? Shocker! Oh no, here comes her backhander, "But nobody cares about legs, darling, especially not men. Men have legs, why would they want another pair, no matter how nice? Men want tits—It's like she's never listened to a word I've ever said." It's as if she is talking a bit to herself, a bit to the spectators, and a bit to nobody.

"Fine." I literally have been driven to the point of agreeing, just so she'll shut up. I don't want to hear her list off my other fatal flaws. I'll be paranoid all evening. "I'll make sure I get a fake tan done before he sees me naked."

"*Good,* darling. There you go, such a good sport," Mother says, getting up, "Ladies, another round of cosmos?"

20. 4:30p.m.

In car with Jess heading back home. Silence. Depletion set in. Energy levels zero. Mother has sucked every last piece out of my being, and I'm sure Jess's, too, like the emotional vampire that she is. Now can barely think coherently. Aware that have mammoth date coming up and should have buoyed spirits, instead am paranoid. Considering pasty white skin with concern. Peeling shirt away from bosoms to survey the damage. Neither here nor there really—semi flat chest. Not completely flat!

"What are you doing?" Jess's voice is monotone. Thankfully she had stopped drinking after that second cosmo and annihilated most of the food in the house, making her now suitable sober. Good from the driving perspective, not so good from the recollection perspective, as the horrors of the passed several hours are probably erupting to the mental surface.

"I'm looking at my boobs."

"Why?" she asks zombie-like.

"Because I'm paranoid, now! What was that last reference she made to them? Like too softly served mozzarella di bufalas?"

"Oh right, yeah, I remember." She sounds feeble.

"Unfortunately, I'm never going to look at them the same again. Not that I ever really considered them. But now—All I can think of is caprese salad."

"Naturally, I can see that."

We're crossing the Harbour Bridge; I'm staring out into the abyss. One always feels like driving straight off it after a visit with Mother. Is that normal? Does everyone think like that about the person that brought them into the world, squeezed them out, ruining their figure in the process … the person who brought them up? Well, that's how I always fucking feel!

"Look, I just wanted to say …" What is she going to say? Not sure I have the strength! "… I'm so sorry about that whole thing. I don't know what came over me. That ridiculous discussion and confession about Pete, and then—you know, telling her about Chad. I'm the worst best friend in the world! I really don't know what I was thinking."

"Oh, don't worry about it." I'm waving away that thought. Done with it. I know what Mother is like; it's not Jess's fault. "She has that effect on people. She sucks them into a *Franny* vortex, they're no longer able to think clearly or of their own volition. I think they have a term for it in a court of law."

"Yes, it really was like I was in a vortex. Under her spell," she is murmuring quietly.

"Indeed. You won't be the first, and you won't be the last, so don't beat yourself up over it."

"She's just …" And she is clearly struggling to find the right description for Mother's behaviour. No matter, I have it all packaged up for her … I know what she's just, and so I shall supply …

"Pure evil!"

"*Yes, yes, yes.*" She obviously agrees. With an incredulous but firm tone, she is now repeating me, "Pure evil."

21. 6:00p.m.

Running late. As usual. Need to be in taxi by 6:30 p.m. to make sure I make it to Freshwater with even the semblance of "on time" or "fashionably late" around me. But running around like chicken without head. None of it makes any sense. Blame Mother, who has brought on paroxysm of self-doubt. Now in the middle of shaving legs with one hand, and applying teeth whitener purchased from corner store with the other.

Still haven't figured out what I'm wearing, or what's clean even. Think will need to focus on assets, despite Mother's jibs … I know I have nice legs, even though apparently not popular with the lads. One needs to play to their strengths, non? Hence the razor!

There, *legs done*. Teeth whitener applied. Okay perhaps it is coming together. Have only nicked legs on a couple of occasions, but not all out arterial bleeds, so safe to apply a coat of moisturiser. Oh nice, a coconut-smelling one that haven't used in years with slightly encrusted lid. Should be fine. I guess the type of lady Chad would be dating would be emitting a lovely and yet delicate fragrance of coconut or vanilla. So I'm on track! Coconut scent subtly wafting from smooth legs!

Time pressing. Running to wardrobe, pulling garments out wildly. What to wear? What to wear? And what look, too? *Edgy and cool?* Short black dress with long sleeves! Very sheike, but too alla Amal Alamuddin? Or floral dress? The strappy, but still short sort, reminiscent of summer days. More Jessica Simpson, but obviously with less breast. Oh, I don't know!

Hey Fred, looking at him now, curled up on the base of my bed, he might have the solution. My focus is date, and I'm sure Fred's is *food,* as always. He's looking back at me as though he's wondering if there's any snacks hidden away in the closet. "No food here, Fred!"

Safe black one; it has to be, as no time to think. Must be decisive. Am cool, calm, in control woman.

Little black dresses are always a winner, right? As long as aptly and possibly boldly accessorised … Hmm? I know—some gold statement pieces should do it—a bangle, and wide necklace—whacking them on. Strapping strappy sandals on. Done.

Time to assess attire, and overall Cee appearance. Standing in front of the full-length mirror. Legs look awesome, tick, however, I do otherwise appear to be flat-chested nun, with ultra short habit. No time to be concerned. Perhaps he has a fetish for pre-pubescent boys. Here's hoping—Or not. Here's *not* hoping actually. Banish thought. Banish thought. Banish thought. *Cee-Project* switching on, looking good, feeling confident!

My phone always rings at the most pressing times. Shit! Really shouldn't answer, no time, but what if it's him? Running out into corridor like lunatic, there's my phone! Oh. No caller ID. Shit! Really must answer.

Be enthusiastic, like woman having fabulous time. "Cecilia speaking."

"Oh, hello, *Cecilia speaking*. It's your mother speaking."

Fuckity, fuck, fuck. What does she want? Another psychotic rant, which will send me into a spin about yet another part of my body no doubt!

"Mother, I really don't have time. I'm running late …"

"Darling, this is important, so just put me on speaker while you do your makeup or whatever you need to do."

Sigh. Hating the thought of it, but clomping back to the bathroom and putting the phone on speaker, flinging it down with vengeance, hoping it'll break and that'll be the end of that.

"Are you there, darling? I just heard the most god awful crash. You didn't fall or anything?"

"No, Mother," I assure her, pulling out foundations and skin brighteners, primers, concealers and a variety of other cover alls, and applying liberally, potentially out of correct order, but who cares really, as long as they make it onto face.

"Good, because the last thing you need is a bruise on your face."

"There's no bruise. So, what was so pressing?" I ask her, moving onto blush.

"Oh, well look, I just wanted to call you because I've had a word with Brad, and apparently this Chad Thompson is rather a *big* deal. Brad's kind of taken aback that you're going on a date with him. In fact, I think he was sort of starstruck. Even asked for his autograph. Of course, I told him it would be completely out of the question for you to ask for his autograph—And if he was shortly going to become part of the family, we wouldn't need his autograph anyway."

Sigh. This is all I need. Added pressure. Keep calm, Cee. Applying liquid eyeliner with the precision of a person who has just learnt to use their hands again following an extended stint in a straight jacket.

"So, what's your point, Mother?" I'm barely engaging in this conversation. Liquid eyeliner job done, and it hardly looks all that bad surprisingly. Onto to the mascara now.

"Well, my point is, darling … He's kind of a big deal. So don't fuck it up."

Lip pencil. Lipstick application. Almost complete!

"Did you hear me, darling? Is this a bad connection? I was saying … he's kind of a big deal … so … "

"Yes, Mother," I'm having to yell loudly, or she's going to repeat it all over again, "I heard you on the first occasion; *he's a big deal, don't fuck it up.*"

"That's exactly what I said. Why did you go all quiet then?"

Pulling out the straightening iron, plugging it in for two seconds, and running it haphazardly through my hair.

"Well, Mother, it's only a first date, so I don't want to make much of it. And the other thing is … Well, I might not even like him! What if he's a total douche? I don't know him from a bar of soap."

Mother is laughing loudly now. "Don't be ridiculous, darling," she says, as though it's the funniest thing she's heard in weeks, and now she's the one yelling (I assume to Brad who must be eavesdropping in the background, hoping he can still extricate an autograph in case this all goes balls up), *"She thinks she might not like him!"*

Lots of laughter. It's echoing through the bathroom from the loud speaker. Trying to apply mascara to that noise is no easy task.

"She'd better like him," I can hear Brad yelling back from a distance.

"Oh, darling, really you are so drole at times." She's in between hiccups as she is speaking. "You're not going to do any better than Chad Thompson!"

More laughter.

"I'm hanging up now, Mother." Just to warn her ... "Goodbye," and I can breath again!

22. 8:00p.m.

Sitting across table from Chad Thompson, Mister Celebrity. Best seat in the house, overlooking the water, of course, because he owns the place. Perks of being with successful restaurateur-ex-footballer-minor-television-star, and more. He must be more than a minor television star because people are looking at us (feels kind of weird), and they have been murmuring things to each other and avoiding eye contact. Wondering momentarily if they're talking about my caprese mozzarella breasts, or lack thereof.

Focus, Cee. Focus.

Managed to only be twenty minutes late. Think it's between borderline *fashionably late* and *she's not going to turn up at all* late. But he didn't seem to mind. When I arrived, he was talking to the chef, Maurizio, from Venice, whom I've been introduced to. More perks. And he commented on my dress, too. "Nice dress," were his exact words, and, "Love when a lady goes all classy." Didn't respond, thinking couldn't agree, given I had more leg out than a standard fee hooker on George Street.

Chad is wearing dark jeans, checkered shirt and a sports jacket. All very *du jour,* and on-trend, but on-trend in that nice, *not trying too hard* way. Not all desperate hipster-like.

Only forty minutes in, and all is going swimmingly. We had the stuffed zucchini flowers for entrée, and are waiting on this squid ink pasta for our main.

"Now I'm worried about the squid ink pasta," I'm flirting. He's leaning in with that pretty smile, as though he's hanging onto every word I'm saying.

"Why would you say that?" Ahh he speaks. Speak again, bright angel!

"Well, you've talked it up. Now I'm expecting something utterly brilliant. You know, a *ten out of ten.* What if it's a nine out of ten? Still great, but not quite the pinnacle! I'll be let down then."

"I can't imagine that happening. It is most definitely a *ten out of ten.* Why would I lie to you?" He is refilling my glass with more champagne, Prosecco, from the region apparently. I'm happy that I treated myself to that expensive bottle of Chardonnay during the week in effort to further my wine knowledge. Not at all linked to Prosecco, but nonetheless part of the continuing education. It's all good research, non?

"Hmm, see?" I say, taking another sip. "You're further bolstering my expectations. You do realise there's a lot riding on this pasta, right?"

"Yeah, I know. My whole credibility could be compromised if this dish comes out and it's just soggy pasta. You'll be like, *who is this guy?* Doesn't know his fettucini from his spaghetti, right?" He's just winked at me. Love it when he winks at me. So inclusive and adorable!

"Agreed. How do you say squid ink pasta in Italian again?"

"Nero di seppia." He's probably saying it in a terrible accent, but I adore it anyway. Having dinner with sexy, stunning celebrity who is speaking Italian to me. Who would have thought?

"I love it when you speak Italian to me." I may just wink back. Yep, the wink has happened. Okay, so the wink isn't usually part of my repertoire, but I'm going to weave it in tonight because it looks so good on him, and I really need to dial the charm up a notch given the calibre of my date and the old caprese salad breasts down there. Maintain sexy eye contact, Cee, and resist looking down at flat chest!

"Doll, if you like that, I've got a lot more to come. Wait till you try the cannoli ripieni di ricotta." Gawwd he even smells nice. All woody and manly, I can smell him from over here.

"You are going straight to the top of my list." I'm finding this flirting super natural, and he's laughing again. Seriously loving it, methinks!

23. 9:30p.m.

Having a grand old time. This guy is fabulous. Funny, hot, and clever. Hoping it's not the alcohol talking. That will teach that Jai about making gross generalisations about people. He might be an ex-footballer, however the pygmy possum comparison was totally uncalled for. On another note, the pasta was utterly sublime. Could have been the effect of having downed potentially the entire first bottle of Prosecco before the meal turned up. Cannoli down, we're now enjoying our short blacks. I'm also enjoying just staring at him. Sad really, isn't it? But when does one get the opportunity to sit opposite such a gorgeous man? Hardly, really! The man market is slim pickings these days and this man could quite possibly be the most handsome man I have ever come across. Ever!

"Has anyone ever told you, Cee, that sometimes you have a terrible habit of staring?" He's speaking with a cheeky smile.

Shit! Must have been for extended period of time. Potentially could have looked like obsessed lunatic. *Note to self:* reduce staring, especially in wistful, lustful manner.

"Yes, I've heard it before. Have considered whether or not I have ADD. I don't think I was properly tested as a child. Sometimes I just get drawn into some bizarre thinking pattern, lots of thoughts, one on top of the other, and forget I'm sitting opposite someone. Sorry!" Feeling like I have to explain myself, feeling rather idiotic.

"Hmm, I've noticed, and it's fine, but that said, it's nice to be out with someone who has a thought in her head, and even, possibly, a few at a time." He's laughing, leaning over the table conspiratorially.

"Do you speak from personal experience?"

"You could call it that. Two failed marriages, a string of very ordinary relationships, an even longer string of very ordinary flirtations—all of whom, during the entire period we were together, probably had one reasonable thought in their head—combined!"

"Cumulatively?"

"Yes, cumulatively. He's reaching across the table and taking my hand. Oh, shit! Quite an intimate gesture, isn't it? Do I let him? Yes. May pee pants! Very much aware now that people's heads are swiveling in our direction.

"It's really quite lovely to be out with an intelligent, witty, beautiful woman—who actually eats her food and doesn't get up mid-meal to vomit in the bathrooms."

Heart soars. Am wonderful, accomplished woman who has attracted (and am currently retaining) glorious ex-footballer-restaurateur-television-personality. Feel briefly like main character in a Jane Austen novel, who has struggled in vain to find nice, normal, well-adjusted man, who will appreciate all of her inherent inner and outer beauty, which up to this point, other men have rejected offhandedly (usually instantly), or feel potentially like character on Sex and the City, or even like Amal Alamuddin sealing the deal with George Clooney. Latter could be a real stretch in the comparison department, given am not renowned human rights lawyer working for United Nations, but close enough is good enough. And right now, I feel good enough.

He's slowly massaging the inside of my hand with his thumb. Should have at least put moisturiser on hands. Maybe some of the coconut rubbed off when I was creaming legs? Am conscious though that hands might be pock-scarred from jabbing myself with Mother's adjoining wedding invitation pins. Hopefully he doesn't think I'm a junky, or a self-harming sort.

"Well, thank you." I'm lurching into motion before I'm sprinted off by another disorienting thought pattern. "I did sneak off to the bathroom while you weren't watching though for a quick power vomit."

He's laughing at my joke, again, and his lovely teeth are flashing in the dim light.

"But what are you thinking during all those moments when you're staring off into oblivion?"

"This and that." Shit! Don't want him to ever know what goes on in this head. "All usually very thought provoking and profound, of course. Typically just about how handsome you are."

Every man likes to have their ego stroked, non? He's throwing his head back and laughing, evidently pleased. I love that he laughs so frequently. Good sign, methinks!

"And here I was thinking you were solving the world's problems. Or the advertising world's problems, at the very least."

"Indeed … *I am,* one handsome man at a time." Oh, the wink is back, and this time it's a conspiratorial one, hoping he likes it! You know what, I think I like it. Happy for said wink to stay and shall continue to incorporate it into my repertoire. Think it's a keeper!

24. 11:30p.m.

Waiting for cab outside of restaurant to take me home. Enveloped in incredibly handsome man's arms. Said handsome man has invited me for coffee at his place, but have declined, given am respectable, intelligent, witty woman who doesn't have sex on the first date. Really? Inwardly dying, want to rip his clothes off at this very moment and discover amazing body (which have previously Googled—and certainly in photos looks ripped and perfect—have noted potential of photoshopping, but think would have been limited, just a little around the edges. And who doesn't need the assistance of photoshopping?). But no, must focus. Steer mind away from raging hormones and desire to fuck. Don't use fuck word, Cee, don't think fuck word, and most definitely don't imagine fuck word in action form.

Shit! Fail! Imagining myself right now entwined in his embrace, naked of course, in his house, room overlooking the ocean. Never been to his house before. Not sure if he has room overlooking the ocean, but think it is safe to imagine it's a possibility.

"Are you sure you don't want to come by for a coffee?" He's looking at me sternly now, only a few centimetres away from my face. Am being overpowered by overwhelming desire for this man. In fact, may pass out in *Scarlett O'Hara* deep south manner.

Focus. Yes, I do want to come for coffee! But declining!

"Oh no," this is so difficult, "I really should be getting home. Have an early start tomorrow." I have to lie!

"It's Sunday." He's wrapping his arms around the small of my back and pulling me tightly towards him. Feel breasts pressed up against him, and momentarily have horrid thought about salad caprese.

"I know, but the advertising world never sleeps. There's a shoot on for a client." And another lie has slipped out! Not a good thing, but surely lying as a last resort to ensure I don't sleep with *man-of-dreams* on first date is pardonable?

Must not weaken. Feeling like jelly! Also, need to remember Mother's stern words of warning, which are swimming now in inebriated state, both alcoholic and hormonal, as I feel own pelvis making contact with his pelvis. Think I can perceive a certain hardening of what may be one very large …

"I suppose you're right." His words are taking my mind away from his penis. Shit! Thought penis. Do not think penis. Do not think penis. Do not think Pe-nis.

Becomes mantra.

"… And who is this client, anyway, who is whisking you away to a shoot on a weekend day? I hope he's not another very attractive footballer completely charmed by your wit and good looks." He's speaking, but his penis is speaking to me more.

"And don't forget my capacity to eat a three course meal and not hock it up at some point."

"Well, how can I forget? One of your other astounding talents."

"Indeed! And it's not a very attractive footballer—In fact, it's an old man with a goiter and a foul temper. Nothing you need to be concerned about," I say, envisaging one of my previous clients in order to create the most disconcerting picture I can imagine. Job well done, Cee! These are promising days, indeed.

But does one detect a hint of jealousy from said ex-footballer? Would that mean he thinks I am a woman of the world, constantly pursued by rich, attractive men? Not at all under the impression that I've been sitting on the shelf (as Mother would refer to it) like old packet of lamington mix?

Phew. Saved by the taxi, which is pulling in beside me. Depressing. But also to some extent feeling buoyed, may have given up to raging hormones and gorgeous man if I'd had a few more moments standing so close to his aroused penis.

"Okay." He's pulling me closer our bodies imprinting on one another, and I can feel the etchings of his *previously spotted via Google stalk* abs and guns. "Well, have fun with your old man."

Unable to respond. Being drawn into never-ending blue eyes and manly smell, which is oh, too divine! His lips are pressing on mine, and I'm being drawn into a passionate embrace. Hmm? Interesting … Not quite the kissing style I was expecting—slightly disappointing, all a bit tongue-jabby and disconcerting. Oh, dear! But perhaps this is what footballers and blondes with fake breasts and zero thoughts in their heads do! So go along with it, Cee! Jab back. Jab here, Jab there. May well have to train him out of this at a later stage though.

Oh, dear, the kiss is coming to a messy end. I can feel it! I want to wipe the saliva away from my mouth. We are staring into each other's eyes now so blissfully. Have heady, weak-kneed feeling. Must get into cab before I make a fool of myself.

Focus, Cee! Focus. As Mother would say, have a plan. Can't believe I'm taking her advice. In this case, the plan is get into the cab, retaining dignity as I do so, a woman of the world, very much planning to continue this at a later stage … not too much of a later stage though!

"Well, thank you for the wonderful evening," I say, trying to sound airy and relaxed as if mind-blowing celebrity has not just kissed me.

Heading towards the door of the cab, wiggling … And what's this? He is bounding ahead of me. Oh, how sweet, he is opening the back door. All very chivalrous! I'm astounded. Previous boyfriend once drove away with me still semi-inside-semi-outside the car in desperate attempt, methinks, to get away from me, almost causing decapitation.

Getting into the cab … Whoops, forgot how short this dress is; may have flashed underpants again. Gosh! Why does that happen to me all the time? At least I'm not going commando today, and decided to wear a lovely pair of black lacy Brazilian cut underpants in case I did not heed Mother's, or own internal, advice, and the evening became amorous.

He doesn't seem to notice. Shame. I think he'd like them.

"I'll call you tomorrow." He's closing the door and stepping back.

Did he just say—*I'll call you tomorrow?* I rather think he did. Means this is some sort of a *thing*, non? Not just a date as such, but a definite thing.

You know, a potential relationship, man-of-dreams, diamond ring on finger sort of thing!

A thing! Heart is soaring to dizzying heights.

"Ma'am. Ma'am. Ma'am," Taxi driver is speaking. I don't hear a word, instead just staring out at Chad like a lunatic for the past few moments while considering "thing" thing.

"Where are you going?" the taxi driver has asked with a rude tone, making it clear he's asked this before, maybe more than once.

"Oh, 9 Hunt Street in Potts Point," I tell him, still staring into oblivion, but feeling more aware of taxi driver.

"Okay," he replies, and begins to pull away. I'm watching Chad distractedly from the window and he's lifting his hand in a Humphrey Bogart waving gesture. I'm so waving back.

"Isn't that in Kings Cross?"

"No, it's not. It's in Potts Point."

Fucking address! When will people understand?

25. Not sure what fucking time it is

oken by phone ringing. Surely the crack of dawn. Rolling around in bed haphazardly. What day is it? What's going on? Who could be calling at this ungodly hour? Recollections flash into mind. It's Sunday, just had awesome date with ex-footballer. Waking up in own bed—good start. Good girl, Cee. Did not sleep with him. But do now have potential "thing" with him. All very good indeed. Phone still ringing, disturbing quiet of morning. Best answer …

There you are mobile. 11:00 a.m. It's an ungodly hour for Sunday, methinks. Oh, already have a number of texts. Interesting. Oh, they're all from Chris. Typical.

I throw the covers off, hunting about for the cordless phone. Must stop incessant ringing. It's a persistent son-of-a-bitch, that's for sure. I conclude at this point that it must be Mother or an actual, real emergency. No, I bet it is Mother!

Consider letting it ring, but she'll just call again.

I left it in the bathroom last night …

"Cecilia speaking," I say, demurely delivered on my part despite incessant ringing having woken me up. My suspicions still say it is Mother, but wouldn't want to frighten off ex-footballer-stud-potential-boyfriend, colleague, or any other emergency caller.

"Hello, *Cecilia speaking*. It's your mother speaking." And … suspicion confirmed.

"Hello, Mother. That's really getting old. Any chance you could stop doing that?" I'm stumbling out of the bathroom with a ripper of a headache, probably caused from the bottle and a half of Prosecco I consumed last night, along with the number of random drinks ingested at Mother's place during the invite collation extravaganza.

"I just don't know why you would answer the phone like that. Really, darling, who else would be speaking? You live alone in an apartment. Unless Fred suddenly becomes ambidextrous and able to not only reach, but also answer the phone, we're all pretty sure it's you," she has summarised.

Why is she calling me at this time of the morning? To deliver some stinging rhetoric about my phone manner?

"Mother, it's just a pleasant way of answering the phone. The person on the other end could not know who they're calling … "

"How could they not know who they're calling? They just called you. Don't be absurd, darling."

"Well, call centres and the like. They always check if it's you, and sometimes people just aren't sure." I'm not sure why I'm even deeming this response-worthy. It must be a result of the wonderful mood I have suddenly discovered I'm in, despite Mother's call. Am in apartment, reasonably sober, have *thing* happening with wonderful, successful man, and am glowing protégé in workplace at the moment (am I too old to be a protégé? Not sure)—but life is looking good since implementing Cee-Project!

"Are you still there?" Oh, must have missed something she just said, as usual.

"Yes, Mother. What did you say? I just woke up."

She is sighing as though I'm the most impertinent, annoying, disdainful child she's ever known, or in this case, birthed. "You really need to get an answering machine so you can screen calls. Why are you taking calls from call centres?"

"I have an answering machine," I say, sticking a pod into the coffee machine and trying to find a clean mug for the coffee to go into. "I just haven't gotten around to recording a message."

Bingo! Clean cup! Really need to put dishwasher on ASAP, kitchen is starting to look unruly.

"It's not that hard, darling. Not sure why you're procrastinating over it."

I'm pressing the happy *go* coffee button. Yum—Just look at that wonderfully syrupy black goodness pouring into my cup.

"What's all that noise, darling?"

"It's the coffee machine, Mother."

"Oh, right! You still have that ancient cheap one you picked up at Aldi.

Darling, you really need to get with the times and get a Nespresso machine. Brad and I bought one a few months ago. Once you go Nespresso, you never go back." She's sounding overjoyed.

"I don't need a Nespresso machine, Mother. The Aldi one works perfectly fine, and it makes great coffee," I say, plucking my cup out and taking a sip. Yep, great coffee!

"Nonsense, darling! Haven't you seen the ads on television for Nespresso? They have *Clooney* doing the publicity. Clooney! I mean if Clooney likes it, how could you not?"

Sigh. There's no sense to be had. Of course if Clooney has a Nespresso machine, I should definitely convert to one, too—since we're all basing our lives on George Clooney's existence!

"Fine, Mother! I'll get a Nespresso machine."

"Oh great, darling! Perfect gift for your birthday, sweetheart! Brad and I will get it for you. What colour are you after? Ours is black, and it looks very slick, but I do like the red and white ones, too. What colour is the rest of the décor in your kitchen?"

Where is this going? Why is she calling?

"I don't really have any other décor in the kitchen." At least I don't think I do, glancing about. Except the toaster, which stands forlornly to the side and hasn't been used in the better part of a decade. Is a toaster décor? Not sure!

"You're always so absurd, darling. But of course you have décor in the kitchen. Everyone has décor in the kitchen!"

"I have a toaster …" I say, taking a seat on one of the stools positioned near the kitchen. Could *they* be described as décor? What exactly does she mean by kitchen décor? *Note to self:* still wearing black lacy underwear from last night … and dress. Must have collapsed straight into bed.

"I'm sure you have more than a toaster there, darling. Other appliances? What colours is the kitchen based on? Any crockery out? Photos? Plants?" She's still going on.

"No other appliances, no crockery, no photos, and definitely no plants. The kitchen colour is a kind of, well it's kind of … grey."

"Grey?"

"Yes, Mother. Grey."

"I'm sure it was burgundy. I could have sworn it was burgundy."

"No, it's grey. I can see it, I'm in it, and it is definitely grey."

"I was there, what, a month ago, and I'm sure it was burgundy." This woman clearly loves the colour burgundy—She must be getting it confused with her wedding theme colour.

"No, grey! I don't think I've ever had a burgundy kitchen before in any of the places I've lived in."

"You're having me on, aren't you? One of those delightful little Cecilia pranks!"

"No, the kitchen's grey—Look, Mother … " I'm tired of the Sunday morning *tete a tete*, whether it be about answering machines, coffee machines or kitchen colours. " … what are you really calling about?"

"Well, don't be stroppy, darling. I was just making conversation." She's being huffy now.

"Yes, I understand. But I have a brunch appointment at noon and I really need to have a shower and freshen up before I go."

"Who with?"

"Does it matter?" I ask, slurping down the rest of my coffee. Christ, I need another one after this discussion.

"Yes, indeed it does. Are you going with Chad? Is he there?" She's sounding panicked, alarmed, but excited at the same time, as though she's having a semi-brush with a celebrity, even if it's over the phone proximity (and even though he's not here).

"No, he's not here, Mother. I'm going to brunch with Chris."

"Well, don't listen to his advice, will you? He's completely off with the pixies, wouldn't know how to ensnare a man even if he had him already on the hook. And don't take that in the wrong way, darling—It's just different in the gay community, you know? That's what they do—They have lots of partners. They're not really interested in the long-term monogamous relationships."

Now she's lecturing me about gay relationships? The pounding headache is getting worse, feeling like my head might explode in similar way to the final episode of *Game of Thrones*, season four, where the prince man has his head quite literally smashed by a giant's hands. Having visual now, not pretty.

"Mother, a lot of gay people have monogamous relationships and are in long-term partnerships. Chris might not be a good example of that," I'm trying to be delicate because Chris is my best friend, "but you're really making a gross generalisation."

"I don't think that's correct, darling."

"Are you speaking from firsthand experience, Mother?" I ask, feeling cross and heading to the coffee machine. I'm going to need more caffeine to cope with this. "When was your last gay relationship?"

"Well, don't be absurd, Cecilia—apart from that dalliance in secondary school ..." Oh no, is she going to continue with some tale of her teenage lesbian love affair? Hell no! Must cut her off now before the damage is done ... Too much imagery for this Sunday morning!

"Okay, Mother—Let's cut to the chase! What's this call about?" I say, popping another coffee pod into the machine (this conversation requires a second cup of coffee!), hoping she forgets about the Nespresso notion. After all, I know what that will involve: countless, pointless conversations about colour, style, milk frothing, grinding ... Really, it's all too much to imagine.

"I was calling to see how last night went."

"Oh, last night. Of course that's what you're after." Oh, of course it is *indeed.* How could I have missed that and thought this was just a Sunday morning courtesy call from mother to daughter? You know, just chewing the Sunday morning fat?

"And so?" She's hanging onto every word! I can tell, and desperately, too. Perhaps even Brad is there. They've probably been up since 6:00 a.m. contemplating when the right time was to make the check-in call and ensure I haven't stuffed it all up with their treasured ex-footballer-celebrity.

I just can't be bothered with this, and it's now almost 11:45 a.m. And while I know Chris will at least be half an hour late on a Sunday morning, I can't bank on anything more.

"It went very well, Mother."

"Very well" she has repeated disdainfully, as though I've just told her to put her foot in her mouth. "What does that mean?"

"Exactly that, Mother." My wonderful morning mood is about to dissipate. Trying to hold on to it; it just feels so good. "We had a great time."

"And ... Do you like him?"

"Yes, Mother, I like him. He's a lovely man."

"Are you seeing him again?" she's asking desperately. I can see her in my mind's eye now clinging onto the phone, eyes wide, schizophrenic look to her, like she's trying to procure her next stash of drugs.

"He said he would call me today, and so yes, I think we're seeing each other again." I can't help myself, but I'm feeling sort of chuffed as the words leave my mouth. A potential second date with a pseudo-celebrity, Cee. Not bad, not bad at all.

"He's calling her today, Brad," Mother is yelling hysterically (obviously at Brad, who must be interested, although evidently not in the vicinity of the phone conversation). *"They're seeing each other again!"*

"Great news!" I can hear him calling back. Honestly, the man sounds gleeful.

"This is good, Cee," Mother is telling me. "Very good."

"Thanks for the verdict."

"And you didn't sleep with him?"

"No." Oh, but I wanted to, and I sure did imagine it!

"Good again! I mean, appearing sluttish on the first date—a complete *no-no.*"

Oh, how lovely. My own mother thinks it was a possibility that I may have acted like a slatternly wench on a first date.

"And besides …" Here we go! I'm preparing for some sort of major insult, veiled as advice. " … You do look rather pale, so make sure you get that tan this week."

Major insult avoided, just minor! I'm surprised by Mother's restraint.

"Yes, I'll book it in."

"And?"

"And what?"

"Well, you know, was there a goodnight kiss or anything like that?" What does *anything like that* involve? I have to stop myself from laughing out loud, but yes there certainly was! There was an embrace, kissing—with tongue jabbage, but kissing nonetheless, and I'm certain a full-on erection was involved.

"Yes, Mother, there was a kiss." I am a thirty-two-year-old woman acting somewhat smug because I've gone on one date and kissed an ex-footballer-pseudo-celebrity (potential *man-of-dreams).* My maturity level—a corpulent ZERO!

"There was a kiss, Brad," Mother is screaming again hysterically clearly in Brad's direction. Mother's maturity level—an even fatter ZERO! Brad's maturity level—triple ZERO!

"Well done, darling," Mother is cooing. "You know I always thought you were a little lost in the *gentlemen* department, but now I see you've just been holding out. Holding out for the big catch!" Her tone is euphoric; it's like I've won an Academy Award.

I'm hearing Brad again, muffled in the background, "Maybe we should invite them round to watch the footy on the weekend?"

OH. MY. GOD. Need to get off the phone as quickly as possible. Realising (potentially too late) that Brad's man crush on Chad borders on stalker-esque, and is most definitely of the schoolgirl variety where one combines their first name with their stalked prey's last name in infinite manners on their school book.

"It might be too soon for that," comes Mother's reply. Phew! But you know you're in deep trouble when Mother's the only person talking sense.

"Got to go, Mother." I literally have to. I can't bare this any longer and

I need to meet Chris. "I have another call coming through."

"Okay, poppet," she's trilling, and in my general fashion (when talking to Mother), I hang up on her before she can say more.

26. 1:00 p.m.

*B*runch. *Is it even considered brunch when it's 1:00 p.m.? When would that make lunch? 3:00 p.m.? Maybe ... It sort of sounds like a typical Sunday. Chris's running spectacularly late! Now sitting alone at table in some hipster locale on South Dowling Street. Waiter has on a number of occasions asked if I'd like to order. Keep repeating I'm waiting on someone else, but he's now glancing at me suspiciously, and clearly thinks I'm most definitely lying. Presuming that, no doubt, I've either been stood up or have no brunch forward slash lunch date, and am taking up a prominent space in his busy section, but am failing to order anything—or to look hip and happening.*

Hipsters everywhere to be seen—with all sorts of facial growths, rolled up jeans, shoes without socks, heavily styled hair, and nonchalant expressions on their faces. Out of my depth.

Sporadic, yet bold, thought enters head now—*I hate Sydney on Sunday.*

Everyone seems to think they're cool on Sundays—more so than usual. As though they've just had a wonderful evening, sharing spectacular moments with spectacular friends (and social media) and now they're catching up, still looking spectacular to discuss last night's events and the coming week's spectacular events.

I hate it. It's so *showy*. Makes me want to vomit.

And finally—Chris is sailing in, looking all handsome and debonair … and short of breath.

He has a boat style hat on his head and massive aviators squashed onto his small face, which he isn't removing now, even though he's indoors. The boat theme continues with a nautical t-shirt, horizontal blue lines, shorts and red loafers. He's holding some green bag over his shoulder … because he's all organic and shit—Whatever!

"I'm so sorry I'm late!" He's flinging himself at me and kissing me dramatically on either cheek.

"I've been sitting here alone for at least forty minutes," I say, potentially a slight exaggeration. More like twenty to thirty, but nonetheless a humiliating experience.

"I'm so sorry." He's sitting opposite me, enunciating the words slowly to inject the appropriate levels of empathy into each sound. "Didn't you get my text?"

"Yeah, but I was here by the time I got your text. The waiter keeps staring at me like I have *leprosy*. Or something far worse—no friends."

Chris is looking at him. "Yes, he does look like the judgmental type."

Think I'll give the waiter a tight-lipped smile, as though to say, *See! I WAS telling the truth*. Waiting until he turns—smile fixed in place … and good, he has seen it! He's smiling back thinly, not sure what he's trying to say in return. Don't care either; I've made my point, methinks!

"I couldn't help it," Chris is whining. "After the events of last night, I could barely get out of bed this morning."

Oh god, dare I say it, "Painful?"

"No, if only!" he's hissing, "More like mortifying." He's speaking to me over the top of his menu.

"Okay, well you'll have to save me the details because I'm starved. I've had two coffees and a whole lot of nothing this morning. I need food."

"You need food! I need to emotionally eat … everything!"

"Well, we're at the wrong place then. Everything here is kale this and organic that. I can barely read the menu, let alone figure out what to order! What's *spelt?*"

"I think it's a type of bread."

"Bread or grain?"

"Oh, I don't fucking care." He's peeved about something, no doubt I shall find out exactly what shortly. "Why can't one just get eggs on toast anymore? Why does every place that is hip need to be such a wank fest?"

I'm shocked by the vehemence of his answer—Sounds more like me than Chris. Sheesh! Must really have been a tough night!

"What's this spelt toast served with chia strawberry compote and organic peanut butter? What is that?" I'm mystified by this *spelt*.

"Oh, ditch the spelt bread already. Here, I'll order for you."

"Fine." I'm too hungry to complain and too mortified by the notion that I need to Google half the menu to understand what it involves to order. Sign of advancing age, no doubt!

Chris is signaling to the waiter with an exasperated nod of his head. The same waiter from before is now fluttering over to us quickly. I shall avoid eye contact.

"We'll have two veggie burgers and two Bloody Maries, doll … And keep them coming." *Doll* is nodding his head, taking the menus swiftly and efficiently.

Maybe that's how one talks to waiters now, abrupt, with some sort of patronising term of endearment like "doll" or "baby". No, actually that might just be Chris. And the *keep it coming comment*, who is he now, Clint Eastwood?

Shall not make the quip, though—I know better than to do that. He's in a royal mood, and at times like these, one needs to move slowly and carefully to not scare the horses.

"So it didn't go well?" Why is he still wearing his sunglasses indoors? Please!

"You could say that, but it would be a gross understatement … In fact, it'll be the last time I ever entertain the idea of having one."

"A what?"

"You know what! I can't even say the word! It brings to mind all sorts of disturbing memories."

Oh dear, that bad, huh? Chris afraid to use the word *threesome*—That, indeed, is the result of a very bad situation.

So he's just ordered me a veggie burger … back to the threesome in a moment. I'm just not sure what a veggie burger is exactly. Would there be a veggie pattie and kale? Would it have a side of hot chips?

"Speaking of bad," he's saying, "what are you even wearing? Are those sweat pants?"

I'm staring at him, giving him my evil eye because he deserves it right now, but it's wasted on his sunglasses, of course, which are still bloody on.

"Yes, they're sweat pants. The reason I look like a homeless person is because I thought I was running late, so I ran out of the house with whatever outfit I could get my hands on."

"Oh, darling, really, next time just be late. Wearing sweats in public! No wonder the waiter was looking at you in such a judgmental fashion."

"Thank you, Chris, for that insightful comment!" I say, clenching my teeth. Why do I even tolerate Chris, or Jess for that matter? How did I befriend them in the first place, and come to think of that, how did I survive in my mother's womb, then exit through her vagina? These questions boggle me often, especially when *said* person in my life is being ungrateful and rude.

"You're welcome," he's responded.

Bloody Maries have arrived—And we are both slurping down half the glass in the first sip.

"Do you want to talk about it?"

"Maybe after two of these," he's telling me, pointing at his drink. "But just to give you the prelude, I'm wearing these sunglasses because I was quite literally kicked out of bed, and now have a bruise on my face as a result. Looks like I've been struck by a biker."

That is bad. Trying to conceal the smirk that is fighting to creep across my face. Drinking more. *Cover mouth, Cee.*

"How did that happen?"

"Well, isn't it obvious? I was the unwanted party. Really! Has that ever happened to you? Have you ever been kicked out of bed because you are the unneeded, or unwanted, person? I don't think so!" He's looking like he might cry. Even with the sunglasses on, his face is crumpling up absurdly.

"Well, come to think of it ..."

"Oh, save me the story," he's cutting me off. "I'm quite sure that you haven't. Nobody has. It's utterly humiliating. How can I show my face anywhere anymore?"

"Well, nobody knows. They can't read it on your face or anything."

"But I know!" He is yelling a bit now, and dramatically, too. That hipster couple at the table next to us is looking over—Obviously we're breaking the *hipster code*, being too loud and evidently indiscrete.

"You're being dramatic."

I am kind of listening to Chris still yapping in the background, watching him flap his arms about, too. But I've also heard the ping that my mobile has made in bag. I'm trying to resist answering ... but it's him, I know it! It's Chad!

I can just feel it in my waters! Not that I know what my waters are, or even where they're located. Or where that saying even comes from, for that matter. Hold back from grabbing phone out of bag, Cee. Feeling like a drowning person needing to reach for their life jacket! Keep hands back, knotted on the table, nodding and smiling on the odd occasion at Chris. I'm even managing to throw random empathetic looks. Of course, I have no idea what he's actually saying. Wanting to focus. Cannot focus!

"Cecilia! Cecilia! Cecilia!" Oh, his mouth is forming in the shape of my name, think he has said my name on a number of occasions. He's talking very loudly—People are looking at us.

"Hello, Cecilia! Did you just have a stroke? What the fuck are you doing?" He's super cranky.

"Oh, I'm so sorry," I say, conscious that people are now staring at us like we have the plague. "I just got a text, and I know I should be listening, but I desperately want to see what it says."

He's raising an eyebrow coldly, as though to indicate this is all completely untoward.

"Fine," he says. His tone is prim. "Look at your phone, then." He's waving his hand towards my bag's direction. "I'll just sit here and nurse my wounds alone."

I ignore the comment and remind myself that he was over an hour late to this exchange, and that this is my world, too, not just Chris's ... So he can wait! Fishing through my bag desperately, heart pounding, I stumble upon the phone almost instantly. It's a sign. I'm convinced.

Glancing at screen ... Gah! It is from him! Hardly containing excitement. Wanting to do *happy dance* in seat.

"Hey, beautiful. How are you doing this morning? Any chance your free for dinner on Wednesday? X"

Heart is soaring! Super excited. Having minor meltdown. Not only is he asking me out on another date (this week might I add), but there's also a kiss at the end of the message AND he's referring to me as *beautiful*. Regrettably, there's a spelling error in the text, *your*, should be a contraction of *you are*, but willing to let even a pesky spelling error slide for ex-footballer-superstar-boyfriend.

"What does it say?" I'm hearing Chris again. "You look like you just had an orgasm." Almost did!

"Maybe I just did," I say, purring.

"Show me!" He's snatching the phone out of my hand—Shame, I wanted to gloat more.

"Looky here—Is this ... the footballer?"

All I can do right now is nod. I'm swooning at the thought of Chad!

"Well, he can't spell, evidently, but what can one expect from the beautiful, athletic people? They all cruise along based on their looks, charm and talent." He's handing me the phone back and now crossing his arms.

"Is that all you're going to say?"

"Yes, it is. Because I'm jealous! I've just been kicked out of bed—and arguably a relationship too—by some twenty-one-year-old twig who has a tiny penis! It looked a little bit like a seahorse. And you're dating some gorgeous ex-footballer-celebrity who probably has a very large penis. What do you expect? I'm bruised and battered and jealous."

Sigh contentedly.

"I know that makes you happy, Cee, because you're a bad person. Inciting jealousy in those around you is an end goal," he's going on in a stroppy manner.

"*En contraire,* my friend, it is not." The waiter has just put down our dishes. Oh, the veggie burger … It looks like a scant burger, and the fries look extremely burnt.

"Excuse me, the fries look burnt." Yes, talking to you little *so-and-so.*

"They're not burnt." He's cocking his head to the side in an *I know better than you* gesture. He has been in my life for hardly over an hour or two and I hate him!

"They are." Chris is slurping away on his drink in the background. "They're so dark they're almost orange." I'm holding one toward his face now as I speak, and it's too stiff to even dangle or swing—It's burnt!

"That's because they're made from sweet potato," he just sighed at me, shaking his head now like I have made the stupidest observation in the entire world. "Nobody eats fries made from potatoes anymore—unless they want to get fat."

Hate him! If Elsie were a boy, she'd be this waiter! He's gone without another word.

Chris is tittering in the background.

"What the hell was that? So now we're paying exorbitant amounts of money for veggie patties and greenery and rude wait staff?" What happened to this world? Fries not even made with normal potatoes anymore. Where's the justice?

"Exactly. It's the new black, Cee. Get some *rude* with your burger."

"Do you think I should complain?"

"No, leave it. Typical fag. He's probably had a rough evening—although couldn't be worse than mine. Or he objects to your sweats, which is understandable."

"You know, this is *my* neighbourhood, so if I want to go to a casual lunch with sweat pants on, I can," I say, biting into this vegetarian mess.

"Oh, darling, no you can't. You're living on another planet. I'm not sure how you've ingratiated yourself with this footballer, but you're going to have to lift the bar because you might start getting papped."

"Firstly, I ingratiated myself with the footballer because I'm charming ... "

"Indeed, I agree. You've always had that subtle charm about you, even when you do have a piece of kale stuck in your teeth."

Ignoring kale in teeth comment ... "And secondly, I hardly think he's popular enough to get papped. We're hardly Bingle and Sam Worthington."

"Oh, he is so bigger than Worthington."

"No, he's not. Worthington was in *Avatar.*"

"Oh, who cares about those giant blue people? And that was years ago, what has he done since, besides beat up some other paps? I tell you, you need to start lifting the bar, doll."

Sigh. There's no sense to be had here!

"So I think I'm in better spirits now and can start talking about last night's incident …" What's with everyone referring to sexual episodes as *incidents?*

Dear God.

"Wait," I say, attempting to stall him. "I need to text him back."

"Oh, don't text him now. Leave it for an hour or so. You can't appear to have been desperately waiting for his invite."

"But I was."

"No matter, doll. He doesn't need to know that. Leave it till 3:00 p.m. at least."

Having a mental reminder of Mother telling me not to follow any of Chris's advice, and she's probably right. After all, this is a man who was just kicked out of bed during a threesome, but … It does seem to make sense. Wouldn't want to appear desperado. Will wait till 3:00 p.m. I slide the phone back into my bag slowly, like it's a time bomb that needs to be eased into position gradually and gently.

"Back to last night …"

Oh shit! Here we go. Bloody Mary, down you go—In need of Dutch courage as his story is finally beginning to unfold.

"It all began when I saw the threesome participant and he was a twig. You know what a twig is, right?"

"Yeah, super skinny, ass like a teenager." One comes to know these things when one's best friend is Chris.

"Exactly, and you know … I'm not into twigs. Pre-pubescent boys are not my thing! Nor am I into men who like twigs …"

Feeling impending doom beginning to unfold. Somehow I just focus on the word *thing*, and yes it is making me flutter at the thought of the very obvious thing between myself, Cee, and said ex-footballer, Chad. Chad and Cee have a thing, indeed!

27. 1:00p.m.

onday. Standing in a beautician's room semi-naked. Well, completely naked, except for terrible paper g-string they have provided me with, and strange paper tea-cozy hat for hair. Trying to cover breasts with hands in awkward gesture, because I'm now paranoid that boobs look like sad mozzarella di bufala. Although, post-fake tan, at very least they'll be brown, and not an unflattering ghostly white colour. Best not cover them then; they can't look like mozzarella if they are brown.

Hear knocking from the door. "Are you ready for me to come in?" *said beautician* is calling.

"Sure." I'm trying to sound relaxed and calm, but voice comes out as yelp. I don't often stand naked in front of women.

Here she is all ready to spray me with some contraption. She looks like she's about twenty-one: thin, short, with clearly enhanced breasts and enough filler in her lips to sink a ship. Perhaps this is the type of woman Chad would usually be dating?

"What colour do you want to be?" She's plugging the contraption in. I bet she'll spray me absentmindedly while she thinks of other stuff and chews on gum. Can't imagine this is a riveting task.

"Brown?" Fuck, I haven't had a fake tan since Jess convinced me to have one before we went to Hawaii so we wouldn't look so ridiculously pale on the beach. That didn't turn out well—but hear the world of fake tanning has radically improved in the last five years and will no doubt look naturally brown and fab after this experience.

"Light brown, medium brown, or dark brown? Also do you want the two or eight hour?"

I'm staring at her like she's speaking Yiddish. What is she talking about, two or eight? Strangely think Mother would be more equipped to be having this fake tan than me. Popular culture is getting away from me ...

"Sorry," my apology is more at her *puffy* lips as opposed to at her, "I haven't had a fake tan in five years. I don't know what two or eight hours means."

Have exposed own lack of knowledge. *Puffy*, my new name for said beautician, is staring back at me like I might be Amish. I can see the cogs moving in her mind ever so slowly (because I imagine that this is the type of woman who would write "your" rather than "you're" when *you are* is implied)—and she thinks I'm nuts.

"Wow! Mind is blown," she's saying with disbelief. "Five years?"

"Yeah," I say, concealing the *capreses* and shifting on my feet with this bloody paper g-string jabbed up my ass. "I'm not really the fake tan type."

"Wow. Mind is blown," she has repeated again, like I'm describing an alien landing, something completely unfathomable in her mind. "Well, two hours means you can wash it off after two hours, and eight means you wash it off after eight hours."

Okay, that sounds simple enough. Would prefer two hours, non? Better than having to sit in stinking mess of fake tan for extended period of time.

"Two hours." There, easy!

"Okay, and colour?"

"I'm not sure. I don't want to look too tanned, you know? I just want to look natural. What would you recommend?"

"What's the occasion?"

Shifting again awkwardly on this same spot, g-string so chaffing me. If I tell her it's for a date, she might think I haven't had a date for five years and then seriously think I'm nutso or part of some obscure, but strict, religious group. But nakedness is stopping the quick thinking part of my brain, and so here goes the truth …

"I'm going on a date on Wednesday night, and he's not the type of guy I usually see, so thought I would put in a bit of an effort."

I feel like a desperate old woman, revealing some body deformity to this young pretty thing with puffy lips.

"Oh, right." She's perked up, probably at the sound of the date. An area of expertise for her, I'm sure. "What type of guy is he?"

Not feeling at all comfortable discussing this with a random beautician I have just met, but am totally compromised right now and desperate to just get fake tan done and get out of here.

"He's an ex-footballer, he's been on television …"

"Shut up!" Her eyes are widening as she speaks, looking conspiratorially at me.

Shut up! Is that like a figure of speech, or is she telling me to shut up? Should I not speak now? Erm?

"Who is he?" she's demanding, as though we're now *besties* and she must know the gossip.

"Oh, I don't think you'd know him ..." Great, I'm stuttering. Wishing I'd never started this conversation. "He's really not that popular."

"Tell me anyway."

"No, really."

"Tell me!"

Oh god! Am sort of afraid of her now, a bit like Char is of Mum. Also naked ... and feeling super vulnerable here, with just a bit of paper protecting my dignity!

"Chad Thompson," I whisper quietly.

"Shut up!" she's yelling. Okay, must be figure of speech. "I love him! He is so gorge. I would die to go on a date with him!"

Okay, all very emphatic, and crazy. She *loves* him. Didn't know his name would solicit this type of response.

"Yeah, he's very sweet." I'm unable to match her level of excitement about it all.

"Oh my god. You're like the luckiest woman in the world. How long have you been seeing him for?"

How long is this going to go on for? Thinking of grabbing clothes and just rushing out of the room. Where are my clothes? Shit, they are in a pile behind her. There's no way I could even get past her without looking utterly crazy.

"It's a new thing. We've only been on a few dates."

"Wow. I'm just totally blown away. I'm going to do the dark on you today because I want you to look fab, and I know he must be the type of guy who likes tans. I can just tell, *you know?*" She's already started strapping on a container to the contraption. "You are totally the luckiest woman in the world. I am dying of envy. Totally dying …" she is continuing on, and now turning the spray gun to the wall, pulling the trigger and releasing a sharp puff of colour.

Oh dear god, why did I let Mother talk me into this?

"Okay, babe," she's saying, because we're now on a "babe" basis, "hands to the side like a scarecrow."

Dropping arms to side of body in ridiculous gesture, she must be looking at the salad capreses now and thinking, *How has this scrawny white thing scored Chad Thompson?* Trying to push thought from mind. Must re-engage *Cee-Project*, which means confidence, right?

"I'm going to make you look amazing!" she's telling me with a super excited tone, and spraying away.

Whoa, that's cold, ice cold actually. Dear god! Smelling like coconut. Just close your eyes, Cee! What ways can I get back at Mother for convincing me into this humiliating experience?

28. 2:30p·m.

ack at work! Looking vaguely like I'm part of some racist parody. Appearing like have painted body brown. Smell like coconut and some other vaguely repugnant odour that I can't quite put my finger on. Clothes sticking to me disgustingly like sweaty, hot day on bus. Looking ridiculous, but nonetheless made it through situation with my life intact, and hence should be thankful. Briefly thought beautician might be obsessed with Chad Thompson and would kill me only to assume my place on date with him. Made it out alive! Even though it was after extended conversation about fillers, and how I should get some in mouth, around eye area, and frown lines. Apparently would give me a more youthful appearance. Doctor Chung does fillers at their studio every week, she told me. They book up fast, but she could get me in, just say the word, and she'd get me a good deal. Politely declined. She looked disappointed. I made a sharp exit.

Oh, yes, just remembered I have a meeting with Swami at 4:00 p.m. Can't go looking like this! He might think I am truly making some racial joke. Will have had shower by then, but somehow think the sum of all these brown parts will have penetrated epidermis and will be ridiculously brown for life. Hope you are happy, Mother!

And here's another thing, spray tanning has not moved at a rapid pace in the last five years at all. And I most certainly do not look natural and glamorous.

"Tina." She's typing away rapidly on her laptop, preparing for the meeting this afternoon no doubt (which I had unprofessionally forgotten about until moments ago).

"Yes?" She's looking up all engaged and excited, as per usual.

"I'm going to need you to go to this meeting with the Swami by yourself this afternoon."

Now she's looking nervous. A moment has passed, and she must be processing thoughts.

"I don't think I can. It's a big one. We're presenting all the social media content. I just don't know how … and you're so good at managing them, and …"

I *am* good at managing Swami and McDutchy; they're not of the easy client variety. She's right about that!

"I know, babe," I say, trying out the lingo the beautician was using in an effort to remain young and cool for as long as possible, "but I just really can't go like this. I look ridiculous and he might think I'm making some sort of racial joke."

"It really doesn't look that bad …" she's trailing off. Even she can't perjure herself to that extent. Great! I must look that bad!

"It does, Tina. No need to lie." She is looking relieved. "I think you need to go it alone."

"Okay," she's agreeing slowly, panic all over her face. She clearly needs more convincing.

"Don't worry, you can do this. You know that content inside and out. And besides, it'll be good for you. Straight into the deep end. You want to stay on, right?" This will no doubt be the major draw card and the most convincing element. Feeling slightly terrible for using it, but desperate times call for desperate measures. This is one of those said times!

She's nodding quickly, emphatically. Good sign, methinks.

"This is a perfect opportunity for you to really shine."

She's still nodding, even more emphatically than a second ago. I fear her head may actually snap right off. I think this is working … Her panic-stricken expression is shifting to one of determination.

Ahh … The young and ambitious, always willing to go forth and give it a go if it means another notch in their belts.

"You're right," she's saying, looking slightly crazed. "Thanks for the opportunity."

"Great, why don't we do a run through?" Getting to my feet and heading to her table, skirt is stuck to bottom, and a waft of coconut odour begins reaching out and spreading across the room like a green gas.

Must have been trapped under bottom. Oh, well!

I take a seat opposite her in an attempt to look as dignified as possible, given the circumstances. There, cosy, next to my intern, ready to further persuade her and instill confidence for meeting. I refuse to attend looking like, and smelling like, this.

"Okay, well I thought I could start with the rich content we're going to produce …"

And suddenly we're disturbed by the sound of someone clearing their throat at the door! Oh, perfect—sarcastic *perfect*, please note! Elsie is leaning against the door frame with a smug smile on her face.

"Yes?" *What do you want?*

"Oh, I was just popping past because I heard through the office grapevine that you'd undergone a bit of a transformation this afternoon … Been on a short trip to Barbados, have we?" She is clearly covering her smile with her hand contritely, despite the derogatory comment.

Are these two stuck at the bloody hip? Surprise, surprise not—to see Jai also now at my door. I haven't seen *him* since our Friday exchange. Glad the pair of them have come together to giggle at my state. They obviously move as a pair, these two little hyenas, sniffing out their prey. *Oh, come on, let's go have a laugh at the little brown girl. The spray tan gone wrong!* Ha! Really, don't they have anything better to do with their day?

"Oh, Elsie," I say quite calmly, considering, "you almost cracked a funny there. So close, but you know humour's not really your thing—One needs to be witty to be humorous, you know?"

It's a bit of a clanger, a clear swipe at her, but honestly, this chick's been chomping at the bit for months, waiting to have a brawl. Not that I'm brawling, I'm not really the brawling type not really. You know, a *word* brawl is really more my thing, than a *brawl* brawl.

Jai and Tina are both laughing, which doesn't help my situation. Oh, here comes the crimson blush from little Elsie. She's turning rather red, beetroot red in fact, and she is looking angry. Oh, dear, sweet Elsie, it would seem I have pushed your buttons? Pressing, and pushing, and loving the result!

"Elsie, you're going a peculiar shade of red. Are you trying to rival my fake tan?" This has welcomed more guffaws of laughter, and a continued reddening of her face.

Silence. She is certainly not a happy camper.

"Did you have anything further you wanted to add, besides the lame Barbados joke? Yes, I've had a fake tan and it's a little bit too brown. What a hoot. You should become a stand-up comedian." Oh, good one, Cee. Now add a crossing of the legs to seal that comment. Very good! I'll just ignore that waft of coconut stench enveloping the office though.

Okay, so I'm going after her, and I'm being a total bitch. So fucking what! One has to look after one's self. My *numero uno* strategy. If someone comes after you, then go straight onto the offensive. Don't let them drag you into the defensive. Lesson well learned from Mother, of all people.

"I hear you have another date with Chad Thompson tomorrow," she's saying to me, snottily.

Has Tina told her? My sidekick betraying me! I'm staring at Tina now, and she is looking way too apologetic, but it's a little too late. *"Again?"* I have to mouth it to her, and all she can do is mouth back, *"I'm sorry …"* Just like Jess spilling it all out with Mother! Can't any fucker in my life keep their mouth zipped? I guess I need to stop verbal diarrhea in Tina's presence, evidently she likes to talk … But wait a second, is it really that bad, after all?

"Yes, I do, Elsie. Really, I don't know why you find my personal life so fascinating. I don't even know your partner's name." I am wearing an expression of disdain on my very brown face. Something else I acquired from my mother.

"Fiancé," she's parroting back quickly.

"Whatever, doll. I don't really care." I'm still calm, unlike her. I'm loving dropping those *dolls* and *babes* left, right, and centre.

Can no longer be bothered to look at her face, which is so red still, so I begin turning away from her—so superior—so taking the upper hand! Conversation logically coming to conclusion! Finished, thank you very much indeed. Time for her to just walk away, tail between her legs … but I know better. Think she is still here—I can sense it. She's a viper; she plays the sweet little bird, but pluck out some of those faux feathers and you'll find some scaly skin. Oh, so rough and hard.

"I was just wanting to tell you … You shouldn't try to change yourself for a man. No matter who he is," she's saying instead, loudly, probably because she is talking to my back now.

Bee-aarch! Now this is getting personal. What the fuck? I really want to resist turning back to her. Too late, looking at her smug face *again!* And she's looking at me like *Let's go to the deuce.*

"Thanks for that sound piece of advice, Elsie …" No longer calm, I'm icy. She's getting the freeze from me as I continue, " … but you know I've only had a fake tan, so maybe you should stop reading into things so much and get on with your own life and your work." Time to show her who really has got the upper hand here. Leaning in closer towards her, I say, "It's just a fake tan, babe." Oh, go on, Cee, give her a smile … and add a raise of an eyebrow. Lovely combination, abso-*bloody*-lutely lovely!

She's just gaping at me now! Oh, go AWAY! She must know that she looks pathetic, like she's investing way too much into some ridiculous analysis of me. Get a life!

"Thanks for stopping by." I'm still smiling as I speak, and it's such a sweet smile, sickly … Feels good! "And thanks for regaling us with your attempted humour, but we've got work to do."

I think I have succeeded in humiliating her ... Yep, pretty sure of it. Off she goes, stalk, stalk stalking away ... Really? Who is this person? First time I've seen her stalk, she must be pissed off!

Oh, and it seems that Jai is still loitering at the door.

"Did you have something to add?" I'm into this mean bitch thing now, and deep, so no point in holding back. Go for it, Cee!

"You know—You didn't have to be so mean to her."

"Me, mean to *her?*" That is a joke. How can he not see that she is a fucking bitch to me? Always appearing, as if by magic, at my office, like she has paid rent or something, and always giving snide comments! He's wrong—massively this time, isn't he? He is! She is the real bitch, and I've bitten my tongue so many times Well, I've had enough of her. "She comes in here all wanting to poke fun at me, and I'm being mean to her?"

"You know what she's like. She's harmless," he's telling me, like he actually believes that.

Harmless, huh! I think not, my friend (and I am being utterly and completely sarcastic with the term *friend* here).

"No, I don't know what she's like because I'm not friends with her. She's like a constant little gnat, annoying me with her commentary." Time to throw my hands up in a gesture of not understanding. It's all I have left!

"Well, take her little obsession as a form of flattery then. She probably wants to be more like you." He's looking his sexy self, all about the loose denim jeans and large t-shirt today. Somehow this man thinks he's untouchable, and always right, doesn't he? DON'T YOU?

Why the hell would she want to be more like me? More late? More single? More living in Kings Cross! More flashing of the underwear to colleagues! She's a completely together person—when I'm, well—I'm not that, I'm me—Cee!

"I don't think it's flattery, Jai." I'm calm now in response, because I'm actually over this ... and Tina and I do have work to do—It's not some random excuse this time!

"Okay then." He's thrown his hands up in a gesture of submission, and he's backing away from the room, out of the door. "See you later."

Good, he's gone. Sexy prick! Prick prick!

Why does Tina always look petrified when I turn my gaze back to her? Am I that scary? People get me so wrong! Sheesh, am I turning into a *crazy*? Potentially? I feel sort of apologetic about the whole thing now! Maybe I did act like a bitch. Should I say something? Fuck!

Oh, I just can't. I'll leave it.

"Let's get started again," I say, forgetting about what just happened! In fact, already forgotten. "So you were going to talk about the content?"

And breathe.

29. 7:00p.m.

Wednesday. Chad is picking me up from apartment. Realise am revealing location of abode in doing so. Slightly run down apartment complex in Potts Point. Yes, indeed a hair's breath away from Kings Cross. Potential turn off? Not sure, but he would have realised it eventually, only so many things one can conceal at a time. You know: general bad character, slovenly behaviour, parents. Those are all I can really handle for the time being.

Considering my appearance in long mirror, alongside Fred. Looking good, methinks. Short sequined skirt, high heels, and winged top—very sophisticated, on-trend, and a little bit sexy, too. Fake tan continues to be ridiculously dark, making blonde hair and whites of eyes stand out in earnest—but perhaps I'm just not used to this new look. Perhaps I've been used to pasty self for too long.

I can't believe I've totally caved. Not only am I sporting a fake tan, but also impractically long acrylic nails in a slightly cliched footballer's girlfriend style. But, am remaining true to self in not having hair extensions, fake breasts or fillers in face. So really, I think the whole thing with Elsie was completely blown out of proportion. *Not changing self for man at all!* These nails are kind of pretty—and really, they no longer look like nails per se—more like odd sort of pretty talons. But they're *du jour*, and everyone is getting them done. It's better to move with the times than be an off-trend, au natural nail woman!

Phone buzzing on bed, I rush over to answer it—all excited about tonight now that I'm ready! Probably Chris or Jess wishing me luck … I need all the luck I can get! Heart pounding already, palms sweating. Shit!

"I'm downstairs. X"

Double shit! It's him. Now I'm seriously nervous. Am thirty-two-year-old woman totally nervous when said man of interest texts!

At the very least, there are no spelling errors in message. Unfortunately, during subsequent flirtatious text exchanges, spelling errors galore have unfolded. But at this point, spelling errors are the least of my concerns.

Focus, Cee.

Have to text back! "Be right down. X"

"Okay, Freddie," I say, patting the little lad on the head, "have a good evening. I'll be home soon."

I just knew he'd jump up on the bed, burying his face into the doona. "Arr, don't give me that sad expression. I'll be back soon!" You know what? He's a Cavoodle—This is his default expression.

Rushing now, *calm down, Cee, deep breaths,* and pulling door closed behind me to head to date …

I'm speeding down the flight of stairs now, clumsily. Oh, might have been those two gin and tonics I had earlier on while getting ready in desperate attempt to buoy spirits and calm nerves. Am not alcoholic! Backing up a fantastic first date is always hard, right? Sometimes said date seems great on the first occasion and then on the second, said date is shit. It's like *Elephant Man* suddenly invades their very person. They're completely different to what you'd remembered, and completely bizzarro—and sometimes they possibly think the same about you. If you ask me, second date is always the hardest. The biggest hurdle! Oh, must not hurtle down last few steps ... Must be sophisticated, demure! Cee-Project engaged!

Whoa, it's hot and clammy out here on the street. Fucking Australian summer, worse still, Sydney city summer. Completely oppressive!

Oh my god. Is that his car? Does he drive a Lamborghini? No, it can't possibly be him. Shit, no—It must be him. No other cars out on the street.

Am currently dating man with Lamborghini. And it's not even in an obnoxious colour. No yellow or orange here, instead a sedate deep red.

Am currently dating man who drives Lamborghini. Who owns Lambor-*fucking*-ghini.

Can't let him see my glee, acting casual, heading towards car as though I get into Lambos all the time. That's it, easy does it!

Need to hold it together. Hold it together, Cee!

Casual Cee, wanting to slide into this beautiful model now, but edging forward for glance in to make sure it's him and not some drug dealer. It's him, *phew*—and looking as handsome and supremely cool as usual.

"Hey, babe," he's saying to me, and I'm sliding low into his

Lamborghini (his Lamborghini for god's sake!)—Wait until Elsie finds out about this!

"Hey, how you doing?" Pleasant, demure, closing the door behind me! In Lamborghini. In Lamborghini. In Lamborghini with *man-of-dreams*. Not sure if mind can compute at this point … CEE! I'm literally screaming inside. Oh, and for some bizarre reason it's my mother's voice right now screaming in my head. *Pull it together! Focus!*

"I'm good." He's leaning across and now he is kissing me, right here, in this Lamborghini.

This is the moment, like in *Pride and Prejudice* where Elizabeth Bennett sees Mr. Darcy's house, the Pemberley Estate, and no matter how much of an ass he is, it's *on* for young and old. And this is *just* his car—Imagine his house, non? And he's not even a stuck-up so-and-so like Mr. Darcy!

"You're looking foxy tonight, Cee. Loving that tan." You are looking rather sexy yourself, driving your Lamborghini, pulling out of the street. Must stop saying Lamborghini, but can not!

He has just shifted his left hand onto my knee. Needing to restrain myself from ripping clothes off again. Composure. Mother was right! Fake tan is a most definite requirement in said situation. Mother and ripping clothes off, two thoughts that should never be uttered in the same realm together—have a fabulous sobering effect on self.

"You look very handsome, as per usual, Mr. Thompson." I'm exuding the usual charm. Feeling très confident right now!

"That's all very *Fifty Shades of Grey* of you," he's saying with a laugh.

Oh shit! Hate that book. Hoping this is not what he's reading or has even read. How can someone have a relationship with someone who actually made it through *Fifty Shades of Grey* from cover to cover without actually turning grey him or herself? Way worse than spelling errors, methinks.

Oh, Christ! And does that mean he has some strange room with whips and other nipple appendages? Shit. Shit. Totally not my thing … Eeek! Best not share my thoughts. Don't want to offend. Stay the sophisticated, fabulous woman that you are, Cee! Do not think about butt plugs!

"Very funny." Good, a safe response, indeed!

"So I'm taking you to this great new restaurant—You'll love it."

"Italian?"

"Of course."

"I'm dreaming of fettuccine right now in a creamy sauce."

"I like where your head's going, babe."

"Or maybe a ragu?"

"I could do a ragu." He's pulling out onto George Street … in the fucking Lamborghini!

"Babe, I'm loving everything about you—except that neighbourhood," he's telling me with a raised eyebrow.

"What about my neighbourhood?" Well, I love plenty about you, including this car, but not your unfortunate taste in literature, or your spelling and grammar errors! But this car—love it!

"I'm surprised you haven't been held-up yet."

"Oh, just a few times."

"Are you joking?"

I think I'll just respond with a nod and raised eyebrow—yes!

"Funny lady." His hand is creeping up my thigh. Oh shit! Might just have orgasm right now. Must save for later. Besides, have fake tan now. Even Mother would approve. Also second date, so no longer sluttish behaviour!

Rule of thumb is three dates, right? But have you seen this guy! Three dates is torture. Besides—I could pretend in my mind, to avoid having self-hating slut feelings, that said first meeting was actually first date. I mean, there was obvious flirting ... not to mention I was knickerless, even though he may not have known. That is kind of date realm, non?

"Seriously, we're busting you out of that place ASAP."

"Whatever you say, Mr. Thompson." Oh, I'm so provocative right now. It's that hand on my thigh, combined with being in this car, and strangely enough, the approval from my mother.

And I've won him over again with my wit and charm, because he is very much laughing—and at the same time has hand on thigh, and is driving his Lamborghini. Love a multi-tasking man!

30. After midnight, methinks. Not quite sure.

Feeling effect of bottle of Chardonnay consumed with fettuccine and being locked in an embrace with Chad. Back in my slummish neighbourhood now, made even more slummish by the fact that we're in my bedroom on unmade bed surrounded by piles of dirty laundry and potentially a few plates with scummish traces of peanut butter or sauce on them. Should have thought about cleaning house instead of having fake tan or acrylics. Wouldn't be here in compromised position, however, without the fake tan.

So not thinking straight right this second as the man is ripping his shirt off—Well, it's more of a very manly unbuttoning—OMG, I might as well die at this very moment, having seen the light. Celestial. He looks like he's been chiseled from stone.

Dating, and about to *sleep* with, incredibly hot man. The type of man who could be paid to take his clothes off.

"Cee." He has startled me from my *vino-pre-sex-Chad-admiration* moment. He's looking at me intently from above—Is that a halo I see circling above his head? Could be another sign that I need to upgrade prescription for glasses or have eyes checked for macular degeneration.

"Cee, you really need to put the dog outside."

What? Possibly the strangest words I've ever heard a man utter pre-coitus.

"What?" Confusion!

"Your dog. *Fred!*"

"What about him?"

"He's staring at us. Look at him." He's just jerked his head in the direction of the corner of the room like there's a spy of some sort sitting there.

It is just Fred—and he is looking at us with that rather sad expression—his usual one.

"He doesn't know what we're doing." Come on stop spoiling the moment! "He's a dog."

"He's staring at us—and it's really putting me off my game."

Don't laugh, Cee! *Note to self:* totally tell Chris and Jess tomorrow. Internalise laughter. Resume composure. Initiate arched back, tense thighs, pointed toes and breezy expression.

Hmm, moment of reflection flooding forth … *I'm really a bad person.* In conclusion, though, I guess it's probably too late to change habits that have been forged over a lifetime.

"I'll put him outside," I say, detangling myself from his musculature.

Semi-naked and grabbing Fred ... He is doing little to resist my endeavours. Shoving Cavoodle outside slummish room ... closing door ... There, easy!

"Better?" I ask, sauntering back towards my god-like chiseled man, waiting for him to re-establish *his game.*

"Much." He's grabbing me by the hand and pulling me on top of him. Whoa, tiger, now that's what I call getting your game on. "I tell you, he was staring with a little demonic expression on his face."

Poor Fred. Demonic would be the last way to describe him. Slow-witted. Potentially a little touched. Epically depressed. *Demonic?* Never!

"An ex gave him to me." I probably shouldn't have said that.

"I knew it!" Chad's voice is emphatic. "Not happy that his dad's been replaced."

Hmm? Not sure if Fred is capable of thinking such complex thoughts.

"Indeed." But I, however, certainly am glad he's been replaced.

He's back to kissing me. Oh dear, it's all rather jerky, a sloppy fashion of kissing, hmm ... Best to ignore it, methinks, given sight of abdominal muscles.

Is that scratching at the door? It's faint, but definitely scratching—Fucking Fred.

Ignore! Ignore! Ignore! Think abs, think muscles, think halo!

31. 9:30a.m.

Epically late for work. Epically late for mid-week WIP with Ian and the rest of the account directors and creative ... again! Usually would be in state of paranoia, running for bus like crazy person, running down street like crazy person, running—a lot like crazy person. Would have thoughts running through mind of being exposed as slovenly, idiotic type who has gotten through all these years based on her wit and charm, only to be unceremoniously fired. Would have mental images of me carrying crates with possessions out of office while Elsie and Jai watch on with smug little smiles on their faces, already thinking about who's going to take over my digs. But not today ...

Instead, despite extreme lateness, supreme calm has descended. How could it not have?

Am sitting in Lamborghini, being driven to work by celebrity ex-footballer boyfriend after having shagged him on a number of occasions last night. Feel like I'm part of some sort of elaborate mirage, and having sporadic moments of realisation. *Hang on, it's all real!*

Post-coitus feeling of love, rainbows and sunshine are all about me. Am thinking of a spring wedding. I'll definitely be wearing Steven Khalil, of course! *Note to self:* start looking through his portfolio of work today to consider dress styles that may suit me.

Plucking mobile out of bag and furtively texting Jess and Chris:

"Oh my gawd. Had wild night of sex with Chad last night and am currently sitting in his—wait for it … Lamborghini, being chauffeured to work!"

Must add a series of smiley faces. I can't scream through the text, hopefully this will give same effect.

"Who are you texting, babe?" he's asking all dreamy and boyfriend-like, putting his hand on my knee and steering car onto work street now. I really want to squeal with excitement. Composure, Cee, that's what got you here and that's what'll keep you here … Composure. Focus.

"Oh, just colleagues." I'm oozing airiness, sharing my prettiest smile. "Letting them know I'm running late."

"You're such a hard worker, babe." He's just winked that sexy wink again.

Hmm?

Phone buzzing at me, I look down at text quickly—It's Chris.

"You're such a fucking bitch. Stop sending me these gloaty texts. Don't you remember what happened to me on the weekend? Am deeply depressed and damaged. BTW, are we still on for lunch?"

"Yes," I text back. "Did I mention I'm getting dropped off in Lamborghini?" I shall, of course in this very case, gloat some more.

Staring out of window at passersby and feeling pretty damn erratically, impossibly, blissfully happy.

Phone buzzing again. Chris. Not sure how he manages to text so quickly.

"If there was a rude finger emoticon, I would be giving it to you right now."

Pulling up outside work building in said Lamborghini, and I can see hipster colleagues hanging about out the front, lattes in hand, sunglasses on, jeans rolled up. Well, suck on this, *hipsters*. Last week I was flashing my underwear, yes I'm fully aware, but this week I'm getting out of a Lamborghini. You don't get flashier than that!

You never know when your luck is going to change. And I feel like I'm certainly on the up, uP, UP!

"Okay, babe, have a good day." How sweet!

No awkwardness! It's all so ordinary and natural. Bizarre—like we've slipped directly into something that works. Shit! I can't believe it. A relationship that could potentially work? Not in my realm of expertise whatsoever. I'm just going with it!

"You, too," I say, grabbing my bag.

"See you on Friday." He's leaning across and brushing my mouth with a kiss. "Pick you up at eight."

"Sure, watch out though. I wouldn't want you to get mugged or anything."

"Silly lady," he's laughing.

Think I shall slide out of the car—sophistication is key here, closing door with a resounding thud behind me. Is it just *moi*, or do Lamborghini doors make a specific sound? Very Lamborghini-esque!

Sigh. So content. Oh, how perfect, ha! There's Jai amongst all the hipsters. Surprise surprise. He's giving me what appears to be a filthy look of thunderclap.

"Hi, Jai," I say, sharing a brilliant smile and very much floating through doors. Am magnanimous today, and I'm sure even the likes of Jai Rodden will feel the far-reaching benefits of my zen.

"Hey." He's following me in through the doors.

How does this always happen? Does he know by telepathy that I'm going to be late and rushes outside to catch me in the act? Almost like he's reading my mind ... "You're late," he says, stating the obvious as we're getting into the lift.

"Thanks for pointing that out, Jai. Didn't realise you were keeping tabs on me."

"I'm not." He's shoving his hands into his pockets in an uncomfortable, angry manner. Sheesh. The guy really needs to lighten up. Needs some zen, probably needs a good shag!

Silence. He's staring ahead. Awkward. Evidently, he's not a happy camper. Not sure if my lateness has somehow contributed to his mood. Why would it though?

He's pissing me off now, too, with all this negative energy, his aura very much pushing into my happy space and crowding it out.

Can't wait to get out of the lift. Finally the door is pinging open— Hurry up door! I'm going with the obvious *push past him* today. He's still not speaking, but following me down the corridor to the executive room. An angry, dark shadow—I can feel his energy still, and hear his shuffling steps.

Opening the door to the meeting room ... Breathe, Cee.

Ian's mid-sentence, but has stopped. Oh no! Now he's looking at the both of us, like we're school kids late for class again!

"So nice of you to join us, Cee, Jai."

"Morning!" I say, so bright and breezy. Jai is heading to a seat and has not responded.

"I would draw attention to your continued lateness, Cecilia, and conscious flouting of the rules, but given you seem to be the flavour of the month, and have just brought in two new accounts, I won't."

"Thank you, Ian." I'm so polite, acutely aware that he's done the very thing that he indicated he wouldn't.

"As per usual, you're welcome, Cee." He's now moving on to another victim.

And I'm having moment of meditative thought. Perhaps effect of Swami influence, or of advancing age. Or because I've been shagged into this state of absolute oneness. Can't be sure, but this feeling was not here yesterday before shag-a-thon.

Besides, Ian's right. I am the flavour of the month. Somehow the odds are in my favour, and I need to stay here … Flavour of the year, making every colleague's mouth water with bitterness, but yet longing for a taste of me and all of my Cee-ness.

It's like a seesaw, isn't it? I may as well just personalise that to Cee-saw, after all, it is my world … and sometimes one's up, and sometimes one's down. Up and down, down and up! And somehow, quite unexpectedly, and for no discernible reason, said seesaw has swung up for Cee.

Happiness is a strange thing. As soon as you realise you have it, you suddenly become afraid of losing it. Oh, shite, sensing fear beginning to drown my glee. Must remain UP here … Suspended in the up!

32. 11:00a.m. Late March

t mall. Terribly tacky formal dress store with Mother and Char—trying on bridesmaids dresses. Mother, in all her wisdom, has decided the colour for this wedding will be burgundy, and hence all related details are to be in this particularly repugnant hue. As a result, we are scouring Sydney city and the wider NSW state to find appropriate bridesmaids dresses in said putrid colour.

Char and I are standing in front of a large mirror wearing identical burgundy silk taffeta numbers. They're spaghetti-strapped in an unflattering a-line cut, which makes us both look like strange, dark red triangles.

Despite our age difference, an odd thirty or so years, Mother is insisting she wants Char and I to wear the same dress because that's what bridesmaids do, and she doesn't want some ridiculously mismatched wedding, open quote close quote.

The result being this—Char and I looking outlandishly ludicrous in everything we try on. It was a struggle pulling the darn ugly thing on in the change room, pushing and pulling straps and taffeta and silk this way and that. We finally waddled out just moments ago together, the odd pair, and well … I want to die!

We are standing now in front of the obligatory mirror. *Alarm* is the only way I can describe the looks on our faces. Utter alarm. Both staring back through the looking glass, reflections big and red.

"Well, what's wrong with this one, ladies?" Mother is being as demanding as ever, speaking with a superior booming voice from behind us, but I can tell she's flustered. "It looks great!"

I'm shooting her a look through the mirror. "You ARE joking, right?" She must be! "We look like Mary Poppins. Mary *bloody* Poppins after she's been cloned thirty years apart, like, like … we might take off into the sky at any moment!"

"Why would you say that? It's a very flattering cut on both of you," Mother is continuing, despite my outburst.

Char isn't saying anything because, of course, she's worried about offending Mother and then incurring her wrath at a later stage, but the look of pure panic on her face is saying it all.

"I wouldn't call this a flattering cut, Mother. We look like slutty nuns."

"Oh, don't be absurd, Cecilia. This is what bridesmaids dresses look like. And besides, let's face it, neither of you are Miranda Kerr. Dresses aren't going to fit you perfectly all the time."

I'm turning around and delivering my death stare—because it is clearly being weakened through the mirror—and she's getting it pure and dark …

There, it is saying *Fuck right off with your comments, and awful fashion sense!*

"That's very rude," I think is a better option. "I'm your daughter and that's your best friend. You should be telling us we *do* look like Miranda Kerr."

"Oh, don't be dramatic, Cee. One needs to be realistic." She is letting out an enormous sigh, like I'm the one being unreasonable.

Confidence crushed. Reluctantly turning back to my reflection. Miranda Kerr isn't that great, is she? Who am I kidding!

"Look Char, I'm sure we can get you a stole or something to cover up your arms. I know you're not comfortable having them out and flapping about," Mother is continuing on …

Oh God. It's a wonder how the poor woman hasn't topped herself yet, what with Mother's constant positive reinforcement and all.

"Where's that sales assistant?" Mother's looking annoyed. "I'm sure they'll have a stole in that exact colour. Where's that little girl? You would think they would be a little more responsive, given the amount of money you have to pay for these dresses—You over there! Yes, you!" she is yelling loudly, gesturing violently at the sales assistant to come our way.

The girl, who is talking to another customer, turns a crimson colour similar to our dresses.

"You, come on, girlie. We don't have all day!" Mother is still going on, like she is royalty.

Feeling deeply mortified, hoping the ground will spontaneously just open up so I can drop into it—right now! It's so mortifying that I'm associated with this display, with this beast of a woman. Oh no, poor girl, she's now looking like she might just cry, but, no, somehow, just like everyone else Mother talks to, she is listening, and scurrying towards us.

"Mother, you can't talk to her like that." Sometimes I have to intervene, and it's coming out as a hiss.

"Of course I bloody well can," she's saying to me. Clearly the bridesmaid dress shopping is taking its toll. "She's here to help us—She needs to help!"

The girl is standing near us now, and she must have caught the tail end of our discussion. Her face is looking pinched and strained, but I suppose she must be used to dealing with psychotic brides. Mother certainly adds another layer to the term *bridezilla* though.

"Do you have a stole in this colour and fabric?" she's asking the girl with a tone which is implying *Let's go to the deuce*. It's one of Mother's favourites.

"A stole?" the girl has just mumbled, not really looking at Mother.

Oh no. She's opening herself up for a blast. The girl's going to need counseling after what's to come.

"Yes, my dear. You do know what a stole is, don't you?"

Oh shit for her, because it's clear she doesn't know, but also probably doesn't want to answer in the negative to Mother. She is opting for a semi-nod, semi-shake of the head.

"It's a fucking shawl, girl."

Whoa! The f-bomb at 11:00 a.m. in a bridal store, to a girl who is probably about seventeen years old and being paid thirteen dollars an hour.

"You know, the ones you put around your shoulders?" Mother is gesticulating like a mad person now.

The girl is barely managing a nod this time.

"So! Do you have it?"

The girl is looking from the dresses and back to Mother. From the dress to Mother. From the dress to Mother.

"So?" Mother is cracking the whip, spinning her out of her crazed ping-pong dress-mother stare-off.

"Yes, I think we do. In the back. I'll … Erm, I'll just go and check," she's stuttering, not surprising really, and now she's pushing past us towards the back room, closing the door behind her—Probably to source an escape route out of here, possibly to hide, most definitely to cry!

"You know she's probably gone in there to cry," I say. Mother needs to know sometimes how nasty she can be to people.

"Frankly, I don't care if she has. She does need to do her job, Cecilia. And you know, how does one not know what a stole is and work in a formal wear store? How do they hire these girls? In my day, not only would she have known what a stole was, but she would have been able to rattle off the fabrics they came in, the stitches, and where they were made. The standard is dropping!" She's tapping her foot self-righteously on the ground.

I think Char might cry, too.

"Well, it's not the *good old days* anymore, Mother, and you just can't go around treating people like that!" I'm hissing now, because the girl's emerging.

And she is looking suitably alarmed, but there's no evidence of any tears or wailing. Interesting. Tougher than she looks, so it seems. She's carrying two stoles, both in the colour Mother's after. Yuck! They are positively hideous.

She's standing in front of us, scarecrow-like, holding out the two stoles to Mother like some sort of peace offering. Strangely Jesus-Christ-on-cross-esque, too.

"I have two of them," she's mumbling, "Which would you prefer?"

Mother is staring at her like she's just told her she has *ebola*, and it's highly contagious.

"Well, why don't you put them on her, girlie, and see which one works better?"

Oh dear God, could this day get any worse?

The girl is walking towards Char like a zombie. She now slowly, and awkwardly, pops one over her shoulders. Char is frozen, as though she knows if she sympathises with the girl it won't bode well with Mother.

Char is clinging onto the first stole and lets Mother assess her. The fabric is strange and sticks out in all directions, like it's been wet, and then left in the sun for too long to dry.

"I don't mind that one, Char." Mother's face softens slightly. "What do you think?"

Char has just gulped. Will she answer? She is looking panicked. "Well, it's rather nice, isn't?" Her voice is prim, submissive.

"Okay. Well, girlie, why don't you pop the second one on?" Mother is commanding imperiously.

The girl is heading over and exchanging the first shawl with the second, a strangely spongy thing, which droops around Char unflatteringly. I hate both of them; they are simply awful!

"I do prefer the first one, Char," Mother is cooing, almost smiling now.

"Yes, indeed, so do I." I think that must have been the sound of Char's teeth rattling as she agreed. Why is she even friends with Mother?

"What do you think, Cee?" Great, now I have to answer Mother's questioning.

"You know what I think, Mother?" I say, being the only one capable to actually voice a negative opinion here. "The dresses look shit, we look shit, and the stole looks like shit. We look like burgundy heaps of shit!"

Oh no, she's doing that staring thing—pursed mouthed, too. She is silent though, so my rant may just have worked … Oh wait, she is turning back to the girl. "We'll take them. The two dresses and the first stole Char tried on."

Wait, there's more … "Did you want a stole, darling?" she says, looking at me in earnest as though she hasn't been completely demonic for the last two hours or so.

"No, Mother, the dress is enough for me." *Phew*, well at least that's a relief, and less burgundy covering I'll have to deal with on her big day.

"Wonderful. Oh, great, ladies! We have the dresses!" Mother is cooing again, and her double personality has been released. The girl is scurrying off to the counter as though her salvation awaits her there.

"Fabulous, isn't it?" I'm being so ironic as I head back to the change room. Char does the same, hanging her head low. I'm suspecting she's ashamed.

Tugging this thing called a dress over my head crossly. What does she want now? Mother's country twang is echoing through to me, through the velvet blind that is separating my nakedness from the store.

"So, darling, you haven't forgotten about lunch tomorrow, right?" Her voice is sounding slightly hysterical.

"Fuck," I whisper to myself, still trying to get out of this god awful fabric.

"What?" How could she have heard that? It's not humanely possible!

"Nothing, Mother." But I actually said FUCK!

"So just confirming, you and Chad will be at my place at around one'ish tomorrow?" she is continuing on.

Fuckity, fuck, fuck, fuck. How does one get one's self out of this? Kind of starting to feel like a dose of the ebola virus would actually be of use at this very moment. I have somehow managed to separate Chad from my familial situation for the past seven wonderful, awesome weeks of dating. But the date of their first encontre is closing in on me. Ready to suffocate and finding it hard to breathe at the thought. I think I need an asthma pump for tomorrow—the set date of complete apocalyptic destruction.

Mother has been planning this for weeks. Quite literally. She virtually held me down and wrote said date in my diary. And of course I've known it's coming, looming over my shoulder like some ominous juggernaut of doom … Utter fucking DOOM! And really, I've just been ignoring it, hoping that I'd be struck down by some random, unknown virus and forced to spend the night and subsequent week in hospital …

Or at the very least that Chad and I would have split up before arrival of said date. Not that I have been hoping at all *that* would happen, but I would prefer a natural conclusion rather than a crazy intervention from Mother.

But that day, nonetheless, is coming. Hard and fast. Someone help *moi!* Now! Please, I beg of thee!

"Cee, are you still in there?" I hear Mother's squawking voice in the background.

"Yes, Mother."

"So, you're still coming, right? You know I have everything teed-up. I even bought a bloody tent for the garden."

"A tent?"

"Oh, you know what I mean, one of those canapé things, all lovely and draped. Brad's going to move the outdoor table there. It'll be all fabulous and *Real Housewives of Orange County* like," she's telling me, and I'm shuddering at the thought. A canapé? She means a canopy surely? Gazebo, perhaps?

"We don't live in Orange County." I'm stalling.

"No, we don't. But it does look that way. I've been planning the menu for weeks, and Brad has been organising the alcohol for longer."

Yanking jeans up, taking frustration out on denim, was that a ripping sound? Hoping not!

"You know Brad absolutely adores him, don't you? Thinks he's an uber-celebrity."

"When did you start saying *uber?*"

"Oh, you know, darling, I'm going with the times now that my daughter is dating a local celebrity."

"Indeed," I say, pulling the curtain of the change room open and coming face-to-face with her winning smile and handing her the dress with a look of disgust.

"So?"

"Of course," I tell her, wishing I *was* in Orange County so I could carry a gun on a daily basis—just for preventative reasons against Mother, mainly. "Didn't I agree to it weeks ago?" I say, stalking towards the counter.

"You did, darling. But, of course, I was a little concerned—Somehow I pick up a vibe that you might be ashamed of introducing your wonderful mother and Brad to your new beau."

Beau! Really? Who is this woman?

Of course I'm ashamed! I feel like screaming at her. Not only am I ashamed, but I'm also worried that he might leave me because you're a complete lunatic, and he might incorrectly assume *like mother like daughter.* Shit!

"Don't be ridiculous, Mother. I just wanted to make sure we were serious before I introduced him to you," I say, fake smile spilling out on face.

"I'm glad you say that, because I was getting a little concerned."

Char is tottering out, avoiding eye contact with the both of us. Mother has snatched the garments away from her grasp and is placing them on the counter.

"Now, are you going to just throw them in the bag or fold them correctly?" Mother is so demanding of this poor girl.

Why would I be ashamed of you, Mother? You're just completely CRAZY! She has psychic, crazy woman powers, and I bet she's heard my inner monologue screaming at her, cursing her. Why else would she be looking at me now so sickly sweet?

"I'm so looking forward to it, darling." She's patting my hand with one of her talons. "And I'm glad you are, too. You should never forget where you came from, dear!" Is there a veiled warning in there, too?

"Never, Mother. Don't be absurd," I say, smiling through clenched teeth.

The girl behind the counter is looking like she may vomit from terror. At least you can when we leave! At least you don't have to endure this woman for the rest of your life, including tomorrow under the new garden tent with Brad and Chad ... Oh god, it even sounds like a disaster waiting to happen!

33. 7:30p.m.

vening before total annihilation of universe, world, and of course, relationship with Chad (i.e. as result of lunch with Mother). Have drunk all alcohol in the house. How is that possible? That includes bottle of Zibbobo, half bottle of gin, and one-quarter Campari. How did that disappear? Not quite sure, desperation has set in massive time.

How is it that all *said* alcohol has now gone, yet I'm still semi-sober? Hmm? But one can't usually tell when one is trashed. In fact, one thinks they're semi-sober until they're … Well, until they are not at all sober on any scale.

"Fred, stop staring at me, looking all alarmed and such."

Must ensure illness strikes tomorrow. And this level of booze is likely to aid that desired effect, non?

Picking up mobile and dialing trusty friend, Jess. Lots of ringing!

Methinks she may be waiting for the call to go to answering machine.

"What?" she answers.

"I need your ha-elpppp!" Slightly slurry, good sign.

"What with?"

"Need to come up with a plan.

"For what? Are you drunk or high?"

"Drunk! I wish I was high."

"You and me both, sister." She's chewing again; at least I think she is.

"Need to stop meeting of Chad, Mother and other weird relations tomorrow," I tell her, leaning on counter for support.

"Oh yeah, totally understand. But you know, Cee, it can't be helped— He will need to meet your mother at some point." This is very irritating logic that she is sharing with *moi*. I dislike a lot, a very a lot!

Aren't friends supposed to help? Supposed to fuel delusional rants?

"Yes—but you've met her ..." I say, trailing off. Sentence gone, unfinished, vision blurry, thin air in front of face looking like obscure pretty flowers.

"Of course, she's beyond nuts. No questions asked. But I guess she has some sort of allure." More chewing. Yep, knew it! Chew, chew, chew away!

"Allure?"

"Yes, allure. It's very arrogant, and a little bit charming. Sort of like her daughter." Did she really just place that comparison out there in the world, and what is this I hear through her chewing? Muffle of a giggle!

"Do NOT compare me to *that* woman," I'm growling now.

"Oh, calm down! She *is* your mother." More laughing. It's like the laughing is more important than the chewing now.

"It's all circumstantial … I have no proof of that."

"Listen, he has to meet your mother eventually. Just do it already. If he loves you, he has to love your mother, right?"

"Wrong! Where did that twisted logic come from?"

"Hmm …" And the munching has returned in full force, and louder.

"Listen, how about some Tex Mex and tequilas?" Yes, get her weakness. Ahh! The spicy flavours of the Cajun world! How can she refuse me?

"I've already eaten dinner."

"When has that stopped you before?" Besides, you are still bloody eating, I can hear you!

"Why do you want to take me to Tex Mex?" She's suspicious.

"Hoping for crazy food poisoning and visit to St Vincent's, or at the very least major indigestion, which will keep me in bed tomorrow, under guise as something more serious!"

"Major indigestion … Sort of sounds like a plan."

"Great!" Spirits are soaring! Am still in business. Attitude for destruction is ripe!

"Okay, I've been dying to try Texmetwo in Newtown." Her excitement is palpable.

"Texmetwo—sounds sort of naff." The naffer, the better. More likelihood of food poisoning!

"Oh, listen here, sweetheart … This is your plan we're executing. We're going to Texmetwo." Munching has stopped. Thankfully.

"O-kay," she's saying super slowly.

"See you in fifteen?"

"Done, doll face."

34. 7:50p.m.

*I*n car with Jess heading towards Newtown and Tex Mex restaurant. *Feeling slightly woozy, like things might be spinning around me. Perhaps more drunk than initially thought, so not semi-sober it seems. But I often find it comes on at a later stage, non? Like half an hour delayed reaction. However, if one continues to drink, then delayed reaction does not occur—until one stops. Then reactions are really not there at all, delayed or otherwise. Should have brought beverage along in car, although thinking that may well be illegal. Not quite sure because don't have car and hence have never needed to consider previously …*

"Cee, Cee, Cee." Name being called on several occasions, snapping me to attention.

"Pardon?" Regal English manner, of course!

"You weren't listening, were you?" she's now asking me.

"No, I wasn't," I respond, evidently too drunk to think about consequences of words. "I was thinking I should have brought a bevvy for the ride."

"Hmm? Maybe not! I think you've had quite a few this evening."

"Indeed," I say, my head flopping to the side in weird erratic manner.

"So, I was saying that Pete and his new squeeze appear to be in *Splitsville.*"

"Oh, really? Is that because you two slept together?" I ask, sans tone. Have no tone at this point, not even monotone, only drunken tone.

"No, she doesn't know about that ... I just think they're poorly suited—and she's a complete and utter idiot. Blonde, young thing that doesn't have a rational thought in her mind."

"Sounds a bit like me at this very moment," I say, slurring, stuttering, and not yet, but maybe soon-to-be spluttering.

"You're not young."

"Excuse me?" I ask her, slapping a hand down on my knee clumsily. "Thirty-two is youngish. What do they say these days, thirty is the new twenty?" Oh dear, do very much sound like Mother now.

"I don't know who says that. Nobody I know. Definitely not my gynecologist, who told me that one's capacity to conceive starts heading downhill after twenty-seven. Something about less eggs—I think it's because one starts rapidly moving towards—well, death," she's finished off resoundingly.

"Indeed—I think you've told me that before. All very morbid," is all I'm managing to say, despite being on rapid descent to death at this very moment according to *Jess's gyno*.

"Are you happy that they're splitting up?" Random question maybe, but it's come out anyway.

"You know, I'm not sure."

"What does that mean? You can only be happy or not happy, non?"

"Well, I guess I would be happy if it makes him unhappy. You know, if he's sobbing into a bowl of ice cream every evening, and having pangs of guilt about leaving me, and thinking where his life is heading now that's he's all alone … Yes, that would make me happy!"

"That makes sense." This woman's flawed logic is sounding completely rational. "One does want their ex to be lonely and unhappy, while one is living it up. That's ideal."

"But I'm not happy in the sense that it puts him back on the market," she is continuing. "You know, he's out there now. Before, he was taken and I couldn't consider him as a prospective mate anymore—but now—now it's harder to do that."

"You can't be serious!" I say, raising an eyebrow. "The man completely demolished your confidence and sense of self. Left you after nearly ten years because it wasn't fun anymore. You cannot possibly be thinking you would pursue that path again."

She isn't responding. Just staring ahead. And I know she's considering it, because she's not willing to confirm or deny the accusation.

"Sheesh, Jess, you have a real *appetite for destruction*."

"I have an *appetite for destruction*? Look at you! You're going on a bender because you need to introduce your new, may I add perfect, rich, hot, boyfriend to your mother. If that's not destruction, then I don't know what is." She's shaking her head as she is speaking.

"I don't think the two things are comparable."

We're on to King Street now, hipster and douche bag central on a Saturday night. Drunken state must be wearing off because I'm now realising I've been talked into coming here—where everyone is wearing double denim (because it's back in style) and mustard coloured pants. Oh god! What have I done! I've sold my soul for a taco and potential food poisoning.

"You know they are comparable!"

"You know what—whatever—I have a real hankering for a Guns N' Roses tune … Do you have anything from *Appetite for Destruction* on your iPhone?"

"No, I don't—Where did that come from? Are you changing the subject?"

"No, I was just distracted by the notion of an appetite for destruction. Weren't you?"

She is shaking her head. "Axl Rose was never really my thing."

"How could you say that!?" Totally startled from my hipster reverie. Completely aghast by her unceremoniously discarding of Axl Rose. "I adored him!"

"You adored him? Hardly seems like your type."

"Well, he was when I was a teenager—I do remember thinking I was going to marry him," I say.

"That didn't work out for you," she has pointed out, trying to parallel park at the same time as talking. Cars whiz past us aggressively as she is trying to manoeuvre this tiny car into that equally tiny space. Suddenly very concerned for life, wanting food poisoning or something that will make me notionally sick. Not wanting car accident at all.

"No, indeed it didn't. Not to mention Axl Rose got fat," I say, noticing the line outside the restaurant we're planning on eating at. Why must one line up to eat? Is this the new craze? You can only eat if your name is on the list—and if it's on the list, it looks like you don't eat at all.

"He did get fat," Jess has acknowledged.

"Like morbidly obese!"

"Maybe not morbidly. But, you know, at the very least—porky."

Sigh. Successful parallel parking on eighth attempt! Great going, Jess. At least she hasn't killed us, I guess!

"Porky, indeed—But, you know, I would have loved him anyway," I say, scrambling out of the car rather inelegantly … Not same as Lamborghini exit.

"You would not," Jess is laughing.

"The depths of my love for Axl Rose are unknown to you," I say, joining the back of the queue for the restaurant.

I can only imagine.

35. 10:30p·m·

estaurant with Jess. Post-mammoth meal. Surrounded by lots of Mexican skulls, which are peering out in the otherwise darkness in a curious manner. Like friendly skulls, really! Smiling skulls. Could be the effect of the Mojitos ingested or psychedelic chilli-con-carne, which wasn't really psychedelic (in the traditional sense of the word) but nonetheless absolutely awesome. A bit concerned about all the beans I've virtually inhaled and after-effects that could potentially occur tomorrow. Trying to remove gruesome thought from mind as Jess and I consider the dessert menu.

"I'm really feeling like something with *dulce de leche* in it."

"Arghh," she's groaning. "Dulce de leche. Totally to die for! If I was told tomorrow that I could either look like Gisele Bundchen, and I mean instantaneously, or have *dulce de leche,* I would go with *dulce de leche.*"

"I would go with Bundchen." I'm serious, who wouldn't—is she joking?

Stuff that fucking dulce de leche. Have you seen Bundchen's tits?

"Noooooo," she is crying out tres-dramatically, face scrunching up into a look of disbelief. Yep, there it is, and it is apparent that she would undoubtedly opt for the dulce de leche.

"Yeah, I would."

"But you already have a great figure."

"Not like Gisele Bundchen's."

She has concurred with a sad nodding of her head. "But great nonetheless, perpetually slim, despite the ongoing inhalation of food like a vacuum."

"Hmm, agreed. But I've been paranoid for months about my breasts."

"Your breasts?"

"Of course, my breasts! Whose breasts would I be otherwise paranoid about?"

"Is this following that bizarre encounter with your mother and the invitations?" She's cocking an eyebrow with an *Inspector Gadget* expression.

"You're onto it. I have been totally paranoid in front of Chad ever since … And, indeed, anyone else!" I'm going to have the classic alfajor cookies: two shortbread-like cookies sandwiching dulce de leche in the middle … Salivating quietly.

"Who else have you been showing your breasts to?"

"Just the spray tanner—She has two massive watermelon breasts. I'm sure she silently judges me for being flat-chested."

"You've had a lot of spray tans of late," she's saying, regarding me closely.

"So what? I like how they look on me. The tanned look is certainly more flattering than the *sickly pale/may have terminal illness* look."

292

"Hmm ... " She is frowning, looking down at her menu. The aura of repressed comments, I can tell when that one's around ... Well I demand to know what her *hmm* means.

"What?"

"Nothing," she says, closing her menu with a snap.

"No, come on. What were you going to say?"

She has let out a sigh. "Just as long as all the spray tans aren't for Chad."

"Why would they be for Chad?" Taking on the inquisitive impetus of my mother, are we, Jess?

"It's just ... There have been a few subtle changes about you as of late."

"Changes? Subtle?"

"Yes," she says, indignant.

"Like what?"

"Well, the spray tan for example, the nails, the outfits—decidedly more stylish and put together. I mean I haven't seen the sweats out for months—and you're always wearing heels now. I never see you in flats!" She is crying out again, as though the kitten heel is complete rubbish and a total sin.

"So I look a little more flash than usual. So what?" Okay, so I've made some minor amendments. What's so bad about that? Striving to look one's best can't be that terrible, can it?

"Nothing wrong with it," she's saying, and I'm thinking: *Make up your damn mind, woman!* "Just making sure you're not changing too much for him."

"Don't be ridiculous," I'm laughing, trying to put that hair extension appointment I've made for mid-next week out of my mind ... I know I vowed it would not happen, but I want to look my best for Chad, and for me, too! "I'm not changing at all for him—I'm just … looking after myself." Am I trying to convince myself, too?

"Okay." She's throwing her hands up. "If that's what it is, I'm all for it."

The waitress has turned up in her traditional South American garb. Why does she look so pissed off? Are the *staffed* always pissed off? Is it normal to be pissed off in the hospitality industry? Does one need the pissed off expression to be serving food at a hip, too cool restaurant?

"I'll have the classic alfajor cookies," I tell her, smiling primly. She hasn't responded, but just jots down the order. Oh no, I got some kind of a look there … Hmm … What does it say exactly? It's sort of a bit of a fuck you expression. Like she might spit on my food before she serves it. Now we're paying for overpriced food, with hepatitis on it. Oh, what joy! Not that she's the type to have hepatitis, maybe she is, one could never really know.

"Can I get the chocolate sheet cake with dulce de leche frosting?" Jess is asking.

The girl has turned to head away, and I've just remembered I also want …

"Oh, can I have two Disaronnos, too, please?" She has turned back quite swiftly, and that withering look is telling me that she might just directly spit on me now, rather than the food. I'm waiting for a response, but nothing … She is writing down the order at least.

"I've drunk too much, babe," Jess is telling me now that *senorita grumpy* is stalking off. "I can't have that Disaronno."

"No worries, babe," I tell her, using her term of endearment loosely. It's natural after all these weeks of practice. "I'll have it."

"Why am I not surprised," she's saying slightly under her breath. I hear you, Jess—Judging again, are we? *Judge Jess*, are we now?

"Hey, what do you make of those ridiculous South American national dress uniforms they're wearing? It's all a bit colonialistic for my taste. A bit conquistador—You know, if they were wearing Brazilian samba outfits with the sequined bras and g-strings and headdresses, I think I'd prefer it much better!"

"I slept with Pete!" Jess has suddenly interjected randomly, interrupting my Brazilian samba outfit chain of thought. Selfish, judging Jess …

"I slept with Pete!" she is snapping at me again like a crazed marionette.

What? What the fuck is she talking about?

"I slept with Pete!" she's repeating for the third time, crazed expression on her face.

"Okay …" I'm grabbing her hand with mine, trying to calm her down before she goes into some endless "I slept with Pete!" (lots of exclamation points) mantra at the top of her lungs for the rest of the evening! Christ! We're not even close to St. Vincent's!

"I heard you the first time!" And the third, and the many more!

"So?" She is wearing this super alarmed look on her face. "Aren't you going to say something?"

"You've already told me this before …" I say, just in case the alcohol has given her amnesia. Is she having a stroke? " … at Mother's house … In fact, you told me in a similar fashion—like you had Tourettes syndrome."

"No."

"No what?" She really is having a stroke.

"No." Again—she has seriously lost it. Glad she turned down the Disaronno before it becomes too messy.

"No what? What are you talking about?"

"That's not the time I'm talking about—I mean I've slept with him again." She is looking pinched and white in the face, as though acknowledging it out loud to me is like acknowledging if for real to herself.

"You slept with him again?" Cannot believe it! Is this not the man who shattered all her dreams, including those of having a baby, ran off with someone else, and then was at least responsible for twenty kilos of weight gain (the rest I suspect might be of her own making)? Is she crazed?

Hang on! Trying to recall conversation in the car. All I'm getting is Axl Rose, but I'm sure there was something else about Pete breaking up with his new squeeze, and then, shit, can't remember. Axl Rose—I would *still* do him, even though I know he's porky. I'm sure he would be amazing in bed. You can just tell these things, especially given the number of women he's shagged. And now, being a fatty patty, he would need to work harder for it.

It's always like that—The good-looking ones are always terrible shags, because they've never had to work for it.

Oh, shit! What does that say about Chad? What am I admitting to here in drunken state?

"Hang on," I say, snapping myself out of reverie before any too frightening revelations are made. Back to Jess and Pete. "Start again, I zoned out."

"Really, Cee?"

"Sorry, I was thinking about Axl Rose." Sheepish look is a must so she doesn't swing for me.

"Oh fuck, not this Axl Rose thing again? You know his name is an anagram for *oral sex?*" she's telling me pointedly, as if this should be a deal breaker for my Axl Rose fetish.

"Indeed, I do. Always fascinated me as a teenager. After all, does he like giving or receiving?" Both, I would imagine. Oh great! The Disaronnos have arrived, and waitress is looking predictably disturbed. I, myself, am rather excited! Spirits have come just in time! Hurrah!

"Could you save the giving and receiving dialogues for your catch-ups with Chris?"

"Sure." Chris will love it. "Okay, back to the sex with Pete. You had sex with him again?"

Am matter-of-fact, after all am sipping Disaronno, and one must speak matter-of-factly when they're sipping Disaronno. It is a rule I have just made up, and it's a good one, isn't it?

"I did—a few times," she says, sheepish look on her face.

"A few times!" Okay, so Disaronno sophistication is completely trashed. Blaming Pete utterly for this sacrilege.

"A few times." She's shrugging her shoulders. "Maybe more than a few times—it's probably in the teens."

I'm staring at her open-mouthed, unable to compute. Unable to speak!

The desserts have arrived. Waitress has just set them down, no interaction, and is now stalking off.

"Say something, or I'll stuff one of those cookies in there." Jess is looking like she might cry.

"F- f- f- for once, *I'm* lost for words."

"Don't say that!" She's putting her head in hands, as though nothing could be worse. And, indeed, it must be a shocking revelation if I'm lost for words.

"I ... I ... I ... " Shit! I really am lost for words!

"We have just been fucking." She's throwing the word around loosely. It just smacked me in the head like a boomerang and is now rebounding off. "On and off."

Apparently like her fucking Pete. Boomerang.

"It just started … I don't know, maybe a few weeks ago. He came over to collect some more of his stuff and then it happened. Boom! Totally unexpected again."

My mouth is still open in sheer horror … I must speak; find words, Cee, any words!

"His penis just fell into your vagina again," I say ironically, starting on my biscuit. Fuck! I need a biscuit after this.

"I don't know how it happened. One minute we were just talking and the next we were in a passionate embrace—and the next I have my skirt up and undies down and we're fucking against the kitchen counter."

I'm not sure I want to hear this, she's turned into Chris—My mouth may well stay this ajar. And hers is, too, like she is hearing it for the first time, mouth gaping—Maybe I should just stick a penis in there right now! Evidently she enjoys sucking cock.

Cee, terrible thought, terrible thought, terrible thought! She's your friend. No matter how misguided! Wipe head clean of obscenity. Besides, she never mentioned sucking cock, just fucking …

Cee! Focus!

"And then it was happening a lot. Like literally booty calls—I would text him in the middle of the night—dirty texts, you know, like …"

"I don't want to know what you texted him." Swift intervention required! "Nor will I ever want to know. Please keep that to yourself."

"It was crazy," she's continuing. It's a juggernaut now—She just wants the truth to come out in some frightening cocking vomit. "We never had a good sex life. We never had good sex. It was like a once a week thing, or whenever I was ovulating. Even back when we first met we never had good sex—And this was the best sex ever—like no inhibitions sex. Like swinging from the chandeliers sex."

She's staring at me wide-eyed, and now she's downing the Disaronno in front of her in one smooth sip. *Hey, that was mine!*

"Oh my god."

"I know, right—so then I'm lying to everyone. I'm fucking this guy constantly and I can't tell anyone, not even you, because I know you'll judge me—and a week ago I tell myself *You have to stop! This man destroyed you. He broke you. He rattled your very core* … And now he's doing it to someone else. He's involved with some other woman and he's cheating on her. Now I'm the fucking bitch cheat! I'm the bitch!" she's repeating.

I'm too entranced to notice if anyone is looking in our direction potentially, because words have been very loud!

"So then I tell him no more. No more! No more sex in the bathroom, in the kitchen, in the car …"

"In the car!" *Gasp.* "Not on my seat?" I ask, sighing with exasperation, wishing she would have told me before I'd bloody gotten in—or not bloody told me at all. In some cases in life, ignorance is, indeed, bliss.

"Yeah, on your seat," she has confirmed. *Groan.* Just great. Oh, it seems there is more … "I say to him, 'No more!'"

"No more." Lame echo delivered from me.

"And he refuses to take my 'no' seriously."

"Son of a bitch," I say, stuffing another biscuit into my mouth.

"He turns up at my door, at the office, calls my phone—but I want none of it."

I'm shaking my head in unison with hers.

"And then," she's going on, "I hear he's going to leave that bimbo. It's over between them. And I think, *fuck*, is that me? Am I the whore he's cheated with on this occasion?"

"Potentially," I say. Not really helping, am I? But hey, it's true. And I'm a friend, and isn't that my responsibility? Telling the truth when required?

"I know, right?" She's shaking her head. "Potentially."

I'm nodding. Fuck, this is some bad shit. But it goes well with the Alfajor cookies. Compliments it almost like a sweet-sour combo.

"The worse thing, Cee, is I'm dying to fuck him again. Dying. All I think about is his cock. His cock inside me … how big and hard it is. How he banged my brains out on the washing machine. And I just want to fuck him again. I want to fucking bang his brains out."

This is entrancing material—it's a fucking revelation! Oh, hang on, think we are no longer alone. Awareness is creeping in—Yes, there is someone standing by the table. Must be the waitress, non? Then why am I afraid to look up? Whoever it is just heard that entire undignified conversation. I'm staring at Jess, shit, and I know she's thinking the same thing as me. She is thinking *SHIT!*

I'm thinking we can make a pact—between this intense eye contact. Please read my message Jess—Look up now, with me, on three. Ready—yes. One, two … And in unison, we are very much looking up towards said person hovering over us.

It's not the waitress—It's Jai, and another equally attractive man. And they're both smiling at us because I'm sure they've heard that whole fucking "fucking" content. Jai is managing to keep a soft smile on his face, and the other guy's face is lighting up like a Christmas tree, like he has a hard-on right now.

Lost my voice. Major embarrassment.

"Cee," Jai speaks with a little laugh.

"Jai," I manage to gasp out. "What are you doing here?" I ask, like it's utterly dubious that he might be in a restaurant in Sydney on a Saturday night.

"Just having dinner," he says, all hot American, stuffing his hands into his pockets. "I've been sitting over there since you got here." He's gesticulating to a few tables away from us.

"I figured you might be snubbing us," he's continuing on. "I tried to say hello a few times—but then I remembered you probably needed your glasses and couldn't see us."

Nodding—and very funny! If I had seen you, Jai, I would have snubbed you, glasses or no fucking glasses. "Indeed, that's likely to be it. Without my glasses I can barely see a half metre in front of me—really should wear them more often, or get laser or something."

Stop right now. Episode of verbal diarrhea coming on strongly ... HALT!

He's smiling that gorgeous *you're so funny* smile. *Angry note to self:* stop thinking about him as being gorgeous! This always comes on when semi-pissed (alcohol not helping in this case). Jai may be annoying and possibly trying to get me fired by revealing my incompetency, but he is also a bit of a looker—and it's not the first time I have thought this. Well, I guess if you like that tattooed, muscular, slightly dark, angry look—Really not my type though. Not like Axl Rose at all ... Oh, and those guns are out. What does that tattoo say on his left bicep? Is that a skull?

"Yeah, I figured as much," he's speaking again. "This is my friend, Mike."

"Nice to meet you, Mike." Sweetly does it. "This is my friend, Jess." She is still looking completely mortified.

Mike is staring at her, and he's grinning like she's a very unique specimen that needs to be investigated quite thoroughly.

"So …" Must interrupt all of this staring before Jess's head quite literally explodes from embarrassment. " … did you enjoy the food?"

"Yeah," Jai is responding. "Love this place."

"The lineup, too?" Humorous, non?

"Oh, we don't do the lineup. I know the owner," Jai has supplied.

Of course he wouldn't have to do the lineup. That's reserved for plebs like me and Jess. Desperate for food on Saturday night, hopping from foot to foot in line as the minutes tick by, getting more and more famished as the evening progresses.

"He's from the same place as me in L.A. You know, we're expats and banding together against you Aussies."

He's from L.A., not sure why I'd never asked where he was from. Probably a result of lack of interest!

Trying to push the thought out of my head of Jess's "fucking" conversation and the lads overhearing it. Oh dear—We're two shameful debauched women talking about sex like wild animals. Only upshot really is that Jess has been doing most of the talking—*Phew!* I have just been eating and nodding and looking startled really. So have been more the participant than the lunatic in this discourse … Don't want to push friend under the bus, but desperate times call for desperate measures.

"Looks like you guys enjoyed your dinner," Jai has commented, and Mike is sniggering in the background. Who is this Mike guy anyway? Someone who just stands and pokes fun at people? Someone who makes no conversation of his own?

"We sure did," I say resoundingly, and with a little bit too much gusto perhaps—I can't believe I have to do this, but here goes … Delivering an equally resounding kick under the table to wake Jess from her humiliated reverie.

My eyes are wide now, and getting wider trying to tell her with the power of osmosis to *pull it together, sister.*

"Yes, lovely dinner," she's managed to stumble out. "I'm a big fan of Tex Mex."

Mike is laughing again, as though he thinks anything she says at this point is a huge joke. He's equally tattooed and muscular as Jai, with an all-fancy, on-trend hair cut. Probably another creative from some upmarket, hoity toity advertising company!

"Well, if you like Tex Mex, you should go to L.A.," Jai is remarking. "Loads of Tex Mex restaurants there."

"Or Mexico," I say with a smile on my face.

"Or Mexico." He is looking at me for a moment too long. I notice for the first time that he's growing his haircut out, which was super short in that shaved sides, longer on top styled hipster look, which every other sheike lad is wearing at the moment. Longer makes it look more blonde and less light brown.

What was that look about? And why am I thinking about his hair? Conversation is becoming suddenly awkward and somewhat silent.

"What are you ladies up to tomorrow?" he's asking a little tightly, as though he knows he's made it awkward with that dissembling look.

"Oh, I have a family barbecue on." Oh shit, how could I nearly forget? "You know, the variety where you want to slit your wrists in an effort not to turn up."

"That bad, huh?"

"Oh, you cannot imagine." A slight laugh from moi, more nervous than anything else. Nerves remaining in preparation for tomorrow!

"What about you, Jess?" he's asking kindly, involving her in the conversation.

"Oh, you know," she has supplied. "This and that."

The men are probably thinking in unison *probably fucking*, but really it equates to *nothing*. But hang on—That's what Jess would usually be doing, but this new, crazy, high libido Jess might indeed be stalking around outside Pete's house pandering for a good fucking.

How did I miss it? How didn't I notice that any of this was going on? What the fuck! I could have saved her from his "fucking" situation ... More "fucking" incidents with that fucking Pete!

"What about you two?" I figure I best ask back, out of politeness.

"Same, this and that," Jai has supplied. Okay, nothing then. Mike is shrugging his shoulders, confirming that he's either mute or a little touched like Fred.

Jai is staring at me again with a prolonged look. I'm looking at Jess, sensing that stare, still, and Jess is looking at me. Mike, well, not sure what Mike is up to, but I'm pretty sure it's irrelevant and somewhat vacant.

"Well ... I guess I'll see you two later," Jai is saying.

"I guess. See you Monday."

"See you," Jess is grunting. I'm sure she's thinking she never wants to see either of them again. Mike the mute has just waved, and they are both hurrying off.

Jess is reaching across the table furtively, grabbing *my* Disaronno, and I can't believe it, but she is downing it in what looks like a single gulp.

"Hey!" How dare she? "That was mine!" Well, they both were—She didn't want one at all, remember? And now she's downed them both.

"Well, get another one," she's yelling at me. "Oh my god, I've never been so humiliated in my life. Do you think they heard the *fucking* conversation?" She's leaning in and whispering the last statement.

"Yes, I think they heard the fucking conversation," I say, leaning in also, and whispering the last two words in a crazed manner. Like whispering makes a difference now!

"Oh god—I'm a regular harlot and whore," she's saying shamefully.

Right, need to flag down the rude waitress, who is at this point ignoring eye contact. Maybe she heard the fucking conversation too, and thinks we're two sex depraved slatterns who she won't dignify waiting on.

"Oh, so what? Just calm down," I tell her, knowing that if it were me in her shoes, there wouldn't be enough vodka in the restaurant to erase the shame.

Oh, finally! Considering referring to this waitress as *girlie* in Mother style.

"Can I get a Grappa?" *Girlie*—shan't say aloud, it's just not me—although it seems to work for Mother and certainly turns otherwise unresponsive wait staff into amenable helpers.

"Make that two," Jess has piped up, and now she's turning to me. "I think we're going to have to walk home tonight."

"Oh, seriously?" *Gasp.* "I have heels on!"

"Well, bloody take them off. We're only in Newtown. It will take us twenty minutes tops!"

Sigh.

36. 10:30a.m.

*S*unday. Wake up startled. Where am I? Who am I? What time is it? Oh yes, there it is, the moment of recollection, when everything comes flooding back. I'm in bed, I'm Cee, it's morning (hopefully) judging from the light. Sunday, post-Saturday evening Tex Mex blow out, and I need to go to barbecue that will end all barbecues today. Did not die, or at very least get all consuming stomach bug to land me in St. Vincent's. Am just ridiculously hungover. Head seriously aching, hard to focus on objects.

It's 10:30 a.m. Haven't missed barbecue, and have sufficient time to prepare for barbecue. Recalling something about needing to bring a salad, specific details unknown. Will need to contact Mother to resolve.

Slowly propping my frail self to upright position. *Whoa!* Epic hangover. Head feeling like it may explode at any moment. Have the shakes, too. I think this might be indicative of body shutting down.

Stumbling to my feet, as I do too often, in an attempt to get myself to the kitchen. Must take a Panadol. Or two. Or three.

Standing is more difficult than I remember, floor appears to be moving beneath me. Shifting. Must be my deep down inner zen, allowing me to maintain balance.

Oh, look at that, I'm still wearing same clothes from last night. No shoes though, always a good thing. But where are my shoes? Not sure. What pair of shoes was I wearing? Not sure. Scanning room furtively, searching for evidence. No evidence is forthcoming.

Shit! Oh no, my handbag. I begin stalking the floor with big Frankenstein steps. The more I enlarge my centre of gravity, the better.

Where's my bag? Christ, surely I didn't lose it, did I? No wait, I somehow got into the house, so must have used keys. Throwing the doona about in a frenzy, checking if it's landed somewhere on the bed.

Bingo! *Phew*—near pillows. Shuffling through precious bag, all essentials are still here: wallet, keys, mobile. No messages on mobile. But here, nonetheless!

God, what happened? Clutching mobile (because of course it's an essential, even when heading to kitchenette). Need Panadol—will help me to think.

Swinging into the kitchen area, clinging onto the wall for support, and throwing pantry door open looking for stash of medication. *Mwah!* Yes, kissing packet of Panadol! Squeezing out two, and popping into mouth.

Need fluid to swallow … Heading towards fridge, but actually probably not appropriate to swig it down with vodka …

Very inappropriate, actually, Cee—Very!

This will suffice: semi-drank Powerade. Not sure when the initial part of the drink was consumed, but it's been in the fridge since, so reckon the remaining surely will be fine.

Ugghh! Pandadols down … Waiting for impact of paracetamol, washing it down with the rest of the Powerade for good measure.

When did I buy blue Powerade? Is this even mine? If it had been me, wouldn't I have bought red or orange flavoured? *Note to self:* these are the colours and not the flavours. But blue Powerade is such a boy's drink. Perhaps Chad left it here?

Must find something to eat. Must reduce state of inebriation as quickly as possible. Scanning the pantry for anything worth eating. Nothing, as per usual, but a random number of condiments, none of which you can eat singularly. Heading back to fridge. Oh good—plenty of cheese. Come here you lovely piece of Gouda!

Opening freezer. It's been a while … And it's heralded with angelic trumpet sounds. Two English breakfast muffins left frozen in their packets. Forgotten from some other morning hangover crisis.

I'll have them! I try wedging them out, struggling a little; they're like ice blocks. They'll be fine after a two minute zap in the microwave. Surely that will thaw them?

Eardrum shattering from ringing of mobile. Closing eyes from pain. Must answer. Peeling eyes open one at a time, and reaching for my little friend, hands shaking, barely able to swipe to answer.

"Hello, Jess," I answer, voice croaky, throat sore. How much talking at a high-pitch did I do last night? Was I aware that I might have been yelling in restaurant or thereafter? Oh shit, recall now that said behaviour was very much witnessed.

"Cee?" Jess has croaked back.

"Yes, it's me. I've semi-lost my voice."

"Oh my gawwwddd," she's groaning. "What happened last night? Were we like crazy drunk? I can barely feel my hands this morning—or my feet."

Hmm! That doesn't sound good. She might actually need to go to St. Vincent's. Must not make mention of said thought.

"I think we were fine." The microwave has just pinged, making me almost jump a mile, the sound was so disturbing. Grabbing the English breakfast muffins, they're a soggy mess. Nothing the toaster won't be able to resuscitate.

Sticking, more like stuffing, actually, soggy muffins into toaster.

Knife already in hand, waiting with anticipation for moment when can shovel food into face.

"We were totally not fine," she's saying to me. "There are literally blanked out parts of the evening for me. Like lost hours."

Hmm—indeed! Moi, too. How did we even get home? But to admit shameless, drunken state would be beneath me. Always retreat to higher ground post-drunkenness; nobody can prove what can't be remembered, right?

"Oh, so we had a few drinks and were a bit noisy. So what?" I say, pulling the muffin out of the toaster and shoving it into my face with half the cheese.

Chewing noisily. Ouch, jaw hurts.

"Oh no—It was totally beyond that. Do you remember when you raced that guy down Oxford Street?"

Swallowing the muffin at the wrong time, evidently, because the thought of said occurrence has made it stick in my throat. It's clogged.

"Not quite," I manage to say, swallowing hard.

"You were talking to some random, who was totally trashed, and spliffed I think. I don't know how you two got onto the topic, but suddenly you both thought you were good runners. And you were insisting you were faster than him—so he dared you to a race, remember?"

Dear God, need to take weight off legs, sitting down on the stool. Yes, I do have some far-flung recollection of removing my shoes somewhere near Hyde Park and then breaking into a sprint.

"He dared you to race him to the Coca-Cola sign."

"Oh my god." Higher ground slowly evaporating under my feet.

"Don't worry, you won," she's laughing, although it has come out like a muted guffaw.

"I won?" I've never won a running race in my life under such circumstance: lack of shoes, elevated alcohol levels ... Confidence induced from alcohol levels is evidently a winning recipe.

"Yeah, ripped him to shreds. I never knew you were that fast."

"Neither did I. Are you sure it was me?"

"Yep, it was certainly you."

"Do you know where my shoes are? I couldn't find them this morning."

"Nope, no idea! Maybe somewhere near Hyde Park? I think they're probably lost to you now, love," she says, her voice woeful. "Were they expensive?"

"Hmm, I don't really remember which pair I was wearing last night," I say, finishing off the last of the Gouda.

"You know this officially makes us alcoholics, right? As in, we should now be seeking help," she's telling me pointedly.

"Oh, calm down," I tell her, shrugging off the thought—Please, alcoholics? At the very worst we're highly functioning ones. "We had one big night, that does not an alcoholic make."

"Suit yourself, but I think I need to go cold turkey."

"Now that's what alcoholics say."

"Really?"

"Indeed."

"Oh gawwwd," she's groaning again. "All these embarrassing thoughts keep crawling into my mind about what went down. Like that hideous sex conversation I had that those two guys overheard."

"That's not the word you were using last night." I love teasing her—in a sly way, of course!

"Oh gaaaaawwd." More groaning. "I know—It was so terrible."

"Oh, don't worry about it. You'll never see them again. Sydney's a big city." I always cheer myself up with this thought after any drunken debauchery.

"I know, but just the thought of being so embarrassing makes my skin crawl."

"You're being too hard on yourself," I say, and she is. "You probably just needed to let off some steam."

"Yeah … I did. But don't you work with that guy?"

"Jai? Indeed I do, Jess, but I don't think his opinion of me would have dropped far as a result of last night's shenanigans. The guy hates me, and he's been trying to show me up at work since he got there. Besides, he's a fly in, fly out. He'll do some creative time in Aus and then just head back to the States," I say, wishing had another muffin. Why, oh why, are my cupboards so barren?

"That guy does *not* hate you," she's saying with a laugh.

"I think you'll find he does!"

"Are you blind? I saw the way he was staring at you—He totally has a *thing* for you."

Feeling a rapid rush of colour to my cheeks—weird! Must be a result of drinking, unstable emotional self, non?

"He doesn't." I'm quite certain of it. "Trust me, he loves to poke fun at me. He has been trying to expose me as an idiot for months now."

"Okay, two things there … The first is he can't expose you as an idiot, because you're not one. That would be a pure fabrication—And the second is you'd have to be totally blind as a bat to not realise he's into you! He was all sweet and starry-eyed when he spoke to you! Besides, I had noticed him way before he came over to talk to us. He had been staring at you all evening!"

What? Shifting uncomfortably in my seat, as though the thought alone makes me exactly that—uncomfortable.

"Probably because he knew I was making a fool of myself and was enjoying the spectacle." That sounds just like me.

"No way, he stares at you like all inspired and in awe … It's kind of cute."

"Oh, don't be absurd …" I'm brushing the thought aside.

"You sound like your mother!"

"Well, I am her daughter," I say, even though most of the time I wish I wasn't.

"Look, I'm just saying—He's a handsome man. I certainly wouldn't be turning him away." She's crunching on something emphatically. Sort of sounds like cereal. It's terrible that I can deduce the food she's eating based on the sounds she's making—This relationship has reached the wrong level of intimacy.

"Okay, I'll use your dictatorial style of discussion," I say, trying to ignore the crunching. "One, I'm already seeing someone, remember! And two, the man has neck tattoos."

"I know, they're pretty hot." She's obviously stuffing more food into her mouth.

"They're not hot, they make him look like a thug."

"A hot thug, though—hmm?" she's saying all lovingly.

"You know what? This conversation is making me nauseas," I say, trying to put it to an end.

"Honey, I don't think it's the conversation."

"Okay, well I need to go. I'm a busy person and I have an important lunch on in an hour," I tell her, checking the clock. It's now past 11:00 a.m., and I'm going to have to scramble to get ready in time. At least the headache is subsiding.

"Oh yeah, good luck with that." She sounds unsympathetic.

"Thanks for the support …" Not! "By the way," I say, gearing up Mother style, "do you remember break dancing in the restaurant post-Disaronnos and Grappas?"

How about those apples, sister!

"No …" Her voice is small now.

"Well, you did, and I tell you what, you have some moves, lady!" Can't help the laughing bursting out of me … And loudly!

"You're so mean. Why did you tell me that?"

"Hey, my usual policy is what happens during the drunken shenanigans, stays with the drunken shenanigans, but since you informed me of my sprint down Oxford Street, I thought I should return the favour."

"Bitch."

"Love ya, too."

"I'm hanging up on you now." She's adopting my style, and I like it … And she's followed through with it!

I may well be a bitch, but does that make me a bad person? I implore you! Does it?

37. 1:00p.m.

Still Sunday. Standing out the front of Mother's house with Chad about to ring bell. No salad. Last shred of dignity remaining! Life about to end in epic display of light. Can imagine burning flesh of the apocalyptic, dismembering, Terminator variety up ahead. Feeling the urge to vomit. Not sure if it's the nausea from last night's shenanigans or from impending doom. Wearing ridiculous floral dress, which is totally wrong for me, but had been desperate, and made decision based on any clean items of clothing, which show some leg (again, let me reiterate, my best asset). If I'm about to lose man-of-dreams, better put best foot forward. Or in this case, best leg.

"It's okay, babe," Chad is speaking all sweet and winningly, squeezing my hand. "I bet I'll love them."

I'm staring at him, trying to communicate a hundred things at once, but still being swept up in his inordinate handsomeness. As a result, the usual osmosis messaging is failing me. Messages are out of sync and chaotic, but along the lines of: *You have no idea what you're getting yourself into, and these people are crazy! You are misjudging the situation terribly!*

I'm so in the midst of trying to mentally convey these thoughts, but my fears are that *it is too late*—Mother has thrown the door open, no knock or door bell required. Had she been watching from the window? Yes, I'm certain of it! I'm turning to face her slowly, as though the making of eye contact with her will peel the flesh directly off my body.

"Oh, hello, darling," she's crying out loudly. Very loudly, as though she's hoping the party inside will hear. "You're here, finally."

She's grabbing me by my arms and pulling me in for a kiss. Oh, no thank you, and very unlike Mother—In fact, the last time she kissed me was probably when I was eight years old and had a wretched day at school. I'm so shocked by this embrace, and combined with my deadly hangover, that it is sending me wheeling back. Luckily, Chad is here to keep me upright with his steady (and muscular, might I add) arm.

"And you must be Chad Thompson?" Mother's voice is so bright that I fear I might be staring at the sun.

"Yes, lovely to meet you—" He has paused, winning smile on his face, but evidently he's forgotten her name, even though I've told him about a hundred times before. But you know what, who wouldn't be put off by Mother's gigantic powers of disassembly?

"Francis," she has supplied already, clearly unable to take her eyes off him, like she's just met Kanye West. "But you can call me *Franny*—or Fran."

"Lovely to meet you, Fran," he says recovering himself, all dimples and blue eyes. How could you not forgive that look? He's just too handsome.

"Well, come on in, you two." She's grabbing Chad by the arm and placing her hand on the small of his back as she guides him through the door. Fine, I'll just waddle in behind, shall I?

Like some lost sheep with a spinning head, I'm following them into the dining room. Oh, what a surprise—There's a gaggle of people: Mother's nearest and dearest, evidently. Most of whom, regrettably, I've met before. Char's over there looking dire straits again eating a cheese cube, the Bradster, wearing a football jersey of some sort (dear god, not sure whose football jersey, but suspect it must be one of the teams Chad played in— Seriously could he be more embarrassing?), the one-eyed chap from the RSL that Mother is trying to push Char into the arms of (even his one eye is fixed on Chad), and there are some other riff-raff friends that Mother and Brad have *Chardies* with on weeknights.

They all, in unison, have just looked up at us, like they have been waiting for us this entire time. And of course, they have been—like desperate psychopaths living in suburbia, waiting for their one brush with fame.

"Chad," Mother's leaning in towards him intimately, like they're old friends, "this is my fiancé, Brad. We're getting married in a few months time. He's a huge fan of yours."

Oh my god, I want to shrink into the ground. She did not just say that? What is the woman thinking? This is social suicide! And just as he's literally walked through the door—No grace!

"Hey, Brad," Chad has replied calmly, extending a hand and another one of those fabulous grins.

Brad is hesitating. Eyes wide. Just staring. And I know—I just fucking know that he's starstruck. Do men get starstruck? Apparently they do very much so.

How long is he going to stare for? It's painful. We're all just watching. I'm feeling that awkward pause in every bone of my body.

Wait, he's moving, steeping forward quite suddenly, looking sheepish. "Mate, nice to meet you." He's shaking his hand. "It's really such an honour."

Oh god, I have to steady myself on the lounge. Did nobody ever teach the pair of them how to play it cool?

"Thanks, man." Chad is evidently used to the adoration. "But I don't play anymore."

"I know—But maaa-ttte, you were so awesome when you did. An absolute legend."

The room is still silent, witnessing this groveling, enjoying every part of it, I'm sure.

"Thanks, Brad." Chad's clapping him on the shoulder amicably. "Why don't we have a beer?"

Gross, Brad actually looks like he may well have just had an orgasm. This is by far the most exciting thing that has ever happened to him. I can read as much on his face. Forget meeting Mother … Even marrying Mother will never live up to this moment.

Chad Thompson is asking him if he wants a beer. It's BIG.

"I'll grab us two *brewskies*, maaaate." Brad's spinning into action.

And just like that, the Chad spell is broken and everyone's talking again.

I'm still watching Brad, though, leading Chad towards a friend of his. "This is my friend Johnno, maaate. Have a chat to him and I'll grab us a few cold ones."

Ahh—My heart is suddenly placid. Calm. Chad has been accepted amongst the pack of lions. True, he's the head lion (or whatever they fucking call them, too hungover to think straight and only watched the *Lion King* once in my teens), but there was a complete possibility that he would be rejected by the pack, being not mediocre enough. Or vice versa, *him rejecting the pack*. But it seems, like Simba, even if it's King Simba, he is being integrated in an appropriate fashion …

Mother is grabbing me by the arm and pulling me aggressively towards the kitchen. "Well, just don't stand there mooning over him," she is hissing in my ear, pushing me towards the dips and prosciutto on the counter. "Really, Cee, don't be so embarrassing."

"I was being embarrassing?" How did the tables suddenly turn, and so quickly?

"Yes," she's still hissing at me like she's an aggressive serpent, "you were just standing there staring. And I understand he's an attractive man … But for god's sake, you've seen him naked … Stop mooning after him!"

My head's throbbing, and I really can't bother refuting this crazy claim.

"Do you need a hand, Mother?" I ask instead, giving her my airy voice.

"Yes I do … Take that cheese and meat to the canopy we've set up. For fuck's sake …"

She is oh so elegant. At least she's not still calling it a *canapé*.

"We've been waiting since noon and we're starving—and boozed up."

"I can tell." Ever so sweetly does it, Cee.

"Don't give me cheek. I don't care who you're dating." She's loading me up with plates.

Sheesh. Hangover and dishes to carry—not a great combination. But chance to get away from Mother, so I will comply immediately.

"And darling …" She's throwing words over her shoulder. I can feel it coming. One of her insult specials! What's it going to be this time? "What the hell are you wearing? I've told you a million times before, don't wear *florals!* Your look is edgy; you look completely absurd when you do sweet. You know, think Gwen Stefani *now*, not Gwen Stefani *then*. You do know who she is, darling?"

I'm turning on my heels and attempting to ignore her. The woman is crazed; one can only acknowledge the fact and move forward.

"Mother, can you fix me a drink when you're done flapping that mouth of yours about? Gin and tonic." *And you better be snappy with it!* There, that should put her in her place.

38. 3:30p.m.

*Still Sunday. Still at the fucking barbecue! Still struggling for survival,
but now having downed enough gin and tonics to sway a small sailor.
Feeling much more at peace with the world, despite sitting in wedding-like
canopy with completely random family members and family friends (equally
random as the former) and man-of-dreams, who may be losing confidence in
our relationship as each second ticks by.*

Man-of-dreams seems to be calm, relaxed, and in his element, despite
having been enveloped by six large males, all severely intoxicated and
enamoured with his very person. Man-of-dreams continues to exchange
clever conversation with them and repertoire about this game or that,
and they continue clapping him on the shoulder at intervals and calling
out, "Maaaa-ttttee," wildly. I'm sitting with the women folk. Conversation
is beyond demonic. I'm vacillating from placid alcohol haze to wanting
to stick blunt object in eye.

"So we're thinking about the Maldives for the honeymoon," Mother is saying, and the rest of the women are cooing (except me, of course, I usually just stare into the distance bitterly—standard response—and I'm doing said staring now).

"Oh, I love the Maldives," Cheryl has responded lovingly, patting Mother's hand. Cheryl, friend to Mother and aging hairdresser, says her name "Che" like Che Guevara, and then "reel," and corrects anyone who might try to pronounce it in a more traditional fashion.

"Me, too," Char has piped up, obviously not wanting to be outdone by Cheryl, given her best friend status.

I'm saying nothing. Zip. Nada. Just staring!

"You know, I recently saw an episode of the *Kardashians* where the entire family went there—and I tell you what, it's complete and utter paradise. Turquoise waters, huts set out in the water, so you can plunge right off ... "

I wish she'd plunge right off.

"... for a swim," she is continuing. "Crystal clear skies, and sunshine all year round."

I'm sure there can't possibly be sunshine all year round. Ignoring the comment! Pick your battles, Cee. Starting to feel like the left out child in this discussion, even though I brought along the star attraction.

You know what, you would think they would be a bit more kind and inclusive, given I'm their only real link to Chad Thompson, local celebrity and sole reason for Sunday barbecue ... But instead, they're all just hanging onto Mother's every word about the fucking Maldives.

Must stop swearing, even in mind. Completely inappropriate! Must wean self off.

"Of course, I'm sure *you'll* be on a honeymoon soon." Oh, Cheryl's talking to me now, is she? All of the sudden I'm visible, am I? She's clutching my knee and leaning in conspiratorially, exposing her wrinkly chest, straining it forward towards me like a well-worn handbag. Definitely drunk, way drunker than my drunken sailor in my drunken head.

I'm staring at her, and I'm petrified. Hopefully Chad won't get wind of any of this … Thank goodness he's completely ensconced by that man huddle of adoration. I don't think he can hear a word.

"Oh, it's a bit soon for that." I'm trying to kill the conversation off, and taking a long draw from the gin and tonic in front of me. God, give me strength.

"Nonsense, dear! You've been seeing him for a few months now—and the man's clearly enamoured with you," she's saying with a laugh, taking another sip of her champagne. Sheesh, lady! Is she winking at me? Like she's in the know! I'm feeling my face screw up at her overdone, heavy-lidded purple eye.

"He is, darling," Mother is concurring. "Look at him listening to Brad and the other men. Let's face it," she's laughing through her words, "we all know they're as boring as bat shit. But look at him tolerating it." The other women are all laughing and nodding.

Good to know they think their significant other halves are as boring as bat shit.

"Darling," Mother is staring at me closely, "it's all because of you. Clearly he adores you. It's time for you to reel him in!" She's recreating a *reeling-in-fish-on-line* action with hands.

The other women are still laughing and nodding.

"Reel him in, baby doll." Cheryl's downing some more champagne.

Char hasn't piped up; just nodding along with the crowd. She's not really experienced in the reeling-in practice, but evidently thinks it might be a good idea, or at the very least is unwilling to contradict.

"Oh my gosh!" Cheryl has begun again. "Could you imagine the ring she's going to get?" she is squawking at Mother. "It's going to be a mother fucking stone and a half."

I'm dying. Must pray, if only silently, to God, Muhammad, fucking Swami Krishnananda, whoever for god's sake will take my plea seriously! *Please let Chad not hear!*

"I know, right?" Mother is going on, clearly relishing every word. "Multi-millionaire he is, it's going to be like Kim Kardashian's ring."

"The Kanye ring," Char has chirped up—So suddenly she's in the know of popular culture ... I suppose she did know who Chad was, even when Mother didn't.

"The Kanye ring," more are cooing, as if entranced by this notion. I'm entranced by the idea that women of this age bracket know who Kim and Kanye are, and are holding them up as a proper example of a relationship, wedding rings, and family holidays.

I'm over this. Have been for hours. Eyes are darting over towards Chad ... *Can he hear?* He's slapping one of the other gents on the back calmly and downing his *brewski*. I don't think he has any idea what sort of nonsense is afoot. I feel like Macbeth surrounded by wicked witches about to cast spell ...

I have no idea how to stop this? Krishnananda! Help me now if you're ever going to help me. I don't even know if you're a religious figure, but you're a Swami, right! And what does that even mean? Not sure ... But please, if you help me now (now that real and true desperation has set in), I will not let your advertising campaign fail. You will be bigger than Bikram! You will. I can promise you that much!

"I always thought she was going to be a spinster." Mother's leaning towards Cheryl and Char as though I'm not really here. "But in reality, she's just a late bloomer. And a practical one! A strategic one! Look at what she has reeled in!"

More hysterical laughing!

Krishnananda—I swear, I will give you television. If you stop this now, you can have tele-*fucking*-vision!

Surely not! It's a miracle. The word *television* must be magical—With just a mere silent utterance in my mind, the skies have opened. There had been no promise, no prediction of rain at all, yet now the torrents are falling. It's pouring. Like the final scene of *November Rain,* washing out the wedding—or in this case, Mother's fucking barbecue.

And there is my Guns N' Roses, Axl Rose comparison. Not sure why, but I guess the band must have had a lasting effect on my psyche.

The canopy isn't holding, and there is screaming coming from women beneath it (and notably a few of the men). It seems everyone is scrambling to their feet, including *moi*. Feeling very powerfully magical right now, I must admit!

Chad is looking towards me in all his marvelous masculine bravado, and rushing my way to save his delicate flower (that's me) from this unexpected downpour, of course.

"Come on, let's get you inside, doll," he's yelling, quite literally sweeping me off my feet, in storybook fashion. Saving damsel in distress from downpour and unfortunate wedding/witch conversation.

Chad—a fairytale prince with shining muscles.

The Swami—possibly a god.

Axl Rose—I'm sure he would have approved.

39. 6:00p·m·

In Lamborghini with hot prince forward slash man-of-dreams (new terms of endearment for Chad). Terribly impressed with him after today's happenings. He is no longer just man-of-dreams, but man-of-epic-dreams. Staring at him wondrously as he's driving to his place in Freshwater, elevating him to god-like status, along with Krishnananda. We have survived lunch with parents—or Mother and starstruck fiancé-of-Mother. And is it possible that we have more than survived? That we have perhaps thrived?

He has just glanced over at me, running his hand down my leg. "What are you looking at all adoringly, baby?"

"Oh, nothing," I'm totally cooing. "Maybe just you."

"So I'm a man to be adored, now, am I?" he's asking with a raised eyebrow, again all blue-eyed and dimples.

"Something like that—But didn't you get enough adoration from the other men folk today?" I'm being sly—Okay, just want to know his thoughts on it all.

"Oh, you noticed?"

I can tell he's proud to the point of arrogance. It's kind of hot. Very Achilles, *hear me roar!* Or something similar to that ...

"Sure did, baby. You are quite the hero."

"Haha," he is laughing. But I know he loves it. Of course he does, can't believe I've not seen it before—that he loves the adoration. Loves being revered by your every day man and woman! Probably misses it now that he's not playing anymore. The whole afternoon has likely done wonders for his ego. He's glowing.

"You know it gets me going when you say that." He's running his hand up my leg.

"Well, you are a bit of a *hero*, baby," I tell him, saying the words softly and sexily, of course.

"Ah–huh. We are totally going straight to my place," he's laughing.

Indeed. What man doesn't love his ego stroked? Or penis. Are they the same thing? Oh, fucking brain! Really! Are they, though?

40. 9:10a.m.

Monday morning. Latte in hand! In office already. Who can complain about a start like that? Boom! Am on fire! What would have made it perfect would be an early morning gym class, like that RPM class attended weeks ago (months ago to be exact). Haven't been to the gym since—Nonetheless, never too late to become a gym enthusiast. Perhaps will schedule one in for later on this week with Jess? Thoughts are of the floaty, sunshine, rainbow-esque variety. Completely fantastical! Am replaying moments from fabulous coitus last night— Perhaps enhancing it, given the rich tapestry of pheromones this morning.

Hmm ... Coffee tastes wonderful, air smells wonderful, world by far is a wonderful place.

Stopping by Tina's desk. Now that she has become a fully-fledged staff member, she has her own desk out on the floor with the rest of the plebs. Nonetheless, her own desk! Feeling somewhat like mother hen with respect to Tina and checking in on her periodically to make sure she's doing okay, surviving the daily grind, is part of said duties, methinks. Perhaps I do flap about her a bit, but, after all, I'm the one responsible for birthing her from the intern space into the advertising employee space, above and beyond all those other interns whose advertising careers (at least for this company) have been aborted. It's the most maternal thing I've ever done ... by far. Besides looking after Fred, of course.

How could Ian not have picked her after we sealed those two new contracts? He had to! Sure, I don't deny it; luck was on my side. But really, it was just a pinch of luck, not a full squeeze or anything.

Tina, I have decided, is my new ally in the office. Given she came to being thanks to *moi*, she needs to repay in kind, i.e. aligning herself with me and leaving the Elsies of the world adrift. She is *Team Cee*. In an office otherwise devoid of allies, even just the *one* comes in handy. Admittedly, Tina is well connected. She's the type to go to after-work drinks or lunch with the team, not flit off at any moment to have sushi with Chris or a fake tan. Yes, I'm still getting them!

I turn the corner to her pod, and find her seated at her desk, latte in hand, hair perfectly coiffed, legs crossed, talking to—you have to be joking! Elsie! Elsie? Really? What's the point of having an ally if they're in bed with your enemy? That little double-faced so and so!

Elsie is looking completely relaxed, leaning against the desk with her glass of warm water and slice of lemon in hands. Legs crossed at ankles, she's wearing cowboy boots, floral skirt and jean jacket. All very nineties with a twist! Hair falling perfectly in loose waves over her shoulders, her face is serene. *Grrr* ... God, can no one else see how demonic this woman actually is?

And what's so private? They're talking quietly, heads bent closely together in an intimate gesture.

Feeling like I have just walked in on two people having sex. That's how intimate this all is. *Vomit.*

Contemplating leaving, but am already in the pod, so if I turn around now and walk away that would look like crazy person activity, wouldn't it?

"Oh, hello, ladies," I say, airily delivered as though the sight of them together doesn't annoy me in the slightest.

"Hey, Cee," Elsie has replied with that stupid, fucking placid smile. Hate. Hate. Hate.

"Hey, Cee." Tina is also looking up, smiling openly, as though there's nothing untoward happening here. Her talking to my archenemy like she's her *bestie* is a bit of a non-event, non?

"Hey." Why did I say that again? Just chiming *heys* about you know!

"How was your weekend, Cee?" Elsie has asked. Oh shit, now stuck in the standard office Monday morning conversations. The ones that are totally arbitrary and that I usually desperately flee from and hide out in my office to avoid.

"Yeah, good. Eventful." *Argghhhh* ... I hate going into the minute descriptions of weekend with colleagues because it's the done thing on Mondays—By the end of it, they're just wearing a glazed expression and you can tell they just want to start talking about themselves and their own weekends. It's enough to put me off the work environment completely.

"We both went wedding dress shopping over the weekend," Elsie's voice is all lovely and cooey. "And we ran into each other at a boutique in Mosman."

Oh, of course Mosman, and boutique and wedding dress shopping.

"Isn't that lovely," I say, trying to feign enthusiasm, but it is coming out as a strange and high-pitched series of sounds.

"It was so much fun!" Tina's saying enthusiastically. "And we both want to wear Monique Lhuillier or Steven Khalil … He's like the *it* designer for wedding dresses, Cee …" she's explaining to me as though I'm some sort of popular culture novice (no, I'm not really!).

"Yes, I know who he is." Neither of them seems to notice I'm being curt.

"Oh, the fabrics and designs—It's all so divine, Cee," Elsie's saying. "There's nothing like planning a wedding!"

"I know, right," Tina has concurred, and is continuing, "I think I've found a new career—wedding planning!"

What? The both of them are grabbing onto each other with clear excitement.

"Me, too!" Elsie has declared.

Oh gawwd this is so frightening. If I didn't have a good gag reflex, I'm sure I would vomit right here, right now. BARF!

I'm now staring at Tina coldly. The girl's just found a career—one that I've orchestrated! And now she's bloody looking for another one? It's like looking the gift horse in the teeth—the teeth? I don't know, whatever that saying is. I'm sure there's something about teeth—Whatever!

Hang on—They're talking to me.

"Cee, wouldn't you like to plan a wedding?" Elsie's voice is ever so sweetly directed at me, but there's a veiled dig in it—I know it. Oh, right—Yeah, I'm still the spinster, even though I have a fabulous footballer boyfriend.

I'm staring at her, and giving her my most winning smile …

"Well, you know, Elsie, it's not really my thing." Lie, sort of, well, not really!

"Oh, you're joking, right?" Elsie's continuing because she doesn't know when the fuck to shut up. "It's everyone's thing. Every girl's been dreaming about her wedding since she was a kid!"

"No, not quite." They're both staring at me incredulously. Okay, so maybe I have had the odd, random wedding dress Google, over the last few months especially, but that does not constitute dreaming about planning my wedding since I was a kid. I was more likely dreaming about pina coladas.

"Jai," Elsie is calling. "Jai! Jai …"

I'm turning around. Yep, it's him walking past, heading towards somewhere and now he's detoured. He's just jumped at Elsie's call—turning into the pod, instead. All very cosy now—*Not at all!* He is all rugged, handsome and disheveled—his usual appearance. Wearing a t-shirt, loose jeans … Shit! Now I'm thinking he's handsome even when I'm sober—bad sign, bad sign, bad sign. This is all Jess's fault—Why did she have to put this thought in my mind?

Luckily, I think he is purposely avoiding eye contact with moi. I wonder why? I'll do the same then. Keep looking towards the ladies, Cee, looking at them both staring up at him all starry-eyed, despite their pending fucking perfect weddings.

"Whattup?" he asks, his hands in his pockets, all street cred and stuff. Now I can look back at him. Whattup? Really? Who are you kidding?

"Settle something for us here," Elsie has begun, and so smugly. This is going nowhere good fast. Why couldn't I just have walked straight into my office? Why couldn't I have just maintained my zen, rainbows, glitter, and cupcakes aura?

"Cee here is trying to tell us that she wouldn't want to plan her wedding. It's never been her dream to get married. Isn't it every girl's dream to get married?" she's saying to him, one hand on hip now.

He's not a girl, so how come she's basing this all on his opinion?

He's looking at me with an amused expression, raising an eyebrow and smirking now, too. And you know what, the thing is I can tell what he's trying to say to me: *How do you get yourself into this sort of thing?*

So I shall just smile back at him and, yes, return raise of eyebrow, too. Mine is conspiratorially telling him with my power of osmosis, which had left me for a while, but has returned thankfully: *Not sure, it just happens!*

Think he got the message. He is now turning back to the pair of them. "I'm sure a woman as intelligent and determined as Cee would not have been dreaming about her wedding since birth. She'd have better things to dream about."

Oh, shit! BOOM! Remark of the century! Exactly, I did dream of better things, like, like … pina coladas.

And he's gone, already turned around and is walking away. *No see you later, no how was your weekend. No shitty small talk, just a whole lot of I have better things to do than talk about this shit* vibe going on. My kind of guy! Not like that, obviously. In a different way … One that I can't think of right now …

I'm so smiling inwardly and outwardly—from every pore in my tanned skin. I am loving the shocked expressions that these two princesses are wearing right now. I want to lean forward and rip off the metaphorical tiaras they both fucking have perched on their young, pretty heads. Calm down, Cee ... Victory has been had!

Returning to rainbows and unicorns. And some more zen. *Note to self:* must stop swearing.

41. 11:30 a.m.

*P*hone ringing while I'm in the middle of investigating hair extensions on Google to make sure my hair will not fall out, or worse, as a result of Wednesday's appointment. Have now read series of horror stories about women having to shave their heads post-hair extensions. Have texted beautician, Chantel (previously known as puffy lips, or simply Puffy), with whom I have now developed some sort of Chad love bond with, and she has assured me that the person she has referred me to does an awesome job. Not shonky at all. Very skilled and talented, even though the salon is located in said person's garage. Phone is still ringing—Must answer in case it is a client or other important person with important question. Why do I know all these people whose names begin with "Ch"—Char, Cheryl, Chantel—Hmm? Is the universe sending me a message?*

"Cecilia speaking."

"Oh, hello, darling. It's your mother," she's saying snottily.

Sigh. Really? She's calling me right before lunch for another exciting installation of general chatter mixed in with obscenities? Should probably give her more of a chance, given she's now stopped using that ridiculous joke—*Oh, hello, Cecilia speaking. It's your mother speaking.* Christ! It took a while to get rid of that one.

"Oh, hello, Mother. Is this important?" I ask, starting to lay the foundations for an easy getaway. "I have a meeting at noon."

"A meeting at noon?" she's parroting back. "Who schedules a meeting over lunch?"

"It happens all the time, Mother." She is getting my high-powered executive manner, when in reality I have lunch blocked out the entire week so I can do exactly what she's referring to: ensure nobody books a meeting over lunch. In fact, it's often been a point of contention with Ian, but I have told him repeatedly that I work better on a full stomach. But now that I'm the golden child of the company, he seldom refers to any of my peccadilloes, other than to indicate how charming they are.

"Indeed. I thought you just had a regular lunch date with Chris scheduled?" Mother's reading between the lines. Reading my mind! The woman knows me too well.

"No, that's not the case—So, why are you calling, Mother?"

"Can't a mother call her only daughter to chat?" She is being defensive.

And it's doubtfully the case with Mother … Never just an innocent chat!

"Yes, Mother, but I was at your place less than twenty-four hours ago. Do you need to update me on anything further?"

"Just a few things, darling."

"Well, okay, let's get into it."

"Darling, I don't appreciate you hurrying me up—but I do understand you're a busy lady," she says, a touch of irony in her voice.

I refuse to respond, checking mobile … There's a message from Chantel, said beautician and fake tan extraordinaire. It reads, "Tara is awesome. She does great extensions, and did mine. Don't worry, you will look fab. Chad will love!"

And lots of emoticons of smooch lips! Somehow she has developed an intimate relationship with Chad (via me) and knows exactly what he's after in a lady. Who am I to question, though?

"… It was such a wonderful day yesterday," Mother is talking nonstop in my ear. "Really, Brad and I just absolutely love Chad. He is such a gentleman, and, you know, completely down-to-earth even though he's a major celebrity. You do know he's a major celebrity, darling? And he just turns up to our house for a barbecue, talks to everyone, is just completely charming …"

"Mother!" Interruption is vital at this point, methinks. "Is this some sort of love fest about Chad? I know how charming he is—I am dating the man. It's now 11:42 a.m.," I say, referring to my monitor for the time. "Could you get a wriggle on?"

"Fine!" she says in her stroppy fashion. "The point of it all is we were hoping to have *him* over to dinner on Saturday night? I thought I could do an Italian-themed evening, given that he has an Italian restaurant."

Dear god! Mother's Italian: a spag bol and chicken parmigiana. How could she think that's appropriate to be feeding a man who has an Italian restaurant with a Michelin Star? Is she out of her goddamn mind?

"Just him?" I ask, noting the reference to having him over to dinner.

"No, don't be ridiculous," she's scoffing. "You, too, darling. Why would I not invite you?"

"Well, it sounds like you're taking him on as your surrogate son."

"And what's wrong with that, darling? Wouldn't you want for me and Brad to love your boyfriend and accept him as one of our own?"

"It's everything I've ever dreamed of," I say, completely sarcastic.

"Don't be sarcastic, darling. It's a terrible trait on women—makes them seem, I don't know, well … bitter."

Okay, so I have a choice. I can allow her to go near the *bitter spinster* subject, which I know she will, given *bitter* reference, or I can cut this off at the knees. Cutting at knees! Chop, axe, and sever!

"We can't do this weekend, Mother. We're going away." That's a lie!

"Going away? You haven't mentioned this before, darling. Where are you going?" She sounds like she's on the scent, on the lie scent that is. Mind fucking reader … How am I ever supposed to quit swearing, mentally or verbally, with people like her and Elsie constantly at me?

"To Polkolbin," I say, too smoothly delivered for her to detect lie. "Up in the Hunter Valley." Luckily Jess's lie to Pete about her weekend away (to avoid sleeping with him after the first *incident)* is still front of mind … And it's a good one, well researched on her part!

"Oh, how lovely! Have you been planning this for long?"

"No, it was very spontaneous. Chad only just mentioned it last night." Come on guys, I'm a seasoned professional! I have been dealing with this lady since the womb. Yes, since then.

"Well, it must be getting serious if he's asking you on weekends away?" Her voice has risen an octave due to clear excitement.

"Indeed," I say, checking the clock on my screen. "I have to go, Mother.

Is that all you wanted to say?"

"No, two more things." She sounds slightly flustered, and I'm feeling mean for putting on the ruse, but, you know, sometimes one needs to do what one needs to do, for self preservation if nothing else.

"So this is an exciting one … Cheryl called me this morning—You know, you remember her from the barbeque, hairdresser, *large rack?*'

Yes, crazy lady with purple eye shadow who almost unraveled my relationship with premature wedding talk. I do remember her. And has large rack become a descriptor now?

"Yes," I say, reserving the mental commentary. I don't have time for this boring ass conversation. I want my lunch!

"Weeellllll," she's drawing out her words annoyingly, "she called me this morning with some verrrry exciting news!" Oh, she's stopped talking. Okay, I get it … She wants me to guess. Very mature of her! Not the first or last time I'll play this game with Mother. And by now, I know all the iterations of it.

"She's getting married?" Most obvious choice.

"No." And she is waiting expectantly …

"Her daughter's getting married."

"Don't be absurd, darling, she doesn't have a daughter. Only two sons." She's sounding harangued. She's harangued? Really!

"Okay, well, one of her sons is getting married?"

"No!"

"She's getting Botox done?" I'm scraping the end of the barrel now.

"No!"

Oh my god, feel like head might explode.

"Just tell me, Mother! I have to go, and we're too old to be playing guessing games!" I'm getting cranky.

"Oh, fine then, take the fun out of it!" She's snotty, like I've just told her Christmas has been cancelled.

"You're in a magazine! My daughter's in a magazine!" Of course, because it's somehow related to her … And that excitement has been regained as quickly as she had lost it!

"What do you mean, Mother?" I ask, racking my brain! Have there been any advertising jobs I might have done which would turn up in magazines? Not just any mags, but those that people like Cheryl would read? I'm sure I didn't tell her enough about my work—and Mother never actually listens to what I'm working on anyway. So I have no idea!

"You're in a magazine. You got papped with Chad!" she's saying, like it's the most exciting thing that's ever happened.

"What? When?"

"You got papped!" she has repeated. "There's a few photos of you and Chad leaving what looks like a restaurant together, holding hands, and then getting into his car, which looks very flashy and expensive …"

"What do I look like?" Oh, Christ, let it not be some goddamn awful photo of me where some part of my underclothing is exposed.

"You look good, darling. Nice high heels on, great legs, white short dress on … The hair probably needs some attention, but otherwise *good.*"

"Can you see my underwear?" Need to be specific to penetrate her excited drivel.

She's paused. "No, darling, they're not those types of photos."

Whatever! Will need to buy magazine myself and ascertain level of attractiveness through careful, assiduous discussion with Jess and Chris.

"What does the copy say?"

"The what?" She's clearly confused.

"The copy … You know, the writing that goes with the picture."

"Hang on! I'll grab my glasses, darling. It's all very complimentary, but I'll read it to you. Don't worry, I've bought twenty of them. I want absolutely everyone to have one and know that my daughter is in a gossip magazine …"

"Mother, what does it say?" *Sigh.*

"Right, back to it," she's saying almost like a little gee-up to herself to keep on track. "It says: *Chad Thompson was seen leaving Vetro e Metallo restaurant in Sydney with a mystery blonde. She might be a mystery blonde to us, but word around town is he's been seeing her for months, and the pair is serious. Thompson's a fast mover; the dust hasn't even settled on his last divorce. This might be wife number three for him!*"

She has stopped reading. That's it?

"Oh my god," I say, standing up. Flapping arms. This is pretty awesome. Have been papped, am in magazine with celebrity ex-footballer boyfriend, and people are talking about me! Little old me! I may be about to become … Oh my god … Dare I say it—a WAG. Certainly not what I've been dreaming about all these years, but it does sort of have a bit of a ring to it when the option is presented.

"I know, right?" Mother is sounding like she might drop dead from excitement. *"Might be wife number three!* Can you believe it? I just couldn't contain myself when Cheryl told me. And to have other people reading about it and calling me—It's really too much!" Mother is beside herself. I'm beside myself!

But, per usual, it's always all about her.

"Mother," I say, snapping out of my reverie, although still standing, "it's noon now, and I have to go. Did you have anything else you wanted to add?" I'm reaching for bag now, desperate to go and buy said magazine. Like right now. I must see it.

"Okay, darling, yes one more thing. Although I kind of expected you to be more excited …"

"What is it?" I ask, cutting her off before another chain of thought unravels in her skittish manner.

"I just wanted to remind you to call your father. As much as I abhor the man, I want to make sure that you two have a relationship, and that that I-talian …" pronounced with an I in the same predictable, racist fashion as always, " … hasn't killed him yet."

And, indeed, she can be a bit fiery. Sometimes even more than Mother.

"When did you speak to him last?" So now, just as I'm about to dash out and buy a magazine where I'm featured, where there's a photo and *copy* about me, she's suddenly interested in my relationship with my father. She hasn't been concerned about that for about thirty years!

"I don't know, Mother," I say, fumbling with bag, wallet and phone.

"Like a month ago?"

"Mother, I have to go." I have to resort to rudeness now; she'll never get off the phone at this rate. Actually considering hanging up, best not though. "I'll call him tonight."

I don't speak to him enough and should put more initiative into it, knowing how *he* is. You know, generally incommunicado. I've just been wrapped up in more important things … like for example, being papped.

"Great. Okay, love you, darling," Mother is trilling.

And now she loves me, does she? Ahh … How the tables have been turned. The power of being papped is extraordinary, isn't it?

42. 3:30p.m.

ack at desk. Feeling slightly untouchable with potential celebrity-status. May also be effect of Spritz Camparis I had with lunch (with Chris of course, yes, official lunch buddy, to Mother's despair). Spritz Camparis—How do the Italians do it so right compared to everyone else? Some Prosecco, some tonic water, a whole lot of Campari, and of course my favourite part—the olive. Adore! Brain has seriously stopped functioning in appropriate manner. Could be linked to number of magazines I've purchased with my very own image in them. Mine! That's right! Mine!

Ten to be exact … Magazines, that is, not images! Yes, may have turned into Mother, but how many times does one turn up in a magazine with very own photo and commentary!

Had initially bought nine, but of course I had to get one extra for Chris, who was beyond ecstatic, and is no doubt telling everyone about his fabulous friend at this very moment.

Because here's the thing about being a celebrity (or like a Z-grade celebrity in this case), when it starts taking off, it zooms off. Everyone wants to be your best friend and everyone wants some sort of association with you. And the celebrity grows like some sort of blooming algae (why the algae metaphor, not quite sure, only one which has sprung to mind) and grows and grows. Suddenly I'm more fabulous, and more beautiful, and more *everything* than the original model actually was or is, because it gains momentum in people's minds.

Mobile buzzing. Oh, it's the beautician,

"OMG is that you in *Famous* magazine? It totally is! I am ripping the page out this very second and pinning it to my fucking wall. Hey there, peeps, this is my client, she's dating Chad Thompson, and her tan, it looks fucking fabulous—AND I DID IT!"

Ha! See, the algae's blooming. Text back.

"It's me, baby. You better believe it! *Prospective wife number three.*"

Okay, maybe that's the Camparis talking.

"Can you get me a better deal on the extensions? $500 seems a bit steep."

Oh my god, I'm already calling in favours. Well, it's at least worth a try!

Phone has just pinged back at me almost instantly—Please say yes!

"Yep, can do, bitch. Texting her right now! She may do it for free if she knows Chad Thompson's new squeeze has her hair extensions in—and will be photographed all over town wearing them!"

Bitch! Is that a term of endearment? Apparently. Might start integrating into dialogue. Must get back to emails. But oh, a distraction to my easily distracted, potentially ADD mind, some light seems to have been blocked out in my office by a large, round shape at door. It's Ian.

Ian never usually makes it out from his office to see the plebs. It's not his thing. He probably does it once a year to make sure people think he's a man of the people. He is not a man of the people! He is a man of social strata. Old school. So this sudden appearance of him at my office door is beyond strange. Monolithic, in fact, in more ways than one!

Looking round office, making sure I'm not doing anything untoward— Oh, I'll just click on and minimise Facebook page quickly, and oh, down you go, too, online shopping.

"Hello, Ian," I say, sounding slightly erratic. Must be the Camparis. Shit! *Note to self:* may be good idea to stop drinking alcoholic beverages at lunchtime. Second note to self: making no commitments right now.

I'm only slightly drunk, but not the best image when one's boss finally leaves their ivory tower to come to your office. "How are you?" Best ask him, eh?

"Good, Cee." It's nice to see his shirt is fully tucked into his pants and no buttons have dislocated themselves from his vestige.

"What can I do you for?" I ask, being quaint and charming.

"Nothing, Cee," he's holding up the *Famous* magazine, "but I wanted to tell you that this is good for business."

"What?" I ask, standing up, somewhat alarmed, looking at the magazine ... How does a man of his age, completely dislodged from popular culture, know that I'm in that magazine? Oh, but he's got teen daughters. I remember the Rita Ora reference now.

"My EA gave it to me," he's telling me. "I like to be abreast of what my staff is doing—even in their private time."

My lips are glued together, and I'm just staring at him, perturbed.

"Don't worry," he's continuing, "this is good. People will love to know that one of our account directors is with Chad Thompson. *Prospective wife*, in fact—They will lap it up, Cee."

Really? They don't even know who I am!

"I've already had an influx of calls. Two big wigs, too. Banks," he's added.

"Banks?" Glue easing off lips enough for whisper to emerge … Cracking the financial market is like cracking the holy grail of advertising.

"Banks," he's confirming. "Nice one—I'll have to move you into a bigger office," he's now calling over his shoulder, and tearing back to his own massive office. Gone. Wow!

"I want the one down the corridor, with views of the bridge!" Must get in there quick while it's all fresh in his mind. I don't think he has heard my desperate call back to him, though.

Easily resolved, I shall email him later.

43. Evening

My house. *Drinking a green juice. Yes, indeed. In desperate cleanse process post-weekend blowout and lunch in China Town blowout, following excitement of appearing in magazine. Cleanse. The word sounds diabolical, even in my thoughts. But clothes have become decidedly tighter of late, and I think it may be a result of incessant boozing and eating over the last month or two (maybe three, or even four if one counts Christmas—Oh dear, could go on with this and include the lead up to Christmas—Need to draw the line at some point). Hence reason for said cleanse, though not sure how exactly said cleanse works. Think you may need to substitute a meal with a juice, or water, or maybe any fluid—Again, not sure. Did not get the chance to investigate during the day seeing as how I spent the morning checking hair extension atrocities and the afternoon looking at magazine, Googling own name to see if any further information had appeared, and fielding phone calls (some of which were from almost complete strangers) who had seen the photo. Strange, the impact of even a tiny bit of celebrity.*

Have not had glass of vino this evening. Big tick. Could possibly turn out to be a booze-less day. Hurrah! Have not had one of those since, well, okay counting back has proved futile, so I don't think I'll do that again. Oh hang on, have forgotten alcohol consumed at lunch. Shit.

Unscrewing top of green juice and pouring glass of thick mess. Gloopy! What's even in here? Looking very much like vomit gone wrong, after liver has shut down, for example. Although, not sure vomit can go right! *Anywho!* What does the label say? Okay, lots of green stuff … Spinach, apples, kale (Oh goddamn you, kale!). I have sunk to new low, haven't I?

Must call Father tonight. Promised myself I would during the course of the day, and inevitably if Mother reminds me, then I know it's long due.

Of course it'll be a terrible, stilted conversation (as result of Father being generally incommunicado) and potential preamble conversation with his wife Maria usually throws me off.

But seeing as I have turned over a new leaf, am eating only leaves, and am now celebrity-dating woman with face in magazine and heavy hitter at work, I figure my life is pretty much together (or as together as it will ever be, or ever has been), and must not fuss or be paranoid about calling Father.

So just dial the number, Cee. No further procrastination or vacillation necessary.

One, two, three rings, starting to feel uncomfortable already, too late to hang up now.

"Hello!" Maria is yelling down the line shrilly.

Taking a moment to recover from hearing loss … "Oh, hello, Maria. It's Cee here. How are you doing?" It's my most resolute adult voice.

Oh—Biggish pause is happening, wondering if she's forgotten who I am altogether, or whether she is gearing up for some retort. Best help her, I guess. "You know, your husband's daughter," I say, sing-song voice implemented. Read today that when people are in love they (unbeknown to themselves) adopt a sing-song, melodic tune with their loved one, which makes them more attractive to the potential mate. I guess like birds or dolphins or something. I've now decided to begin sociological study and use sing-song tone with anyone who is being strange, abrupt, or rude to see if it lulls them into a false sense of adoration. Did read the article on *news.com*, but no matter, still worth a try.

"I know who you are," she's snapping at me, seemingly crankily. Hmm … Sing-song tune has not worked on first occasion, but shall persist. "I just didn't recognise your voice, given you haven't called in so long."

And that's not at all because you make me feel so comfortable, is it? I think not! Maria is potentially even crazier than Mother on the lunatic scale—Hard to believe, isn't it? But very true. When you think about it, she's bound to be; after all, she is Italian, and, well … Italians do everything better: food, men, women, sex, Spritz Camparis … and levels of craziness.

"I've just been so busy, Maria, it's just slipped my mind," I say, continuing the ruse. "I've been meaning to call for the last fortnight or so."

"You haven't called for more than that—I think we last spoke in January," she's telling me. She has a mind like a steel trap, something about that whole Italian guilt thing. Apparently it's very important to remember every detail of encounters so you can use evidence against people, even if *said people* include your daughter-in-law.

"Oh, has it been that long!" Still merry. Keep it lighthearted, Cee.

"Yes, it has," she's snapping with that lilting Italian accent of hers. It's all very Sofia Vergara, you know sexy, but super annoying and nasally at the same time. Indeed, Sofia Vergara is South American and Maria is Italian—But you get the point, I'm sure.

"Your father has been worried about you," she's telling me.

I'm picturing her right now, standing in the corridor of their home in Five Dock where the phone is stationed, hand on meaty hip, glaring, crazily, at nothing in particular.

Phone is cordless, but nonetheless, in my mind she is stationed, rooted to the spot. Perhaps the lack of movement increases her intensity.

"Dad doesn't worry." Seriously, Dad doesn't worry! Half the time he doesn't remember what I do, where I live, or how old I am! Not because he's senile or anything, he's just the easy-going type and doesn't need to keep tabs on my every waking moment.

"He does worry!" she's yelling at me in return. Wow, she is loud. Having to hold the phone away from ear about thirty centimeters to ensure hearing is not seriously impaired as a result of this conversation.

"Your father ..." she has begun again, and here we go into the guilt lecture. See, this is why I don't call. I don't understand why he doesn't just pick up the phone for once. Oh, that's right, because she polices the corridors like a Nazi! " ... pretends he doesn't care, but inside, his heart is breaking. He is waiting to be loved. Wanting to be loved. A man doesn't ask to be loved—He just expects to be loved!"

Not sure if this is some Italian proverb that doesn't translate correctly into English, but it doesn't quite sound like my father, a man who awkwardly shakes my hand instead of giving me a hug. Not that I mind—He's old school, that's all.

"I know that you're all busy and important now that you're seeing that footballer—"

How does she know? Does she keep tabs on me, too? She had a private detective on Father once when she was convinced he was cheating. Then it turned out he was just driving out to some secluded location off Parramatta Road (didn't know one existed, but he had certainly managed to find it) and was just sitting in his car. Staring. Then there was the whole inquisition about that. Frankly, I think he just needed some bloody peace and quiet, but Maria packed him up and sent him off to see a psychiatrist …

"Being photographed around town …"

That's how she knows! Bloody magazine!

"But the thing is, the man's still your father. And he is old." She is enunciating the last few words in staccato. "You should be here looking after him, loving him …"

She is continuing to rattle off a list of things I should be doing. Hmm? Think now is apt time to interrupt before timpani bursts.

"He's not that old, Maria. He's seventy. It's not like he's ready to be put in a home or anything." *Sigh.* There goes the light-heartedness, straight out the door. But I did manage to maintain it for what has felt like a very long time.

"Ahh!" she is crying out, and it's a guttural sound, like she's just been garrotted. "You want to put your father in a home! Is that why you're calling? You and your mother, always up to something!"

"I don't want to put him into a home. I said he's *not* that old, like not old enough to be put into a home." I'm not sure why I'm trying to clarify this, because the woman turns my words in some sort of Shakespearean villain manner. Should just remain silent, less opportunity for her to construe something against me. Maybe that's why Father doesn't talk much anymore—But I guess he's always been a man of few words …

"Ye-ahhhh," she's drawing out the word in victory. "That's it, you and your fancy boyfriend and your mother with her new husband. You want to put your father in a home—But I won't stand for it. I love him. I love the man—" she is violently yelling now. Oh, dear. Have caused ruckus, which will likely impact badly on father later on tonight.

Taking sip of restorative green juice. Fucking shit! Tastes awful. Gawwdddd! Why are people drinking these things? Staring at green juice now like it really is the devil incarnate. Can't possibly drink more of this. It's not happening!

Impetuously, it seems I'm losing my cleanse resolve. It hasn't taken much really, has it? Screaming stepmother and revolting green juice has flung me over the edge. Heading to fridge to see if can find a more appropriate drink for the situation.

"Maria, Maria!" I'm hearing Dad calling in the background. "Who's that on the phone?" Her renewed screams have obviously roused him away from the television where he was no doubt stationed. "I will not stand for it! I will not stand for it!" she's yelling at me still … Seriously, everyone seems to just fucking yell. No wonder I'm literally on the verge of alcoholism …

Yes, orange juice located—tick! Pulling out the vodka bottle bought at the same time as green juice this afternoon for emergency situation. I think this could potentially be categorised as such an emergency. Don't you?

"Nobody's putting him in a home," I say, slugging half a glass of vodka out and topping it up with juice.

"You're putting him in a home!" she's yelling like she's in a Broadway show, some sort of theatre production where you need to overact and really project in order for the audience to hear you.

"Who's going into a home?" Dad sounds closer to the phone now. He's probably right near her, trying to make sense of it all.

"You!" she's now yelling at him. "Your daughter wants to put you in a home."

"Don't be ridiculous," I hear Father saying.

"Me, ridiculous!" she's crying out with disbelief. "You're ridiculous, you ridiculous old man! Your daughter is going to put you in a home. Don't you realise I'm trying to protect you!"

I'm sitting down on the stool with my drink … *This could go on for a while.* No wonder I don't call him as often as I should, or even want to, because these calls take a serious mental toll. Feeling like I may need to be put into straitjacket after this one.

"Give me the phone, Maria," I can hear him saying.

"No!" she's crying emphatically. Oh, that sounds like some sort of scuffle. There's a lot of muffled sounds and *Give me the phone* from Father, and swearing, that's her, it's in Italian. *Testa di cazzo.* Not sure what those dull thud noises are though, potentially Maria beating up Father.

I shall sip and wait patiently. Yum, thank you for saving me again, dear vodka. At last, sounds of clean air, scuffle free, and now some heavy breathing on the other end of the phone.

"Oh, hello, darling. It's your father here. How are you?" Evidently he's managed to wrestle the phone off her, and is now affecting a super calm tone as though I couldn't have possibly witnessed (over the phone) their brawl.

"Sei un scemo!" I can hear her screaming in the background still. Oh, give it a rest, woman! Honestly, my father's choice in wives is shocking, simply shocking! "Vaffanculo scemo!"

Think he is shuffling to a quieter location; either that, or he's thrown a bag over her head. I'm happy with either, so long as the shouting stops.

"I'm doing well, Dad. Really well, actually," I say, trying to ignore the muffled ruckus in the background. Yes, she is still there!

"Oh, well that's good to hear." His voice is calm—the calmness of a hostage who is just about to kill their jailer in cold blood. It's his usual tone, though. "What's this about putting me into a home?"

"I said to her you're not that old, not old enough to be put in a home or anything, and she took it completely the wrong way," I say, trying to explain.

"Oh yes, that makes sense. You know, try not to say anything that inflames her, even when you're saying the opposite. Words just set her off," he's instructing me in his gruff, matter-of-fact manner.

"I know, Dad. But really, I don't know how you deal with her."

"Oh, dear, don't be silly," he's saying in a sing-song voice. Okay, newsflash to *news.com*, sing-song voice is not voice of love, but voice of lunatic. "We all have our cross to bare," he is hissing now like a man possessed. "So don't say things like that … She might be listening on the other phone."

Oh, right. Wouldn't want to get him into any more trouble this evening.

Wouldn't want to read about his homicide tomorrow morning online, knowing I may have had a part to play in the whole bloody end of it.

"And how are you, Dad?"

"Great, darling—Doing really well. Thinking about going back to the office for a few days a week."

"But you're retired, Dad." It's completely counterintuitive to me for anyone to contemplate going back into the workforce.

"Oh, I know. I think it will be good for me, though."

This is when I think it would be a good time to read between the lines. So ... *Good for him.* Yes, of course, good for him to get away from Maria for a few days. Understood. Might stave off the madness for another few years.

"Indeed, you might be right, Dad."

Not a fan of these awkward pauses during phone conversations ... They don't work for me! Not when I'm not off on my own tangent, anyway.

"And how's the new boyfriend going? I saw your photos in a magazine today." Well, if Dad knows, that's a fucking coup. The man hasn't engaged with popular culture since the eighties.

"Good, Dad! It's going really well."

"I'm glad my little girl's happy. I always knew she was going to make it big."

He makes me smile, poor Dad, still has illusions that I'm concealing Madonna-esque talent. Ahh ... To those that wear rose-coloured glasses, I tip my hat. If only I had a hat ... or said glasses ... Wouldn't wear though—too vain.

"I am happy, Dad." It makes me sad that we talk through stilted code sometimes, a) because his wife is a crazed lunatic and b) because we both find it hard to communicate with each other.

Another awkward pause.

"Okay, darling, thanks for your call," he's telling me merrily. *That's it?* "Let's speak soon."

"Yes, darling, love you, too."

I can hear a torrent of abuse from Maria. "Testa di cazzo! Ma che fai? Sei veramente un uomo ridicolo …"

OVER, and out!

Oh dear, my heart has sunk a little. May be getting softer with advanced age … Why did he marry that woman? Note to self: do not look at online news tomorrow morning in case homicide case catches attention.

44. 10:35a.m.

ednesday morning. Tapping email out to Chris along the lines of, "Going to random girl's house this evening to get hair extensions done in suburbs. May not make it out alive. Last supper (or lunch, in this case)?" Oh, and here's Tina, having appeared at my door, all enthusiastic and beautiful, short skirt and espadrilles on.

I'm still unhappy from seeing the exchange between her and Elsie the other day and feeling like third wheel. But I've elected not to be all *I'll get you back,* crazy bitch style—I shall, instead, take higher ground, given that I'm now a sophisticated woman with a celebrity boyfriend and winning job. And a soon-to-be new office (might I add)! I am a clever woman of zen. Crazy bitch no longer fits my persona, not since the implementation of *Cee Project.*

"Hey, Cee," she's calling.

What it it with the sing-song voice? Did everyone read the article on *news.com?* Oh my gosh!

"Hey, Tina." I'm opting for a smoother, more articulate voice. A *woman of the world* voice. "How are you doing?"

"Good." She's leaning on the door hinge in a relaxed manner. "Can I come in?"

"Of course, my door's always open," not true, not for everyone, or anyone, "at least to you." Thinking should clarify in case here on after I start getting every youngster and their hipster dog in here wanting some sort of advice. Not happening.

She's smiling, taking her usual seat at the table.

I'm waiting for her to start talking. Despite her enthusiasm, the girl is very measured and wouldn't be wandering into my office if she didn't have something to say.

"I miss being in here," she has finally shared.

Hmm … That's unexpected and strange. I'm narrowing my eyes at her. Somehow I don't quite believe it—I thought she would revel out there on the floor with all those other hipsters driving for success. "Why do you say that?"

"Oh, no reason, I guess." Such a weird choice of words from her, because there's always a reason, isn't there? "It was just nice in here; we were like a little team … comrades almost."

Comrades? I can't see her as any type of socialist, even a Chardonnay socialist. She doesn't even drink! One couldn't be left-wing and sip hot water and lemon at their comrade meetings.

"You don't have much camaraderie out there?" I ask her, feeling like I'm taking on the psychologist role. This is unfamiliar, but somehow, strangely fitting. Crossing legs, I begin tapping my pen on my lip in a psychologist-like fashion, as though I'm considering her shared thoughts deeply.

"No, not really! I mean ... I have a lot of friends out there. A lot of friends ..." she's repeating. Okay, good for you! I know you're a popular girl, you don't need my vote, missy.

"But everyone's also a little bit bitchy, you know?" She is staring at me, wide, dark eyes a bit like Bambi's. *Sigh* ... She must have had some sort of run-in. So, who cares? Welcome to the industry sweet-bloody-heart. Dog eat dog, stab in the back. Bitchy is tame. You're either prepared for them and let whatever happens wash straight over you—or you're not going to make it. Simple. Rule of industry! Rule of office! Rule of *fucking* LIFE!

"Yeah, I know—But it's like anything ..." I say, feeling like adding "kid" at end of the sentence but realising it's wildly paternalistic and also brings to attention my advanced age. "I'm sure people were bitchy at university and at school, non? It's like that everywhere—You've got to be prepared, doll." *Doll* is better than *kid*. You know, for good measure now that I'm *woman of the world,* giving advice.

"I know ..." She has let out a sigh. "I figured it just would have been different at work. I don't know, more ... erm ..." She is clearly searching for a specific word, wonder what it is? Oh, here it comes ... professional."

Smiling. *Professional!* Is she joking?

"The workplace is not professional, Tina! It's the furthest thing from the word. It's a bloody jungle ..."

Another Guns N' Roses song has sprung to mind, and I'm visualising Axl Rose in white bike shorts, leather jacket, and bandana, thrusting pelvis of course. Trying to push it out of thoughts ... No, still very much in mind. Much of my advice is based on lyrics from Guns N' Roses songs. Some may consider this disturbing. I would say, in a way, it's poignant. Indeed.

"It's a jungle," I say, recovering my thoughts. "They will sling anything at you. Sometimes what they'll sling at you will be true. And sometimes it will be bullshit. So? Who cares? You remember *you* are who you are. You have to let it wash over you, water off a duck's back."

Good metaphor not relating to early nineties rock.

She's staring at me. Wide-eyed, still. Maybe she is struggling out there, but she doesn't seem like the type of girl who would. You know, all private school bitch and all.

"Has something happened?"

"No, nothing," she's shaking her head. "I just sometimes wish I could rewind and come back in here."

Hmm … Sounds like something did happen, but I'm not going to press her for it.

"But you have friends out there," I say, thinking how blatantly obvious she made this a few moments ago. "I saw you talking to Elsie the other day—You seem close."

Cee, you are the adult. Take the higher ground. Do not delve into the Elsie scenario because you're still sort of smarting from it, but concealing it under your rugged exterior. Nice self-awareness, non?

"Yeah, I guess." She's picking at her skirt. "But you know, I don't know if we are … I think she might just be … "

"A bit of a bitch," I say with a knowing expression on my face.

Oh good, she's nodding at me, like, *That's exactly it. You've hit the nail on the head.*

"Well, so what?" She's not the only bitch in the world. "There will always be an Elsie around, trust me. Bitches be bitches. You just need to be stronger than them."

Listen to me, totally turned over new leaf here.

Screen has just pinged with message from Chris. She'll have to wait a second, need to read this …

"You are totally going all Jenny from da block. Backyard extensions in the suburbs? Love it, it's so gangsta. Can I come, too?"

"Okay, I should go," she's saying to me. "By the way … "

Oh god, has she been warming me up for something? So I would be soft and cuddly for the *actual* big question?

"Yes?" I'm a little suspicious.

"Can you come to one of Krishnananda's classes next week with me? He wants us to visit the studio." She's at the door now, looking at me slightly desperately.

"Oh, really?" *Groan.* "It's not my thing." My voice is becoming whiny almost instantly. Doesn't he use some trapeze like contraption in his classes?

"Oh, I'm sure he would go easy for you on the first occasion. It'll be fine … "

She is trying to reassure me, which I guess is sweet, but I have a vivid vision creeping into mind of myself hanging from the trapeze and then falling and breaking my neck. I'm a fabulous woman, providing advice to troubled young minds, and have work, romantic relationship, and the rest of it *all* in check—So I don't think I'm going to allow it to all be taken from me in some sick trapeze forward slash yoga injury exclamation mark!

"Please." Oh, dear lord, she's pleading with me.

"Why don't you take Elsie?" *Your new wedding buddy.* "She's, like, all yogarrific—and stuff!"

Can't believe I'm throwing Tina into Lex Luther's path, but, you know, sometimes there's collateral damage, and I do not want to be hanging from groin, upside down, suspended a few metres up … Why would one do that to one's self?

"No, I can't take her … I really can't." She's panic-stricken.

"Okay, fine," I say, only because she is looking like she might have a stroke. "What about Jai?"

Light bulb moment! Only name that crops up in mind other than Ian's, and well, let's just say that is no pretty sight.

"I can't. He's going back to L.A. next week …"

Hold up! Jai's going back to L.A.?

Regurgitating thought into verbal realm. "Jai's going back to L.A.?"

"Yes, personal leave or something … He's heading back on Monday morning."

Don't question why she's so informed—and evidently I'm out of the loop again. I'm trying to grab onto the basics of the situation here, and ignoring why I'm so interested in it.

"Is he coming back?"

"It's indefinite, some sort of family situation. Nobody knows what it is—There's a lot of speculation out on the floor about what's going on though …"

Don't fucking care about the speculation! Cut her off, Cee.

"When did this happen?"

"I don't know … I think Monday," she's telling me. "So will you come?"

she asks again.

Confusion—unable to put together a convincing argument as to why I shouldn't go, or to even construct a well thought out lie.

"Fine, I'll go."

"Great!" She's clapping her hands together in an enthused fashion. I've kind of missed that. "Tuesday at 6:30 p.m. Wear some Lululemon."

"I don't own fucking Lululemon …"

She got what she wanted, and so she has gone. Left my office just like that.

And I'm left with an impending sense of doom, probably because of the death apparatus I'll be suspended from next week, but maybe it is linked to the news about Jai leaving. Why didn't he tell me? Why would he tell me? It's not like we're that close or anything. Christ, I've never even broken bread with the man, only had half a drink with him in the boardroom that one time, but somehow I thought we had—I don't know what I think …

Something stupid, evidently!

Sigh. Turning back to my screen, typing to Chris, "No, going with Chantel the beautician. We're like besties now. She'll be cut if I bring my other bestie along … Lunch?"

45. 6:00p.m.

Out in front of random looking house in Alexandria with Chantel. Several cars parked on lawn (all slightly hotted-up ... Is that what they say these days? You know when cars are lowered and have large exhausts? Not quite sure). Chantel's car looks like this, and has been spray-painted some weird colour which changes depending on the light—It's referred to as a "chameleon" colour, so she says. Think it looks more like an oil slick, but not going to tell her this. Despite her sweet-as-pie façade, think she might be a "bad bitch" when required, as per the "Nicki Minaj" song, which was blaring from the speakers during the drive. One day you get dropped off at work in a Lamborghini, the next you get picked up in a hotted-up Skyline. Tried to avoid eye contact with Jai, who left the building at the exact right time to catch me getting into said vehicle, which was blasting gangsta music at the time. Caught his smug little grin.

Chantel is knocking on the door loudly again.

"Quite a few cars here," I say. Take the hint, will you? Sharing thoughts with her via osmosis again: *Is she a drug dealer, also?*

She never gets the thought sharing process; just always stares back at me with her ever-contented expression. Probably a result of excessive Botox, but also the vapidity of her mind, I imagine!

"Yeah, she's like super busy."

Door is flying open, I almost had to step back then, half expecting a *Sons of Anarchy* scene, with Katey Sagal smoking a fat one and holding a firearm. *Phew*, none of that luckily—It's another blonde clone, short, big-breasted, blue-eyed, and hair down to her ample ass (can see it sticking out from the side, despite front-on vision—So the booty is the new thing for definite, as previously established).

"Hey, sweetheart." She's cooing and hugging Chantel.

"Hey, baby, long time no see," Chantel has replied. Tara, (blonde number two) hair extension extraordinaire, is smoking a cigarette, although not a fat one, and her cigarette arm is held up at a comical angle as she hugs Chantel close.

"This is my friend Cee." Chantel's extricating herself from the embrace and gesticulating towards me with a wide-eyed look, as to say, *Can you believe it!*

"Oh, hey." Tara's leaning in, I think to give me a kiss. It's all about the hugs and kisses at this locale clearly.

"Nice to meet you," I say, nodding my head a few times.

"Oh, yeah, super great to meet you." She's looking starstruck. "Come on in, doll face. So excited to be doing your hair." She's ushering me in, and I step closely behind her into the dark corridor. Fuck, why am I the one that has to go in first? How well do I know Chantel anyway? I don't even know her surname? Shit … I didn't even tell anyone the address of this place. They won't be able to find me if I don't turn up at work tomorrow. Desperately thinking I should have accepted Chris's invite, at least that way we could have worked together in the event of any hostage situation.

"Oh my god," I can hear Tara (Blonde Two) whispering in the background. "She's, like, so classy … And she looks taller than in the magazine. Like six foot or something," she says, tone full of awe.

Despite potential hostage situation, I can't help smiling. Really? Did she think I wasn't going to hear that? And I'm five foot eight on a good day, but I can't help walking taller as a result. Am now statuesque glamazon with celebrity boyfriend.

Blonde Two has just pushed past me, her ass nearly launching me into the corridor. "This way," she's telling me like a flight attendant.

She leads me into what appears to be the garage. Wait. Heart stopping moment, life flashing before my very eyes!

The door is sweeping open ever so slowly, and I'm preparing myself for the part when someone pulls a gun … Here it comes … Oh wait, I may have overreacted … Yes, indeed. I'm being led into a pristine white world with about ten hair work stations, almost completely packed with customers. It's a garage transformed into a sweatshop. Every woman has turned to look at me.

"She's here," Blonde Two is trilling.

They're continuing to stare.

"Oh, hello, everyone," I say, sing-song voice in place. Okay, so no empirical data has suggested that it works, but I'm going with it anyway. Lots of smiling back towards me, nodding and still more staring.

Blonde Two is ushering me towards a seat.

I'm slowly lowering myself into it, very aware that they're all still looking at me. Clinging my handbag to my chest as comfort gesture.

"So I'm going to do your hair today," Blonde Two is telling me, "and I've ordered you all Russian hair, okay?" Like this is supposed to mean something to me. It must be the blank expression on my face that is forcing her into further dialogue. "So Russian hair is, like, the best. None of that *nasty shit from China* for you! I'll only do the best for you, doll face."

I'm hideously aware that the other women in the room may be having that nasty shit from China glued into their heads right now. Ignore. Embracing the thought of having Russian prostitute's hair glued to my own.

Ignore that thought, too, Cee. Focus on the notion that you will have luscious blonde hair in a matter of … Actually, how long am I going to be here? How long do these things take?

"Oh, wonderful," I'm cooing. "Thanks so much."

Evidently Blonde Two is happy with this because she is nodding emphatically and stubbing her cigarette out. Thankfully … Oh no, she's just lit up another one, and is starting to lay out hair over my shoulders.

"Don't worry." She's waving around the cigarette and the hair at the same time. "It's real hair, not acrylic, so you won't go up in smoke," she's laughing. I'm laughing, too, desperately. It's coming out as strange, hysterical, nervous giggle.

"You're so lucky." Chantel is leaning in from where she's hovering at my side. "She's totally the best extension lady in Sydney."

"Shit, doll." Blonde Two is looking chuffed. "She's such a sweetheart," she is saying to me, gesticulating towards Chantel.

"Now, what do you want to drink?" Blonde Two is leaning close in to my face; her hideously swollen trout pout is at my eye level.

"Oh, what do you have?"

"Do you want a champagne? You look like a champagne type of lady," she's telling me, still nodding vigorously; the trout pout does not flap around, but remains frozen in place.

"Champagne sounds wonderful." At least it will take the edge off.

"Get her a champagne," Blonde Two is barking at one of the apprentices in a dissembling change of personality. The apprentice is scurrying off.

"So," Blonde Two has begun, "we have your pic on the wall." She's pointing a talon towards a wall with various pages from magazines ripped out. Can't quite make out my image given general blindness, but can make out images of other women in provocative positions and swimsuits. Hmm—Does the wall denote the type of lady who gets hair extensions?

"Tell us then," she's saying, turning a conspiratorial eye as the apprentice runs out with a glass of champagne and hands it to me.

Oh, there's the ping of mobile. Looking down at it, it's been clutched in my hand in case I needed to make an emergency call. It's Jess:

"I need to see you tonight. Total emergency. See! Emergency!"

Tapping back, and Blonde Two has started sectioning off my hair. She hasn't continued her chatter, which means she must be forfeiting to my texts.

"Err …" I begin to tap back. "Kind of in the middle of something."

Blonde Two is clearly trying to angle gaze to get a look at what I'm writing; I can see her in the mirror.

Ping. Jess's reponse! "Is it sex?"

"No," I've responded. What's she thinking? Why would I even consider texting during sex?

"Well, it's urgent. Can I meet you at your place in a few hours?"

Sigh. When did friends become so demanding!

"Do you think I'll be finished by eight?" I'm looking at Blonde Two, who is in turn looking completely enthralled, probably trying to figure out the text drama at hand.

"Oh yeah, totally. I'll have you out in an hour, *doll face.*" She's starting to stick things into my hair. Hmm … Not sure if I like this *doll face* terminology. Know may have used term in past, but am not doll face!

"Okay," I text back. "8:00 p.m., my place."

"Done," Jess replies back quickly.

Putting phone away. Taking well deserved sip of champagne. Looking up, and they're all still staring at me. For fuck's sake!

"Was that *him?*" Blonde Two has asked.

"Who?" What is she talking about? Did I miss something?

"Chad Thompson." Oh, right! That him. My claim to fame!

"No." I'm being honest for once. "Just a friend of mine. She's having some crisis."

"Oh, tell me about it, doll face … Aren't we all!" she says, giving a conspiratorial look around, and now everyone is laughing, so best I laugh, too. Only polite! You know, going back to my jungle metaphor, when one is in the jungle, one must act like part of the pack.

"So back to Chad," Blonde Two has quickly shifted the topic. After all, she only has an hour with me, no doubt she needs to pump me for information ASAP. "What's he like?"

Not surprised that the whole room has fallen silent, and that the ladies with half-glued-in nasty Chinese shit are obviously waiting for my response. They're practically quivering with excitement.

"Yeah, he's a lovely man." Standard response, non? Really gives nothing away, but there's a collective sigh in the room and a few of them are moving a little nervously—crossing and uncrossing their legs, adjusting clothes, picking at manicured nails—that kind of itchy, anticipation-filled movement.

The oracle has spoken. Yes, she has!

"He's ripped, right?" Blonde Two just asked.

"Pardon?" Well, that's a bit personal, non?

"Ripped, you know, ab-wise," she's explaining, as though I might not know what ripped is, given I'm not a *bad bitch* that drives a skyline chameleon … or any car at all for that matter.

Oh shit, I'm totally not going to get myself out of this, am I? What could I possibly say in this situation which wouldn't make me sound like I have a stick shoved far up my ass? Or that wouldn't negate the *free hair* situation Chantel has negotiated for me?

Do not want to pay $500 for Russian hair glued into head in garage. At least you can offer is some *ab* chat, Cee.

"Yes, indeed," I say, finishing off the champagne. "He is totally ripped."

There is a fluttering of excitement, and the women are looking around, making little faces at each other: winking of eyes, opening of mouths, and all the rest of it. I've totally become *Jenny from da block* this evening. May be bad bitch, too … without booty, of course, but *bad bitch with flat ass nonetheless …*

46. 7:50p.m.

*A*t home inspecting hair whilst drinking Coke Zero. In an effort to cut down number of alcoholic beverages consumed on daily basis, am now drinking sugary carbonated drinks instead (or in this case, diet sugary carbonated drink). Not sure which is better or worse, but having ingested a sip of green juice, have decided green juice is, indeed, not for me, and perhaps should move on to zero calorie drink fad. Staring at reflection in bathroom mirror, considering hair. Can one have too much Coke Zero? Not sure. Shall Google.

Chantel, Tara, and other colourful participants in garage salon all said my hair looks fantastic. In fact, they told me quite a few times, with lots of cooing and remarks about how stunning I am.

Has certainly been an ego boost, but now in the house staring in the mirror, I'm not quite sure about the whole hair thing—Have look of

Daenerys Targaryen from Game of Thrones. Might start wearing mythical flowing garb. However, not sure if hair is Targaryen enough, or more like a porn star? Yes, more a merger of both said examples.

Swishing hair from side to side in Marsha Brady style. Maybe it'll just take some getting used to, methinks. Head is decidedly heavy, like having a helmet on it, but am unable to remove.

Oh, text from Jess.

"Can you meet me at the bar on the corner of your street instead? Lucky's?" I know what bar is at the corner of the street, she didn't need to add the name.

"Why don't you just come to my place!" I text back.

Am already in sweats, and will now need to locate an appropriate pair of shoes to go with sweats if I need to go to Lucky's. Besides, now that I'm getting papped, I need to really ramp up the appearance during downtime, i.e. moments when I just pop down the street to get groceries or to have brunch with dirty hair, track pants, and thongs. Need to at least buy designer track pants, wear hat to cover dirty hair, and sunglasses to cover face.

"Oh, come on. I really want a drink," she has texted back, and is persistent, non? What is wrong with her tonight? Suddenly she demands that I meet her tonight urgently, and then she won't even come to my place! Is there an emergency at Lucky's?

"I have alcohol at my place. Have you forgotten who you're talking to? And I look like shit, dressed like dag. What if I get papped?"

Fred is staring at me sadly, as per usual, from the ground near my feet … He certainly doesn't like the new me. When I walked in, he started barking at me like he had no idea who I was. Then when I picked him up to console the poor little thing, he tried to eat my new hair. I literally had to remove clumps from his tiny mouth. Perhaps new hair means that I've joined part of the animal kingdom, or that he was a Russian pimp in another life. Could explain why he has rebirthed as slightly demented, melancholy dog.

"Oh, come on! You're not going to get papped. Especially not without him. I've already gotten us a table. See you in five."

Sigh. Insistent, and persistent indeed! Best swig down remaining Coke Zero for the road. Okay, appropriate footwear—Hmm ... What goes with sweat pants other than Ugg boots? Nothing really, other than runners ... Not feeling the runner vibe!

Damn it! Desperately pulling on a pair of dirty jeans that have at some point found their home on the floor of my closet, slipping on thongs. Baseball hat on for good measure, and grabbing handbag ...

"Sorry, Fred," I say, heading out, and hopefully he'll be more pleased to see me when I return than he was earlier on today.

It's dark already. Descent into winter is upon me. Hate winter, means another layer of clothes that I need to coordinate. Winter style is decidedly worse than summer style, where you can just slip on some jean shorts and a tee and it's all acceptable. Once coats, gloves, boots, and scarves are involved, it all turns a little pear-shaped. You can certainly discern the stylish from the style-less in winter; naturally, I fall into the latter category.

Wishing I lived in a city with perennial summer. Should move to Caribbean. But what would one do there? And I really find Caribbean accents very annoying. Not quite sure why, but they're a little bit too jaunty for my liking. Note to self: Caribbean idea is a bad one—Don't move there!

Turning into Lucky's, a seedy bar on the corner of my street with booths, and sticky floors, and sticky menus. Constant beer smell!

There she is in the corner, sitting furtively in a booth with menu open in front of her, and a beverage. Looks like a long gin and tonic. Must really be an emergency!

Sliding onto the seat opposite hers.

"What have you done to your hair?" she's asking instantly.

"Nothing." Obvious lie, I mean, It couldn't possible have grown to this length since the last time I saw her. "What are you talking about?" I ask, removing baseball cap and smoothing hair down in an elegant manner, befitting hoody, jeans, and thongs.

"Have you had extensions put in?"

"No," I continue to lie.

"Why are you lying to me? Your hair didn't grow six inches overnight, did it?" She's looking at me like I've gone completely bonkers.

"So I've had hair extensions put in." I'm defensive, and so what! "So?"

"Have you lost it?" She has slapped the menu down onto the table and is judging me quite openly.

"No, I haven't. Everyone's doing it," I say, taking hold of the menu. Sheesh, you wouldn't want to think that your friends are supposed to be supportive or anything.

"Who? Who is doing it?"

We're still on this. "A lot of ladies are. I know heaps." I'm not willing to say that the majority of whom are those I've met through my now almost obsessive fake tans and, of course, wives and partners of Chad's friends.

"What, like characters on the *Real Housewives of Beverly Hills* or something?" She's being ironic.

"No, Jess, people I actually know. Just because you don't have friends who have hair extensions doesn't mean I don't."

"I assume you mean Chad's friends, or the women who fawn over Chad?"

"I'm not going to dignify that with a response," I say, sticking my nose in the air.

The waitress has stopped at our booth. She looks like a junky, but hey, I'm not really the judgmental type. I'll leave that to Jess.

"Can I get a gin and tonic?" Coke Zero is just not going to cut it right now. "And in a long glass." Long glass required at this point.

"Could I get some fries, please?" Jess is asking. "I'm fine with my drink."

The waitress has taken our menus and sniffs at us, wiping her nose wildly. Oh, dear … Junky, indeed. Right, refocusing attention on Jess, and still feeling cranky. Her judgmental tone has been apparent for weeks now, months in fact—since I started dating Chad. The implication being I'm changing into something he wants, a WAG of some description.

Can't a woman look after herself without her motives being judged? And even if I was turning into a WAG, which I am NOT, isn't she supposed to be my friend? Chris hasn't had any issue with my hair extensions—In fact, I think he probably could have been talked into getting some of his own. You know, like a Rastafarian look.

"Fine," she's saying to me grimly, crossing her arms. "I'll drop it."

"Thank you!"

"Just as long …" Oh, here we go. Feminist rant 101 from Jess. " … as you know that you're a perfectly beautiful woman and don't need to conform to some sort of modern day notion of good looks just because you're dating this man."

"Thanks, Mum!"

"That's sort of ironic, because I'm sure your mother would be supporting your transformation in some Victorian era sentiment of getting a ring on your finger before the year's out." Her manner is all crazed now.

Whoa! What is wrong with her? This is what she was like when she was on all the mad hormones trying to get pregnant. Erratic. Judgmental. Greer-esque in her delivery!

"What's wrong with you, lady?"

"Sorry … I'm really out of sorts." She has an apologetic look on her face.

"Well, what's wrong? What's the emergency?"

Junky has brought my drink. I'm smiling at her graciously, hoping she won't pull a shank on me at some point. She hasn't smiled back. And, whoops, a few judgmental points there—Oh, well!

"Oh, it's terrible," she's begun, "I just don't know how to tell you … I think I need some chips in my stomach first to calm the nerves."

Oh shit, really? I thought Mother was the only person who liked to play *guess the surprise,* or *bad news* in this case.

Racking my brains, trying to think of the worst possible life occurrence for Jess. I bet it's …

"You're back with Pete?" Option one!

She's shaking her head, good sign! "No," and yet she is looking sad at the same time.

"Pete left the girl he's been seeing?" I thought they were breaking up … Option two!

"No, he's still with her," she says, looking sad again. Her expression is taking on Fred-like proportions, which is bad, to say the least. The dog's chronically depressed; I'll have to put him on meds soon, methinks.

"You lost your job?" Let's have a look at what's behind door number three, shall we?

"I wish."

Oh, thank Christ—The fries are here. The guessing game can now cease. Junky has tossed them down, and they are skidding across the table. Coming to a definitive stop in front of Jess ... Junky is quite skilled, it seems!

Jess has already started to plunge into them, grabbing a fistful and stuffing them into her mouth. And I am happily sipping on my gin and tonic, though still somewhat confused. So good! Junky has done a good job, heavy on the gin, easy on the tonic.

"Okay." Jess is still swallowing a mouthful of fries, but managing to speak also. "I don't want you to judge me when I tell you this because you need to be there for me and you need to support me." More fries in face.

"But you were just judging me a moment ago." *So that makes you a hypocrite.*

"But this is different," she is telling me in between bites—How so? It's you, and not me? Luckily, verbal diarrhea doesn't occur. I'm opting for head nodding, and as woman of substance, I take the moral high ground again.

"Of course, I won't judge you," I say, clenching teeth a little. Why are relationships so difficult?

"And you'll support me no matter what?"

"Indeed," I say, equally calmly. Although I feel like screaming at her, *What the fuck is it?* But I manage to maintain a reserved, zen-like exterior.

She is doing some deep breathing in and out … "I'm pregnant."

Okay, was not expecting that she is expecting … Not at all!

"But you're drinking gin and tonic." I don't know why this is the first thought that has come into my head, but here it is, and already out of mouth.

"No, it's just tonic … But I did, however, go on a bender with you over the weekend, and now think I may have caused irreparable damage to the baby."

"Did you know?"

"Of course not!" she's snapping. "I mean, I'd skipped my period, sure. But I've always been irregular, and you know I've been told for years now that my eggs aren't fertile, and that sometimes there are no eggs—years! I thought it was like every other time I'd missed my period."

"Oh, shit!" The gravity of it all is hitting me … Jess is pregnant. Wow, this is all very strangely adult … unchartered adult territory.

"You think I've caused irreparable brain damage, too, don't you?" She's clapping her hand over her mouth.

"No, of course not," I say, flapping a hand around and shooing away the thought. "That's how people usually get pregnant—alcohol. I'm sure if you've stopped now, it'll be fine," I tell her, you know, being a medical professional and all, which I'm clearly not! But good advice, Cee!

"That's what the doctor said," she says, still covering her mouth, eyes wide.

"See?" There you go. No need for medical degree in this case.

"But I just can't believe it—After all these years of trying and hormones and bullshit, and then I stopped trying—and bam, I get pregnant! I don't even have a fucking partner, Cee!" She's yelling at me like I'm the one that caused her to be impregnated.

Okay, I'm a friend, so what to do? Yes, shall cover her hand with mine in empathetic gesture. Patrons are looking at us. As per usual! This might not be the moment to tell her to keep her voice down though.

"Is it Pete's?"

"Of course it's Pete's," she is hissing. "Who else's would it be?"

Trying not to point out that it could have been any number of people's, given she's not actually in a relationship with Pete anymore and he's seeing someone else. And given her new wild, sexual libido.

"Have you told him?"

"No, I can't," she says, stuffing more chips into her face. "I haven't spoken to him in a week. Not since we stopped shagging, at least—and I heard through the grapevine that him leaving that girl was just a rumour, and that they're going strong now." She's raising her eyebrow.

"He needs to know."

"No, he doesn't, Cee. And I'm sure if you were in my shoes, you wouldn't say anything to him either."

Hmm, maybe she's right. It's easy to take the moral high ground when it's not you.

"Well, what are you going to do?"

"Keep it, of course! I've wanted a baby since I was—Well, since always. I've always wanted to be a mum."

I'm nodding, knowing it's true. Me, though, yes—Cee over here on the red seat with the token G&T—not a maternal instinct in my body. Not one! Maybe it will just ping on at some point like a text message—Who knows? That's what everyone says … when the body clock starts ticking. Still bloody waiting over here … When is that ping going to happen?

"Cee, are you listening?"

Oh, she has been talking.

"So I need to know you'll be there for me. I know things between you and Chad are like … epic, or whatever."

Is there a tone of irony in her voice?

"But I seriously need you. I don't have anyone else!"

"Don't be ridiculous. I'm your best friend. Of course I'm here for you," I assure her, and I am! One hundred percent.

"Thanks." She's sitting back in the booth, less tense now.

"But those hair extensions, Cee, they've got to go. Seriously, you look like a porn star," she says, shaking her head.

"I'm willing to forgive that remark, given you're pregnant and everything and your hormones are going wild. But I have two words for you … Fuck you."

"So classy," she laughs through her words.

"Indeed."

"Why did you want to meet here anyway? You're not actually drinking!"

"I thought you would be less likely to make a scene in public."

47. 3:30p·m·

hursday. Day after extensions and pregnancy bombshell! Have endured day full of jibes regarding extensions and potential new careers suggested by colleagues as result of hair extensions. Brushing off remarks like confetti at a wedding. Let the plebs have their moment in the sun. I am now zen woman (of the intellectual sort) with high profile job, man-of-dreams, cameos in magazines as "mystery blonde," shoulder to cry on for struggling friends, and aunt to baby (who may or may not be scarred from alcohol-induced bender I forced friend on last weekend, prior to her, or my, knowledge of pregnancy situation). All summed up, and am running on an absolute high.

Have also managed to drink Coke Zero at lunch, much to Chris's disappointment, who is concerned because he may have lost his lunchtime drinking buddy. Chris, however, likes the extensions of the hair variety—So much so because they remind him of a transsexual dancer's hair from *The Fairy*, his locale of choice on Saturday nights.

Hair reminds people of either porn star or transsexuals. But who am I to judge these two groups of people and their lustrous manes?

I'm in the process of packing up my office, as I am now moving into a new, larger office down the corridor, with a window and a teeny tiny view of the city. Initially thought moving would be easy, a few boxes, and in and out I go. Instead, I have discovered that I have amounted a load of shit in my filing cabinets and drawers over the years. Mostly it's of the useless variety, which I should have turfed the moment after it was used instead of lazily stuffing it into a drawer. The thought process at the start of packing was to locate any useful documents from the mess and turf the rest. However, said process has become more and more arduous as day has worn on, so have now wheeled in the confidential bin, and am shoving everything in that.

As I'm stuffing a ring binder into the bin, clearly flouting the rules of only putting paper in (because it gets shredded at a later stage), Elsie has walked in, all floaty and smelling of Jasmines.

"Hi, Cee," she's cooing as she watches my handy work.

"Hello, Elsie," I reply in the manner of Jerry Seinfeld addressing his arch nemesis, Newman.

"You do know you can only put paper in that bin, right?" she says in her deprecating manner, like I'm an idiot.

"Oh, really?" I ask, shoving a plastic sleeve in at the same time as speaking with the bitch.

"Yes, it says it on the front of the bin." She's gesticulating towards the large sign on top of it, which reads: "Paper only. Foreign objects will jam the shredder."

"Oh, dear. I must have missed that."

She is so rude, the way she just stares at me, and is now crossing her arms so prim and proper. Evidently her display of liking me has come to an end. It obviously irks her that despite all my quirks, all my rule breaking, my tardiness, slovenliness, and the rest of it, I'm the one who is getting promoted onto the bigger accounts and into the bigger office. It's clear she thinks it's because of my personal relationships, my said *charm*, and that it has nothing to do with my competence.

Well, why don't you go cry about it? I continue shoving paper recklessly into the bin, like Jess does with food in her face.

"Was there anything else you wanted?" I ask, looking up snottily at her now.

"Yes, I wanted to see if you were coming to Jai's farewell on Friday night ... given you're the only person who hasn't bothered to respond to the invitation, even though I sent it earlier on in the week. I need to confirm numbers."

"And one person makes a difference?" I ask, buying myself some time. I'm sure I have something else going on tomorrow night—Racking brain, which works far less effectively without glass of champagne (or two) in the middle of the day. Yes, dinner with Chad! Could probably reschedule—but I haven't seen him for the majority of the week, and I need to maintain presence and momentum. Shit, what to do?

"Yes, it does," she's telling to me. "Unlike other people, I take planning very seriously."

Ignore the jibe, Cee, as it is evidently directed towards you and your scattered, erratic approach to life.

"Well, I can't make it. I'm busy," I say, not letting on what said engagement is. I know it will irk her since she needs to know everything that's going on so she can maintain some sort of sense of control.

"Okay, then," she's saying breezily. Oh, there's more … "I'm surprised you're not going to bother turning up. I always thought you and Jai … got along quite well."

What's she getting at? "We do get along," be cautious, Cee, she's manipulative, remember—feeling like I'm stepping into a trap, "but I get along with most people in the office."

"Yes, I know you do. I just thought you two—had an understanding." She's grappling to find an appropriate word to describe her perception of my and Jai's relationship. She's clearly muting what she really thinks, but what does she really think exactly?

"I don't know what you mean," I say, and I don't. I'm not going to entertain her dissembling bullshit late afternoon on a Thursday either.

"Okay," she says, her voice bright and fake. ""Really, I'm not surprised you wouldn't turn up. Since you've been seeing Chad and become a socialite and all, you seem sort of distracted."

I feel like saying to her, *I'm always distracted, Elsie, now piss off!* No, I must remain cool and calm, because I know she hates it, like any mean girl. It bothers her that she can't get a rise out of me.

"Well, thanks for the observation, Elsie! I'm really kind of busy at the moment, though, if you haven't noticed—moving into my new office and all," I say, putting in the knife, "and besides, don't you have a wedding to plan on work time?"

Smiling at her coquettishly, her face begins to shrink up into a very unattractive expression. Funny, I thought Elsie couldn't be unattractive even if she tried—but I was wrong.

Goodbye.

Off she stalks, angrily. I'm grabbing another binder and stuffing it into the bin, almost in defiance. But you know what, her words have bothered me, despite all other appearances. Why would she think I was closer to Jai than the rest of them? The man has annoyed me for the majority of his stay here, constantly drawing attention to my tardiness and lack of concern about his creative. Maybe of late we've fallen into some sort of uneasy understanding of each other, but I wouldn't say we were *close*. Not at all!

If I were to be honest, and of course only to myself, the thought of him leaving has played on my mind since I found out earlier on in the week. And I'm not even quite sure why. It bothers me that he didn't tell me personally … And I guess it bothers me that he might not be back.

I mean, it's a leave of absence. He could potentially be back, right? And he could potentially not come back. It kind of would be a sadder place without him here, periodically popping into my office to make snide little remarks and smile at my silly jokes in his ever so sexy way.

Can't think about this. I'm a woman in a fulfilling, relevant relationship with man-of-dreams—Can't be considering Jai in any other context other than as a colleague.

Anyway, why is he going back to the States? Family matter, maybe? Keep thinking he has pregnant girlfriend back home who is about to deliver baby or something. Not sure why this jealous thought is the only one in mind. Ashamed that last night I was desperately checking his relationship status on Facebook. It says nothing—so I've drawn a blank with that one.

That didn't help.

Probably can reschedule the date with Chad. The whole notion of momentums and presence is my mother's, and I'm just invoking it for my purposes for this occasion. I think, really, I just don't want to go to Jai's farewell party. Something tells me to steer clear.

Steer clear—Don't muddy the waters! Be smart, Cee.

But I should say something to him before he goes, surely. It would be rude of me to let him walk out of the place without a single *ciao*, or *see you later*, an *au revoir* even? Rude, and it would be an indication that there had been something between us, something I have been trying to avoid, perhaps.

Okay, so going to head around to his office now. Get it over with before *thank god it's Friday* sets in. That's tomorrow but creeping up stealthily.

Standing up, adjusting skirt and smoothing hair … Now having a skirmish with the contents of my handbag … There it is, pulling out lip gloss. Applying layer of said lip gloss on lips. Straightening clothes again to be on the safe side. After all, my clothes always seem to have a mind of their own, flipping here, popping open, sliding there, or slipping up at inopportune times.

Heading down corridor, effecting calm demeanor. Am woman of world with own executive office! Now, where is Jai's office? Have never visited it before, but I'm sure it's close by. Hmm, interesting that I've never been to his office, isn't it? Considering he has been to my office on countless occasions, sometimes multiple times in a single day. Perhaps due to lazy, slovenly nature, I have never bothered getting off my ass to go to his— Instead, I've evidently preferred holding court in mine.

Turning the corner towards area where creatives sit. It's creative, indeed. Lime green tiles on the wall, designs tacked up everywhere, and a general smell of body odour, the type that usually comes with creatives, who have been up all night coming up with ideas and so personal hygiene has gone out the window, being replaced by pure genius. Of the smelly variety! There's a pod of them staring at me now, all hunched over, wearing black or fluros. They're looking up at me, like bats in a cave, all pierced, and, well, bored looking.

Straightening clothes again, feeling like I've turned a wrong corner and stepped down a dangerous, unknown side alley with many the street urchin.

"Oh, hello … Which one's Jai's office?" Okay, so really don't know which one is his office. Being head creative, he's one of the few that gets to be separated from the other pleb creatives.

One of them, with a ring through his nose and cut-off black gloves, the kind that were big in the nineties that expose your digits but not the rest of your hands, is pointing at an office without a word.

"Oh, thank you!" I'll just scoot on over there then. Sheesh, talk about a hostile crew.

Heading into said room, and here he is, the man in question—Jai, leaning over a table, looking at some drawings with a pencil in his mouth. Heart has suddenly fluttered, not sure why, but he's so damn sexy, especially when he's all concentrated in a creative way, and still flexing his guns. Wish he would wear long shirt, or at least a jacket, so I'd be less distracted during conversations.

"Hey," I say from the doorway, in the same manner that he lingers in mine usually.

"Hey." He's removed the pencil from his mouth and is looking in my direction with a surprised expression.

I close the door behind me ...

"Why are you closing the door?"

"Because those people outside scare me," I whisper, gesticulating towards the bat children out there.

He's smiling. "Why?"

"They're like the children of darkness or something. I feel like I've entered their lair ... No wonder nobody comes around here. It's very ominous ... Semi-expected a skeleton to drop out from the ceiling."

Okay, stop verbal diarrhea now, Cee. He's still smiling, so good sign— but he's also giving me a confused look. Must be a result of my feverish chatter.

"They're fine. Just kids."

"One of them looked at least forty-five."

"Oh, yeah ... That's Mike. You probably should be concerned about him—Take a seat." He's gesturing towards the table.

"Okay," I say, edging towards seat, sitting down awkwardly, holding down sides of skirt. Unfortunately, I've worn the notorious skirt that I flashed underwear in earlier on in year. Apparently have not learned my lesson.

He has just sat opposite me. "So, what brings you out my way? I don't think you've ever been in my office before. To what do I owe the pleasure?" He's messing his hair up in what (I could be wrong) seems to be a nervous gesture, an *I'm not sure what I look like at this very moment, it could be terrible, should do something to fix it* gesture. It's very familiar ... I do such gestures all the time.

"Ahh ..." I've begun, good start, not sure where it's going ... I guess I have failed to think about what exactly I was going to say while marching over here in all my glory. *What am I going to say?* Slightly lost looking into his grey eyes … He's wedged a ring into his eyebrow today, didn't even know he had a piercing.

See, Cee, the man is not your type. He has facial piercings and neck tattoos …

"Did I have some creative owing you?" He's looking lost. Oh shit, now I'm forcing someone else to play the guessing game. Hate the guessing game.

"No," I manage, finally pulling myself together. "Just thought I would pop past to see you because you're leaving tomorrow."

"Oh, that," he's saying with an ironic smile, putting the pencil down on the table and nodding his head. Apparently what I've said makes sense. "You came to say bye."

"Yeah, something like that."

Awkward silence. My favourite! I'm scanning brain to find exactly what I had been intending on saying. Looking around his office, there's stuff everywhere. He's so messy. Way messier than I am! Desk is covered in papers, empty coffee cups form a tower installation, skull earphones flung down, CD cases, books, sheesh … His bin is towering with rubbish, like he hasn't emptied it since he's worked here.

"You're really messy," I blurt out, clearly having a thought to mouth moment.

"Yah," he's nodding. "I am. I'm a creative person, we're always messy."

"No … I mean, like, really messy. There could seriously be a homeless person living under the desk and you wouldn't notice."

"Well you're messy, too."

"Yeah, but not this messy! This takes it to new levels. I need like a Hep shot just coming in here."

"It's not that bad." He's glancing about like he's never noticed before.

"It is. How are you going to clean this up by tomorrow?"

"I don't know. I figured I would just leave it like this. I mean, once I'm out of the country, what are they going to do, send me a cleaning bill?"

Sounds like something I would do.

"Nice hair, by the way," he has supplied, changing the subject, and with a little ironic smile, too.

He's such a shit. "Thanks, please spare me the stripper, forward slash transvestite, jokes. They're a dime a dozen at the moment."

"I kind of liked your hair before."

"What, looking like I'd just been hit by lightening?"

"Yeah, it was sort of … edgy."

Indeed, it was edgy, in more ways than one.

"So when are you leaving?"

"Sunday."

"Is it for good?"

"I don't know. I'll have to wait and see."

"That's a vague response."

"Yeah, well I don't have all the answers at the moment." He's rubbing his face. *What does that even mean?*

And there's the appeal of being with someone like Chad. Sure he may not be as smart or as *creative* as a Jai equivalent, but at the very least he's fairly obvious and clear. You don't have to stumble through a minefield of options relating to what he's thinking, doing, or saying. Sometimes *simple* is so much easier than complex.

Maybe this conversation will help put any Jai-esque thoughts to bed.

Don't think bed. Do not think bed.

"Where are you from in L.A., anyway?" I ask, changing the subject a little. No point trying to wheedle something out of him that he doesn't want to give away. *Pregnant girlfriend* thought now becoming less likely, and is replaced with drug cartel option.

"Hollywood."

"You're from Hollywood?" No way, he must be joking. Who is from Hollywood? Is Hollywood even a legitimate housing suburb in L.A.?

"Yah, I'm from Hollywood."

"Do you live in the Hollywood Hills or something?" I can't help the sarcasm.

He's nodding his handsome head.

"You're joking?"

"No, I'm not joking ... I mean, I don't live there. My dad lives there, and I used to live with my dad. He's a screenwriter ... kind of a big deal." He's raising an eyebrow like he's daring me to care.

"Is he, like, Steven Spielberg?" I'm so immature, but I've said it now.

"No, he's not Steven Spielberg ... You're such a funny girl," he says, shaking his head.

"What does that mean?"

"You just say *stuff* as soon as it comes into your head ... It's really funny to hear and to watch."

"I'm glad it entertains you," I say, getting to my feet. Shit, whoops, should have just held down skirt. Hope I haven't flashed. Distinct possibility that I have, but it's time to go. I'm not even sure why I'm here, and he's certainly not giving anything away, and I'm not about to hang around and just be ... well, insulted or something.

Well this has been a sociological experiment and a half, should have just sat in new office and done nothing about his whole leaving thing.

"I meant it as a compliment," he's telling me, getting to his feet, too.

"It didn't sound like a compliment."

"It was. You're honest and funny, and not many girls are."

I'm nodding, because indeed I am. *"Funny* in a silly, laugh at but not with, kind of a way?"* I ask, heading towards the door …

This has been a waste of time!

"Wait." He's grabbing my arm and turning me back towards him. "I'm not sure what you want me to tell you. Yeah, I'm leaving, okay? It's the way it has to be."

"What does that even mean, Jai? Like, am I supposed to sort through that riddle and figure it out?"

"It's not a riddle! And besides, how come you're suddenly taking so much interest in my movements? You couldn't have cared less for the last six months. I don't think you even knew who I was until a few months ago—And now you're so wrapped up in Chad!"

"Well, he's my boyfriend." *Where is this even going?* But he just said *Chad* in a way that spells out something to me, just not quite sure what.

"Yah, he's your boyfriend." *Yeah, I just said that, what is this?*

Feeling a little awkward now, he's really close to me, and still holding onto my arm. I think, yes, pretty certain that we're almost touching with other parts of our body. Feeling flustered, tension very much rising between the small spaces between us … And, well, he's so fucking pretty. Why does he have to be so pretty?

Need to move.

"I just wanted to say bye." *I'm sure that's why I'm here!*

"Yeah, bye, whatever." He has dropped my arm.

Right, chance to leave. Turning and opening the door, going to do just that ... But why am I stuck to this spot? I think I want him to call me back, hmm? Don't think he is going to. I'll just leave then ... Out the door now, and iconic stalking is very much happening, stalking away from him.

48. 8:00p.m.

*F*riday night. At dinner with Chad, a friend of his, and friend's partner at The Green Room. New hip locale in Sydney city. Feeling like I'm surrounded by shrubbery. So much shrubbery around that the waiter literally needs to part the wilderness to get our order. Yes, lots of plants, indeed. It is possible might start shortly hearing the sound of macaw or the like flapping about. Don't think Chad and company are happy with locale, potentially because of obscured vision of other patronage through to table as result of flora and fauna. I've come to the conclusion that "these people" like to be looked at. I keep envisaging some Godzilla-like spider suddenly crawling out of the greenery and embedding itself in my fake hair, where it will never be discovered, but instead will lay eggs and Godzilla-like baby spiders will tunnel way into brain. Will then become another extension horror story on Internet. Scary! Yes—but not quite enough to turn the average punter off of having extensions.

With extensions on my mind now, Georgia, partner to Jayden (Chad's friend and also ex-footballer), is leaning across me and has given my leg a little squeeze.

"Darling, did I tell you I love your extensions? They just look stunning on you … You'll have to give me the details of the salon you went to. I'm starting to hate the place I'm going to at the moment—They just can't seem to get the balayage right. And you know if balayage goes wrong—It just looks trashy."

"Indeed," I say, as convincingly as I can. Of course if balayage goes wrong, well, it's so wrong, isn't it? No idea what balayage is, will need to Google when get home. Will need to figure out how to spell it, too.

Can't imagine Georgia getting into a Chameleon Skyline and heading out to the suburbs to have her hair done in a sweat store garage by Tara (Blonde Two).

"I bet Chad loves them," she says with a knowing expression on her face.

"He sure does." A little bit too much, in fact. He fawned over them. Adored them. Made me think, *What about my old hair?* Did he think it was edgy like Jai thinks it was?

"They never love short hair, darling," she's telling me. "They always pretend to, but really they want what they can't have."

Didn't I have a similar dialogue with Mother? Is Georgia just a younger version of her? Gawwwd, the thought frightens me.

Georgia has taken a strange liking to me. By strange, I mean I've only met her twice, this being the second occasion, but she acts like I'm her *bestie*. She's spent most of this evening whispering furtively in my ear and telling me how *us girls need to stick together*. We've already exchanged numbers, and I've been cajoled into some miracle spa appointment in a month's time where one is wrapped in plastic and then placed in a hot room—Apparently one can lose an entire dress size.

At the point of said conversation, I had sort of wanted to tell her that it's probably due to extreme dehydration. I personally wouldn't want to risk my own life just to lose a dress size, but she was so emphatic about the whole thing and excited, too, that I couldn't deny her such small pleasures. The men folk seem pleased by our obvious kindred spirit state, and continue on their conversation about football, or some other league, sport, code, not sure—Nonplused.

This, I've discovered, is how the double dating scene works in the *Chad* world. Some other celebrity football or restaurant couple turns up, he's all ripped and attractive, wearing the latest Hugo Boss suit, she's teetering on impossibly high heels and squeezed into a teeny dress, which makes her breasts looking impossibly large. Then we have dinner, the women folk together, me scoffing down food and drinking vino like tomorrow might never come, her pushing food around plate and not eating anything and drinking Perrier, talking about salon treatments, pregnancies and generally gossiping. The men folk instead drink boutique beer and nosh on, talking about the good old days—when they were playing—like they're trapped there.

There's usually not much cross-pollination between conversations.

It was fun for the first two occasions, like some sort of new sociological experiment where I was thrust into the world of footballers and their wives, and was sussing out the patterns and behaviours … But it has rapidly gotten old and tedious.

Right now … I'm super bored. Also, I'm sure Chad mentioned we were going to have dinner alone tonight, but then these two turned up amongst the fernery, peeping through like two meerkats.

Sigh!

"So, darling, have you heard about the L.A. trip?" *Is she talking about Jai?* Can't be! There is no way there could be any cross-pollination between those two either. I'm shaking my head.

"Chad! Chad!" she is over-enthusiastically calling across the table, flapping a hand in his direction.

Chad is looking up mid-conversation, expression slightly annoyed that the barriers have come down even momentarily.

"You haven't told Cee about L.A. yet?" she's calling.

What is this—Two men not telling me something about L.A.? Is this some sort of L.A. vortex?

"Shit! I completely forgot. It all happened so quickly today that I forgot to call you." He's pushing some meat from his fillet into his mouth.

"You're going to be so excited about this!" Georgia's squeezing my knee, harder this time.

Why does she know and I don't know? Feeling slightly annoyed. Also annoyed by her constant handling of my legs.

"So remember how I told you way back when we met that I have a friend, Craig Derning, who lives in Malibu and has a restaurant over there, too?"

Nodding head. But do I remember? Perhaps, vaguely! Wonder why all these ex-footballers are going into the food industry post-career—May not be pertinent time to ask him right now.

"Well, he wants to catch up. Talk about the franchising. He's buying a vineyard over there. A vineyard!'

I can tell he's super excited about the whole thing, and you know, having a friend in the wine business and all is not such a bad thing. Especially with my habit—I mean my hobby.

"He wants us to go over there to talk food and franchise ideas—So we're all leaving on the weekend." He's extending his hands out like he's a magician doing a *ta-da* gesture.

All three of them are staring at me with big smiles on their faces, expecting me to be overjoyed, I guess …

But what is he even fucking talking about? *We're leaving on the weekend? Who's* leaving on the weekend?

Not sure what to do, to say, just pasting a little smile on my face because I know they're just waiting for acclamations, and this is the best I can do at this point.

"Who's leaving?" I ask, still smiling, teeth semi-clenched and jaw aching. Fake smiles are hard work!

"Us!" He's gesturing around the table as he's speaking, and the other two are nodding at me with gigantic smiles on their perfectly symmetrical faces. Beautiful people are so off-putting, aren't they? "Jayden, Georgia, you, and me," he's now telling me.

I know who we at the table are! Does he really think I'm that confused?

"Well," he's continuing, "actually you're leaving on Monday because my travel agent needs your passport number to finalise the flight details. But they're holding a seat for you on Monday—It's only a fortnight!" he's added, probably because I don't look supremely overjoyed right now.

It's only a fortnight! Feeling a hot flush of crazed anger wanting to creep across my face—Stifle it, Cee! He didn't think about telling me this sooner? Okay, so he's only known for a day, but surely he should have asked me if I am free to go, or if I even want to go.

"I don't even know if my passport's still valid," I say, stumbling my words out.

"Oh, of course it will be, darling. Otherwise we'll fix it by Monday," Georgia's telling me warmly, and is handling my leg again in an almost too intimate gesture. Less of a squeeze, definitely more of a caress …

"You see," Chad is continuing, "Jayden was keen on coming because he wants in on the business, too, and Georgia's surgeon is in L.A. …"

" … So I thought I could get a little something-something done while I was there … " she has interjected.

"So we thought *let's all go together* …" he's finished off with an over-the-moon tone.

Okay, they've officially lost it. Not sure how to contain expression and thoughts. I mean, on the one hand it's great. Who wouldn't want to go to L.A. on some vineyard/restaurant tour with man-of-dreams, right? Awesome time to be had by all! Plus, obviously he's thinking seriously about me if I'm going on this trip with him and his friends—And I'll likely get papped (excitement levels soaring now)—But why didn't he at the very least ask? Damn it! What if I'd had other plans? And I do have to go to work, am high-powered executive now with fabulous office …

Oh, it seems I have failed to disguise my feelings through the expression on my face; he has more to say. "Darling," he starts, reaching across the table and taking my hand, "of course I would have called to ask you, but your phone at work was off the hook or something …"

"That's because I'm moving offices; it was disconnected." But he just said a moment ago that he forgot to call … So did he forget, or did he try?

"See?" he's saying. "I was going to text you, but then I got carried away

... " He's trailing off and looking sort of Fred-like, like he knows he's somehow screwed up his wonderful surprise.

And it is a wonderful surprise.

"He's flying you first-class," Georgia is telling me, as though she's sure this will make a difference. And well, it sort of does ... A lot!

First? First? First! Chris, Mother and Chantel will die when they find out—Jess, less so. Oh my gosh! I'm imagining the look on Elsie's face. Am now officially part of the lives of the *rich and famous*. Woman of substance, similar to Amal Amaluddin, living sheike life with fabulous partner ... Going on mini-breaks to the States and flying first class.

"Of course, darling," I say, smiling more sincerely now. "What a fabulous surprise!"

He's just winked at me, that winning wink. "I knew you would love it, doll. Get ready for the wines and the food; we are going to live it up."

A small sound of glee has escaped Georgia. "Oh, darling, I wish we were flying together," she's saying, arm slung casually around my shoulder. "Are you sure you can't get her on the same flight as us, Chad? I just adore this girl."

I'm not quite sure why or how I've earned this evident adoration and loyalty, but it's there, and how can one say no to it?

"Sorry, Georgia," Chad has told her, and is now explaining. "Tried, but Pete couldn't do it. Babe," he says, looking at me a little apologetically, "I'll have to give you Pete's number, the travel agent; he's waiting for your call tomorrow. You give him the passport details and he'll organise the rest for you—Simple!"

"Oh, so awesome, Chad!" Georgia is crying out. "The best!"

Weird interlude, because it's as if that conversation has not just happened

… The men are already resuming their football chat and Georgia has begun pushing food around her plate and smiling emphatically like a complete lunatic. I'm trying to smile, too, but have a slight destabilising feeling as well.

"I'm going to have to tell work tomorrow then, Georgia." I have no choice now, and I need to pack. What to pack for living it up vacation in L.A.?

"Oh, don't worry about that, babe. As if they could say *no*. Besides, once you and Chad are married—and let's admit, we know that's happening soon; I've never seen him so besotted before—Well, once that happens, you won't have to work at all," she's telling me brightly. "None of their ladies work."

Another off-putting statement from the profound fluorescent Georgia … Why wouldn't I work anymore? And why am I even concerned about this? I've spent half my life, my entire adult time working in my career, trying to figure out a way that I can extricate myself from the work environment. Why am I suddenly concerned that that day might be just around the corner?

Moment of clarity flooding in … It's because we're not as important as they are. Our careers aren't as important as theirs, nor are our opinions! We don't even get consulted about a major trip overseas. We just do what they say. We are the average folk, *we* are the wives, and I'm a *we* now, am I?

Is that a terrible compromise? After all, it comes with so many perks!

I have the worrying sentiment that it is, actually, and that a shit-storm lies ahead.

"I'm so glad Chad's with you now," Georgia is continuing to talk, oblivious to my inner turmoil. "That *Grace Rose* was such a total bitch."

I'm smiling at her, knowing she means it as a compliment, that I'm now a sworn and solid member of the crew, but it just doesn't sit right. Maybe Grace Rose is nice, but just didn't want all of this!

"You know," she says, still going on with her chatter, "maybe you can get a little something-something done in the States, too. Wouldn't that be fun? We can be plastic surgery buddies!" She is laughing now. It's forced, but I'm not quite sure if she knows that it is. Maybe she has forgotten what real laughter feels like.

"Mmm," I mumble, stuffing a bread role into my mouth so that is the only sound that I'm able to articulate. What the fuck is she talking about? I feel like Jess at this moment. Comfort food right in there … Need carbohydrates to deal with this!

"Have you ever thought about getting your boobs done?"

Oh no! Not caprese salad! Obviously she's noticed that the mozzarellas are not up to scale. Stuffing rest of bread roll into mouth and swallowing hard, semi-choking myself, dry bread clogging in throat.

"Nooo," I manage, chugging down half the glass of Chardonnay.

"You should—Once you've got them, you'd never go back—I'm sure Chad will love them!"

And just like that, I know the pendulum is shifting, swinging in the opposite direction … NO! Screaming in head, *You can't swing back, Cee!* I'm at the top of the seesaw—the very pinnacle of the fucking ascent—I will not—I cannot go back down.

But I know I can't stop it. It's fucking gravity. I don't have a say in it because the thing about being up is—The only way to go is down!

49. 11:30a·m·

*A*t home, packing bag. Hair pulled into messy ponytail. Singlet top on and yoga pants. Even though do not practise yoga, have pair of yoga pants, which wear at home on days when have eaten too much night before and require stretchy waste band. Nervous eating has continued—Literally eating all day, thus yoga pants have been put to good use. Note to self: yoga pants are not of the Lululemon variety, so need Lululemon variety. Trying to pack bag, has become conundrum. Well, to begin with, do not really have appropriate bag for L.A. trip. Have either smallish bag for short breaks, which is leather and slightly stylish in a beaten-up, I travel a lot (even though I don't) kind of way, or have large bag for overseas travel, made of old fabric with unidentifiable stain on side. Have opted for latter even though completely daggy and embarrassing, and can envision people staring at it and then at me, and then asking, "Are you sure you're in first class?" In order to bring *appropriate number of clothes for fortnight I must carry unfashionable bag. Other option requires re-wearing (a lot) or adopting new nudist approach to life. Neither of which are particularly appealing.*

At least I've found my passport, which is still valid. Must be result of Hawaii trip with Jess a few years ago. So I've contacted travel agent and provided details, and flight details have been forwarded to my email account.

I also called Ian on his mobile (when he is at home), which he was evidently displeased about, and I told him I'd need to take abrupt leave from Monday for a fortnight. Explained that Chad had had brain wave about business and needed me by his side, both within a partner capacity and within a work capacity, to broker deal and discuss communication options. Whilst initially put out, I managed to convince, using said sway and charm, that it was good business for the agency, and that I would be endeavouring to make good contacts and bring back some international work—Total lie, given plan to spend the entire holiday in alcohol-fuelled haze.

Plan worked! Good going, Cee! Ian has approved leave and given me his blessing. I'm slightly concerned about leaving new office alone for a fortnight, given the vultures in the building. Fear I may find squatters there when I return—Can't think of that now, need to continue with preparation for L.A. trip.

Doing well, as have already left message with Jess and Mother, who were both mysteriously absent this afternoon. Chris, on the other hand, was mysteriously present today (a shock, given he usually needs to sleep off Friday night's shenanigans till late afternoon or evening on Saturday in order to prepare for a Saturday night of wild partying). Even more shocking, he's agreed to come and help me pack for the trip, and, wait for it, look after Fred while I'm gone. *Love him!*

Besides potential office squatters, am now concerned about Fred's wellbeing, too. *Note to self:* Chris is a responsible thirty-something year old with own pet, and pet has never shown any signs of neglect, except that time he was dyed pink for Mardi Gras. But Chris assured me that he had used organic dye.

Scheduled time of arrival for Chris is 8:30 p.m.—Likely time of arrival knowing Chris, 10:30 p.m.!

Now staring at wardrobe in horror. I'm sure I have nothing to wear that is appropriate for celebrity lifestyle in Malibu. Still staring. Hmm? Possibly been staring for around five minutes, maybe more, and am slightly discombobulated by it all.

Oh good, have needed a welcomed distraction from clothes nightmare and from distracting stare … I've been saved once again by the ringing of landline, so reaching forward for cordless on unmade bed.

"Cecilia speaking."

"Hello, darling, it's your mother," I hear, using her usual snotty tone. "Sorry I've missed your call. I've been at Char's place all day, and then the hospital—She's gotten herself into a spot of bother and broken her hip. Really, can you imagine only a month and a bit out from the wedding?" She's speaking as though the wedding is the main concern, not the busted hip.

"Oh no, that's terrible!" Poor Char has probably taken a forceful tumble to get herself out of the wedding. Why didn't I think of that? "How did she do it?"

"I don't know—something ridiculous. She slipped over in the kitchen.

Her dog has a terrible problem with licking the floor in some desperate attempt to find leftovers. The floor, as a result, becomes a bit slobbery— and she's slipped and gone down like a lead balloon."

There's so much wrong with that story, but trying not to delve in too deeply—at all actually.

"I've told her," Mother is continuing, "a million times before to have that dog put down. He's such a nuisance really. Always digging things up and slobbering. But she insists she won't do it, stubborn really. She can be really stubborn. Sometimes I think she loves the dog more than she loves me."

Oh dear, and here's Mum trying to eliminate any competitors, further evidence of her trying to control every element of Char's life. *Sigh*. Hoping the stalker/psychotic gene has not passed from Mother to me.

"And look what's happened now!" Mother's saying. "What am I going to do about the bridesmaids? I mean, she can't possibly be a bridesmaid now. She has surgery in a week's time, and then she'll be on fucking crutches or in a wheelchair! I mean fucking Char, how self-centered can she get?"

I cannot believe she's just uttered those words, but then again this is Mother, so who am I kidding?

"Poor Char," I say, imagining that dear old lady in a hospital bed right this minute, worrying about when Mother's wrath will strike her down.

"Oh, stop the *poor fucking Char* business," Mother's saying rudely. "What am I going to do?"

There's no point in indicating to her that she's a completely selfish megalomaniac, who might be a clinical narcissist, is there? No! I've tried that one before. It always backfires, and then I have to endure an hour's long conversation about how I'm the most terrible daughter in the world.

"Why don't you ask Cheryl, you know, your hairdresser friend from the barbecue?"

"Oh, fucking Cheryl ... She'll try to take over the entire wedding and make it the *Cheryl Show*. Have you seen the plunging necklines she wears? I mean, I understand she still has a semi-good *rack*, but does one need to show that sort of thing when one is seventy? No."

Closing eyes, attempting to count to ten. It may calm me down and get the image of Cheryl's rack out of my mind. Recall her lunging towards me at the barbecue with her heavily exposed said rack—Dear god!

"Well then, just have one bridesmaid." That's enough, not like she's not been married before ... Why, oh why, am I even taking part in this discussion?

"Don't be absurd, darling. I have two groomsmen teed-up, so I need two bridesmaids. And if I only have one I'll look like I have no friends, quite literally, because my bridesmaid is my daughter!"

There are no words suitable for me to share—The woman obviously doesn't want to be helped. I shall resume previous position in front of my wardrobe, back to the staring at my clothes, waiting for Malibu-esque attire to jump out towards me at will.

"I suppose you're right," she's saying. It has taken her a while to respond, and I have way more important things to do than to listen to her again. "I may have to invite Cheryl ... Given the wedding is so close, she won't have enough time to take over. And I suppose I have that fucking stole from Char's dress to cover her cleavage with—I mean, really, I can't believe it! I almost feel like Char might have done this on purpose to ruin my big day!"

Closing my eyes, desisting from the staring exercise. Her voice seems even louder with my eyes closed. Weird.

"She did not do it on purpose, Mother. She just fucking slipped over, could you give the woman some sympathy?"

"Well, no need to be so rude, darling. I've told you a million times swearing is so very inelegant on a woman."

Oh my god, I'm about to completely flip out. The woman says *fuck* in every other sentence—Does she not notice this? Does she have Tourettes syndrome?

"Listen, Mother, I don't have time for this. I'm very busy packing …"

"Packing? For where? Polkolbin?"

Oh shit, forgot the Polkolbin lie. How could I be so careless? Must be stress from random, unplanned trip to L.A. clouding my judgment— Luckily she's reminded me!

"Not Polkolbin, Mother, we've had to cancel that—which really gets to the point of why I was calling earlier. I wanted to let you know that I'm flying out with Chad and a few friends to L.A. on Monday for a fortnight."

"On Monday?" She is sounding perplexed.

"Yes, it's all very sudden. Chad wants to catch up with a friend of his about franchising the restaurant and thought it would be a nice holiday for us, too. It's only a fortnight." Not sure why, but thinking the Char thing might have destabilised Mother.

"Well, that is sudden, darling. When did he book it?"

"Yesterday." What does it matter? "We're flying first-class," I add, hoping this might be some sort of boon she can latch onto.

"Oh, well, I'm very surprised—and shocked really." She seems to be gathering her thoughts, not a good sign. "I mean, it sounds fabulous, and I'm sure it's a great sign for you two that he's taking you on a trip to the States with friends, but it's so close to the wedding and I need your help."

Oh, the fucking wedding! She doesn't need my help. She's a chronic organiser—She has everything under control!

"Well, it can't be helped." Good option, Cee, to the point! "And I'm sure you've got everything planned. You're very good at planning." A compliment always helps.

"I'm not sure I'm pleased about this, darling. I mean, really, now that Char is out, I need you to be about. I can't do it all myself. This sounds like a ridiculous idea. I mean, who books a trip with a day's notice? I don't like the sound of that at all. It all sounds very spur of the moment and unplanned, and unplanned things never go well—Really, it surprises me that an upstanding chap like Chad would be involved in this sort of thing. In fact, it's starting to change my perspective on him. He can't just demand that you do things at the drop of a hat ..."

"Mother," I say, interrupting her endless chain of thought, which is heading nowhere positive, fast, "this is great news—And you can't judge someone's whole character on how they book a holiday ... I'm leaving first-class on a fabulous trip on Monday. How can you not be happy for me!"

"Because I'm fucking getting married and you should be focused on that."

Sigh. "Mother, I know you've become accustomed to the fact that I was single and could do things for you at the drop of a hat," very apt to borrow her expression, methinks, "like Char, for example. But I am not your hostage, and I do have my own life. And now you're going to have to get used to the fact that Chad's in it, and he's my top priority …"

"He's your top priority?"

"Yes, Mother—That's what relationships are about."

"I really don't like where this is heading, Cee. In fact, I think Chad might be having some sort of adverse effect on you. You're turning into something different. Sure he's a celebrity and everything, but nobody's worth changing your very person for …"

"Are you joking, Mother? That day of the wedding invitations, you wanted me to change everything about myself so that Chad would find me appealing! Where has that person disappeared to?" I yell at her, fuming and feeling pretty unfairly judged.

"Change your appearance, sure!" she is crying out. "But don't change who you are. And don't change where your priorities should be, i.e. with me."

"Okay, Mother, I'm hanging up now because I think you're a narcissist and should seek medical assistance for that. I'll be away for a fortnight from Monday, but will have international roaming on my phone. So you can still call me."

I'm so trying to hang up, but can still hear her yelling.

"You're the fucking narcissist!"

Oh, how inelegant!

I'm shaking my head, the woman is impossible! Now Char and I are both abandoning her before the altar. Char because she has a broken hip and her daughter because she's going on a two week holiday and finally has a life of her own.

For Christ's sake, I have been in the dating tundra for over a decade now, meeting crazy after crazy in some endless display of romantic oddities. The Christian, the one who had a penchant for feet (and feet alone), the financier who put most of his paychecks (and some of mine) up his nose, the architect who was concealing a family with children in another state—Haven't I suffered enough? I've finally located and ensnared (as Mother would say) man of means, man of career, man of looks, and man without any creepy back stories ... And they all turn on me! Suddenly, I'm not there for them anymore. Suddenly they need me.

Well, you know what, it's *tough titties!* They'll just have to fend for themselves. Maybe I've spent too long babying these people because I've had nothing else in my life of substance to focus on. Not sure who these people are exactly, but am now raging and throwing everyone together in the same pile ... But both Mother and Jess have said I'm changing for Chad—and so they are definitely in said pile.

Things change, and just as I've supported them, they'll need to support me. But clearly that is too much to ask!

Now what? Jess is buzzing my mobile. Should I answer? Am convinced she'll judge me now post-Mother's response to it all. Not even perks of first-class travel seem enough to convince them that I should be going. But I need to tell her that at very least I'm going—given the whole pregnancy thing ... because unlike others, I am supportive!

"Hello?"

"Hey, how are you doing?" Her voice is calm, non-confrontational. Still, I'm geed up from my altercation with Mother a couple of minutes ago.

"Hey, I've been trying to call you. Where have you been?" I'm demanding.

"Oh, I went to watch a movie."

"With Pete?" I'm being accusatory. Ha! They're all the same, looking after their own interests and dragging me along behind them like some sort of decapitated side-car!

"No," her tone is strange, "I went by myself. You know I like to catch the odd movie by myself."

Okay, so that's true. She has an inner passion for ridiculous teen dramas about vampires and angels, and so rather than dragging a mature friend along to that sort of thing, she goes it alone. Thankfully. If I have to sit with her through one more *Twilight* film, I will gouge my eyes out …

"Right," I say, trying to recoup my inner fire and rage for friends and family.

"What's wrong with you? You sound sort of crazy. Have you been drinking?"

"NO!" Of course she would say that. Crazy Cee, always having a *bevvy*, sometimes even before midday, she'll never change. "I haven't had anything to drink all day, I'll have you know."

"Well, that's a change," she's laughing.

Okay, am about to really rage. I am aware that potentially over the years, particularly in more recent months, the alcohol has mellowed me out and that exorbitant consumption of Coke Zero could be having the opposite effect.

"Very funny! Because I'm such an alcoholic, right?"

"Calm down! What's wrong with you?"

"Listen, I have just had a very disturbing phone conversation with Mother and am quite sick of being judged by friends and family who should be supporting me." There, I've said it!

Buzzer has just rang … It must be Chris downstairs.

9:00 p.m. Sheesh! He's almost early by his standards.

"Well, what did you tell her? What's going on?" Jess has continued on. "You're not making any sense."

"I'm going on a holiday with Chad and some of his friends on Monday. We're going to L.A. for a fortnight and he's flying me first-class. We'll be there to meet with a friend of his who wants to invest in the franchise—And yes, we decided …"

I'm lying. Well, starting to … because no, we didn't decide, *he* decided, but she doesn't need to know who was significant in the decision-making process, does she? She'll go off all half-cocked in her feminist way if I say he decided for us. Can a feminist be half-cocked? Is that a feminist slur to begin with?

No matter, must continue dialogue; she is still on the other end of the phone, after all.

"… on Friday—Yes, it was spur of the moment, but whatever happened to being spontaneous? Why can't one be spontaneous in their relationships?" I continue, pressing the green button into the building willy-nilly, hoping it's Chris and not some junky from out on the road about to stab me to death and steal any leftover cash in the apartment (which is very little, mind you).

"There's nothing wrong with that, babe," she's telling me. "It sounds great. Good for you."

"I'll have you know …" Hmm? Not really understanding that she's not actually angry with me. My rage is semi-blinding, although I can sense she's not angry, and I'm finding it difficult to resist stamping my feet. Oh, and my voice is getting louder. " … that I will still be there for you and the baby even in L.A. In fact, I've had international roaming put onto my phone so that you can contact me at any time, at my cost."

"Doll, it's fine," she has continued before I've finished. "It's only a fortnight. I'm sure I'll be fine. I don't even have a doctor's appointment in that period of time. Go, have a great time with your man, just stop yelling at me."

"Oh." Full realisation has just sunken in, and am feeling somewhat premature in my ranting—She's okay with it all! I've clearly severely misjudged the situation. Damn Coke Zero.

There is knocking at the door. Yes, I just jumped. Well, wouldn't you? I'm still not sure if it is Chris, or potential killer forward slash junky. It is quite odd that he would be here so early. The likelihood of it being killer-junky type is higher than it being Chris …

"Oh, right," I say, mumbling into the phone and heading to the door anxiously.

"Sounds like a great trip," she's saying. "You need to get away. You haven't been away in years."

"Indeed," I agree, hovering at the door. "Not since our trip to Hawaii."

"That's right, it'll be great for you."

I throw the door open in a surprise attempt to startle the junky, just in case I need to run like an Olympic athlete past him … I'm good at running, even when drunk and barefoot, remember! Phew, it's Chris— He's looking rather startled. He's holding up hands like, *Please don't kill me,* and I'm nodding my head at him in a gesture of apology. *I'm SORRY, I thought you were a junky!* I hold the door wide for him to come through.

He has a bag with him, on wheels, in a monogrammed Louis Vuitton pattern. Love it. Looks rather expensive. Very appropriate for trip! Love him. Must be a response to the phone rant earlier on today about stained suitcase.

Closing door behind him clearly to avoid any other potential junky scenarios.

"I thought you didn't like him." I'm talking to Jess again now (allowing Chris to recover), who is still on the phone.

"Why would I not like him? I haven't even met the guy."

Very true! Which triggers the thought, *Why haven't I introduced him to my friends?*

"Sorry." I mean it, too.

I follow Chris into my room. He's laying the beautiful Louis Vuitton out onto my bed, opening her up almost like she isn't a suitcase, certainly not a *she* at all, but a man he is pursuing! And, oh, another reason why I love this man—He has just pulled out a bottle of Prosecco. He's making a shocked expression at me like he didn't know it was in there. I must return it with a hammed-up smile at his pantomime, and begin gesturing spasmodically to him to open ASAP. Like, right this second!

He's winked. Message clearly understood. Off he goes, undoubtedly heading to the kitchenette.

"Sorry, babe, Mother just got me all worked up," I say, feeling apologetic. It's obviously the emotion of the evening.

"No worries! I've had first-hand experience with her. She's completely nuts. Listen, you relax tonight and have a vino. Get off the Coke Zeros. They are making you nuts. I'll call you tomorrow."

It's the most sense she's made in years. Pregnancy suits her, methinks.

"Indeed. Coke Zero will be the end of me."

"Ciao."

Hung-up. Chris has just appeared with two glasses of Prosecco. Yum!

"Who were you apologising to?" he's asking, handing me a glass.

"Jess."

"What for?" he asks. I clink my glass to his, swigging away semi-violently. So much better than Coke Zero. *Gasp of pleasure!*

"Oh, I just feel like she's judging me for my relationship with Chad. Thinks I'm changing into a WAG or something—And then I called Mother to tell her about the trip and she's got the shits with me because I'm not going to be here for her wedding prep, and she also thinks Chad is changing me into something I'm not, that I have all my priorities mixed up." *Sigh.*

"Listen here … Those ladies are jealous bitches," he's saying emphatically.

"Are you calling my mother a jealous bitch?" Not sure if I should be offended. No, well, he's certainly right about the bitch part.

"Yes, I am. And she is. Of course women are going to be jealous. I'm a bit jealous, doll … You're dating Chad Thompson, hot celebrity ex-footballer with enormous penis—"

What? I've never mentioned his dick size to Chris, and it certainly isn't enormous. I'm raising my eyebrow at him.

"Go with me here, even if his penis is not enormous … They are imagining it is."

I'm nodding along with the narrative now like he is speaking gospel from real life experience.

"You're driving around in a Lamborghini now," he's continuing, and you know what? I'm letting him speak because I'm just enjoying this drink. "Going on first-class flights to L.A.—They are jealous bitches. All women are … Luckily, you have a gay best friend, who is not a bitch, and is just waiting to go on holiday with you and said boyfriend on his yacht."

I'm listening to him, I really am, but I'm a little distracted, too. "Don't think he has a yacht," is my vague response.

"No matter. Drink up, and stop bloody drinking that Coke Zero—I noticed your fridge is full of it, and I'm turfing it before I go tonight. It is making you crazy. Could you enjoy yourself for once? Fuck, you've been *papped*. Can you believe it?"

Shaking my head.

"I guess." He is sort of making sense in that crazed Chris fashion, and he did bring me an expensive looking bag, and a bottle of Prosecco. How can I say *no* to that?

"No! You don't *guess*. You know! Now show me your fucking wardrobe so I can apply my expert assistance to that."

I'm leading him to the wardrobe, and now we are both staring into it. I'm feeling slightly frightened, and he's looking more than slightly frightened, but he's begun diving in like a bull at the gates ... pulling clothes and hangers aside in a frenzy.

"You know," I say, not sure if he can hear me with his head in the cupboard, "he didn't even ask me if I wanted to go."

"Oh, shut the fuck up," he's shouting back as he continues his battle with my clothes. "If fucking Chad Thompson booked my flight to L.A. first-class tomorrow, I'd be there, no ifs, buts, or maybes. Stop making an issue when one doesn't exist!"

Potentially *shrewd!* But shrewd coming from Chris? C'est possible?

"What *is* an issue is your wardrobe. There's fucking nothing in here we can work with," he's telling me, turning and looking at me with an expression that says, *How dare you have so much shit in your wardrobe?* Don't know why he doesn't just say it; he doesn't normally hold back.

"I know, right? Epic disaster."

"Not epic disaster … Tonight we finish the Prosecco and whatever else you have in the house, and tomorrow … We shop for Malibu."

He is pushing past me, heading out towards the kitchen again—Refilling his glass must be his agenda. And filling mine back up is on my agenda, too, and it does make sense! I'm following him to the kitchen, sold on his cache and arrogance! But why am I struggling with shaking the feeling that there's something not quite right in the mix?

50. 7:00p.m.

Qantas first lounge in Sydney. Waiting for flight. Feeling like relaxed woman of world, jet-setting about, looking fabulous. Hair has just been blow-dried and falls in stunning waves across shoulders—If only it would hold for length of trip. Have faith in fake hair to keep up its end of the bargain, but not in my own. Sipping champagne and snacking on chip-like things (of course one wouldn't have normal chips in the Qantas first lounge), trying to not make too much of a guts of myself given am in said lounge and playing executive, high-roller woman jet-setting about.

Managing to focus on my cool exterior, but am so fucking excited I could literally pee pants. Have just put up Facebook status: *In Qantas first lounge on way to LAX airport.* Little plane image has popped up alongside status. Love that little plane image.

Keep checking *likes*, which are coming in at slow, but steady, intervals.

Have brought duty free perfume, which shall be fragrance for trip. *Shalimar.* An old one, I know, but a good one. Refined, sophisticated, and just a little bit edgy. Have slight panic that fragrance may not be summery enough for Malibu. In fact, it's not summery at all, more Middle Eastern—Oh dear, have I selected the wrong fragrance for trip? Wish Chris were here with his cutthroat buying skills and innate style. He managed to whip us through Pitt Street Mall yesterday like some Gok Wan pro buying swimsuits and casual jumpsuits, shorts and tees, like he had been planning for weeks, and all was done with such decisiveness.

My perfume purchase had involved the spraying on of around twenty fragrances, and finally elected to go with Shalimar—Now, at least forty-five minutes later, I think it still might be the wrong scent. Wonder if I can return and perhaps substitute with more floral, *beachy* fragrance?

Ringing of mobile sounds very loud in first lounge … It's Tina, *how strange.* She doesn't call me, usually at all, unless she's having some work-related panic. May be a work emergency, so I will answer. Given I'm a busy executive woman flying to L.A., must take work call in Qantas first lounge.

"Tina?" I say in an assured, woman of the world voice.

"Hey, Cee," she responds, her voice cloaked in what I can tell is fake cheerfulness.

"How you doing?" Maybe she's not very pleased I won't be around for the yoga sesh I said I'd go to with her?

"Yeah, good … Sort of good," she has quickly adjusted her statement. "What about you?"

"Fabulous." I'm totally Samantha Jones, *Sex in the City* style, uh-huh!

"Sitting in the Qantas first lounge waiting for my flight. I'm flying first-class, you know." Is it not classy to say aloud? Sure woman of the world would not be lording her first class tickets over underlings, but you know? One must do what one must do.

"Oh, great … Yeah, I heard you were flying first-class and everything. Office gossip and all," she has supplied.

And I'm totally excited, like shifting in seat excited. Wonderful! Let the plebs chitter-chatter about my first-class tickets. Not sure how that got out, maybe my Facebook status gave it all away? It obviously did! Or Ian has turned out to be a gossiper like I've always somehow known he is. He probably wears a fat suit and actually has a body like a stripper— Mysterious, that one! Wouldn't put anything past him at all!

"I'm so sorry to call you while you're on holiday—but I really need to talk to someone, and I just didn't know who. I don't really trust anyone anymore!"

What is she babbling about?

"I'm just so stressed about going to the Swami's class on Wednesday— I'm stressed about seeing the Swami. I'm stressed about being in the office, because I know they're all talking about me … I think I need to hand over the Swami account." It's all vomiting out of her, one word on top of the other. I can barely understand what she's talking about.

"What!" Exclamation mark times ten! "I worked long and hard to get that Swami account, and so did you for that matter! You're not handing it over!" I say, trying to take my voice down a notch. Professional appearance has evaporated, and people are now staring at me over their professional glasses. Oh, yes, glasses, still too vain. Choose to struggle with vision instead.

"I know," she's gasping, sounding desperate, "but I just can't deal with it! I can't deal with what people are saying about me."

I can hear her sobbing quietly on the other end of phone. Must make effort to extract information in a more appropriate manner.

"Okay, calm down." I don't sound calm at all. "What are people saying about you?"

"You mean you haven't heard?" she asks in between quiet sobs.

"No." Being social pariah in the office means you usually get the office gossip around two weeks too late, and by that time it's been and gone.

"Well, they're saying … They're saying—Oh, I don't know if I can tell you …"

"Oh, spit it out, girl. People saw my undies earlier on this year. If I can weather that, I'm sure you can weather what this is," I say, trying to ignore the imperious glance from the elderly gentleman a few seats up.

"They're saying I slept with him … with the Swami," she has finally spat out … And it's ludicrous, non?

"Well, don't worry about that. It's obviously bullshit." God, this girl is so naïve, I can see a *furphy* like that from a mile away, even without my prescription glasses.

"No, you see—It's actually true," she is sobbing out.

"What!" I'm screeching, getting to my feet. Lots of people are staring! Now using a quieter tone, in vain, to avoid seeming like Qantas first lounge pariah. "You slept with the Swami?"

"Yes. It was just the one time, but I did."

"That's—That's—That's so gross, and once is enough!" Whoops, maybe insensitive to spurt out! But seriously, has the girl gone nuts? The man is of a non-descript age, with long beard and robes on. He's a religious man, for god's sake; he even brought the rains when I called for them at Mother's house!

"It was just once," she's whispering.

Like that makes it any better. Trying to keep coitus thought of Tina and Swami out of mind—But here it is, obliterating all happy thoughts. Utterly disgusting! Feel the urge to vomit.

"He didn't take advantage of you, did he?" Oh god, he'll have a lawsuit on his hands. How else could this happen?

"No, I was just spending a lot of time with him, practising a lot, working on his account, and he's truly such an amazing man ..." she's gushing.

Oh, vomit.

"... And, I don't know, one evening after class one thing lead to another and we had sex," she's telling me breathlessly, like she's at a confessional. I'm the priest and she's finally shedding her skin.

"He's a religious man," I say, *and old!* "You can't just fuck the Swami."

I think people must have heard that. Heads are very much swiveling.

"I know, I know," she's still sobbing. "Things just got out of control, and it happened ... And then I panicked because I'm supposed to be getting married soon and I just cheated on the guy I've been with since high school. How could I do that?"

Indeed. *In-fucking-deed* ... How could you do that? And with the Swami, too! Oh, gross, please disappear, mental image of the Swami lifting his robes ... So deeply disturbing.

"And I felt so guilty, I needed someone's advice ..." she has trailed off.

Puzzle pieces fitting together in shocked, grossed-out mind. On said puzzle is an image of Elsie's little, bent head, all pretty and with a bitchy expression. "You told Elsie."

"Yes, because I thought I could trust her—And … Well, she told everyone. The whole fucking office knows. I'm so ashamed."

That double-crossing bitch … That little hipster, sweetheart, Bondi piece of shit! I knew her heart was made of stone from the very beginning.

"Why didn't you tell me?" I say, a little heartbroken by the fact she had turned to Elsie instead of me.

"Because you were my mentor, and so fantastic … You're like the office superstar. Ian loves you, Jai loves you—You date some fucking celebrity. I just couldn't do it. The fall from grace was too much."

Hmm! Well she's obviously wearing rose-coloured glasses. *Office superstar, my ass!*

"You should have told me," I tell her, and she should have. I would have helped her, smoothed it over, and not told everyone because unlike Elsie, I don't thrive on sucking other people's lives from them … like a vampire, a leech. I want to rip her tongue out.

"Well, I didn't. And it's done now … Everyone thinks I'm some little *Swami whore.*"

Indeed. This is very bad. Swami whore thing is very bad.

"I need to give up the account," she's pleading now.

"No." I have to be firm; this is business, too. "At this point, all they know is that it's a rumour. If you give up the account, they'll know it's true."

"It is true!" she is crying out.

"No, it's fucking not. It's not true until everyone believes it," I say, applying some George Costanza lying logic.

"You need to act like this never happened. In your mind, it never happened."

"But it did. I'm thinking of telling Matt." *Shit. Drawing a blank—Who the fuck is Matt?* "My fiancé," she has now supplied.

"Don't." As a mentor, this is something I must share. "Before you do anything rash, you need to take a breath and think about it. Don't do anything in the spur of the moment."

"But it's dishonest," she's saying weepily.

"Yes, it's dishonest. So what? Who hasn't been dishonest before?" Those who say they haven't are the most dishonest, lying to themselves, right? "I have certainly done worse than this in my time ..." And there's some dishonesty, too. Sleeping with the Swami? Pretty bad. There's certainly nothing of that variety in my books. " ... Everyone survives. Don't tell anyone else, okay? You need to decide what you want to do before anyone else can get into your head and instruct you on what to do. Because trust me, they'll be wrong."

She is silent, but I have to go because my flight number is flashing red on the screen. It's boarding. Shit!

"Listen, I've got to go. They're boarding my flight. But remember to stay strong, don't tell anyone, and don't do anything rash, okay?"

"Okay," she says in a small voice.

"I'll call you once I'm in L.A." I'll have to, she clearly needs me. "And for god's sake, have a vino tonight!"

God knows she'll need one after sleeping with the Swami. Oh, gross—mental image again. Keep thinking about his penis. Think it may look like some sort of shriveled seahorse, similar to the threesome twig's one ... Oh dear god—Wipe thoughts clean. Wipe thoughts clean!

The injustice of it all!

427

51. LAX. Not sure what time it is. Potentially afternoon.

*T*hink it's afternoon, and sure, flight attendant might have said it was, but could not hear anything over roaring headache. Majorly hungover. Severely hungover. Diabolically hungover. Whoever said that you can't get drunk from expensive champagne was so completely wrong. One can certainly get momentously drunk as a result of numerous flutes of Veuve Clicquot. Lost count after fourth, and then it was all downhill from there. Although, it did appear to be uphill while it was occurring. Had the first to calm the nerves prior to takeoff, the second because one was flying first-class to L.A. and it was all very exciting, the third in anticipation of meal, the fourth with the meal, and wasn't the meal fabulous? I mean you actually had a choice of entrée, main and dessert, and it was all served on wonderfully elegant plates, with actual *forks and knives (which were of the expensive, heavy variety), and there was a fucking cheese platter—and I do love cheese! And then my little party of one just continued on into the evening as we flew against time.*

Effect of air travel and alcohol—truly, truly horrendous! Feeling like a mess as I walk through LAX with sunglasses on to collect luggage from belt. Not because I think I might be a pseudo-celebrity (because clearly I am not), but because I'm so hungover that the thought of bright light truly terrifies me.

Prior to landing, swooped into bathroom like epic rock star, i.e. hardly able to stand up, to examine appearance because after ingesting copious amounts of alcohol, I then fell into drunken stupor of sleep and only woke up when flight attendant shook my shoulders (quite violently, might I add) to tell me we were landing.

"Of course," I just about managed to mumble out in the most elegant way possible, despite drunken stupor.

Had then swooped to bathroom to evaluate damage. Analysis had concluded that hair held up remarkably well. However, as predicted, fake hair held up its end of the bargain while real hair tried its hardest to escape and do its own electrocuted look. All in all, though, the good outweighs the bad, and hair looks pretty good despite air travel and drunkenness. Face has held up, too, makeup still in place, and I'm not looking as droopy or blood shot-eyed as initially anticipated. Must have been some weird, suspended, mid-air, time-zone thing, which had kept appearance from disheveling completely and utterly.

The only thing is, that weird, suspended, mid-air, time-zone thing did not assist with hangover—In fact, I think it might be amplified by one hundred, at the very least.

Have already stuffed half a pack of Panadol down my throat, along with the bottled water I should have been drinking on the plane rather than drinking alcohol. Hands are shaking excessively.

Calm. Remain calm, Cee. Heading towards claim belt. You'll be able to sleep it off once you get to Chad's friend's place. Whatever his name is? Was it Craig? Can't recall. For now, just collect the bag …

There are a few lonely bags spinning around at the moment ever so slowly on the conveyer belt. Evidently, they haven't yet unloaded the plane.

Shifting from foot to foot like strange flightless bird. Oh, I know. I'll switch phone on. Maybe Chad's tried to text, he's supposed to be collecting me from here.

Am flooded by strange sense of dread, but not quite sure why. Think it might be a result of drunk-induced paranoia—But then it's probably because I'm going to have to talk to Georgia and Jayden in the next hour or so—and admittedly to Chad, who becomes very much like Georgia and Jayden when he's around them. Not sure how much longer I can put up with the inane chatter about football, houses, deals, breasts, Botox, handbags, and the incessant preening that goes on as result of them wanting and waiting to be papped.

Shit, Cee! What are you thinking? Drunken paranoia and judgment have definitely set in. Cannot think of man-of-dreams in such manner! Also, have just signed up to this two-week holiday with said people in Malibu. Cannot start off thinking negative thoughts about them. Cannot—Must not! Focus, Cee. Focus!

My trusted mobile is slowly coming to life. Screen flickering on and off as it clearly tries to recalibrate locations, continents, those sorts of things (or potentially could be result of spilling champagne on flight, on phone, and on passport).

Nope, it's working! Thank god! It's buzzing at me randomly. Two new messages:

Opening the first from Chad.

"Hey, babe! Welcome to L.A.! This is going to be awesome! Listen, traffic is a killer here and will take a lifetime to get to the airport, so catch a cab. Will send you text with the address. Can't wait to see you!"

Staring at phone, wanting to annihilate it with eyes. *What?* I just flew for fourteen hours and he can't bother picking me up? Is the man serious? Sure, it probably makes sense that I take a cab. I mean, I know it's a bit of a hike from Malibu to LAX, especially with traffic, but surely man-of-dreams, or man that warrants that title, would be fine with it? Would be racing to airport to collect me with the greatest anticipation of seeing me—Would already be here! Evidently not in this case!

Okay, perhaps drunkenness is setting off rage and unsubstantiated claims, forward slash, emotional behaviour, full stop.

Breathe deeply, Cee. In and out! No, don't hold breath!

What is that extreme ringing noise? Shit! What is it? Is it an alarm? Is there a bomb? Terrorists? Head is feeling like it might explode like familiar *Game of Thrones* episode previously stored and recalled from mind. I really want to put hands to ears to cover, but fear other travellers waiting for bags will think I'm nuts, or worse still, I might miss some sort of anti-terrorist alarm announcement directing me to safe passage.

Oh, hang on—Hang on! It's just the conveyor belt swinging to life. I see a large flashing light atop it spinning. Oh right—Calm down. Just the bloody conveyor belt—but why does everything have to be so noisy and bright in the States? Why can't the conveyor belt just start moving and dispensing bags without the light and sound act?

Bags are starting to drop out at random. The crowd that has formed around me is lurching forward in some great zombie bag wave. I'm getting pushed to the front of the bag mosh pit. The person behind me has something jammed between my shoulders, and I'm hoping it's not a gun, although it feels more like an aggressive elbow. Maybe I should turn around and tell them that I'm extremely close to vomiting so they might want to reconsider such close proximity.

Don't. After all, if it happens, it will be their loss.

Hurrah! Miraculously, my bag is one of the first off and onto the belt. I'm sure it is the Louis Vuitton effect. Had it been the dowdy bag with the stain, it would have been the last. Not sure how that works in the great realm of karma, but I'm sure Vuitton comes up trumps, even in that jurisdiction.

Wedging bag off in slightly psychopathic manner—Whoops, almost just struck elderly woman in the head next to me. Wow, she is tiny.

"Sorry." I best apologise, as I did nearly knock her off her feet.

She is giving me daggers—Fine! I swagger off as quickly as possible, yanking my bag behind me, heading to customs. The line is dissembling shortly at this point and I might make it through quickly.

Oh, that wave is for me. Yes, a portly, middle-aged man is waving me forward. Go, go, go … He is doing that back-forth staring thing—at my passport and back at me. Passport, now to me. Passport and back to me.

"I'm pretty sure it's me." I'm rather amusing, even in this state of alcohol recovery.

"Just making sure," he's telling me. Uggghhh. American accent. Now I'm going to have to hear this accent all the time—reminding me of Jai!

Why am I even thinking of Jai? Flight and hangover have had discombobulating effect.

"Just stare into that camera and we'll take a pic of you. Don't forget the sunglasses, ma'am."

Just remembered that I haven't taken the sunglasses off. Shit! No wonder he was staring at me. Double shit! Need to encounter light. I slowly remove sunglasses, and an ethereal glow penetrates my eyes. If only it felt ethereal, and not like shards of glass jabbing into my pupils.

Squint.

"Done, ma'am," he's telling me. "You can put the sunglasses back on." He's just shared a smile and raised an eyebrow. "Had one too many drinks on the flight, did we?"

Smart guy, is he? "Hmm—something like that." Aren't they supposed to not make conversation? And shouldn't he be insisting that my sunglasses stay off for the full "customs" experience?

"Thumb and index finger up here," he's gesturing towards a screen on the counter. I'm trying to follow the directions, indicating how my hand should be splayed to get imprints on screen, but I've never been particularly good with directions. Whoops second, no third failed attempt—He is reaching over to me now and pushing my hand down into an uncomfortable spread-eagled position. I will not deny this feels awfully intrusive.

"And then the other." His tone is bored now.

Follow instructions, Cee, concentrate. Only just barely, but somehow have scraped through the second hand.

"Are you here for a holiday or work?"

"Holiday." A living it up vacation, actually. "My boyfriend's here, staying in Malibu with some friends."

"Grand," he says, his voice oozing an ironic tone. "Do you have the address of where you're staying?"

Handing him my mobile with the open text message for him to read. He's just staring at me like, *You could have just read it out.* He's letting out a long sigh, obviously over having to endure strange exchanges on a daily basis, and tired of challenging them.

"Thanks, lady." Well, at least that's better than "ma'am." When does one get to the ma'am age? And how did I reach it without knowing it? "Okay, move along." He's waving me through … "Next!" he's calling loudly, almost shattering my eardrum.

I'm stumbling forward like a woman possessed, wheeling luggage behind me. I'm starting to sweat. Is it hot in here, or am I experiencing the first warning signs of early menopause? I know it's a bit soon, but it happens to some women when they're still young. I can feel myself sweating, like literally having a hot flash. Hmm—also potentially a result of alcohol, but no longer thinking straight.

A customs official is waving me through the large double doors, nonplussed about checking my luggage. I've either been marked as a priority customer, i.e. unlikely to be carrying or smuggling anything into the country (probably given the *ma'am* demographic), or they don't want to deal with some hungover, potentially still drunk, ma'am with a serious sweating issue.

Out into the main airport department I go. Have strange sentiment that I'm watching myself from afar.

It's not pretty.

Somehow I've made it to the cab without maiming anyone in my path, despite erratic walking and pulling of Louis Vuitton. Suspecting people might be getting out of the *ma'am's* way. Feeling slightly like Courtney Love when coming back from a gig—only slightly less glamorous (yes, indeed, that's how seedy I am this afternoon)!

Hefting bag into boot of car, I take a seat at the back of the cab, feeling like I've at the very least made it through the airport gauntlet.

"Where to, ma'am?" the driver is asking.

What's with the ma'am? Do I look that disheveled and decrepit as a result of drunken state and flight? But I checked before I left the plane, didn't I? And I had looked semi-passable—So what's happened since?

Pressing phone up to the Perspex that divides us so he can see the address. He's leaning over his shoulder, putting on glasses and reading address.

"Okay, got it."

I'm nodding my head, unwilling to speak in case when I open mouth I involuntarily vomit instead. He should be happy with my selective muteness—In fact, he doesn't seem to mind.

I'm staring out the window, but the whizzing of the cars and traffic around me is making me even more nauseous. Look away! Look away!

Locating mobile again, it's time to check Facebook. Realising that international roaming and plan charges will be exorbitant and should keep checking of Facey to a minimum, but what other options do I have here? Staring out of the window might result in vomit, a hefty fine, and being kicked out of car in a foreign city with friend's very expensive luggage. Shall focus on Facey instead.

Have record number of likes on LAX post. Feeling like well-traveled woman of the world again—with severe hangover.

Have two personal messages. The first is from Tina:

"Are you there yet? Panicking, can you call me?"

Okay, there is no way I can stomach another conversation about fucking the Swami, office gossip, and a broken engagement at this very moment. The thought of it makes my stomach churn, and I'm having a hard time getting rid of the visual image of a seahorse *you-know-what* again.

"I've just arrived, babe. Hang in there, will call you as soon as I get to Chad's friend's place."

Write back and then enter as an after thought:

"Do not tell anyone!"

Second message … from Jai! Having fluttery feeling in stomach—It's different to churning. Open message:

"Are you stalking me now (followed by a smiley face)?"

Hmm—Less complimentary than I would have liked, but nonetheless a little funny … He must be wondering why I'm in town the same time as him. Admittedly, sounds slightly stalker-esque, doesn't it? But really just mammoth coincidence … Not sign from universe, I tell myself. Just a coincidence!

"I'm stalking you?" I'm messaging back. "More like you're stalking me! Why are you here, anyway?"

After all, he didn't actually tell me. He only acted very evasive about the topic and talked in wild conundrums. He could be here marrying his childhood sweetheart, and well, I have already explored the drug cartel *and* baby-mother options, so I know it's not either of those!

Phone is buzzing. He's responded already, keen bean.

"Are you serious? I left before you. That's the whole thing about stalking—It's usually the person that does the following who is the stalker! In this case—you!"

Smiley face.

I like how he throws in the smiley face, sort of takes the edge off the otherwise unflattering commentary … What did people do before emoticons existed? They must have been in a constant state of confusion about misinterpreted emails and texts!

"And what constitutes the 'stalk-ee' exactly?" I'm tapping out.

"The pursued," is his response.

"And wouldn't you like that!" I respond.

Pause. Receiving nothing instantaneously. Bad sign, because he was rapidly responding a moment ago, wasn't he? Perhaps I've pushed flirtatious commentary too far, or he really does think I'm a stalker, and was just masking it all with hyperbole. Was it hyperbole? He was pretty frank? Maybe I misinterpreted? But there were smiley faces involved! Smiley faces!

Mental rant over, incoming message …

"Yah, I kind of would."

Blushing. Oh my god. Am blushing in cab as result of PM from non-boyfriend. Smiling sillily to myself despite semi-drunken state. Must stop. He must have been thinking about his response, that's why he paused, non? Can't send crushing comment now, need to ease out of flirtatious mode.

Me: "I imagined that would be the case." Emoticon of wink.

Still me: "Am here on spur of the moment holiday with Chad and his friends."

Now start vomiting out responses in usual manner.

Me again: "He has an old friend who's interested in the franchise."

437

Pause. Long pause. Staring at phone. Come on, write back already! Really, you're going to be pissed about me being here with Chad? Shifting in seat uncomfortably, wishing he would write back. Write back! Write back! Trying to will phone to do so, and in reality, Jai, through exceptional mind power made only more exceptional by booze bender on flight.

He has written back: "Sounds like a blast."

No emoticon. Is he serious? Ironic? Not sure, the last conversation we had about Chad he told me the man reminded him of a possum pygmy, and I'm actually sure he meant pygmy pygmy, but pulled back on it because it was a potentially racial slur. Now he thinks I'm going to have a "blast" with him? That doesn't seem right.

Phone pings again.

Him: "We should catch up, though, since you're here and everything."

Staring at it. And what does that bloody mean? God, I wish he would be clear about things. I mean, seriously, does this man hate me, love me, or just want to be my friend? Who fucking knows!

Cecilia, voice in head is hissing, with remarkably akin tone to Mother's voice, *you shouldn't want this man to love you. You have man-of-dreams already. You should want this man to hate you, or at very least be your friend!*

Sigh.

"Sure. I'm on international roaming, so just call my mobile." Best supply number in case he doesn't already have it. I mean, it was in my signature block at work, but it would be slightly stalker-esque of him to be noting that down, right?

Phone pings almost instantly.

Him: "Okay, I'll buzz you. Here's mine," and said number has ensued.

438

Finding myself staring at phone again. Have I just committed some sort of relationship faux pas? Am I now treading on dangerous territory? Am I suddenly in the cheating court? I've never been in the cheating court. Never. That said—I've never been in a relationship long enough for the cheating court to exist.

Maybe I'm on par with Tina? Swiping thought away. No way am I on par with that. The fucking Swami, are you serious?

Weird, it's as though I've summoned her to life. The phone has started buzzing: unknown number. I can feel it—Again with arcane vision into the future and universe gained through alcohol buzz, *it's her*.

"Hello?" I say, forgetting my usual "Cecilia speaking" routine in this ESP moment.

"Cee!" It's her. It's official, have ESP. Am psychic. Or at very least, psycho. "I know you said you'd call me, but I'm desperate to talk to someone," she's pleading.

"Yes, indeed," I respond, hand cradling head already. "That's fine, speak away, but lower your voice. I have a splitting headache."

"Did you drink too much on the plane?"

Oh, for fuck's sake, am I that transparent?

"No."

"So I think I have to tell him." She is sounding quite desperate.

"Who?"

"My fiancé," she is crying out plaintively.

Oh, for double fuck's say, we're back here again, are we?

52. 11:00a.m.

ay one (or are we classifying this as two, given I arrived yesterday? But this is really the first day I've woken up here, so really that makes today day one, non?) … In bed. Think I may be under house arrest, or possible hostage, of a number of very ridiculous ex-footballers and WAGs with no sense of humour and epic levels of self-esteem, no intelligent conversation, and a shitload of whatever fabricant exists in implants.

Am aware that I'm being judgmental. I try shifting in bed, but I'm quite literally pinned down by one of those large muscular instruments Chad calls arms. A fortnight ago, I would have luxuriated in this moment. Waking up in bed with man-of-dreams who drives Lamborghini, has face like angel, a wonderful personality, and a kind heart. I would have laid here under the weight of his arm planning our wedding because sure, as explained to Elsie, I have not been dreaming about my wedding since childhood, and, indeed, I have not (only spasmodically, and at times). But in the throes of an epic romance, one can't hold back from imagining walking down the aisle with a Stephen Khalil strapless dress on, garland of roses in hair, similar to Kate Moss at her wedding, and lilies in arm— Okay, perhaps have been planning wedding (just a little).

But that was a fortnight ago, and now I'm feeling the weight of that arm baring down on me like a torture tool. Am trapped. Trapped! TRAPPED!

Man-of-dreams has turned into hideous ogre. Maybe not hideous ogre, but lecherous ex-footballer who wants wife to stay home and not work after wedding and get breast implants the size of volleyballs. Yes, volley-fucking-balls—almighty, hard, balls that would keep one afloat if one were in a drowning situation.

How did I miss that? Not quite sure, think I may have been in some sort of post-coitus with extremely attractive, cashed-up man, and ignored all signs and symptoms of underlying ogre-dom. But am quite sure that he made intelligent conversation at some point, and he was sort of funny. He wasn't always demanding that I become Pamela Anderson overnight ... *Was he?* Or did I just not see that either! Hmm?

And hey, BUDDY! Yes, I'm screaming in my mind at you, Chad, because I'm too something to actually do it out loud! I'm turning my face towards him with a filthy expression—I still have a job! Yes I do ... despite the boobs resembling mozzarella!

He's not reacting to my *antagonism by osmosis.*

How have I been so blind? I think it was because everything was always done so subtly, nothing was ever overt. He was always on the cusp of being smart, on the cusp of being funny, on the cusp of being kind, on the cusp of wanting to transform me into a glamazon. Never once did he request the hair extensions or the fake tans or the nails, never once, but instead, subtly encouraged me like a hamster trainer when I'd had them done.

"Oh, you look stunning, darling," he would coo. "You should have had the hair extensions done aaggges ago."

And I, like a very well-trained hamster, went along with it all. How stupid of me! How quickly to trust … how suckered in by this idiotic pygmy! And I'm, well, a little ashamed at being so caught up by the whole glamour, the fakeness of it all … But who wouldn't be awed by that shit?

Trying to thrust the thoughts from last night from my mind, but they keep recurring, vomiting forth like usual verbal diarrhea, scarring inner eye …

When I arrived at this gorgeous beachside shack, three stories tall modern exterior, pool, gym, library, sauna, you name it … *Oh my god*, I had thought, *staying in house akin to lifestyles of rich and famous.* Feeling like Brooke Forrester and the like— I had decided to just turn a blind eye to the forcing self on trip, the no airport pick-up, the stupid fucking friends …

And it all seemed to go that way for a wee while—Of course, when I got into the house, I realised they were all blind drunk. I also realised why these people don't usually drink lots, because they're messy and disgusting when drunk.

Okay, so have been accused of being messy when drunk before, but racing down Oxford Street sans shoes to beat your new *bestie* to the Coke sign doesn't really equate to everyone getting into the Jacuzzi naked. It was a veritable orgy of fake tits, all floating on the water like bizarre one-eyed flotation devices.

To make matters worse, Georgia suddenly took it upon herself to announce that she was taking me to Dr. Someone (not sure, Jewish surname) to get a consultation about fake breasts tomorrow (which, may I add, is now today), and she knew I would absolutely love them. How can she know that? I might just love my mozzarellas, for all she knows.

Of course, I politely indicated I wouldn't be attending the appointment, at which point man-of-dreams, sophisticated, elegant man, whom I had been planning to spend the rest of my life with announced ... Wait for it:

"Yes you are. I'm not marrying a woman with small tits!"

To everyone's applause and laughter—except, of course, my own. At which point I realised this guy is a total asshole, had been from the start, only I'd never gotten him drunk enough to realise it.

Here's the long and the short of it: you only really know someone and what they're capable of when you've been drunk with them, and they've shown you their true colours. Unfortunately, because I'd spent most of my relationship with Chad drunk myself, I had never really realised how much of a tosser he is.

Knocking at door. Oh, who the fuck is this? Like, seriously, this is not the Playboy Mansion. If I see someone's boobs (and they're not my own) I am going to—I am going to—Oh, I don't fucking know!

Yanking myself out from his arm forcibly ... Who cares if he wakes up? Have been mooning over this idiot for way too long, protecting him against the harsh realities of this world and how much of a dickhead he is.

He has just abruptly startled awake-ish—Good! He's looking up at me, still semi-asleep.

"There's someone at the door." I'm not going to hide my crossness.

"You get it, baby," he's saying to me—patting my arm, and flopping back into his sleeping position ...

Fucking pygmy!

Fine, I'll get it, babe! Sarcasm of course ... I head to the door and open it just a crack, just in case there are foreign boobs awaiting me out there. It's Georgia, all dressed up, handbag on wrist, looking a bit sheepish.

"What?" So sick of the vacant, vapid pleasantries!

"Oh hey, babe," she's saying sweetly and ignoring my tone. "We have an appointment with Dr. Epstein at noon, and I don't want us to run late."

You are kidding me! "The boob guy?"

"He doesn't just do boobs, he does all sorts of plastic surgery."

I'm staring at her—That doesn't help. But the thing is, she doesn't realise, nor does she recall the breast soup I escaped from last night. She was way too gone.

"Come on, sweets, let's go," she's instructing me.

"I'll meet you downstairs." She has just blown me a kiss and is now pulling the door shut.

Seriously? The boob guy! Staring at Chad, who is semi-awake, but still snoring. I would actually rather go see the boob guy than spend the morning with him.

Oh, how the mighty have crumbled.

Opening bag aggressively and starting to pull on clothes—shorts, t-shirt, wedges—Who cares if *the look* doesn't work? I'm going to see Dr. Boobies, after all—He won't be focused on my clothes.

"Where are you going, babe?" Chad has piped up, obviously aware of movement like any other primitive beast.

"To Dr. Boobies with Georgia." Not sure if he senses the anger in my tone, probably fucking not, too blinded by the notion that my mozzarellas are going to be big balls of Edam.

And as predicted, my tone has been very much misjudged. "Oh great, babe. I knew you'd come around. You'll love them, doll." He's hammering his face into the cushion, evidently wishing sleep back. "See you later."

Feeling homicidal thoughts of smothering him with pillow right here, right now, while I have the opportunity. It would be so easy, I could just creep around the side of the bed and he'll not even notice. I'm sure of it.

Breath. Count to ten, Cee. Do they have the death penalty in the States? Potentially—Not sure, as it's not something one investigates before coming on trip to the States with fucking man-of-fucking-dreams. Who would have thought feelings of love could be transformed to homicide so quickly?

This guy is a douche. Certainly not man-of-dreams … Shit!

Grabbing jacket and bag and heading out of the room to meet Boob Soup. This is what my fucking life has come to. You think you shack up with a celebrity ex-footballer with a face like Leonardo DiCaprio that it's going to be all rainbows and flowers—But you know what it is in reality? It's all boobs and hair extensions …

… And really, really, *really* dumb people.

53. 12:15p.m.

r. Epstein's office. Alone, except for around five other Fred-like looking women with faces full of filler, hair-bouffants of various heights and lengths (but nonetheless bouffants), and breasts, lots of breasts, indeed. Georgia has gone in for appointment. I'm next up, apparently. She'd gushed at me with enough enthusiasm to drown a cat. Conclude am definite hostage in situation.

How is this possible? In cab ride down to Epstein's Surgery, I kept thinking how beautiful it was—the mountains, the ocean, the houses, and the wineries. Why couldn't I be at one of those wineries? Isn't that what I had been promised? *Vino* and *food!* Instead, I got boobs, plastic surgery, and women with terribly sad faces akin to my uber-melancholy Cavoodle.

I didn't sign up for this! Not at all!

The woman to the left of me is paging restlessly through a *Vogue* magazine. Looking at her from the corner of my eye to ascertain amount of work she's had done. Definitely breasts (but that's a given in this haven of tit-soup), there are certainly fillers in the lips and potentially in cheeks—Oh, think she senses my observation. She's looking up at me— Yes, I've been caught out in analytical plastic surgery stare.

Oh, shite!

She doesn't seem annoyed; instead, she's smiling at me now. Of course her lips form a smile and I can see teeth, but the rest of her face has remained perfectly still. It's like staring at a scary mannequin that's sort of moving and trying to communicate with the living.

"Hi, there," she has begun.

Oh, double shit. She's going to start talking to me. I am not the type of person who makes conversation with strangers on public transport, in supermarkets, and certainly not at plastic surgery waiting rooms. But it's too late to politely smile and avoid eye contact now—She's already said something because evidently, she is the type to have a discussion with total strangers in restricted places where possibility of escape is limited.

"Hi." I have to say something, I guess, elegant smile on my face, of course.

"Where are you from?"

How did she detect an accent? Surely my Australian twang can't be deciphered from just one word!

"I'm Australian."

"Oh, I love Australia," she's saying in a gushy voice. "It's always been my dream to go there."

She is smiling again, face remaining fucking frozen. Am I staring into a mirror of the future? Will I look this way a year down the relationship path with Chad?

"It's a beautiful place." And it is, I love Australia, but may be bias!

Is that enough? Can I now look back down at magazine? Will mannequin care? Or does she want to keep on talking? It's always such a fine line—When does chit-chat officially end? I am wishing that it already has!

"What are you doing in the States?"

Well, apparently not then.

"Umm, I'm here with my boyfriend," soon to be ex-boyfriend, methinks, "and some friends of his—on holiday really."

Friends of his, not of mine, that would be a loose description of relationship with Georgia, Jayden, and the rest of them. I mean, I've seen them naked now, but still I don't like them. How could I appropriately refer to that? Intimate acquaintances?

"Well, good for you." She's patting my knee. What's with everyone and the manhandling? "You will have a blast." Again with the blast!

Nodding head—Now can I look down?

"And you just thought you'd see Dr. Epstein while you were here?"

No, no I can't. I really can't continue with this.

"He is the best," she is continuing, nonetheless. "The best in L.A. You will love him."

"Oh, I'm really just here with a friend," I tell her, desperately not wanting to be lumped with the rest of this crew of blondes and plastic surgeon miscreants.

She's looking at me knowingly. "Oh yes, darling. That's what they all say on their first time," she says to me, patting my knee again with a perfectly manicured hand.

"No, seriously, I'm just really here with a friend." I don't want to go in there!

She's staring at me closely like she can't quite understand my accent and has no idea what I'm saying. It doesn't compute. Her eyes have glazed over.

Georgia is bounding out of the doctor's office looking absolutely ecstatic, like she's just about to have a mammoth orgasm, or at the very least been allowed to eat carbs again.

"Here she is right now." I'm turning to the random stranger, getting to my feet quickly, and grabbing Georgia by the arm.

"Oh." Random stranger is looking slightly perplexed but could be the expression her face is frozen in.

"Hey, doll," Georgia has begun. "Oh my god, you won't believe it—He's going to do some lypo on my thighs. By the time I head back to Sydney, I'm going to have pencil-thin legs. A bit like yours really—but maybe with less muscle."

Her face is looking hysterical, and it's so close to mine. I'm not enjoying the smell of her sickly sweet perfume. And her breasts are almost jabbing into mine—Oh god, remembering last night, and those great big things bobbing on the surface of the Jacuzzi.

Clear said mental image. Clear mental image! Cleanse mind, Cee!

"Oh, that's great." I'm not sure why I'm saying this, the whole surgery thing seems so barbaric in a way. "Now, we need to go."

I begin tugging her in the direction of the door.

"But wait," she's resisting, "what about your appointment?"

I'm shaking my head at her and still tugging. "I'm not going in there."

Hopefully I'm being firm enough for her to understand.

"But what about your new boobs?" She's putting on a firm fight, worthy of a Krav Maga professional, really.

"I don't want new boobs," I say, and I really don't. I know I've called mine names, but I wouldn't have them any other way—not now that I've seen the alternative!

"Oh, come on, you can't possibly be happy with those?" Luckily I know she doesn't mean it as a jibe. She's just completely vapid and stupid, and probably thinks everyone wants watermelon-sized boobs.

"I am," I say, tugging her out the door … Yes, I'm winning.

"Cecilia Binner?" Shit, someone is calling my name, must turn around slowly … Shit, shit … It's Dr. Boobies, a tall man of nondescript age and appearance, and he's heading out into the waiting room and calling my name again, louder this time.

But we're through the doors now, and I'm pulling her out into the sun, a summer's day in L.A. Thank fuck for that! *Sigh.*

"Cecilia Binner?" he's calling again with a confused tone …

Sigh. Leaning up against the wall behind me, I feel like I've just escaped being shanked by *my* jailer.

"What's gotten into you?" Georgia has asked, a look of utter concern on face. "I didn't even pay for my visit, or book in for the surgery."

"Well, you'll have to do that on another day." I'm so irritated now.

We are staring at each other, fake hair extensions and tans, one woman having upgraded to an upmarket model of body, and the other still in the same one nature has given her.

She has let out a sigh, one of defeat, I hope. "You really don't want to be a part of this, do you?"

Shaking my head, "No, I don't." Maybe she is smarter than I've given her credit for!

"Well what are we going to do now?'

"We're going to have a fucking drink." Of course, my solution to all problems.

"Sounds like a plan, doll," she's agreeing. "Do you think we can get some fags, too?"

"I don't smoke—gives me asthma."

"Well, you can just fucking smoke on this occasion—because I'm taking it's the last time I'll see you."

"Fine." She's right. "I hope you have a fucking puffer then."

"Ventolin?"

"Yep!"

"Sure do, let's get this show on the road."

54. 5:00p.m.

ineyards. Somewhere near Malibu. Wine fountain and largish sign out the front spelling out WINE—all promising signs. With Georgia, who has turned out to be more fun than immediately imagined without Jayden. Amazing view of vineyards, Tuscan style mansion, and surrounding arid hills. Finishing up an amazing bottle of Chardonnay and cheese plate. Now this is what I'm talking about, this is what I came to L.A. for—not bloody plastic surgeons and tit soup!

"Oh, doll," she's saying, afternoon sun beating down on us, "let's take a selfie."

I've had just enough vinos to take the perfect selfie. Somehow quality of selfie grows exponentially in accordance with vinos consumed. She is turning the phone towards us, and we're squeezing together, pouting for the perfect selfie. Or at least through wine goggles, it appears to be the case.

"I'm posting it to Facebook," she's telling me. "I'll tag you in it."

Yes, we are thirty-something women taking selfies and posting them on Facebook—Did I hear someone say, *Grow up?* Never! Fun is young forever. And that's the only thing that is.

Nodding head in accordance with affirmation and taking a swig of vino. "Love this place."

"Me, too," she's agreeing, typing Facebook post. "And it's so good to be away from the boys—and gawwdd having a vino and some cheese. Totally perfect." She finishes up her message and is putting her phone down.

"Do you think Jayden would have a problem with your drinking of vino and having some cheese?" Whoops, voice is becoming slightly slurred, but 'tis a vacation, non? If the moment for boozing it up on a weekday ever occurred, it would be right now.

"Totally," she's saying, lighting up another cigarette. "He would never come right out and say it, but you know he says it in his own little way— like, *Oh darling, do you really want that piece of cheese? Really? You know you'll complain about it tomorrow.* But the only reason why I complain about it is because of him."

She's handing me the pack. Oh, go on then! I'm plucking out another cigarette for myself. Smoking has now become habit of the day. Have smoked three, and fear potentially addicted at this point. Also feeling slight constriction of lungs—Black lung coming on.

Does *Medicare* cover hospital visits in States?

Lighting up again, anyway. The hell with it! We're talking men now, in L.A.! Ridiculous ex-footballer, ogre-like men who demand fake breasts from their ladies! It calls for vino, cheese, and fags …

Not of the homosexual sort, of course, but rather of the cigarette sort.

"Oh, fuck really? But you're rake thin." And she *is* tiny. "Except for the boobs, of course," I say, reinforcing that much, knowing how important they are to her. Tit soup and all!

"I am not. I'm a size ten at best, and that's not fucking thin—Wish I was a size six or eight. I see him looking at those young things, size six with breasts, of course, and I know he's thinking about fucking them," she's telling me with a great degree of anguish.

"Really, who are these women?" I'm intrigued to know more, having only been exposed to the young hipster-thing variety with green tea and kale in their hair.

Kale in their head! Well, makes more sense than ingesting it.

"They're out there ..." she answering me, "and they're after him. You know, watched him on television when he was like some hot shot—Those girls are the ones who will fuck anyone in the bathrooms of some nightclub as long as they played league or NRL." She's shoving a piece of cheese in her face, and very much resembling Jess as this discussion progresses—The food shoving, the swearing ...

"Really?" I say perplexed, wondering what NRL is? Is there a difference? Are there NRL groupies and league groupies? Are they separate? Or do they cross-pollinate? Not sure Georgia is in the state of mind to respond to *said* questions.

"Yeah, they're everywhere! Haven't you noticed?"

Shaking head, I actually haven't.

"Of course you wouldn't," she's saying to me. "You're smart and have legs up to your fucking vagina ..."

Isn't that where they're supposed to end?

"I mean, you're different from the rest of us. You're not like the usual footballer's gal. You're all funny and shit. Charming, whatever," she has declared.

Where is she going with this?

"Chad was besotted from day one when he met you," she's telling me. "He only had eyes for you. Because you're different and, like, cool or whatever."

What's the *whatever* part? Not sure, too trashed to figure out. But there appears to be lots of whatevers in this dialogue.

Focus on the problem at hand instead.

"Yeah—But he still wants to change me. He wants me to have fake boobs, and be all blonde and fabulous—For fuck's sake, he didn't even tell me he'd booked me on a trip to L.A. He expected me to drop everything and just come on this trip." And I did, I dropped everything, and I'm here. What does that say about me?

"But surely you can make some compromises?" She's looking confused.

"They're too big though—They're huge!" Sadly, as much for me, as for her. I know the realisation is just happening in my beverage-induced mind, but it's clear, and evident—and here. And I'm sure it is the thing I've sensed since even before coming out here to the States … slowly creeping up, tapping me on the shoulder, and yet I've just brushed it off and gone along with Chad's world because, well, because I guess I thought it would make me happy, that is was what I wanted … And I guess I was wrong …

Have reached destination, end of relationship. *Sigh*. Have been here many a time before. It's a familiar locale.

"How are they big?" she's pressing me, slowly propping herself up from her awesome yellow reclining chair.

Perhaps they're not big to her, but they're big to me. Maybe Mother's right, am holding out for perfect man who doesn't exist. Even when presented with perfect man, I toss said perfect man aside, restlessly finding new fault. But surely having equal say in a relationship is not finding a ridiculous flaw. It is a flaw! Of the epic variety! Lots of exclamations in thoughts! Most definitely due to advanced drunken stage.

Georgia is trying to pour another glass into her flute, but the bottle's empty.

"Shit!" she has declared.

"Don't worry," I tell her, clumsily propping myself up, too. "I'll buy another." I reach for my handbag in a demented manner. Why so trashed? Why? Is it the sun? Am I getting dehydrated, as well as awfully sunburned, increasing rate of drunkenness in exponential fashion? Similar to air travel, I suspect.

"I'll get it, babe." She's reaching for her handbag now. "I'll put it on Jayden's card—After all, you won't be around for much longer."

Indeed. *Note to self:* never fly to the other side of the world to be with man on holiday that you hardly know, in case it goes pear-shaped. What to do after that? Do you go straight back home? Or do you continue on with holiday alone?

Ahh—the shame! Imagine walking back into office a week and a half in advance! Elsie will have a field day. The rumours will fly like nobody's business. At the very least they'll take over the Swami fucking incident, non?

Georgia is waving the very cute waiter over. He's all Santa Monica charm and tattoos—and reminds me of Jai. Pushing thought of him away—Can't deal with it right now.

"We'll have another bottle of the same," she's telling him, winking flirtatiously and handing him her card.

"Sure, ladies." He's winking back at Georgia and sauntering away.

"See that," I say, popping on my sunglasses and reclining back into my seat, looking out to the glaring sun through my shades. "You're a hot piece of ass, Georgia. Look at that little boy just lapping it up. You could get anyone!"

She's smiling at me. "Thanks, babe. You've got such a kind heart."

"What?" I'm accustomed to playing the villain—This is a new area for moi.

"That's why I liked you from the start. You're not after the money or the celebrity status—you're just you—and I guess you just liked him."

"I did." She is smarter than I thought. Or is that just the epiphany-like quality that alcohol has? But if I am honest with myself, there have still been moments when that material shit, and even Mother's and Chris's reactions to it all, had gotten me excited … But yes, it was because I actually liked him … But now, well, that's a completely different matter altogether.

We've stopped talking for a moment—I think she's in same spaced-out trance like I am. I'm looking up at the sky—*Fuck, this is fab*, even if I am in L.A. with *Boob Soup*. I'm living the dream—or something like it. I'm sure the dream doesn't involve boob soup and partner sending me to surgeon to be cosmetically enhanced—but something close to the dream anyway.

At very least, as good as it gets right now.

"Hey, babe," she has startled me from my reverie. "Who's Jai?"

What?

"How do you know his name?" is escaping my mouth before I can think about what I'm saying. Oh dear … I really am *drank*. Erm drunk, really am drunk, I mean.

L.A. dream waiter has dropped off bottle, and has winked at Georgia again. She is now smiling coquettishly at him—Oh shite, something or someone is going to go down here.

"Jai?" she is asking again, pouring the drink clumsily now, spilling half out of her flute. And she is pouring mine equally as clumsily.

"Oh—I work with him … Why?" I say, clinking our glasses.

"He just commented on our selfie," she's telling me, glancing at her phone distractedly.

"What did he say?" I'm demanding like a lunatic.

"Beautiful ladies."

Smiling. *Aww*—so sweet!

"He's kind of hot, too."

"How do you know?"

"Perving on his pictures right now … Mmmmhmmmm," she's murmuring. "Give me some of that."

"Oh, put it back in your pants," I say, laughing. "If you want to go after someone, go after the waiter. He's been eyeing you all afternoon."

She's throwing a look towards said waiter who's watching from a distance, but definitely looking in her direction.

"I know, right? He's hot!" she's laughing through her words.

"Indeed," I say, dropping half glass of Chardonnay down top—Whoops … Wish I could lick it up, but maybe not appropriate behaviour to pull my top to my mouth in bid not to waste good vino.

"Oh, shit …" she is declaring, still laughing, more of a giggle now. "He's looking."

She's sitting further down in her seat, and I'm looking over at him, not so discretely.

"Umm … He sure is." I'm still laughing. "You should totally give that a whirl." Oh shit; too much wine has made me too naughty. Also need to throw Boob Soup off the Jai path.

"I shouldn't—But then I think, *I'm sure Jayden would.* You know?" She's looking towards me, almost for further approval. "I found a g-string in his bed this month," she's telling me unsteadily, yet drinking her glass down rather steadily. "Like a fucking lacy Victoria Secret g-string—that was not my own."

"Oh, shit!"

"I know, right?" She's sliding down in her deck-like chair looking Fred-like again. Fred is now my barometer in the sadness status. Wondering how he is doing with Chris? Has he yet been transformed into fag-dog? An odd shade of pink, perhaps!

"And so—Did you confront him about it?" Collected thoughts, and back to conversation. Should be incensed for Boob Soup, instead of thinking about Fred.

"No," she has replied resolutely.

"No! Why the fuck not?"

"Because it's not the first time! And you know you've got to put up with this shit." She has raised an eyebrow and her shoulders, like a *move with the times already, sister* gesture.

"You are joking," I say, articulating the words carefully.

Pause. She is staring at me with swimming, drunken eyes. Hmm? Where is my cigarette? Have I dropped it? Hope not, because it's an arid climate here and could start bush fire, but in bar. Bar fire—Not good!

"No—I mean, I have it all: the lifestyle, the money, the holidays, the status. You have to give something in return." She seems sad.

So sad! It breaks my heart it's that sad. One should never have to give up that much, surely!

"I mean, everyone wants to be like us, don't they!" she's telling me, and there's no question mark in her voice, even though it's posed as a question. She totally believes this.

She must know that I don't agree, or at the very least, I don't want to be that person. And through our wine-soaked spectacles, I'm sure that we understand each other. Boob Soup and I.

Alcohol, the fucking great equaliser!

I'm smiling at her. "You go after that guy," I say, gesturing my head towards the waiter.

"Really?"

"Do it—I'll never breathe a word," I say, winking at her.

Seriously, it's the least she should do. Who finds potentially dirty g-strings in their bed (which are not their own, damn it) and just shuts up and puts up? That can't be right.

She's swinging her legs around to a sitting position and is squeezing my knee, but looking in his direction, again coquettishly, and he is shifting on the spot, obviously knowing he has her attention.

Ahh—young love. Lust, whatever!

"Babe, why can't you stay?" she has suddenly demanded. "Be part of it. I need someone like you," she's saying, manhandling my legs again.

I'm shaking my head.

"Love you, doll," I tell her in the loosest sense of the declaration. But vino-fuelled, and current situation taken into account, no, don't really love her—In fact, can barely tolerate her, but you know, it seems to be the right thing to say at this moment. "And you're better than this—but I can't be part of it."

We are staring intently at each other. There always seems to be a lot of intent staring and searching of the soul after a few too many *bevvies*. More manhandling from her also ... But she is now getting to her feet, letting out a sigh, and putting her drink down.

"Indeed, you are better than this!" She's heading towards twenty-one-year-old gorgeous tattooed thing. Who is smiling back at her!

Indeed, I am.

55. 7:00p.m.

Still at vineyards. Alone, though. Sun is going down. Wonder if I should be concerned about Georgia. She's been gone for a few hours. Does that mean she's having the best sex in her life with young thing or she's been whacked by young thing? Hmm … not sure! Have sobered up, well, almost completely, and am hungry. Stomach rumbling, hunk of cheese not enough to stave away hunger pains. Dinner crowd about to arrive, women dressed elegantly and men wearing slacks and loafers. Definitely need to leave. Have been sitting in yellow reclining outdoor chair looking out at the view for too long now. I must look like a modern day cowboy staring out to the horizon, pontificating the world and one's own place in it.

Pontificating, indeed. Now with the clarity of no longer man-of-dreams being that, I need to figure out a way to get home—And I mean really home. Not boob soup location in Malibu, but back to Sydney.

Sigh. Oh gawwd, will have to face Elsie, office gossip, Swami sex scandal, Mother's wedding extravaganza, baby prep, and Chris—well, and any number of potential threesomes on his end. And, of course, if I don't return with his expensive handbag (which is now the only thing that remains hostage at the Playboy Mansion), I'll also need to front up to his wrath.

Sigh. It's almost too much to deal with.

Will need to tell him I was in a desperate situation, with blondes and bimbos and potential plastic surgery, and had to make desperate run for it. Although, I'll know he'll say to me, *Why would you run from that? Sounds like paradise—and all set in the idyllic panorama of Malibu!*

That's what I will need to contend with.

Well, would prefer to contend with the known than navigate this shit-storm. Am, I've just decided, now back in the *single jungle,* as a primate of the creeping to mid-thirties range with sizeable amounts of prior relationship baggage (not of the Louis Vuitton variety), making me, I am sure, dating pariah.

Mother's hopes for a spring wedding (for me in this case) will be shattered for an extended period—one might think … if not forever.

Wish women who didn't marry had far more fashionable title than spinster. Doesn't really have a cache to it, does it? Not like *bachelor.* Will need to workshop some other titles to bring into vogue and overtake out-of-date, Jane Austen-like *spinster* term.

"Ma'am," someone is saying and touching my shoulder, startling me from my replacement brainstorm session of spinster term, "we'll need these seats," the kindly man from the bar is telling me.

"Oh, yes, indeed."

Okay, so external factors, i.e. being kicked out of vineyard because am lonely drunk and friend has disappeared to shag waiter, have set chain of events into motion. Need to figure out what to do in the immediate.

Should I call cab and go to a hotel somewhere in Santa Monica? Can't even stomach going to hotel in Malibu in case I make sighting of hideous eyesore of Playboy Mansion while driving down there. There's no way I will be able to change flights and get directly on plane tonight. Will probably need to wait till later on this week.

Wait a second; is this a glimmer of hope? Perhaps! Should contact Jai! He's here, and might be available to help. Don't really want to come across as damsel in distress type—am not damsel in distress type, after all, am woman of the world, living, well, nowhere at this point. Dream has shattered around the inflated sense of me, and shards are being flung at me like confetti in some ridiculous imitation of post-wedding proceedings ...

Okay, right ... Just call the man! Other options are bleak, not even sure what the cab number is here, would need to Google. Cab did drop off, which means they do come here, but at this time of the evening?

Where's Jai's number? I did prudently save it—you know, in case homicidal situation arose and needed to contact someone. It turns out to have been a good decision, non?

Phone is ringing, and stomach is involuntarily clenching. One ring, two rings, three rings ...

"Yep?"

Heart fluttering, but also have sinking feeling. Why am I calling this person? Shit! Why did he pick up? Why would he even want to help me? Am able woman who shouldn't need man's help ...

"Hello," he's calling into the phone again. Whoops, sidetracked by thoughts—That makes a change. *Note to self:* focus during telephone calls.

"Hey, Jai," I manage, recovering self. "It's Cee, how you doing?" Trying to affect a relaxed tone of voice, but it sounds more like a baying sound.

"Yeah, good—"

There's a lot of noise in the background. Maybe he's at a party, or dinner, or some other social engagement. This was a bad idea!

"Oh, sorry," I'm spitting out. "You must be out. If it's not a good time …"

"No, no, no," he is saying hurriedly. "Hold on, I'll just go outside."

Can hear background din and clamor as he is evidently moving through a throng of people. Now silence. No, now street sounds.

"Hey, sorry," he is back talking to me. "I'm just in a bar. How you doing?"

"Sorry." Why do we both keep saying *sorry?* "Maybe now's not a good time …" Not sure why I'm trying to extricate self from situation, but I hate being a nuisance.

"No, it's totally fine. What's up?" He's laughing a little, seeming pleased that I have called.

"Oh, you know—this and that." Oh, fuck! What am I saying? *This and that?* Mind is totally slow at the moment. Has slowed down from warp speed to Georgia and Jayden standard in sympathetic pack animal gesture.

"Okay, what does that mean?"

"Weelllll," I say, drawing word out in a sing-song voice. "It's not really going that well." There, I've said it. I hope he is reading it as HELP!

"No?"

"No." *No, not at all!* "In fact, I'm sort of stuck at the moment." Oh dear, liberated, emancipated woman that can handle own affairs has gone out of the window.

"What do you mean?" Evidently I'm not making much sense either.

"Oh, I'm just out at some vineyard in Malibu," I say in a relaxed tone, as one does. "But really, I have nowhere to go now. I mean, I probably need a lift to a hotel in Santa Monica for tonight and then will need to change flights from there and go home."

Well, that's really the long and the short of it, non?

"What happened to Chad? Aren't you supposed to be here for two weeks?"

Pause. "That didn't really turn out as planned."

"The Chad thing didn't turn out, or the two weeks?"

"Both."

Long pause. Don't really want to explain the details over phone.

"Do you want me to pick you up?"

"Yeah … Sort of. Like now, if that's not too much of a hassle," I say, pulling face on my end is sort of a bit demanding. He is out somewhere—potentially with someone. What if he and Malibu Stacy are out having a drink celebrating their ten year anniversary? Or the birth of their baby! Can one drink directly after having baby? Not sure!

"Yeah, no problem." He just said *yes*. My heart is soaring. "It might take half an hour or so, traffic's a bitch here," he's added. "What vineyard are you at?"

"Hmm … Not sure! Has a sign out the front, big metallic letters that say WINE, and a wine fountain …" I say, looking around and scanning for any other distinctive details, noting I have not brought spectacles and am as blind as a bat at this point.

"I know the one," he's already responded. It seems that WINE sign and fountain are distinctive enough in this case. "Be there soon."

"Okay, bye." I'm feeling awkward, but relieved. He's hung up and on his way to get me, to rescue me. Thank fuck for that!

Staring out at horizon again, cowboy-esque, pondering the big questions ... Did I do the right thing? What's happened to Georgia? Do I just leave my stuff in Malibu and take off?

"Ma'am." It's the barman again. "You're really going to have to move," he's telling me now, haranguing expression on face.

"Oh, sure," I say, getting to my feet.

My cowboy pontification days are clearly very much over.

56. 7:45p.m.

Sitting on stone wall outside vineyard. Alone. Sort of feel like the type of girl who sits on a wall … Not quite sure what type of girl that is, but it sort of brings to mind wild child, ditching school and wearing school jacket tied around waist with knotted sleeves. Feeling comfortable in new wild child, rebellious teenager role.

Waiting for Jai. What if he doesn't turn up? Slightly panicked. Maybe he was suddenly distracted or is the type of person who says they're going to do something and then doesn't, and doesn't even tell said person they're no longer taking part in said agreed activity, just switches phone off or infuriatingly won't answer phone at all.

Maybe. He doesn't seem the type though.

Phone pings, and I pull it out from bag. It's Georgia:

"Hey, babe. Sorry, got to bail with Jaime. Will get him to drop me home later. Ciao. Xo."

Fickle is her name. Well, it's not, it's Georgia, but nonetheless the woman is fickle. Who is Jaime? Must be tattooed, young American thing. Hope the text has come from her, and not said Jaime as he drags her body through the hills of Malibu looking to bury her in a shallow grave. Image in my head now, as is tit soup.

No, it must be her. How would he know my name, find my number in her phone, and then write such an affected, but careless, text? It has definitely been penned by her own hand!

Yellow Mustang is pulling into parking lot—staring after it—potentially Jai. Looks like the type of car he would be driving, flashy, but hip at the same time. Squinting eyelids together to see who is getting out of the car, it would appear to be an adult male, but given state of eyesight, I can't really come up with many more descriptors from this distance …

He is approaching me—waving at me—definitely him (or accomplice in Jaime forward slash Georgia scenario).

"Hey," he's calling, all tattooed and swarthy and hot. Black jeans, army boots, chain, and t-shirt, with sleeves rolled to shoulders, revealing very relevant musculature.

Heart fluttering.

"Hey," I say, jumping down from wall, slightly inelegantly, but at very least have landed on feet. Think girl who sits on wall type would have definitely made a more sophisticated, yet edgy, descent.

Awkward moment. He is just a few feet away from me. Not sure if we should hug, kiss on the cheek, shake hands—all very, very awkward. Resulting in some strange disjointed robot-like dance with one of us moving forward and the other moving back at the same time, and vice versa. This is stupid. I'll just smile at him, and he is tucking his hands into his pockets, flexing his muscles in a masculine manner, evidently displayed to hide awkwardness on his part of said encounter.

"Sorry about this," I say, still feeling awkward.

"No, that's totally fine," he says, shaking his head. "I really wasn't up to anything anyway." He's rubbing the back of his head now. "I'm glad you called."

"It sounded like you were at a bar or something?" It didn't seem like nothing—In fact, it certainly felt like I was interrupting something.

"Oh, that," he's saying. "Yeah, just catching up with some buddies. No big deal."

"Okay." I don't want to press the point—I mean, he's here, isn't he? "I just ..." Oh no, I just what? Train of thought is becoming all muddled with pheromones and thoughts about his new haircut (which did I mention is short again, no more blonde, just a light brown) and that musculature ... Stop thinking about musculature, Cee, even though I love saying the word, even in my mind. Could say it all day long— musculature, musculature, musculature ...

Off on bizarre tangent!

"... I just didn't really know who else to call." *The truth.*

"And here I was thinking I was your first choice," he has said with an ironic smile.

"That, too ..." Hmm ... Perhaps initial statement was a little offensive. Pause. This is a rather uncomfortable silence.

"We should probably go." *Go where, though?* "I have been hanging around for a while now—I think the owners might forcibly remove me soon."

"Sure." He's extending an arm towards the car in an *after you* gesture. Hoisting bag over shoulder, I start walking towards it.

"How'd you get here anyway?" he has continued to talk, probably because I'm not saying anything, I'm just tumbling into this hip car. He is sitting in the drivers seat with far more coordination than I'm demonstrating right now, that's for sure.

"Cab—I came with a friend of mine for a few drinks."

"Did they leave?"

"I suppose you could say that." *With my encouragement.* "She sort of left with one of the bartenders—a few hours ago."

"As you do." He's turning the key in the ignition.

"Indeed. Kept thinking she was going to come back, but that didn't turn out to be the case."

"Evidently—So, where am I taking you?"

Interesting question. *Where is he taking me?* Where exactly am I going? I should just go back to the house in Malibu and suck it up for another day or so, which will give me enough time to change flights and the rest of it. I mean, that would be the sensible option, wouldn't it? And if I were a sensible person, I would probably do that—but have never been really that much of a sensible person.

"Is that a hard one?" he's asking, smiling. Very funny!

"Well, it sort of is … Don't really have anywhere to go," I say, trying to take the needy edge out of my voice. Wanting to remain empowered, secure woman who does have home, abode or the like—somewhere out there. Am not homeless person!

"What happened?" He's frowning, looking at me like a basket case.

Thoughts of myself being a rebellious school girl have disappeared and feeling more Winona Ryder-esque post-shoplifting escapade.

"Oh, nothing really—Well, it just didn't work out with Chad." I mean, really, how long can I keep this *nothing's wrong thing* going for? "And I don't really want to go back to the house in Malibu."

"Did he do something?" He's narrowing his eyes, being all manly and protective so it seems.

"No," I say, shaking my head. "I just misread him. I've been giving the man too much credit—and evidently too much of my time."

"Intellectual pygmy?" he has asked, smiling.

"Of the possum variety—of the possum variety who drags their significant other on a trip to L.A., giving her a day's notice, and instructs her to have a boob job, otherwise he couldn't possibly be seen dating her."

"Shit, really?" He's still smiling. He must think it's funny.

"Well, they were the real deal breakers, but you know there was a whole lot of vapid, senseless shit in there, too—preening, self-absorption, naked Jacuzzi episodes with a throng of other people, and ..."

"Naked Jacuzzi episodes?" He seems startled.

"You know, being a man and all, I can see how that would spike your interest, so let me just tell you—It wasn't pretty. Still struggling to eradicate the episode in my mind. It keeps creeping up on me at unwanted moments, and suddenly I have mental images of breasts and penises bobbing in the water ..."

He's laughing out loud now, like he's having a good old hysterical moment at my expense.

"Well, I'm glad it seems funny to you because I'm literally scarred for life. For LIFE!"

"I'm not laughing at you … You're just a funny girl, that's all. I mean, you ditch some rich dude in L.A., end up blind drunk at some winery, and then tell me some crazy orgy story."

"It's just another day in the extraordinary life of Cecilia Binner." *Sigh*. Like really, could the guy not make fun of me? It's just a little more than I can take right now. But he's still laughing. "So onwards and upwards," I say, my voice bright and cheery. "Can you just drop me off at a hotel in Santa Monica? I can stay there overnight and change my flight tomorrow."

I can totally tell he is trying to stop laughing, but evidently it's stronger than him. I mean, really, I've just ended a relationship here. I could be really cut-up, you know—and about to go on a chick-flick, ice cream, doona depression binge. I'm thirty-two years old and unlikely to meet man-of-dreams again. This could be classed as epic failure—He could be more sensitive, or at least try a bit harder.

So I'm not cut-up at all, he doesn't know that. I don't even know why I'm not cut-up!

"Okay, let's get this show on the road," I say, clapping my hands in a Tina-like gesture. Maybe that will snap him out of hysterics.

Oh good, he has stopped the laughing, and now he's just looking at me (he needs to keep his eyes on the road). He is still smiling, and that smile keeps threatening to turn into hysterical laughter. He's very cute when he smiles, even if he's annoying the shit out of me.

"Why don't you just stay at my place?"

Frowning at him, I say, "Because I don't really know you."

"But you didn't know that guy either," he's saying, laughing again.

"Oh, come on. Stop it." *I'm over it now.* "I'm going to take offence soon.

Just take me to the hotel."

"No, seriously." He's clearly making a radical effort to pull himself together. "It's my dad's place anyway, and there are like eight bedrooms. It will be totally fine. We won't bother you at all—and you can change your flights and the rest of it from there."

"That's very kind of you, but I really don't want to impose …" I don't even know why he's here. It could be for any manner of reasons …

"You won't be imposing. It'll be fine," he's telling me, steering the car out onto the highway.

"But I don't know if you're some crazed psychopath—I mean, maybe you had to come back to the States because you're running a drug cartel, or …"

"A drug cartel?" He's giving me an incredulous look. "How likely would that be? And besides, do I look like I run a drug cartel? I'm a Creative Director, Cee."

"Indeed, the perfect cover—And sometimes with the way you dress, you look like you might be running a drug cartel."

He has just shrugged his shoulders. "Well, at the very least, I'm not doing any flashing of my underwear. At very least, my clothes provide adequate coverage."

"You didn't just bring that up, did you?" I say, narrowing my eyes.

"I did … I went there," he's laughing. "You know, I do enjoy our banter, Cee," he's telling me. "In fact, I've missed your little jibes and witty comments."

Heart has just stopped, like actually, and it's back pumping again. Am still able to function thankfully. Did he just say he missed something about me? Does that mean he's been thinking about me while he's been gone?

"Does that mean you've been thinking about me?" Shit, it just came straight out, didn't it? Thought to mouth!

Pause. Static electricity in car!

"Yeah, I mean, I guess I have been." He's trying to sound relaxed with remark, but doesn't quite make the mark. "Wondering when you would give that ridiculous pygmy the flick."

Promising, very promising indeed, methinks. He's been trying to get rid of competitor. Need to fish to find out if the man has a girlfriend, but how to do so in cool, nonchalant way? Am not cool and nonchalant to begin with, so I can't imagine what would ensue when trying. Besides, why am I thinking about this, am literally fresh out of a relationship by a couple of hours. Surely I can be an independent woman for a period of time, woman of the world, woman of business ... And there's no other evidence this man is interested in me ...

"Cee? Cee?" Oh, he's saying my name. Must have asked me a question. "Pardon?"

"So, you're okay to go to my place? Promise I will not throw myself at you, or turn into crazed lunatic."

"Are you very sure?" I ask, inwardly hoping he will throw himself at me.

"Yes, I promise." *Drat!*

"Okay, fine then—But let it be noted on the register that you invited me, and I didn't oblige you to take me back to your place." I'm flirting in a snotty way.

"There's no register, Cee."

"Hmm ... There always is. Besides, I don't want to interrupt anything with you and your *girlfriend* …" I say, glancing over at him. That was so not slick. Beyond not slick, it was like serving up a turd and covering it with ice cream to hide the odour, appearance, and consistency.

"What girlfriend?" He's looking perplexed.

"Your girlfriend," I say, adding some ownership to the girlfriend word.

"What are you talking about, Cee? I don't have a girlfriend."

"Oh, it was just one of my hypotheses around why you came home. You know, potential nuptials, pregnant girlfriend, wife, that sort of thing." I'm trying to say it as though it's the type of thought that would cross anyone's mind … a plausible reason for him coming back to the States and taking a *leave of absence*. I mean, they are plausible thoughts because they occurred, at very least, to me …

"There's no girlfriend, wife, or illegitimate or legitimate children that I'm coming to care for," he's saying. "In fact, my life is quite barren of women altogether. No mother, sisters, etc. I'm actually here for my dad— He's not well."

"Oh." Shit, have I pried too much? Not quite sure how to take that at all. Well, there's no significant others of the female sort, so that's good. Is it? Is that what I was after? I've definitely pried too much into his personal life and that's sort of not very cool. Obviously he hasn't wanted to tell anyone about his dad.

"I'm sorry about your dad."

"Yeah, thanks."

Silence. I'm staring out the window, trying to make something out in the darkness. We've evidently reached the Hollywood Hills and are now starting an ascent. Still can't believe he's from here, and his father is some screenwriter. Maybe like Arthur Miller. How cool would that have been to grow up with? Sort of beats the old crazy Franny upbringing in suburban Sydney.

The streets are getting narrower and narrower, and the houses are getting bigger and bigger, like some sort of exponential graph of streets to houses … Modern houses, Tuscan houses, perching out on ledges of hills, dominating the night's sky with light.

"It's kind of nice you've been thinking about that though," he's suddenly said.

"What?" What is he talking about? "These houses are fucking huge."

"Oh yeah, I know right. I guess I'm used to seeing them," he's telling me.

Craning head to get a better view. "So what were you talking about— Nice, what?" I ask, wondering if we're driving passed Vin Diesel's house at this very moment, or Kurt Sutter! OMG could die.

"I meant it's kind of nice you were thinking about whether or not I had a girlfriend."

Still distracted. "Oh yeah, that." The streets are so tight now, like hairpin turns. Hoping one of these movie stars hasn't had too much cocaine and is about to get in their Porsche, in *Wolf of Wall Street* style, and plummet straight into us. "I checked your Facebook status, too."

Oh, shit! Did I just say that? No, I totally did not? NO!

"What?" He's pulling into a driveway.

The house is huge, like some sort of seventies style, *Mad Men* bungalow split on a number of levels, with said Porsche from *Wolf of Wall Street* parked in the driveway.

"This is your house!" I say, feeling sort of like Elizabeth Bennet when she first sees Pemberley … But to be frank, this is way better than

Pemberley. I mean, hello, house on Hollywood Hills kicks Pemberley to the curb any day of the week.

"What did you say?"

"Your house is gi-normous," I say, wide-eyed. "I don't think that's an accurate term of measurement, but this house makes it one."

"No, before that," he's shaking his head.

"I don't remember," I mumble, staring back at the house.

"About Facebook," he's prompting.

Oh, that, shit. I actually said that ... "I didn't say anything about Facebook."

"Yes, *you did.*" He's enunciating the last two words.

I'm shaking my head at him. "Why don't we go inside?" I say, scrambling out of the car.

"Oh, so now you want to go inside?" He's getting out of the car, too.

"Yah."

He's heading towards the front door. "I'm sure you said something about Facebook," he's saying, getting his house keys out.

"No. No, I didn't. You're totally imagining it."

57. 3:00a.m.

ide awake! Tossing around in extremely large bed in extremely large guestroom, decked out in Cuban-like styling. Think a Havana club. The Che stares back at me from a billboard-like wall. His revolutionary eyes are gazing out towards an unknown fixed point somewhere atop the bed. His face is set in a resolute, stern expression. He's bothering me, even though he's not looking in my direction. Tossing again, sigh, tossing again, sigh. Fucking Che!

Had elected to go straight to bed after arriving at Jai's house, an overwhelming tiredness had swamped me (also needed to get away from inappropriate Facebook comment before further questions were raised). Probably effect of jet lag and number of drinks consumed in sunshine earlier on in the day. Jai hadn't objected, just led me through this mammoth house where we passed what appeared to be a library with enough stuffed antler heads and watching eyes to spook anyone, a sun room, and then into the guest room (with a deck, mind you, and a view of the Hollywood Hills, a little different to my place in Potts Point, that's for sure).

Mia casa, e sua casa is basically what he'd told me. Not in Spanish, of course, but the usual basics: bathroom, kitchen and logistics of getting around the super mansion. I was pretty sure he is sleeping on some other floor of the house, in another huge bedroom, so I'd probably need to call him on my mobile if I needed anything else.

"Dad sleeps all the time, so you probably won't see him," he'd said to me. *Okay.*

Had then just tumbled straight into bed wearing current clothes—not that I had other clothes to change into—and had a few hours of blissful, out like a light sleep, before I woke up at 1:30 a.m. stark awake, as though it was the middle of the day. I'd checked my phone, and had a few messages from Chad, including, "Where are you," "I'm worried," "Georgia just called and said she doesn't think you're coming back! What's going on? Call me," then, "Please call me." You know, that sort of thing. Finally texted because I figured even though he is a complete and utter ass, he probably had the right to know I wasn't dead in a ditch somewhere.

"I'm with a friend. No, I won't be coming back. This was totally wrong, Chad. My mistake, your mistake. It doesn't work. Will call you tomorrow."

I tried to make it as clear as possible given text restrictions. You know, you just can't pour out your heart in text even if you do have an infinite amount of characters to use. It's just not right. The man deserves a conversation. Tomorrow, though.

The thing is, the more I've sat up and been thinking about it in bed, the more I've realised that this was all really of my own making. I had wanted to be wound up in the whole celebrity life, the man-of-dreams life. Whatever he said or did, I spun it into something fabulous because I wanted it to be. I'd been wearing rose-coloured glasses the entire relationship, and been completely suckered into the whole thing.

Fuck! I even went to Dr. Epstein's!

Chad wasn't really to blame. Well, yes he was an epic ass, forward slash megalomaniac, forward slash *possum pygmy*, but it's not like he had ever promised to be anything else. I had just been projecting all the other qualities I wanted out of a relationship onto him, because I'd decided in my mind that he was man-of-dreams.

I'm thirty-two going on fourteen.

At very least nobody can criticise me for acting too old for my age.

I'm hearing movement outside on the deck. Perhaps it's possum pygmy come to take revenge after all my unflattering commentary on its behaviour and character! Listening carefully. Hearing noise again. There's someone out there.

Perhaps it's Jai come to declare his love? Or at very least come to console me with his musculature?

Slowly getting out of bed and creeping towards sliding doors … Spreading curtain, and peering out, furtively, like spy assassin. Can't see anybody or anything, including any pygmy for that matter.

… But hearing noise again! A rustling of some sort.

Opening door sharply and stepping out onto balcony, ready to perform well-honed Krav Maga skills that I've developed from watching YouTube videos.

Looking from left to right, and on the right hand side … one elderly man, sitting on the edge of the deck, legs hanging precariously from the drop, with a suspicious looking fag hanging from his mouth.

He's just pulled said fag from his mouth and said with a matter-of-fact tone, "Who the fuck are you?"

I'm staring at him, and it's been longer than a moment, wide-eyed— Am I dreaming this? Or am I awake? He seems very tangible, and sort of pissed off, and I can also smell the ganja, terribly pungent on a summer's night—definitely not a dream.

"I'm Cecilia."

"Is that supposed to mean something?" he's asking antagonistically.

"I think so—It's my name."

"Well, that's great, doll." He's taking a drag on his big fat one. "I'm Larry. What the fuck does that mean?"

"I don't know," I say, wracking brain. Larry, Larry, *Larry*. Not ringing any bells! "Is this some sort of existential conversation that I don't understand?" I ask, slowly creeping towards him.

Perhaps I should be keeping my distance, but Larry doesn't strike me as a crazed psychopath, and anyway, the ganja would slow him down.

He has suddenly started to laugh. "You're funny," he says, pointing at me with a stubby finger.

"Indeed, people always say that."

"I bet." His response is pleasant, pissed off attitude subsiding, potentially result of ganja. "Do you want a spliff?"

Hmm—Have not been offered a *spliff* in at least five years. What's the harm in having a spliff with some complete stranger in the middle of the night, early hours of the morning, whatever time it is now, at a random friend's house in the Hollywood Hills?

"Why not?" I decide, sitting down opposite him cross-legged. The fuck with it, what more could go wrong on this trip anyway?

Could be going home in a body bag. Disposing of that little thought, quickly.

He's putting his fat one down on the deck like a seasoned professional, smoking end hanging off the side. He has produced marijuana from a plastic packet tucked under his shirt, like a magician pulling out a white rabbit. Pulling paper from under his thigh, he is now rolling me a spliff, and I'm watching him as he expertly licks it closed and then hands it over to me.

"You must be one of Jai's friends." He's leaning across with his lighter as I'm putting said spliff in mouth.

Oh shit, now engaging in illegal activity in States. Have not thought this through properly ... pros, cons, all that sort of thing. And I'm not even drunk, am making this call cold.

I'm nodding my head, and now he's lighting said spliff.

Well, here goes nothing. I take a drag ... Fuck! It burns through me instantly, providing that wonderful little spliffed-out hit. I remember this ...

So, the *fuck* with it all. What does it mean anyway? What does it matter? Who even cares?

"Who are you?"

"I'm his dad," he's saying, taking a drag.

Oh, okay, that explains a lot of stuff. Like why he's here acting like it's his house and demanding to know who I am ...

"Oh, right ... He said you would be sleeping." My mind is already bending in all sorts of directions.

"Is that how he gets the ladies to come back to his place?"

Laughing. "You're funny." Compliment back at you, old dude.

"Yeah, I've heard that before, too."

Feeling like I need to explain the situation to him … I *am not some hussy Jai's picked up at a club and brought home to shag*. "We're just friends. He was just doing me a favour, letting me sleep at your house."

"Well, that's a shame." He's finishing off his fat one, stubbing it out on the balcony and flinging it over the edge carelessly.

"Indeed. I think so, too." Oh god, what am I saying to Jai's father? Christ, revealing self to be a harlot, taken in by son's musculature. Maybe not the best way to meet potential father-in-law.

Is that what I'm thinking? That I want to be with Jai? Random thought indeed … or just one that's been hanging around and has resurfaced as a result of the spliff!

"So, why aren't you two, you know, getting it on?" He's popping new spliff into his mouth.

"Hmm—because I was seeing someone else."

"Oh, right. He's turning towards me, engrossed in conversation, or at the very least seemingly so. He has the same grey eyes as Jai and that ironic smile.

"Yah, so I came to the States with this other guy—but he was a total douche bag … So I had to make a run for it. Now I'm homeless. Well, sort of. I have a home in Australia …"

"Shit yeah, but that's far away."

Nodding head sadly.

"Well, it's a good way to be."

"What? Homeless?"

"Yeah—means you don't have to worry about the other stuff, you know, possessions and shit. You're free as a bird." He's making flapping movements with his arms.

"I have no clothes," I say, as though it's the worst part of the scenario.

"So what are you wearing?"

"I only have these clothes," I clarify, stubbing out the finished-off spliff and rubbing nose—very spaced out.

"Do you want another?"

"Sure." Why stop at one? "How come you have all this ganja?" He's already started rolling another spliff.

"Oh, you know, one of the only perks of having stage three cancer."

"Oh, shit. Really?"

"Mmm-hmm. The rest of it's total bullshit," he says, handing me the spliff and leaning over to light it.

"That's why Jai's here," he's telling me. "Looking after his old man before he carks it."

"Shit. I thought he was coming back here to run a drug cartel."

Larry is laughing. "How do you know him anyway?"

"We work together in Aus," I tell him, taking another drag. Whoosh-ka, feeling amazing!

"Oh yeah, I see. He's so fucking serious, that boy."

"Jai?" *Doesn't seem like the serious type to me.*

"Yeah, covered in tats and piercings and shit, but deep down he can't let any of it go. Let himself go."

"Doesn't take after his dad?" I say ironically.

He's shaking his head.

"So you're dying, huh?" Oh fuck, did that just come out of my mouth?

485

What am I thinking? Nothing, evidently! I've never really known anyone that has been *dying*. Been to a few funerals, always cried, considered my lot in life, but after a few days it goes. Here before me sits a spliffed-out man who's making his exit.

"Yeah, my body's shutting down," he's telling me.

"Oh, shit." My words are quiet now. He's dying—too much to take!

"I know, right? I wouldn't care as much if I wasn't in so much pain. Otherwise, fuck, we're all supposed to die … Who fucking cares?"

"That's bleak."

"Well, you know, I'm a writer. I'm a bleak fucking person," he says sarcastically.

"There's just one thing I want to do before I die …" He's stubbing out the second spliff and flicking it. Shit, he smokes fast.

"What?" I'm leaning in, intrigued.

"I want to get a good fuck in." He's nodding. Men—all the fucking same, no matter how deep.

I'm giving him a raised eyebrow. "I'm not fucking you." At least that one is clear, so sorry to shatter your dying wish—but not happening, old man.

"Really?" He is looking perturbed.

"No, no matter how funny you are."

"Damn it!"

"I'm hungry." I said that rather abruptly—but I'm literally starving.

"Yeah, me, too. Let's go get some nosh." He's slowly getting to his feet in a geriatric manner. Like really? How is this guy going to fuck someone? He'll die in the middle of it. Probably his dream—Probably any man's dream!

Stubbing out spliff and handing the half that's left back to him. He's popping it into his jacket and extending a hand to help me up. Like I need a hand? But I'll take it anyway.

He's now leading me into the house.

"You'd prefer to fuck my son?" he says, more as a statement than a question.

"Yeah, probably." Ganja is reducing care factor of acting like whore in front potential new boyfriend's father to zero. Although, I meant *yeah definitely*, so still a little filter left.

58· 3:30a·m·

n mammoth Tuscan kitchen with Larry, chowing down on some cheese,
prosciutto and crackers … very civilized munchies food. No chips,
cereal without milk, or tomato sauce (sans anything) going on here. We're all
classy, Hollywood Hills munchies business. Larry has made me a gin and tonic
and declared that he makes a great beef lo mein and has hit the nine-burner
stove with all sorts of ingredients. He's flinging things in like a chef
extraordinaire, shoving cheese into his mouth and chatting away.

"What's your favourite series on television at the moment?" he has
asked, tossing some sort of Asian sauce into the pan.

"Definitely *Sons of Anarchy.*"

"Oh yeah, Kurt Sutter … Great fucking writer."

"Do you know him?" As per usual, starstruck. *Note to self:* said behaviour
leads to all sorts of shitty situations, including tit soup.

"Yeah, I do. He was here last weekend."

"Did he have a spliff?" Oh my god, have I been having a spliff in the same place Kurt Sutter was having a spliff?

"No. No he didn't," he has said with a laugh, and he's continuing, "What else?" *Let me think, what else do I like watching?*

"Oh, probably *Game of Thrones.*" Yep. "But it's a bit complex for me—way too many characters does my head in. Wish they were still on the whole Daenerys Targaryen and Khal Drogo thing—Now that was a hot couple."

"Drogo?" He's looking over at me perplexed. "Who the fuck is that?"

Finally, I've found a man who swears more than I do.

"He was like the king of the horse people. Like a huge Maori guy, ripped and stuff."

"See!" he's saying, pointing the spatula at me. "That's the type that the young girls want to be fucking."

"Yah." Agreed. Who wouldn't want to fuck the Khal Drogo?

"What are you two doing?" comes Jai's voice from behind me. I spin around in my stool to face him. He's looking like he's just woken up, wearing a *t-shirt* and shorts, hair slightly askew, looking from me to his father, me to his father.

"Oh hey, son," Larry has called out. "I'm making some beef lo mein. Do you want some?" he's saying as though it's the most regular thing in the world to be serving up Chinese food at 4:00 in the morning.

"No, I'll give it a miss." Jai's still staring at his dad, looking perplexed.

"I met your dad," I say, brightly delivered, especially at this wee hour of the morning, methinks. He's looking at me with equally troubled eyes.

"Here, son." Larry's heading over to the drinks cart near the fridge. "I'll fix you a drink. Cee's having a gin and tonic. Do you want one, too?"

I'm patting the stool next to mine invitingly, looking at Jai.

"Sure," Jai is saying really slowly, heading over to the stool.

I'm smiling at him, and he's sitting next to me now, all calm, looking at me, and his eyes are screaming—*What the hell is going on?*

Larry has placed a gin and tonic in front of Jai and is now heading back to the beef lo mein.

"Don't worry, son, we didn't sleep together," Larry has suddenly announced, and Jai is looking deeply troubled by the announcement. "She said she would prefer to fuck you."

Was taking a sip of drink and almost spit it out. Oh shit, so embarrassing, but so ridiculous. Starting to laugh. Larry is laughing, too. And now we're both bent over hysterically laughing.

"Oh, I see," Jai is saying, not laughing. "You two have been smoking joints."

"No!" I'm shaking my head, and shaking with laughter at the same time. Grabbing Jai's arm imploringly, I look into his eyes, telling him—*No, totally untrue!*

"Sure have." Larry's not backing me up whatsoever.

"Here, Jai, I'll roll you one," Larry is continuing instead. "I can do two things at the same time, cook and supply."

Am dying for that beef lo mein. Starving.

"No, Dad, really," Jai has replied.

"Oh, I insist." Larry's rolling away already.

"I'm so starving, Larry," I'm announcing. "Do not burn that lo mein." I'm concerned about the state of the food while he's handing out spliffs.

"I have it under control, Cee," he's telling me, and quite convincingly.

"Oh, shit." Jai's shaking his head.

Larry has just put the spliff in front of Jai on the island bench, with a lighter. "Ready when you want it," he's saying to him as he walks back to the lo mein, *thankfully*.

"I found him on the deck, Jai." Good enough explanation, methinks, grabbing his leg in manhandling sort of way as a means of connection. Must have rubbed off from Boob Soup. He doesn't seem to mind, although he's still looking at me like I've lost it.

He's so handsome though …

"So," Larry has begun, "I think she's the girl you've been talking about from Australia … you know, the one you said you liked …"

"Shit, Dad," Jai's interrupting, but Larry has continued regardless …

"You said she had awesome legs, a beautiful face, terrible hair—and she was funny. Super funny. This is her, right?" he says, shoving the spatula towards me.

I'm staring at Jai, and he has turned bright red. Crimson red. And he is clearly avoiding eye contact.

"It's her, right?" Larry is going on, no filter, and Jai is sighing … He has started lighting up on the joint. Defeated. "At first I thought *not possible* when she came walking out on the deck with those legs and that accent—but then she's funny. *And* she came home with you. It must be her!"

Jai is saying nothing in response, just taking a long drag on the joint, and now he's looking at me, grey eyes, ironic, saying *I'm sorry*.

"I do not have fucking terrible hair."

59. Wake up groggily. Can't remember date, time, nothing.

*C*an't even recall who I am. The usual hangover experience ... only spiked with something else. Oh, shit! Recall the spliffs. Oh, shit! Recall bits of the episode with Jai's father. Oh, shit! Shit! Shite! No, really? How embarrassing? Want to die. Lying on Chesterfield lounge in library. Pulling self into sitting position ... Oh, fuck, head is aching. Swinging legs off Chesterfield and hitting blunt object, I look down, assessing object—not object—person. It's Jai sleeping at feet on carpet below Chesterfield. Oh, shit!

Fuckity! Fuck! Fuck! How old am I supposed to be again?

He's stirring under my feet. Potential result of said feet ...

Trying to recall what went down last night. I think despite being ridiculously embarrassing, did not sleep with Jai or Larry or kiss Jai or Larry. Just finished spliffs, drinks, and beef lo mein and passed out in library—I think I was reading something aloud …

I think I had insisted on going to library to find favourite book and read passage to Jai. What was favourite book? Don't have favourite book.

Looking around, head spinning, light piercing eyes, there is said book just laying around. It's Frankenstein, and it's open at a random page.

Oh, shit. Why, oh why, Frankenstein? Just dropped book on ground. Whoops, annoying, at least it missed Jai's head, unlike feet!

Jai is now awake, looking up at me. He's got the same perplexed expression on his face, as I'm sure I had a few moments ago. I'm watching his face go through same realisations as I did, *What am I doing here? What the fuck went down? Oh, shit, that did not happen!* Yes, it did—dying of embarrassment!

I'm smiling at him. "It wasn't that bad," I say, trying to reassure him with a little laugh thrown in to add lightheartedness.

Oh, is that a smile? Yes, delayed, but he's now smiling back at me. *Phew.* "No, it was worse than bad." Oh! How?

"Oh, come on," I say, shaking my head.

"Why the hell were you reading me that bit from *Frankenstein?* Is it supposed to mean something? I was trying so hard to understand what you were trying to tell me—"

"I have no clue," I say, still shaking my head. "*Frankenstein* is not my favourite book at all. I'm sorry," I tell him with an apologetic expression. "Was just spliffed."

He's laughing.

"And you didn't sleep with Larry?" He's leveling his eyes at me.

"God no!" He is of course joking, must be, right?

"When I saw you two in the kitchen and him making lo mein ... I thought, *Fuck, I'm screwed.* The woman of my dreams just had sex with my dad. He always makes lo mein post-sex—like always—no matter what time! So easy deduction to make."

I'm staring at him, and he's looking back at me with a perplexed expression, like he doesn't realise he's said something huge. Massive. GI-NORMOUS!

"I'm the woman of your dreams?" I say, pointing at self. Is he serious? I'm the woman of someone's dreams—and his dreams? No, it can't be!

He's looking embarrassed, no, now he doesn't. "Yeah, you sort of are."

Completely rattled! Starstruck! And feeling a little bit—no, correct that, A LOT in lust.

"But you were always being a complete dickhead at work. Checking up on me, trying to catch me out. Checking where I was in the morning, where my work was up to—I thought you thought I was totally incompetent and wanted to reveal me to everyone, as—as—I don't know! You were completely *team Elsie.*"

"I was never team Elsie." He's grabbing one of my legs, sort of a manhandle, sort of a fondle, sort of a connection. "She was nice to me from the start. God, I know what she's like. It was just nice to have, you know, a friend in a place where I'm foreign and don't know anyone!"

I'm still staring, feeling perplexed, but fuck he's pretty and makes the loins stir even post-spliff.

"I ... I just wanted to be around you," he's telling me. "That's why I hung around, not because I wanted to expose you. I mean ... From the start, I thought you were a super hot chick and everything—But then you just grew on me, like being funny and ironic, and not taking shit. I just liked everything about you," he's saying sort of sheepishly.

"Except my hair," I say, still pissed about the hair remark. I do not have *terrible* hair. Okay, so it's not gorgeous, but it's not terrible.

"So you don't have great hair …"

Okay, it's sort of true.

"You said to my dad that you wanted to fuck me last night. Who says that to someone's dad?" He's laughing.

"Well, firstly," I'm ready to rebut, "I said I would prefer to fuck you rather than Larry. That's hardy conclusive. And secondly, I was spliffed!"

"You also said I was really pretty," he's reminding me.

"Did I?" Really? I don't remember actually saying that. But he is really pretty—Sounds like something I would say.

"Yeah, before you started reading some obscure passage from *Frankenstein.*"

Okay, totally sounds like me.

Annoyed, a little … So am total trollop, reading random bits from Frankenstein. What of it?

BUT he claims I'm *woman of dreams. Not trollop of dreams!* So, what do you want to do?

"You know what I want to do," he's telling me directly, eyebrow raised.

Very candid, Jai, but he is clearly forgetting I've been recently burnt, and not about to have sex with him right here in the library.

"Hmm," I murmur, getting to feet and stretching. Extending my hand to him, and he's slowly getting to his feet, too. He's centimetres away from me, and I'm feeling unrelenting urge to just grab him and have my way with him … But I'm going to say, instead, "I really feel like a burger."

No, that is not a euphemism! "Could do with something to soak up alcohol and the rest of it."

"Sure." He's recovering himself.

"I know a great place. Burgers and beers. You'll love it." He's turning away from me and heading to the door Fred-like.

Really, Fred-like? That's sad!

The thing is—Fuck, I like this guy. He even respects the moments when I can't be everything, when all I want is a burger and a beer because I'm spent.

"Great," I say, heading his way and grabbing his arm tightly.

He has turned around and I'm kissing him. I'm actually kissing his lips. It has taken him off guard, and me, too, actually ... But it has not stopped him from responding quickly—raunchy, sexual kissing, lots of soft tongue and open mouth. Melting. Floating.

I have to pull away from him, although I'm wanting it to go on further because he's a fucking master. A creative genius! No tongue darting in and out and no jabbing or messiness.

Totally perfect ... But this all needs to wait—just for a little bit longer. Pull back, Cee.

And I'm away from him.

"I kind of like you, too." That kiss must be enough to show him how I feel. I feel so lightheaded, and not because of the hangover or effects of the spliffs.

"Yeah, I figured as much." He's smiling with his ironic mouth and his grey eyes ... at me, *woman of dreams.*

"I just need a bit of time."

He's nodding, smiling, clearly pleased and no longer Fred-like. "That's fine ... and maybe a burger, huh?"

He's not *man of dreams* ...

He's just *it*.

No down. No up ... On the even!

60. 10:00a.m.

Morning of Mother's wedding. Sitting in her French provincial lounge room with robe on and slippers, waiting for the hairdresser and makeup artist to get round to me. Of course I'm the last cab off the rank because it is Mother's big day and Cheryl is ridiculously dramatic and is monopolising attention of both makeup artist and hairdresser as they buzz about. Mother is starting to look furious, like she may soon have emotional outburst of epic proportions. Sipping champagne calmly, wondering if we're in the eye of the storm at this very moment.

"I really think this foundation is too light for me," Cheryl is announcing, holding a mirror up to her face and examining it closely.

Char is in a wheelchair following her hip injury, but still here with us for the wedding prep, despite being demoted from bridesmaid to *special guest*. She is looking as unsettled as ever, like she knows Cheryl is pressing

Mother's buttons and a fight of war-like lengths will no doubt ensue.

Jess is also in attendance, looking rather rounder than usual given pregnant status. She's here to provide support. Ever since I came back from the disastrous L.A. trip that will live on in peoples' minds (friends', family's, and colleagues') in infamy, she thinks I'm like a tiny time bomb waiting to go off. That I've been emotionally repressing violent sentiments around the Chad breakup and will at any moment have a complete meltdown that will include the need for psychiatric assistance ... She's told me all this in so many words, but of course I'm happy to have my best friend at my side.

And I keep assuring her that won't be the case, and am indeed completely *fine*. But she won't have a bar of it. "You were so wrapped up in this guy, and now you just don't care at all?" she has said to me. It's just too hard for her to understand or to stomach—Maybe if it were wrapped in prosciutto, it would be easier to ingest. Not that she's eating cold meats, now, given the baby ...

Am also only person in social circle going to wedding alone. Am the last *single* left standing. Wow—I didn't think it would be me. I always thought my friends had far greater fatal flaws than I did, which would preclude them from having relationships, or at very least maintaining relationships. In fact, it's evidently me with the fatal flaw—I don't even know what it is!

In my short-lived absence, and the following weeks of concern for wellbeing, Jess has managed to get back with Pete. Hmm ... That's all I have to say about it, and will not be giving further opinions on the topic even if requested. Except ... That's what happens when one leaves best friend in order to take a disastrous trip to L.A. ... I guess it is kind of good in some ways, considering they are having a baby together. Nothing more to say though!

Chris has somehow patched together a relationship with some new beefcake he met on Grindr. And wait for it … Even Tina, a girl who started as an intern, subsequently cheated on her long-term partner with Swami-fucking-Krishnananda and then decided to come clean to said partner, who then kicked her to the curb (not physically, but metaphorically), has managed to find a date for Mother's wedding. Really! The injustice! Don't know who, I'll find out soon enough, I guess … But the girl has certainly moved on from Krishnananda, forward slash, office pariah status, and has met someone new. Ahh—the confidence of the young!

I, myself, and moi, on the other hand, am single for Mother's fourth wedding. Really, statistically speaking, I shouldn't be surprised, given I've also been single for the other three weddings—one of which I was not born yet, but still.

Sigh.

"Really, this foundation is too light," Cheryl is continuing on, and clearly ignoring the look on Mother's face, which suggests steam is about to start coming out of her ears full pelt.

Foundation is by far not too light, in fact it's now bordering on far too dark. Cheryl is obsessed with looking tanned for the wedding. *"All* of us should look tanned," she had informed us. So we had all marched off to get indecently fake tans a few days ago, and now look an interesting discoloured orange shade. But in addition to that, Cheryl is also insisting on having dark foundation, you know to give that extra bit of "oomph," or so she has continued to tell us.

"I don't think we should go any darker than that," the makeup artist is frowning at Cheryl. The thirty-something year old is looking like she knows she's happened upon some difficult customers and would have preferred not to take this job, but presumably it is the allure of a few hundred dollars cash-in-hand that keeps her in the game.

"I do!" Cheryl has declared emphatically. "We all look like we're going to the morgue, not a wedding. Cee," she's saying now, turning to me obviously for support. "Don't you think this colour's too light?"

"No," I say, watching the clock tick. It's a fucking 11:30 a.m. wedding, I wish they'd get their wriggle on with the makeup and hair; otherwise, we're going to be unfashionably late—like the guests might start leaving. "I think it's fine." *Just hurry up!*

Cheryl is looking at me like she wants to throttle me and is now saying to the hairdresser, "She's not really with it at the moment—She's just had a terrible breakup with a celebrity. Chad Thompson, do you know him?"

"Yeah, I think I do. Ex-footy player," she has responded.

Cheryl is nodding her very orange head, and now she has returned her gaze to me, shaking her head, as though to say, *Poor, demented little thing—Can't even get makeup colours right anymore.*

"I'd really prefer you don't discuss my daughter's breakup with the makeup artist," Mother has piped up. Oh god, want to sink into the ground and die. "It's none of her business ... or yours, in fact! And besides, she's right, that makeup is already too dark on you. Now hurry on. They need to finish up with me and you and then move on to Cee."

Well, that was actually quite controlled knowing what Mother's capable of, no loose swears or crazed remarks. And also uncharacteristically supportive of daughter, non? It is likely she doesn't want the gossip circulating on her big day though, I know her too well. But maybe she's

501

turned over a new leaf?

Waiting around is annoying! I keep checking my mobile … and still no text. Jai has been oddly absent for the last day or so. Not sure what's going on. He's been texting and calling since I'd left the States regularly, on a daily basis, in fact, and sometimes multiple times a day. I'm missing my dose of silly banter, and in addition, now worried that something's gone wrong. Maybe he has realised I am demented creature as Cheryl clearly thinks, and shouldn't be engaging in some transatlantic pseudo-relationship via texts and calls. Really should be worried that something has happened to Larry, but instead am coldhearted person who is more concerned about state of own pseudo-relationship.

I'm frustrated with all of this. Jess is staring at me. I can tell she thinks I'm up to something, probably thinks the meltdown is just around the corner. Have not told her about Jai situation, or anyone else for that matter. Don't know why I've opted for silence when I'm usually a minute detail sharer—But I just haven't wanted to share it, it's sort of my thing. Besides, not sure what it all means. I haven't even had the headspace to process it.

What am I going to say to her anyway? Oh, after everything went down with Chad, I ended up contacting Jai from work—who was also in the States at the time looking after his father who is dying of cancer. You remember, that guy from the Tex Mex place you made a fool of yourself in front of? Yes, of course you do. And then I spent the night at his place, got spliffed with his dad, ate beef lo mein, but didn't fuck the dad, passed out in the library, had pash with Jai where he revealed I was *woman of his dreams, yes, woman of dreams,* had other subsequent pashes with him, and then headed home early, leaving luggage (including terrible relationship with Chad) behind. So have been texting and calling Jai since, not sure what exactly that is—potential pseudo-international-relationship? And now he's dropped off the face of the planet, okay so maybe just for a day or so, but nonetheless, what do you think?

What would she say? Why would I tell her that now?

Staring at phone again. Nothing.

Should have slept with him. Feeling like character in *Atonement* who doesn't sleep with star-crossed lover and then he's shafted off to jail, courtesy of her nosy sister, and then to war front, and then he dies! So she never gets to sleep with him. Is that the narrative? Can't quite remember! Although, maybe she does sleep with him—and potentially in the library!

See! The library had been the perfect location! Should have done it in the fucking library—even though wasn't wearing stunning green dress like Keira Knightley in *Atonement* the movie, and did really want a burger.

Looking up again because can still sense Jess staring at me. Char is looking at ground, and Mother is advancing towards Cheryl with a threatening look. Hairdresser and makeup artist are standing back looking appalled. Oh, shit! What did I miss here while was thinking of missed sexual opportunity with Jai? Something bad! Evidently something very bad …

Oh, Christ! Must avert biff between Mother and Cheryl an hour before the former's nuptials and wedded bliss.

Right! Getting to feet and throwing myself between the pair of them, but Mother is being particularly aggressive and shoving me forward, clearly wanting me to land on Cheryl, and I have. Well, my fall has been broken by her rather large rack, that is.

Mother's still pushing forward now, but Jess has sprung into action now, and is grabbing her by the arm.

"Sorry," I'm mumbling to Cheryl as I'm very much trying to detangle myself from her breasts … And the harrowing memories of floating tits in Jacuzzi have returned. Shake away, Cee. Shake away!

"Mother!" Dear god, she is writhing in the background like a woman possessed, and I'm crying out to her, "Pull yourself together!"

"I will not pull myself together!" she's thundering. "Did you hear what that bitch said to me on the day of my wedding?"

No, not really, was thinking obscene thoughts involving Jai and Keira Knightley. Well, not Jai and Keira … Never mind! How could I have blanked out so much of what was going on in reality? Is this how I live my life?

"She told me," Mother begins, wedging her arm away from Jess at the same time, "that I didn't want her in the bridal party because I was afraid Brad would run off with her. Like Brad would give two hoots about that mutton dressed up as lamb."

"Oh, is that right, Fran?" Cheryl is saying, getting to her feet and drawing herself up into her full buxom glory. "I have caught him having a perve a few times before."

Are these ladies serious? They're seventy, already! Who is perving on what?

And here we go again. Mother is lurching at her, and I'm throwing myself at Mother, but apparently a woman possessed is no match for another half her age. She is thrusting me aside like a paper cup. Ouch, that hurt a bit. Mother is grabbing Cheryl's hair and pulling it hard, as though she's trying to yank it straight out of her head …

But it appears that Cheryl's not having any of these girly fighting techniques. Shit, it looks like she's going to throw a … Yep, she has just thrown a punch, which has connected (rather loudly, might I add) with Mother's face. Mother is reeling back in obvious shock, hands up to her eye.

"You bitch!" she's yelling now. "And on my wedding day!" Oh no, she is going for her again … Jess is stepping in, *phew*, and managing to hold her back.

"You come at me, bitch," Cheryl is yelling, putting her dukes up like a seasoned fighter.

"Mother, leave it!" *Cheryl is crazy!* "She's totally nuts. You're going to get hurt … and Jess, be careful. The last thing we need is Jess injured in her fragile state.

I'm hoping Cheryl hasn't heard the *nuts* part because she might come at me, too.

My words have had some sort of impact on Mother—At least I think they have. Perhaps it has dawned on her that she can't take Cheryl. That woman clearly has some fighting prowess.

"Get out of my house, right this minute!" she's yelling instead, spittle flying from her mouth in a very unfeminine manner.

"I will, you disgusting little turd." Cheryl's face is changing into a grotesque grimace. Oh dear, *disgusting little turd!* Who is this woman? Shit, it was my suggestion for her to be Mother's bridesmaid. Push thought aside, Cee!

"Get your things." She's got to go, feeling a little responsible. "Now!"

She is glowering at me! Good, go! She's stalking off into the bedroom where I assume her bag is. I'm looking back at Mother with a shocked expression; her face mirrors my feeling of disbelief, although with an underlining current of rage. A large red welt is already starting to form near her eye. Shit! She's going to have a shiner for the wedding.

"You," I'm pointing at the hairdresser, who is hiding behind the lounge, "grab some ice or peas or something from the fridge for Mother's face."

She is slowly getting up from crouching position and is scurrying into the kitchen, can of hairspray still in hand.

The front door has just slammed shut. Evidently Cheryl has gone through the family room to avoid us. Hearing a car revving and accelerating out of the driveway, hot-tailing it down the street.

Mother is looking like she might collapse. Think Char is rocking in fetal position even though she's in a wheelchair.

"Sit down, Mother." I'm actually feeling sorry for her. Fourth wedding or not, no one deserves that stress, and a fucking shiner on the day they're getting married. Jess and I are guiding her to the lounge. "Fix her a drink, Jess, something strong."

Jess has already sprung into action.

"Mother, are you okay?" I ask her, pressing the peas the hairdresser has handed me to Mother's face. I'm kneeling down so I'm closer to her, and look at her to ascertain the level of damage. Her mouth has fallen open into a strange "O"-shaped shocked expression. But at the very least she's holding the peas to her eye.

"I can't believe the bitch hit me."

"Well, you were advancing on her like a crazed person." *And she was.*

"I'd just had enough, she's just been such a fucking pain—And then when she tells me she's had the dress altered so she could show some more cleavage, I saw red, and I told her I wanted her out of the bridal party, and then she claims I want her out because Brad's been perving on her? The woman has lost it!"

Okay, so that's what I missed. A biff over a seventy-year-old woman's cleavage! Does anyone ever grow up?

"You didn't need to fly at her like a cage fighter."

"I just saw red, Cee—I don't know what came over me. It's lucky I didn't kill the woman!"

Well, actually, Mother, the fighting was more one-sided than you think. It's actually lucky she didn't kill you. Not going to actually say that out loud though, am I?

"Try to control yourself, Mother." I'm looking up at the clock. Fuck, 10:45 a.m. "Ladies," I'm turning to the hairdresser and the makeup artist, "quickly do your best and fix Mother up, otherwise we're not going to make her fucking wedding."

They're staring at me with perplexed expressions, as though I'm speaking in a foreign language.

"Chop, chop," I say, clapping my hands to emphasise the need to hurry. Good, they're spinning into action, pulling out hair wands and brushes and the like.

"I'm going to need the heavy-duty concealer to cover the eye," the makeup artist is saying to me.

"Do what you can," I say, suspecting she'll need more than the heavy-duty concealer. The eye is already swelling up—substantially. "Sorry about this." Sorry, indeed, that my mother is a psychopath and has friends who have equally psychopathic tendencies, and evidently cage fighting experience.

"I've seen worse on wedding days," she's telling me, and she has already started lathering Mother's face with the brown paint. Wow, well that is a shocker to hear! Worse than two seventy-year-olds fighting liked caged animals—I've lived a sheltered life it now seems.

"In the meantime, I'll do my makeup and hair so we can still make it on time." I could have already done mine by the now—Here goes the rush job!

"I'll do your hair," Jess is saying to me with a raised eyebrow.

"Oh, really." *So her, too* … "Does everyone think my hair is terrible?"

"Only sometimes." Jess is rubbing my arm and giving me a *it's for your own good* look.

"Most of the time," Mother has managed to concur.

61. 11:15a.m.

other's wedding day, still. One shiner down—delivered from bridesmaid to bride. And also (perhaps unremarkably) one bridesmaid down. Fifteen minutes before service. Limo waiting outside. Luckily will only take ten minutes to get Mother to church, and Mother is already dressed in her white meringue fru-fru with a rather large fascinator clasped to her head. She is sitting in the lounge room literally drinking from the bottle now, lamenting her swollen face, the photos, the guests that will see her, etc., etc. I'm thinking about taking the bottle from her before she gets too messy and obliterated (i.e. no longer capable to say vows at church), but am concerned that she, too, might fly at me in a rage.

Jess is finishing my hair in the bathroom. Hairdresser and makeup artist have left.

"Oh, fucking shit!" I hear Mother yelling from the lounge room …

Perhaps I really should forcibly remove the bottle from her. "I only have one bridesmaid!"

Oh dear, was wondering when this would occur to her. Evidently the pin has just dropped.

"What am I going to do?" she's still yelling, and with more despair now.

"Mother," I'm doing the same yelling now, too, "at this point, we just need to get to the fucking church."

She's coming in. I'm hearing the heavy *clompy* footsteps heading in the bathroom's direction, yes, and here she is having appeared like magic, shiner and all, at the door, still clutching bottle. Fascinator slightly askew.

"No, that will never work." She's clutching the door. "There will be three lads at the altar and only two ladies. It will look ridiculous!"

What's more ridiculous than a drunken bride who looks like she's done five rounds in the boxing ring?

"It'll just have to be, Mother. We'll just need to control the controllable," I say, spitting out some sort of quote I read on Facebook earlier on this morning.

"No. I won't stand for that. Someone else will need to do it." She's looking Jess up and down with maniacal expression. *Really?*

"Mother— " I begin, delivered with my most effective warning tone.

"Jess, what about you?" Mother has ignored me, makes a change! "I think we could squeeze you into that dress, maybe with the assistance of some scotch tape and scissors."

"Mother!" I'm mortified—Why does she never learn?

"Oh, no," Jess has begun, already ready in her formal dress and heels. "I'd really prefer to give it a miss." Probably thinks Mother might rush at her, too, and take a swing if she's on the bridal party.

"Nonsense!" Mother's setting the bottle down on the ground unsteadily. "I'll just go grab the dresses," she says, tottering off

"I'm so sorry about this, Jess." I'm keeping my apology quiet and brief, as I don't want Mother to hear it, but it's sincere. I am sorry!

"Not your fault—You didn't pick her out for a mother."

Earth shattering scream ensuing from the bedroom. Still screaming, like blood curdling variety that only Mother can achieve in a non-blood curdling situation. What now? Looking at Jess and shaking head. Really, could the woman be more dramatic?

"I think your hair's done," Jess has said calmly, unplugging the iron.

"Thanks," I say, peering at it in the mirror. She's straightened it out wonderfully so that it flops casually around my face in a relaxed Jennifer Aniston type do. Sort of miss the extensions. Somehow miss that porn star, exotic dancer look … but I know it wasn't really me!

Oh, more screaming. I guess she wants a response from us then.

Sigh. "I'll go see what's wrong." I best! Heading to the bedroom.

And here's Mother, standing in the middle of the room, covering mouth with horrified expression like she's just witnessed a murder.

"What, Mother?' hands on hips.

She is staring at me disbelievingly, shaking her head.

"Tell me, Mother?" I say, feeling like on a show featuring *Skippy* the talking kangaroo (am now really showing advanced age with Skippy reference). Waiting for her to twitch at me, or show some sort of sign of what's going on. *What direction is the bushfire, old girl, come on already?*

"The bitch has taken the dresses," she finally blurts out, re-covering her mouth after the words are out.

What? Looking around, I remember the bridesmaids' dresses being on the bed. They're clearly not on the bed now. Looking around room some more, just in case they've been misplaced, hung elsewhere—*I don't know.* Something logical.

Indeed, not the case. Bitch stole the dresses! No wonder she was in a hurry to get out of the house so fast. Fucking bitch is pushing my buttons, too, now. Wishing I would have swung at her myself!

"Oh, shit!" How could this go so wrong?

Jess has appeared at the door, no doubt wondering what's gone down. Mother is sitting on the bed looking disconcerted.

Long silence.

"I just can't do this," Mother is saying, shaking her head. "It must be some cataclysmic message from the universe that we shouldn't get married."

I'm staring at her, and I'm heartbroken, watching this grand old dame being completely destroyed by some insipid, large-racked bitch. Okay, so maybe Brad isn't her soulmate. Who knows with Mum, she's been married three times already! But one thing's for sure, no one, not even crazy Cheryl, is reducing my equally crazy-assed Mother to this state. Not on any of her wedding days!

"Don't be ridiculous." Good start, Cee.

"Oh, come on, Cee! Who are we kidding? This wedding is a disaster! It must mean something. Christ—I've been married three times already. You'd think I would have learned my lesson," she says, putting her head in her hands.

"Mother," I say, grabbing onto her hands and looking her square in the face, "you have learned nothing from those marriages. You're the eternal optimist—And that's awesome, that's how we should all be."

"Oh, fuck, I'm an idiot." She's smacking a hand into her face and starting to cry.

"Mother, you are not ruining that fucking makeup." I'm shaking her, hoping to return her usual cruel, psychotic self.

She has moved her hands, and is staring at me wide-eyed, clearly trying to hold back tears.

"You paid a fucking fortune for that makeup, and you are not crying it off. Don't let that bitch get to you. If you think Brad is the man-of-your-dreams, then you pursue it. Don't listen to anyone." I am centimetres away from her face.

Who am I at this moment? Some crazy Oprah, all-thinking, all-perceiving figure? Must be!

"You think?" she asks, letting out a gasp.

"Yes!" And I mean it. Her face is bloated and banged up, but I don't want her to feel like that inside, too. "You go for it. You deserve your happiness."

"I deserve *my* happiness." She is nodding and repeating my words.

"That's right," I tell her, pulling myself up to full height. I feel like an evangelist in religious amnesia and frenzy. "You deserve it, Mother, and if your own flesh and blood, your own daughter thinks you do—Then you fucking well do!"

She's nodding her head, and I can tell she's now entranced by it all.

"I do, don't I?" She is directing her attention over to Jess.

"You sure do," Jess is agreeing and nodding her head emphatically, too.

"I do," Mother is chanting—totally sold.

"Now open your fucking wardrobe," I tell her (we need bridesmaid dresses, and we need them fast), "so Jess and I can find more appropriate dresses for the ceremony. I'm sure you have the right sort of shit in there!"

Mother is getting to her feet now and vigorously throwing the doors open to her wardrobe.

Okay, so maybe, not the right shit. But it is shit of some sort …

62. 6:30p.m.

Mother is married. That was an undertaking. I should get a Nobel Peace Prize for this. Despite the swollen face, evident boozing, and random bridesmaids wearing 1980s attire on -size too small, Mother made it down the aisle, to the adoring eyes, of course, of Brad. And they were married, one hour later than expected.

Photos ensued at Circular Quay. Sort of embarrassing, given attire. Short black dress and stockings, with shoulder pads and plunging neckline. Hmm ... lots of Asian tourists staring—Not, *methinks*, for the right reasons. Jess, as per usual, put on a dazzling performance, despite *Pretty in Pink* laced outfit and matching gloves.

Oh, dear!

Now standing out the front of the reception venue in Darling Harbour with Jess. I'm slugging down a glass of champagne, and she's staring out towards the Harbour with a harrowed expression.

"Wish I could drink."

"Indeed." Yep, that must suck! "Really takes the edge off."

"Hmm … biggest downfall of pregnancy. You'd think, in this day and age, they'd come up with some sort of miracle alcohol to be consumed during pregnancy." She's clutching some sparkling water in her gloved hands.

"Yes, totally agree."

Silence falls between us as guests are heading into the venue, and complimenting us for the themed wedding. Hmm—themed wedding, indeed!

"You know, you were good with your mother," Jess is saying now that group of people have found their way inside.

I'm nodding my head. "I'm not quite sure why—It, well, it kind of just happened." "I guess after all is said and done, she is my mother."

"And how are you doing with the Pete and I thing?"

Oh, we're there now, are we? Only she has an advantage being totally sober, and me having consumed a few celebratory beverages. *I got through the day sort of drinks.*

"Oh, it's a difficult one, babe." I can be nothing but honest with Jess, especially after alcohol consumption.

"How so?" She's leaning forward in her spangly dress with a worried expression on her slightly puffy face.

"I don't know—I know he's the father of your baby and everything, and that is good in a way, you know, but he just treated you so badly." And he did, and I had to pick the pieces up after he cheated!

"God, I know," she's nodding her head. "But you know, everyone makes mistakes."

"That's a big fucking mistake." Another car-oad of people has just turned up. We are both turning their way, ready to smile and make nice chit-chat. After all, this is a wedding, right? A themed one, apparently. And it's my mother's wedding, her fourth one, yes, she's seventy, and a crazy bitch, and she is also sort of fun and, well … that's it!

It's Tina—and Chris! Okay, kind of strange—and another gay man with purple hair. The new beef cake! Must be! OH MY FUCKING GOD! It's the Swami. No, it is not! But it is, it's the Swami. Have almost dropped my drink. Recover self, Cee. Lift jaw, Cee.

"Hello, ladies," Chris is calling and flapping his arms. Okay, already one too many drinks. "What a fabulous wedding," he is screaming, and hugging me violently.

"This is Dave." Okay, so despite purple hair, Dave is kind of a stunner.

"So good to meet you," I say, giving him a hug, tip-toeing and attempting to peer over his shoulder to catch a glimpse of his bottom, so I can assess Chris's brand new BF.

"We're getting in there to have some cocktails, doll," Chris has announced, throwing a careless arm around Dave's shoulder, and Dave is smiling empathetically. "Fabulous wedding, doll, but what did happen to your mother's face?"

Shaking head and raising eyebrows at Chris in an expression of, *Please don't ask again.* Like *ever* again!

"Okay then, it's a brunch conversation." He's waggling his hand at me. Dave is following, looking apologetically back towards me. "And P.S.," Chris is yelling back, "I have not forgotten that you owe me a Louis Vuitton!"

Sigh. Yeah, I know. Give it up, boyfriend; you're never getting it back! Like ever again!

Tina is stepping up towards me, kiss hello from her, kiss back on the cheek from me. "First question, how do you know Chris?" I might be a little envious, after all, she was my intern, he is my best friend.

"I don't." She's clapping her hands together as she speaks. "We hit it off at the wedding and then went to drinks together."

Feeling less green now. I guess it's good they get along!

"But the Swami doesn't drink," I whisper into her ear, afraid he'll hear and put some Swami spell on me. Do they even do that?

"Sometimes, he does," she has whispered back. OMG! Is she serious? But who am I to judge? A Swami though, really?

The Swami is bowing slightly, hands in a prayer position at me. They are walking off together, which is enough for me to drink this entire glass of Champagne in one hit. Right now! That's better!

What the fuck? The Krishnananda? Question mark and lots of exclamation marks, lots!

"So?" Jess has piped up.

"So, what?" Tipsy now, and deeply concerned about the Swami and Tina situation.

"Are you going to accept the Pete thing?" She's looking concerned.

Oh yeah, right, back to Pete. The fact is she's the bestest friend I have in the entire world. The girl who goes to 6:00 a.m. spin classes with me and watches me chase some guy down Oxford Street barefoot on a night out. I have to have her back, you know, support her, even though I think Pete is a total douche bag, insipid, disgusting thing. Can't be worse than the Swami though—Oh shit, seahorse penis in head, vision not good!

WHY? So scary it hurts.

"Whatever makes you happy, babe." And that is the only answer, right? As long as she's happy!

She certainly looks happy to me now, hugging me tightly, her baby belly pressing into me.

"Let's go in," she's telling me, arm snugly around me.

Okay, so I have no man. Don't have imagined *man-of-dreams*, or real man guised as *man-of-dreams*, aka said footballer, ex-celebrity, beautiful thing. But I have fabulous friends, always have had, and have crazy mother, always have had.

And you know what else I have? Tonight I have fabulously-styled and beautiful looking hair.

63. Maybe past midnight? Not sure?

Mother's wedding reception. Everyone's dancing. Band is ripping up some awesome jazz tunes. Mother, despite swollen face, is shaking some moves with Bradster—OMG, and so is the Swami. Can Swamis dance? Totally thought they were all about the meditation and shit? He is pressing up against my beautiful little Tina with seahorse penis—cannot forgive. Sipping gin and tonic, drink of preference, and shaking some grooves in seat. Yes I am single, seated, wallflower dancer sort at Mother's fourth wedding, but it's been a fun night. Cake has been cut, speeches made, love declared. Isn't that what weddings are all about?

Waiter is heading over in my direction—because I'm the *sensible party* at this operation! When the fuck did that happen? When did I become the sensible party?

Am past sensible at this stage, one too many gins, but must make effort to listen to what waiter needs to tell me.

Said waiter is leaning in and yelling at me over the music, "You're Cecilia Binner, right?"

Nodding head. That much I know. He's young, earnest, and cute, if you look past the acne and all … which must be chronic, as even I can see it without spectacles on.

"There's a guy at the door for you. He's been trying to get in for a bit— but we're not sure if he's supposed to be here. Sort of insistent, though—Do you mind coming out to take a look?"

Frowning at him, I'm thinking I'm not in the mood to partake or witness another brawl. But I need to check this out … for curiosity alone, really.

Nodding my head. "Sure," I say, finishing off gin and tonic and getting to feet.

Following him, slightly unsteadily (and slowly) to the front. Staggering, not my usual stalking by any means.

Outside. The breeze out here is cool and sharp, wishing I had brought a jacket. The sky is clear and black, and the passerby's are drunk at this hour, vapid or laughing.

The waiter is pointing me in the man's direction. Said man is wearing a suit, but he's turned away looking at the harbour.

Heading towards him. A few metres away now so I best call out, methinks … "Hey," I yell, and he is turning around. Who is it? Looks good in a suit, whoever it is. Squinting. Making my stagger more of a saunter.

No! Really? Eyes widening … It's Jai. Jai! And he is smiling at me, looking all sheepish. All sexy. All it! Wearing suit, no tie of course, revealing tats on neck, but looking so damn hot.

Heart is leaping from chest. Overcome with emotion. It's Jai! Jai!

"Hey." His hands are in his pockets, very shamefaced. "I've been trying to get in for twenty minutes. These clowns won't let me in," he says, gesturing towards the waiters.

"Probably the neck tattoos." I'm smiling, and wanting to touch him, to reach forward, to kiss those neck tattoos.

Reaching his side now, and melting into his eyes, those grey eyes. He has just grabbed me by my arm. He feels strong.

"I tried to make it for the wedding, but the flights were delayed," he's saying to me, and I'm standing so close to him now—our bodies touch. I'm smiling sort of stupidly, because he has this effect on me.

"What are you doing, you crazy boy?" He smells so good, of skin and fragrance, and this magnetism between us is overpowering.

"I wanted to be here for your mother's wedding. For you." He's grabbing my other arm. Fuck, I could really just fuck him right here, right now. Banish thought! Banish thought!

"Is Larry okay?" I ask, pressing into him.

"Yeah, he's okay—Shit, he's dying, but he insisted I come here—to see you, of course."

"I like Larry." Our lips are almost meeting; cold air the only thing between us.

"I hope you like me more than you like Larry." He's so softly spoken, hands pressing into the small of my back and against the terrible eighties dress.

"I certainly do." And I really really *really* do.

"Good."

His grey eyes so close and honest, and here comes the kissing. I am kissing him right back, like a full-on *Fifty Shades of Grey* raunchy kiss … Not that I like that book, or have even read it all. Okay, so maybe I have! But who hasn't?

OMG, eyes flicking open, sensing observation. Yes, the waiters are staring at us like we're putting on an open-air porn show for them.

"Come on, let's go inside." We have plenty more time for kissing, methinks.

"Okay." He's still looking down at me, and I'm looking up at him. What is he about to say? My heart is still pounding. I'm smiling with every inch of my body and face … "Cee … You are one awesome lady."

The fact is …. I think he is one awesome guy. In fact, beyond awesome … But I shall tell him later. *Why?* Well, a *woman of world* always has a good reason to keep a secret—*Right?* And it's a good secret, kept in a balanced place. A place where there are no scoreboards, no back and forth, no ups or downs, and no seesaw—a place where I am *woman of dreams*, a place where he is just *it*, and a place where everything else just *is*.

www.ingramcontent.com/pod-product-compliance
Lightning Source LLC
Chambersburg PA
CBHW022150260626
47155CB00017B/1